BETRAYALS

BLACK CIPHER FILES #2

LISA HUGHEY

SALTY KISSES PRESS

BETRAYALS

by
Lisa Hughey

Lisa Hughey

February 2012

ISBN: 97809840428381

Print ISBN: 9781950359080

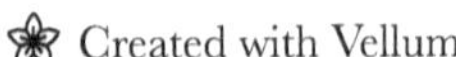 Created with Vellum

This story is, at its core, about parental sacrifice and the lengths we will go to, obsess over, and ultimately employ to protect our children. I don't think our children ever fully understand the powerful swell of love we feel for them, hidden beneath the nagging to clean up their room and do their homework. Every hug we give them, every shoulder to cry on, every word of praise still doesn't impart the tremendous and awesome impact of that love in our hearts.

To R, K, and R, I love you so much. Thank you for loving me back and leaving me alone to write.

CHAPTER 1

Disinformation n. Deliberate spreading of false information with intent to mislead.
August 31, Afghanistan

SOMETHING SNUFFLED IN THE CORNER.

I curled my arm protectively around the meager bowl of whatever they'd brought me. No stinking rodent was going to touch my daily ration.

The dank smell of urine-soaked sand, feces, and human sweat filled the fetid air. A thin layer of grit and despair coated everything, including my tongue. I vowed never to set foot on a beach again.

Probably wouldn't anyway. As I was likely to die in this godforsaken rat hole of a prison. I scooped the cooked until mush food into my mouth greedily, careful not to spill a single grain.

Hard to believe that just a month ago, Jordan and I had been dining on spice-rubbed porterhouse and chipotle garlic mashed potatoes in D.C.

That life was long gone. The contrast between then and now was laughable.

Then, I'd dabbed daintily at my mouth with a soft linen napkin. Now, I lapped the bowl with my sand-coated tongue and carefully sucked on each dirt-crusted finger.

If malnutrition didn't kill me, the germs probably would.

I could hear the woman, our chef, server, and general attendant, coming. But I wasn't finished.

Fuuuuuccckkkkk. I screamed the expletive silently. I'd learned brutally fast that cursing out loud, especially from a woman, in this prison was taboo.

One by one, the locks clicked open. I huddled over the tiny tin bowl, licking with short, frantic strokes, trying to eat it all before she took my food away. My arm chains clanked as they swung together, ringing in the silence. I ignored the stabs of extreme pain in my left arm.

The woman scurried in furtively and eased the door closed.

This was a change in routine. Subtly, I shifted to a higher state of alertness. The bruises, aches, and burns from the last 'change in routine' still hadn't healed. I hadn't had a beating or torture session in a few days. They'd left me alone.

I was pretty sure the radius bone in my left forearm arm was broken. Fortunately not the ulna and not my shooting arm.

"Miss," she whispered in Pashto.

I didn't answer. I didn't know how much they knew about my background and I wasn't about to give anything away.

"Miss." This time she whispered in Dari.

I remained silent.

"Miss." Next it was Modern Standard Arabic.

Something must have flickered in my eyes because she continued in Modern Standard. "Come. I will let you go."

My brain whirred. It had to be a trap. The were going to let me go and then follow me. Thinking I'd lead them to whatever they thought I had.

Common torture tactic. Slowly break down all barriers to civilized behavior until the prisoner was more animal than human. Then dangle the carrot of freedom and watch the animal lunge for it.

If I was in their shoes, that was what I would do.

I sat quietly, waiting for her next move.

She started to strip off her burkha.

That wasn't right. A woman showing her face, her arms, her legs was not tolerated. Especially not in front of the prisoners. Walking around without the covering meant certain death.

Maybe that was the test.

They were waiting to see if I'd react with compassion. Would I think of someone else before myself? I analyzed each possible reaction and action for this situation.

One. Take the burkha and take my chances. But what about the woman?

Two. Help her put the burkha back on. And stay.

Three. Stay still and do nothing.

Inaction was always my least favorite response. And I'd been trapped in this prison for two weeks. But I stayed still.

As she lifted the veiled hood from her face, she was crying. They'd coerced her into doing this. She knew as well as I, she'd be dead if she set foot out of this cell without the covering.

"Put the burkha back on," I whispered in Pashto.

"They are going to kill you." The rough wool tangled in her hair, muffling her voice.

And what do you think they're going to do to you?

I wanted to be free. But not at the expense of this woman. I wrapped my arms over my chest, stifling a gasp as the wrist cuff banged my injured forearm. "Go back to your duties."

"My slavery." She spit. She knelt beside me and jiggled the key to open the shackles. "You must go."

The glob of mucus lay in the middle of the sand and dirt floor. "No."

"They killed my *xawand*." She stood in the middle of the room, proud and fierce, dressed exactly like me in a grey cotton shift. "They killed my *mashums*."

Her husband. Her babies. Her family.

I understood that kind of loss.

I understood the rage and the grief. I understood the unquenchable lust for revenge. I'd used the emotions on more than one occasion to recruit agents for the CIA.

The same had been used on me.

I shouldn't trust her. Maybe this was all an elaborate ruse, and I was falling straight into a dangerous con, but somehow her words rang true. The grief and rage in her eyes was not fake. She gripped my hands with a fierce strength.

But I still couldn't trust her.

"Why did they kill them?"

"They forced my *xawand* to carry the drugs across the border. He didn't want to do it, but the village warlord, his own father, wanted the money."

Her situation wasn't uncommon. The number of widows was on the rise because of men being forced to be drug mules. So it was possible....

"My *xawand*, he left and never returned. He was a shepherd, a farmer, not a drug dealer."

And her babies? Somehow I couldn't ask. The logical assumption was malnutrition, starvation, or sad victim of exploding land mines.

De-mining was the main focus of the work I did with UNOCHA.

"Why let me go?"

Her body was stiff with the measure of her rage. In her eyes, I didn't see fear or desperation, only a deep, unwavering resolve.

"A woman should not be a prisoner. A woman should have rights. A woman's children should be safe." Her voice broke.

"You're right." I still couldn't figure out what was in it for her. "But what does letting me go accomplish?"

"They speak of you with fear. With awe. You have the power to help change this life, this country." She gripped my hands more tightly. "You will see. You will make them stop."

"I don't have that kind of power." Was she saying she knew I worked for the CIA? Or was she referencing my ties to UNOCHA?

"You have far more power than I." A calm settled over her face. "What they are doing is wrong. You must stop them."

"What about you?"

She shook her head. "If you leave now, you will have one day before they realize you are missing. Go now."

I looked at her. For some reason, she had latched onto me as her salvation. I knew, if I left, she would be doomed.

"Why now?"

"They are going to kill you. In the morning."

That statement tipped the scale. Fighting the injustices of these people's lives was my crusade, but justice for myself was a reason to survive. A reason for revenge. A reason to live.

Someone had set me up. Someone had wanted me to die.

However, I couldn't let this woman be punished.

My heart thumped in my chest. "Come with me."

"No. There must be a body here for the middle of the night check."

She was right. There was a night check, usually when the moon was high, so the guards could see without a light inside the small rectangular cell built halfway into the ground.

"What will happen to you?"

"They will beat me." She gently un-shackled my wrists. "But the punishment will be worth your freedom. This is the only way I can make a difference."

And wasn't that what we all wanted? To make a difference? She had no power in her world. This gesture was the one thing she could do, the one action she could undertake of her own free will, to influence the world around her, to hopefully bring peace and safety to this region.

How could I take that away from her? Her power to choose?

I couldn't.

It spoke to how worn down, how completely exhausted I was that I let her put the burkha over me. I listened mutely as she gave me detailed directions to her village and instructions for once I arrived.

"My father-in-law is the warlord. Do not let him catch you," she cautioned. "He does not believe in the rights of women."

In the back of my mind, I kept waiting for my

tormentors to burst in, to grab us both. I steeled myself for the final betrayal. But the halls, if you could call them that, stayed blessedly silent.

What the hell. If I was going to die, it might as well be trying to escape rather than being eaten alive by the rats in my cell or beaten to death by my captors. "What is your name?"

"Fariya."

"*Shukran.*" Thank you, I whispered.

She cradled my face in her raw, work-roughened hands and kissed both of my filthy cheeks tenderly, like a mother blessing a child.

"*Asalamu alaykum.*" Peace on you.

"*Alaykum asalam.*" And on you peace.

Unable to shake the feeling that something was terribly wrong, I asked her again. "Are you okay?"

"I will be as soon as you are gone." She bowed her head in deference.

I refused to put the chains on her. I closed the door, locked the locks and ascended the primitive stairs to the exit. I gripped the keys between my fingers, ready to gouge out the eyes of any attackers. Ready to defend myself from the onslaught I was sure must be coming.

This was too easy.

A puddle of Afghani wine, with its sickly sweet odor, was soaking into the dirt floor in front of the exit. She'd drugged the guards. They slumped back against the wall, white ceramic mugs with a blue kite logo loosely clasped in their hands.

Fantastic. Apparently corporate sponsorship had traveled all the way to rural Afghanistan.

I peered out the arched doorway into the late evening sky. Nothing moved. A slight breeze whistled through a sparse copse of ash trees. Somewhere a small rodent scuttled away as the laughing cackle of hyenas tore through the air. Nothing human moved in the dead of night.

I stepped out of the doorway, pausing. I still had the keys clenched in my hand. I could turn around, return to the cell before anyone missed me, and save Fariya.

Reflexively my fingers went to the hollow in my neck, but my mother's amulet wasn't there. I thought of Fariya, her commitment, her sacrifice. My promise. Was I really going to do this?

I was.

I took a tentative step, then another. I stared up at the clear night sky, orienting myself by the constellations. I needed to travel east. Fariya's village was ten miles away. I had minimal time to make my way there, steal food, clothing, and weapons, and be gone.

Using their primitive yet effective warning system, I kept track of the painted white rocks marking the border between safety and sudden death, and kept clear of the painted red rocks, indicating land mines. I stared hard at the ground, looking for other footprints to lead me in safe passage.

Soon I was running, a loping awkward gait from the still tender wound in my right leg. But I was free.

For the first time in two weeks, I was free.

CHAPTER 2

September 1, Afghanistan
6:00 am

ARABIC LETTERS in peeling paint over the arched wooden doors proclaimed this the village of Zaman Khalili.

I crouched behind a gooseberry bush and surveyed the walled compound. Behind me and to the right was a giant field of freshly harvested poppy plants. The bulbous cheerful heads bobbed in the morning breeze.

The sun would rise soon. Light had begun to bleed up from the rocky desert.

Fariya's sandals had been too small for me, so I'd left them behind. Now my bare feet were raw from the harsh, unforgiving sand and miles of agony. I glanced behind me again, to be sure I wasn't leaving giant bloody footprints like a big, fat arrow pointing to my position.

I assessed the compound but couldn't wait much longer. Just as Fariya had described, a six foot high wall circled the living quarters, the only entrance and exit, the enormous locked gates.

The sun had crested the horizon and soon the village would wake for the day.

And the guards would be posted.

I needed to get in, get out, and get gone.

So far, Fariya's directions had been perfect. I found the small dip in the ground along the far wall where children snuck out to play.

I slid head first into the depression in the ground. If I hadn't been nearly starved for the last two weeks, I would have gotten stuck. As it was my butt barely cleared the bottom of the wall.

When most of my body had emerged on the other side, I lay bowed in the hole with my right cheek flat on the cool morning sand, maintaining surveillance. Waiting, watching. A snake, hopefully not poisonous, slithered along my burkha trying to absorb some of my body heat. I ignored it.

My main problem right now was the dogs.

Not 'cute, cuddly be-your-best-friend' dogs. But 'get-too-close-and-I'll-rip-your-head-off' dogs. These dogs would not be domesticated or friendly.

I sniffed the air. No tea brewing yet. I had some time.

After locating Fariya's home from her description, I wriggled the rest of the way in, and slid up the wall, brushing the dirt from the front of the blue garment. I tiptoed toward the clay building, trying to ignore the painful burning of my feet.

With luck, Fariya still had a pair of her husband's shoes or sandals.

I peered into the dark cell of a room. All night long, I'd traveled in the open space, thankful to be out of my purgatory. Thankful to breathe fresh, clean air. Now an irrational fear of going inside gripped me.

My heart thumped against my breastbone, shaking the sides of my ribs. I forced myself to reach for the shovel propped against the open doorway and watched with detachment as my bony hand trembled; angry blue, purple, and yellow welts circled my emaciated wrists.

The shovel seemed unbearably heavy. In early morning air, the village sheep bleated and doves cooed. The sounds forced me into action. If I didn't haul ass, Fariya's sacrifice would be for nothing.

I owed her.

From the doorway, I counted paces, five to the center of the small room and then turned left as she'd instructed, and paced off another five steps.

The hard-packed ground looked as though it hadn't been disturbed since the hut was constructed, but Fariya had sworn her father-in-law had weapons buried in the main room. I jabbed the hard dirt and pain sang up my left arm.

I couldn't dig until I stabilized the bone.

Using my toe, I marked the spot with an X then prowled the spartan room. In the corner sat a wooden crate of supplies, marked with symbols of the United States Military Civil Affairs Battalion, a goodwill package designed as a part of *Operation: Rebuild* to deliver aid to the villages and ensure cooperation against the Taliban and al-Qaeda.

I opened the crate and found a long wooden spoon. In a basket on the other side of the room near the pallet, I unearthed a long strip of fabric woven into stripes of brown, ocher, and deep blue. Hopefully, Fariya didn't need it.

Crafting a makeshift splint, I awkwardly tied the wool, criss-crossing along the spoon until my arm felt immediately better.

I hustled back to the X and started digging, ignoring the zing of pain every time the shovel hit the hardened dirt. The process was slow, and I could only trust the cache wasn't buried deeply.

The small village came to life as I worked at the hard earth. Then a gong tolled and all activity stopped.

Morning prayer.

I huddled beneath the single window, a small oddly-shaped hole in the middle of the wall. Melodic chanting resonated in the morning air, taking me back to my childhood and a yearning for the simple pleasure of listening to my mother sing.

Although I didn't have a prayer rug, I knelt on the hard-packed dirt and bowed to the West.

Musical voices raised in thanks and praise hummed in the air.

I couldn't chant. It might give me away.

Instead, I gave thanks for my freedom, I gave thanks for my life. As I glanced at the shallow hole I'd dug, in the shifting dirt and sand, a burlap bag with the outline of guns caught my eye, and I gave thanks for the weapons to aid my escape.

As the gong tolled again, signifying the end of prayer time, I crawled over to the shovel and scooped at the dirt again and again.

I dug faster, praying no one would look in Fariya's hut while she was away at work. A dog barked and women in burkhas bustled quietly past the window, not far from me.

With short strokes of the shovel, I uncovered the hidden stash. I pulled out the burlap bag and emptied the contents onto the dirt floor.

The bag contained a virtual United Nations of firepower. Two Russian rifles. One AK-47, a Kalashnikov

7.62 x 39 mm assault rifle weighing in at nine and a half pounds without the magazine. No way could I carry it.

An AK-101, a compact assault rifle, standard for NATO forces. Much lighter. And there were more of the 101 cartridges buried with the weapon.

Two handguns. One Italian pistol, Beretta 92G, with no safety, used by the French military, a little over two pounds. And lastly, an Austrian Glock 17, a favorite of the Afghan National Police force, and a full 12 ounces lighter than the Beretta.

I hoped I didn't need to use any of them because the recoil just might knock me on my ass and I didn't know if I could even hold the damn thing to fire it.

No way could I bring all four. I couldn't carry them all. Carefully I lifted the AK-101 rifle out of the bag.

I didn't see the "jingles", a cascade of little bells attached to the stock, until I heard them jangle. I held in my breath, waiting for discovery.

As I crouched low to the ground, I heard another jingle and my pulse stuttered again. I realized it wasn't from the weapon I had, as my fingers were still slick with sweat and gripping the jingles on the AK. A guard patrolled by outside, his bells masking my own thumping heart.

When he was past the window, I carefully removed the bells, then lifted the smaller, lighter Glock 17 out of the shallow hole. Sweat trickled between my breasts as I tried to keep my breathing slow and even.

I laid the weapons in a Keffiyeh scarf and fashioned a sling to carry the assault rifle and handgun. Quickly I scraped the dirt back over the bag with the remaining weapons and then pulled a small rug from the corner to cover the slight impression.

Rummaging through Fariya's bride trunk, I found a pair of men's sandals and slipped them on my abused feet.

The pungent scent of Chai tea drifted in the air. My stomach growled in response. The aroma of sizzling sheep's meat from a wood-burning fire assaulted my senses. My mouth watered but my stomach revolted.

I swallowed hard, hoping to keep down the little bit of rice I'd eaten last night. I needed all of my strength to survive. I put the pre-wrapped package of bread and dried fruit she had left for me in my pocket. I would eat later.

The women would be serving the men, then the children, and it seemed a perfect time to escape. Now that the sun was up I could slip out of the walled complex with little notice.

Most everyone should be in the main compound area eating. There would be guards posted at the massive front doors and the back area, but Fariya had promised that the East side of the complex would not be well-guarded. The current group of men forced to be drug mules were gone, so the guards would be very young men, in their early teens and the least experienced.

I skirted the edge of the compound, almost to my exit point, when a dog started barking furiously.

Shit.

Had the dog somehow noticed me? Smelled me? I wasn't moving with my usual agility or speed, but I hadn't thought I was that out of place.

Perhaps the dogs had caught my scent, as my body still carried the stink of the prison.

Someone approached. My body quivered with tension as I continued to walk slowly. A wizened old man scurried past me with a worried expression.

As if he recognized me, he reared back. Then, he

grabbed me, whispered harshly. I only caught every other word, he spoke so quickly.

"Fariya...sacrifice...don't let...catch...go, go...."

I nodded, thinking him demented as I pretended to be Fariya and trying to pull away, until the content of his rambling penetrated.

His eyes were tortured. "Go...before...find...here."

Realization dawned. He knew who I was. Which meant Fariya had told someone of her plan.

He knew who I was. And he was telling me to go before they found me.

A sonorous bang, bang, bang, ripped through the morning chatter. Male shouts pierced the air.

A cry rose from the center of the compound.

"*Amreekees.*"

Soldiers. American soldiers were here.

CHAPTER 3

Americans. Soldiers. Here.

For a moment, my spirit soared. I could be out of here and on military transport home in a matter of hours.

Back in my townhouse in Alexandria, back in my cramped little cubicle in Georgetown, back in Jordan's arms.

Jordan.

My heart beat faster. Maybe we still had a shot.

Our last words, right before I was captured, had been stilted, awkward. But Fariya's love for her family highlighted the emptiness of my personal life. I needed to let go of my fears and take a chance with him.

First I had to get the hell out of here.

My impulse was to scale the wall and sprint for the ground convoy trucks. I picked up my pace, making a beeline for the unguarded side wall.

A sunburst of joy spread through me. I could go home.

The sudden rattle of metal detectors as the Special Forces guys searched the compound for weapons grated on my ears. Then, the bark and growl of the dogs and the commands from the Spec Warrior leader drowned out the annoying noise. The additional sounds and distractions made my escape easier.

As I climbed to the top of the wall one-handed, I protected my arm as best I could. I straddled the two-foot-wide wall, hugged the flat top to keep my profile low, and canted my head to listen as the soldiers raided the compound.

They were calling to each other in some sort of code, but I wasn't close enough to hear actual words. The general mood seemed to be relaxed, the villagers ignoring the soldiers, except for the kids begging for pencils and pens.

The fact that they were here so soon after my escape nagged at me. What were the odds that they would be inspecting this compound, on this day, at this time?

I dropped down on the other side of the wall and fell off-balance. The muffled landing stung my sore feet as if I'd pressed thousands of tiny shards of glass into my soles. I bent into a crouch, the sling with the rifle banged against my back and jabbed into a semi-healed bruise over my kidney. White spots danced in my eyes. I held still, desperately trying to clear my vision.

The rough wool of the burkha abraded the cigarette burns on my arms. The frantic words of the old man beat in my ears, pounding at my thoughts. *Fariya, sacrifice.*

Something was not right.

The paranoia I'd experienced and disregarded right before my capture came raging back. If these soldiers had been in the area, why hadn't they come to get me out of prison? In those two long weeks, why hadn't the CIA facilitated my release?

Two weeks.

Two fucking weeks.

I eased the Glock out of the homemade sling and

clutched the weapon in my right hand, thankful my left arm was broken, not my right.

I couldn't shoot for shit with my left hand.

I needed to find a place to conceal myself until after the Americans were done in the compound. If I could make the run to the poppy fields, I could hide there. Assuming they weren't here to plow them under. The plows must be coming since the village showed signs of American aid.

I crept along, hugging the side of the wall. When I got to the corner, I lay down flat in the sand, my cheek on the ground, my head facing the wall and edged forward inch by inch.

After a quick visual inspection, I saw only one soldier to guard two vehicles. Finally things were looking up. I surveyed the two vehicles, one *Mine Resistant Ambush Protected* RG-31 and one hard topped, open convoy truck. After I watched the guard's pattern take him across the front and around one truck twice as often as the other, I deduced the MRAP had the weapons.

Jordan had been in Afghanistan. He had talked about performing surveillance on villages and known enemies from three hundred yards away. If the soldiers had snipers in the hills, I'd be dead before the shot echoed.

A pang of sorrow filled me.

I'd never told Jordan how much he meant to me. How much I was beginning to care. Now I wished that I had grabbed the courage to move our relationship to the next level.

I shoved aside the tender feelings. I could wallow later.

Slowly, I lowered my bundle to the ground. I ignored the weapons truck. I needed what was in the second truck.

I had sixty seconds before the guard would be around again.

As the guard rounded the MRAP, the one with the weapons, I moved.

Five. I scurried toward the second, zig-zagging, trying to forget about snipers and Jordan, as I counted off the seconds in my head.

Twenty, twenty-one, twenty-two. I put my right foot on the bumper, grabbed the handle on the open side, and pulled myself up and over the tailgate, stifling a groan at the sharp pain in my left arm.

Thirty, thirty-one.... Carefully, I eased down and stretched along the floor, flat on my back.

Forty, forty-one, forty-two.... I moved only my gaze, methodically cataloguing the truck's contents. And there in the corner, mounted on the wall above my head, was my prize.

The red cross on the white box identified the medic kit.

Fifty-five. Five seconds.

I couldn't get the kit down before the guard's next pass. With effort, I slowed my breathing. The exertion had taken more out of me than it should have. I needed water as well as medicine.

Outside the truck, the young soldier's measured pace scuffed the hard-packed desert sand. The heat grew more intense as the sun rose in the clear blue sky. No rain today.

The guard was almost around the corner. An insect buzzed above my head.

Sweat--hydration I couldn't afford to lose--rolled down my forehead, past my eyebrows to the bridge of my nose, and hovered there.

In my mind's eye, I placed him mid-way around the tailgate. No further than thirty inches away from me. I closed my eyes, not wanting anything to draw attention to the shadowed interior of the truck bed.

The hard metal pressed into my back, the sharp blades of my shoulders pinched my skin. I'd always been fit and solid. Now I was neither. And the lack was agony.

I inhaled slowly, meditating on the covered top that offered cool shade from the already blistering sun.

I ticked off the seconds in my head and hoped the guard hadn't noticed the wake of my burkha in the sand.

When I determined he'd rounded the corner, I counted out ten more seconds. I had to wait until he was far enough away from this truck before I moved.

I eased up gingerly, struggling with the effort needed to rise from the prone position. I lifted the kit from the hook and counted off seconds while I grabbed what I needed.

Eureka. My salvation.

Antibiotics.

I shoved two vials into my pocket along with a syringe, then swiped a roll of bandages and antiseptic salve.

I stared for a moment at the painkillers, Tylenol with Codeine then closed the lid with a quiet snap. I couldn't afford to lose any more clarity.

A shout sounded--much closer than I would have liked. *Shit.*

I hunched back down. Landed on my injured arm. Pain, sharp and insistent, throbbed through me. The shout had triggered my flight or fight instinct. Adrenaline pumped through me, raising my blood sugar, depleting energy I could ill afford to lose.

I listened to the soldiers shouting. I could only hope they hadn't found the half empty bag I'd just buried.

I struggled to switch over to English. The words, sounds were foreign me after several weeks of hearing and speaking Arab dialects.

"Riot, escapees, reacquire." They repeated the words

over and over, in English, Dari, Pashto and Modern Standard.

Wanting information from the warlord?

Think, Staci. Use your brain. Use your training. I forced myself to focus on their words.

Escapee. That was me.

Riot? That wasn't right.

Reacquire? A fancy word for putting me back in that jail...or worse.

Then their words struck me. Escapees? Multiple? Fariya wouldn't have done that. Letting other prisoners go meant certain death.

The old man's words came back to me. Sacrifice.

Shit. Shit. Shit.

Moisture leaked from my eyes. Dammit. I couldn't afford to lose any more. Yet tears continued to roll down my face. I didn't have time for grief. I didn't have time for this choking rage festering in my chest. I had to get out of here. Quietly. Silently.

Reacquire?

No fucking way.

Fariya had given her own life to insure I helped her, helped her village, helped her country. She had given her life for mine.

Someone had set me up. Someone engineered my capture. Someone wanted me dead.

I wasn't going to let them succeed.

CHAPTER 4

S eptember 6
    Washington, D.C.

STACI IS DEAD.

Jordan Ramirez stared at the official, high-level, high security clearance report from Afghanistan. A succinct, thirty-two word brutal recitation of her death.

Cigarette burns, barbed wire tearing of dermis, mole on her collarbone burned off, decapitated (head missing), skull found in ashes outside the prison. Body showed signs of pre- and post-mortem torture.

He couldn't bear to look at the second page yet.

Photographs.

Frank McClellan, his boss, gestured to the two-page report he had just handed to Jordan. "An American woman we've been keeping track of was killed."

The normal sounds of the office filtered through his consciousness. But the everyday murmur of conversation, the hum of computers and fax machines, the muted ringing of phones seemed distorted, far away.

22

The smell of coffee left too long on a Bunn warmer, the subtle mix of fabric softener, floral perfume, and the slight under-scent of perspiration twisted into a surreal throb behind his left eye.

Staci. Dead.

He refused to believe it. She had such life, such energy, such sheer presence. She couldn't be dead. They weren't done yet. He was still mad at her. She couldn't fucking go away and not finish their argument.

He loved her.

When was he supposed to get that out? And why the hell hadn't he told her instead of arguing with her for misleading him about her job?

And shit, didn't that just say it all.

Inside his pocket, Jordan clenched her mother's amulet in his left hand, running his thumb over the delicately carved scarab. Beyond shifting his thumb he didn't move, didn't twitch a muscle. He couldn't have even if a sniper had a bead on him.

Something in Jordan's very stillness must have given him away. "You okay, man?" Frank's question ripped him out of his misery, and Jordan realized he'd been silent too long. And it was critical he not show any more reaction than he'd already betrayed.

No one knew about his relationship with Staci, and if they found out, he wouldn't be able to access this report. Jordan dropped heavily into a chair at the lunch table, before his knees gave out. "Yeah. Touch of food poisoning."

Frank took a surreptitious step back.

Jordan tapped the sheets of paper against the forearm of his Egyptian cotton shirt and forced himself to focus. He had to start asking the right questions. "What was she doing in that area of Afghanistan anyway?"

As if he didn't already know. As if he and Staci hadn't had the mother of all arguments when he'd discovered she was going there. And that had been before he'd found out she worked for the fucking C.I. of A.

"She was a do-gooder, working for United Nations Office for the Coordination of Human Affairs. Humanitarian mission for de-mining." Frank snorted. "The land mines have been there for years. It's not like they're going anywhere."

Jordan had nearly had a heart attack when he realized which region of Afghanistan she was in. Supposedly she truly had been on a humanitarian mission. But the enormity of her previous lies, omissions really, had made it impossible for him to believe her.

He'd been keeping tabs on Afghanistan ever since he found out she was going, surreptitiously reading the hourly updates his office received from the government's shared intelligence network, Intelink.

He'd seen the carefully worded communiqué, a capture report that detailed the woman, her general description, the request for ransom from the Afghan warlords who oversaw the prison, and the known methods of torture they employed. And he feared it was Staci. He'd tried multiple times to contact her by email without success.

When he couldn't get hold of her, he was certain she was the woman in the report. He'd wanted to grab the first transport to Kabul armed with his Remington M24SWS sniper rifle and the intelligence to get her out.

Instead, he had assumed she would be quietly liberated and returned to the U.S. by the CIA. Because that's what the CIA did, they protected their own.

Dammit, he should have done more. But Jordan no longer did hostage rescue for the FBI. He didn't have the clearance or the manpower to get her out of that prison anymore.

Now he worked the other side, for the Franklin Group, a highly distinguished, well-connected think tank. Trying to anticipate problems before they happened. Analyzing data and generating reports to prevent this kind of incident from occurring. Advising the military, the government, anyone who would listen about the motives and operations of their enemies or even allies, and the possible repercussions of any U.S. actions.

He'd retired his ghillie suit and rifle in favor of thousand-dollar Hugo Boss and the weapon of knowledge. Now he was trying to protect and prevent, rather than react to, threats.

Most days, it worked for him.

But not today. *Dios*, not today.

Right now, his inability to act chafed. The need to be there, to be able to bring her body, Jesus, her body, home, was like acid burning in his gut. The carvings cut into the skin on his palm as he clenched her amulet too tightly.

Jordan couldn't claim her even in death.

Initially they'd kept their relationship private. He'd almost gotten to the point where he thought maybe she was ashamed of him, of their relationship. Of course when he'd discovered she was CIA, her refusal made a lot more sense. And he couldn't jeopardize her memory or her standing at the CIA by acknowledging their relationship now.

It was a forbidden, opposite attraction because while their views on just about everything matched, their methods of solving problems contradicted on many levels. Yet, their passion for each other had overruled and overcome all the reasons why they shouldn't be together.

She couldn't be dead.

How would he live without her?

He forced his throat muscles to relax before he spoke again. "Are they sure it's her?"

Frank shrugged. "Positive I.D."

Frank didn't care, didn't know, that Jordan's world had just imploded.

"The prison riot is being heavily covered by the press. It's only a matter of time before they figure out one of the dead prisoners is American. The guys on the Hill are freaking out."

"What kind of response do the politicians want?"

"They want a solid position on why this isn't our government's fault." Frank ambled toward the coffee pot on the granite counter. "Senator Jordan of the Senate Select Committee on Intelligence sent out the high-level transmission request. They'd like to keep it quiet as long as they can and get their ducks in a row."

Senator Jordan and his committee. Wasn't that just the fucking icing on his personal hell cupcake?

"Of course they want to deny any sort of responsibility." Even as he spoke, he knew that wasn't fair. Jordan resisted the urge to smash the flat of his hand up into Frank's nose and break something. It wasn't Frank's fault politicians worried more about covering their asses and did whatever was politically expedient rather than acknowledging that someone had made a mistake.

"Well it doesn't look good to have American civilians and registered voters worried about traveling." Frank grimaced, but then he forced a smile. "Even if the Travel Warning from the State Department has recommended avoiding Afghanistan for years."

He knew that. He'd begged Staci not to go.

"Although...that region should be safe." Frank stirred sweetener into his coffee.

Jordan watched the spoon go round and round, the clink of metal against ceramic tink-tink-tinking to the rapid beat of his heart. He wanted to wrap his hands around Frank's throat and shake him until he spit out whatever he wanted to impart.

Frank did that--paused for dramatic effect--as if he could make people hang on his words. Most of the time Jordan ignored the tactic. But today, Jordan needed the information Frank had and if he didn't get it soon, Jordan would be forced to ask again. He couldn't show undue interest, but he needed any information he could get on Staci's death.

"This particular area is basically controlled by our military. They are part of Operation: Rebuild. After the fiasco of just plowing under their fields, now we pay the warlord villages not to grow opium and we give them supplies." Frank sipped at the coffee, then lectured, "Then we foot the bill to replant the fields with orchards, whatever, so they still have a way to make a living. The Franklin Group suggested the program."

Jordan's stomach clenched. "So if that's true, why did they imprison her?" Jordan tried to make his voice sound interested in an offhand manner.

Just me wondering about this 'obscure and tragic but unimportant in my world' situation. Instead of the truly cataclysmic event it was. Staci had been in the wrong place at the right time and that had cost her everything. And him too. He couldn't even mourn in public. Because she'd kept their relationship a secret, he couldn't chance that somehow he could damage her reputation posthumously.

"Our intelligence indicates she was turned in by a local warlord for inappropriate dress. Usually they're a little more lax about the dress code but with the recent resurgence of Taliban in that area, some of the natives have reverted back to the customs of keeping the women robed."

"Why the hell wasn't she wearing her burkha?" Jordan bit out. She knew better. They'd discussed it loudly. He'd seen her pack the damn thing himself.

"There's no hard intelligence on the exact circumstances of her capture. And her murder is being blamed on the prisoners during the riot." Frank said, "The situation feels a little funny, but I can't put my finger on what's wrong."

As annoying as Frank was, his analysis was usually dead on.

"Want me to take a closer look at it?" Jordan offered casually and prayed Frank agreed. Otherwise he would have to make a copy of the report when the office cleared out.

"You wanna write the position paper, go for it. You've got more background experience with the country anyway." Frank shrugged and took a gulp of coffee. "We've been told there's no official analysis needed on her death, but it wouldn't hurt to work up a short post-mortem. Especially since we advised on this region. If the politicians change their minds, we'll be on top of it."

"Sure." Jordan curled his fingers around the sheath of papers. If there was anything unusual in her capture or death, he'd find it.

He might not be able to claim Staci, but at least he'd be able to avenge her.

"One thing doesn't make sense." Jordan mentally scrolled through all of the information he'd read on Afghanistan since she'd left. "Why would the escaping prisoners take the time to kill her and chop off her head? I would think escaping was more important."

"Yeah. But the warlords had no reason to kill her. They

wanted the ransom." Frank steepled his hands together and pressed them against his lips. "Why kill her and risk retaliation from the government, both theirs and ours?"

It didn't make sense.

Jordan smoothed a hand down his shirt, his fingers dipping past his ribcage to the concave hollow of his stomach. He'd lost weight since Staci left.

He'd been working like a demon, trying to lose himself in something other than worry and fear for Staci's safety. Turned out the worry and fear had been justified.

His mind raced. She had told him that her trip was humanitarian and had nothing to do with the CIA. But what if her capture had nothing to do with how she dressed and everything to do with her work for the CIA? If the prisoners really had killed her, perhaps they had discovered she was CIA.

Did the CIA know more about her death? Did the Senate Select Committee on Intelligence know that Staci was CIA?

He couldn't tell Frank that Staci was CIA. Jordan shouldn't have that intel.

"There's a visual in the file. It may give you some clues," Frank commented as he stood. "It isn't pretty, but nothing you haven't seen before."

Frank was wrong. He'd seen Staci many ways: happy, angry, flush with desire, sparkling with vitality and good humor, even mischievous.

But he'd never seen her tortured, decapitated.

His stomach lurched at the thought of looking at the pictures. He needed to honor her memory, but he couldn't sit here calmly and look at photographs of her dead body with Frank McClellan sitting across the break room table from him.

He couldn't.

"You okay? You look a little green."

"Bad sushi." Jordan deliberately set the file on the table.

"Never touch that stuff." Frank paused in the doorway. "Back to the grind. Let me know if you come with any ideas."

Jordan went back to his office and closed the door carefully. He reached for the file, and observed with detachment that his fingers trembled.

It was too late to save her.

But he could find out why her life had been sacrificed. It would be his final tribute to the woman who'd invaded every part of his life. He touched the thick paper and flipped the page to look at the visual confirmation of his lover's dead body. Forcing the bile back down his throat, he meticulously catalogued every detail of the torture.

The burn marks on her skin, the scrapes and signs of abuse clearly visible in the stark, graphic photos. There were four close-up shots of her naked corpse.

With his finger, he traced the lines of her body as if he could caress her one last time.

Her feet were battered and scraped. There were abrasions along the bones in her shins. Bruises, fist marks on her back and stomach.

He looked at the bones in her shoulders, noted where the mole had been burned off. Sickness rose in his throat again at the clear evidence of physical abuse and torture.

His hand shook at the violence. Her skin in the photo was so white, her body looked much lighter than her mixed heritage, and very pale against his darker hand.

The angle of the shots showed her breasts, flaccid in death. He paused, rubbed back and forth at the underside of her right breast, as if he could feel the raised scar tissue from the procedure she'd had to remove a cyst as a teenager.

The scar wasn't there.

He pulled a magnifying glass out of his desk drawer, slowly, purposefully, afraid to let elation build as he examined the stark picture.

The scar wasn't there.

Relief gushed through him, and he could barely contain his joy. He wanted to whoop with glee, he wanted to scream from the top of his lungs.

The woman in the picture wasn't Staci.

Did the CIA know? Had they already sent a team in to extract her? Except if they had, wouldn't Intelink have some chatter about the extraction?

But what if they didn't know Staci wasn't dead? She'd been keeping their relationship a secret from the agency. He couldn't do anything that would jeopardize her cover. So how did he let them know without a whole lot of questions that could get her in a whole lot of trouble?

He sobered as a final thought struck.

If she wasn't dead...where was she?

CHAPTER 5

J ordan sat at his desk and remembered the exact moment three and a half weeks ago, when his life changed. When Staci had ripped his world apart. They'd been at her house and she'd been packing for her trip.

"Afghanistan?" he said the word calmly, as if he didn't want to run over and pull the clothes out of her duffel bag.

As if she hadn't just gutted him with a serrated edge, Ka-Bar combat knife and left him to bleed out on the floor in front of her.

Fuck.

He waited, needing a moment, as she carefully rolled a satellite phone into a heavy, hooded sweatshirt and tried not to let the steam building burst through the top of his head.

Frustration beat through his body.

She tossed bundles of pencils for the kids into her pack as more than food, candy, or even basic necessities, the kids would want writing supplies.

"I wish I could bring some books," she muttered,

apparently oblivious to the absolute fury swirling within him.

"Why would you want to go to Afghanistan--right now?"

"Because it's my job." She calmly folded a pair of tan pants with multiple zippers and little hidey pockets for storing everything you might need to carry on your person. He tried to ignore the multi-tool Swiss Army knife she tucked into the interior pocket. It was as if she knew she'd be searched and hoped they'd miss the weapon and general emergency aid.

"I can think of ten different reports with warnings on my desk right now." *Did he freakin' shout that or had he been calm?* "Reports that strongly suggest all civilians stay the hell away from the entire country."

"I know."

"Is this job really worth your life?" Apparently, he'd shouted, based on her frown, but he couldn't bring himself to tone it down.

If ever there was a time for shouting, now was it.

Staci waved away his concerns with a careless flick of her fingers. "The region I'm going to is fairly safe. The local warlords are allies and our military has a strong presence."

"Honey, I have news for you. That kind of crap might make for good public relations in the media and photo ops for the Secretary of State, but anyone who has been there knows things are completely different."

"I have good sources. It's fine."

"Sources?" He heard the derision in his voice. She was a freaking college professor. How accurate could her "sources" be? Jordan bunched his hands into fists, and his muscles tensed into classic defensive readiness.

She stopped folding her clothes and propped her hands on her hips. "How long have we been together?"

With visible effort, he relaxed. Sometimes he really, really did not understand the female brain. Even though he'd been raised solely by his mother and aunt, a woman's intricate thought process escaped him. "What does that have to do with going to a violence-riddled country?"

"Do I ever do anything without having a plan, without a clear direction and plenty of forethought?" She held a palm up. "Really think about it before you answer."

He had to admit that she was meticulous and thorough and one damn fine researcher. But.... "All the research and academics in the world--"

"I'm damn good at physically defending myself. We spar every night." She talked over his objections with less heat than when they'd had a raging argument about the ramifications of foreign aid to countries who walked a fine line between ally and enemy.

"Yes. You can hold your own against an instructor or mugger, but sparring can't protect you from the business end of a Russian-made AK 47 or an armor-piercing round from a tank."

Not to mention fucking IED's.

He balled his fists in a lame attempt to keep his hands to himself. Dammit. He did not want her going to Afghanistan.

"I'm more likely to be attacked on the streets of D.C. or New York," her voice broke, "like my grandparents."

A low blow in his opinion. Lately she'd been obsessed with the violent death of her grandparents. But Jordan let her argue, because he was too upset to speak.

"Than I am on the streets of Kabul, as long as I wear my burkha." She folded the faded blue fabric into a neat, precise rectangle.

"But you aren't just going to be in Kabul."

He couldn't stand it any longer. Jordan stopped her

efficient packing with the simple pressure of his palms against her shoulders, bare except for the thin straps of a soft cotton tank top.

Savoring the warmth of her satin skin, slick with lotion and the scent of gardenias, he curled his fingers into the muscles on her arms and gently squeezed.

"Don't go."

"This is one of the things I do." Although her voice was low, calm, the tension in her body transmitted to his hands as she turned around to face him. Her gaze was a mixture of apology and defiance. "This is for UNOCHA."

"Land mines?" His voice rose.

"I don't have anything to do with the actual de-mining or detonation of the explosives." She skirted the subject.

"Could you pick anything more fucking dangerous?"

Her gaze slid away from his for a mere instant before returning and holding.

"What the fuck," his voice got lower, quieter, "was that?"

He couldn't believe her involuntary flinch from what should have been a completely rhetorical question. Not much else could be more dangerous than going to Afghanistan in the middle of a fucking civil war.

With that one telling gesture, he knew something bigger was coming. For a bare flicker of time, he wanted to cover his ears, he didn't want to know, didn't want to hear what was coming next.

He knew her, knew by the look in her eyes he wasn't going to like it. Strike that. He was going to hate whatever came out of her mouth next. And yet, he had to ask. "What?"

"I work for the CIA," she announced baldly.

What?

He knew she'd been keeping secrets...but he couldn't

even be sure he'd heard correctly. "Tell me my girlfriend didn't just tell me that she works for the CIA?"

The fucking Central Intelligence Agency?

You couldn't trust a spook. Most of the time they were lying. Either by omission or because their information was classified. With her confession, he realized the first woman he'd ever considered taking home to meet his mother and aunt, the first woman he'd opened up to, had secrets he wouldn't ever tap.

He despised secrets and lies. And he realized that he'd been in the biggest lie of all since they'd met. "Has anything you told me been the truth?" He couldn't keep the bitterness out of his voice.

"Yes," she practically shouted. "How can you ask me that?"

"Fuck." Jordan closed his eyes, reached for his usual calm. "Because I really don't know you at all."

And fuck him, but he really didn't.

How could he judge anything, present or past, without filtering it through the reality that Staci Grant, his girlfriend worked for the CIA. "Was our relationship a cover for something else?"

"No!" Her gaze was wild, desperate.

He let his disbelief bleed through. Frankly, he'd lived through enough weird political dynamics before he was ten years old and finally understood asking about his father was a really bad idea and some things were better left unexplained. And with that thought he had to wonder...she couldn't be trying to get information about his father, could she?

Or what if she'd been trying to get information about his job?

He couldn't seem to grasp anything, as if his mind was

clouded with static. Trying to make sense of the past few months, he reviewed their interactions, and everything took on new meaning and implication. He'd only ever discussed his work in hypotheticals, but she would have had access to his laptop and his files at home. It would not be good for his career if the Franklin Group discovered he'd been fraternizing with a CIA employee.

"The CIA can get access to the Franklin Group's work through Intelink. You didn't need to fuck me to get information."

Her arm swung out, palm open as the flat of her hand smacked against his cheek. "That cheapens both of us," she said hotly.

Okay, yeah. The insult was uncalled for, but at the same time he couldn't bring himself to apologize. As he analyzed every interaction, he kept coming back to the one truth. She'd lied. About everything.

"Maybe. Of course, I'm not the one who based this," he gestured between the two of them, "on lies."

As she bent her head, remorse pricked at his conscience. He hadn't been entirely truthful either. But his relationship with his father didn't have anything to do with Staci--or himself.

He was an accident of biology and lack of birth control. And a product of his mother's refusal to cave in and have an abortion when she'd ended up pregnant and unemployed. The truth was Jordan wouldn't be here if his mother hadn't had the moral and religious constitution to tackle the stigma of being a Mexican-Catholic unwed parent.

"I was planning on telling you," she started. "After...."

"What? You, maybe, come back from a war zone?" He tried to temper his response but didn't succeed. His voice was harsh and accusing.

He'd been to Afghanistan. He knew what the country was like, and the thought of her spending any time there completely freaked him out. "Is this a working trip?"

"Yes. I'm going to volunteer with UNOCHA for two weeks."

"That's not what I meant," he replied patiently.

"Even if it were, I couldn't tell you." She closed her eyes, an expression of pure frustration on her face. "This work is strictly for my parents."

"Your parents are dead."

She flinched and part of him felt sorry for pushing, but the other part, the one who knew too much about the way the CIA operated, needed to know.

"Every year I take two weeks and work for this organization." Her fingers brushed at the amulet resting in the hollow of her throat. The amber scarab bumped subtly to the beat of her pulse. "My family is big on giving back and this particular cause was especially important to my mother. It has nothing to do with the CIA."

Yeah. He'd heard this before. "Truth?"

"Truth."

Was he going to have to ask for a pledge of veracity every time they had a conversation?

Staci reached out, her fingers tentatively trailing down the length of his arm, the gesture uncharacteristic and somehow vulnerable.

He tried to ignore the tactile sensation but the brush of her touch ignited every nerve ending in his body.

She wasn't a tentative person. It was one thing he admired most about her. She knew her mind and went after what she wanted. Even if he didn't always agree with her, he appreciated her passion.

Staci lifted her hand away from his wrist and crossed her

arms protectively over her stomach. She would know the non-verbal communication showed her defensiveness and her need to protect herself from whatever came next.

The move galvanized him and he reached for her. His biological imperative was to protect. He'd been raised by his aunt and mother to cherish and revere women.

Not attack.

He slid his arm around her shoulders, the heat of her skin zapping his nerve endings. From the first time they met, before they'd even been introduced, swear to God, the electricity had arced twenty feet between them.

Together they were combustible.

They would have to discuss her trip, her job, her lies again later, but right now he chose to burn.

Jordan gripped the back of her neck, fingers twining in the leather chain, and pulled her to him, their bodies sliding together as if reassembling pieces of a well-oiled, field-stripped rifle.

"I don't want to fight before I leave," she whispered, her breath hot against his neck. "Please."

Her mouth brushed against his collarbone and his body responded with pre-conditioned reflex, the slight flick of her tongue against his skin sent lightning bolts straight down to his groin.

The rush of adrenaline from his earlier anger transformed into a buzz of arousal. It was irrational and stupid. He was mad at her and still all it took was the soft, wet heat of her mouth for his scruples and his hurt to take a hike.

She subtly shifted her hips and the cradle of her concave stomach rubbed sensuously along his already hardened length. Jordan ran his hands firmly along her spine, stilling the movement of her hips as he cupped her ass and lifted her against him to increase the pressure.

She nailed him with a hard and near-violent kiss, and her hands gripped his shoulders with an intensity more powerful than lies. The heavy scent of her musk crowded out the lighter fragrance of gardenia. He slipped his hand underneath the smooth cotton of her shorts, traced his middle finger along the elastic lace of her thong, his fingers trapped by the tight thong against her aroused sex.

He slid his middle finger inside of her, his other fingers slipping along her folds and reveling in the fact she was already wet.

God, he could spend all day just rubbing and playing with her, listening to her soft moans, feeling the sound rumble through her body.

Just touching her turned him on so intensely, he could come right there, with her pubic bone pressing against his cock and the hard berries of her nipples stabbing into the muscles of his chest.

She moaned low in her throat and nipped at the curve of his neck as her hands headed south toward the erection popping out of his thin shorts.

He lifted her up so his hand could have better access and ran his tongue down the center of her breastbone, tasting the sweat, barely cooled, on her skin. Her head tilted back even as her legs came up to grip his hips. She rocked back and forth, as he nipped his way down to the beautiful globes of her breasts.

Her nipples peaked through the gray tank top, begging for his touch. He sucked one swollen tip into his mouth and tongued hard while his fingers plucked a similar melody on her clitoris.

Her arms corded and strong, held his head to her breast as her hips pumped faster.

Damn, she was close.

No way was she going over that edge without him.

She pushed his shorts down as they tumbled to the bed, her palm hot against his engorged cock.

His brain short-circuited. Protection.

No way. You're mine. He squeezed her butt, shoved the thong aside, keeping the material tight against her clitoris and slammed into her.

She seized his ass with her hands and yanked him toward her, pistoning her hips into his. Staci came in a violent burst as he slammed in and out of her slick channel, the head of his erection rubbing against her sweet spot inside.

"Unh," she moaned. Her legs gripped his body as she bowed under the force of her orgasm.

The rhythmic contractions pulled on his erection and he shoved over the edge with an explosion of light and sensation, semen jetting out of him in sharp pulses.

The union of their bodies was always incredible, but this sex was better and hotter than anything they'd ever shared.

They lay there, hearts still pounding, bodies slick with sweat and come. The glow of sexual satisfaction shimmered around them, but the blood that had vacated his brain began to return.

Afghanistan, the CIA, her growing obsession with her grandparents' deaths. He pressed his cheek to hers and tried to forget about Afghanistan, tried to forget about the monumental lie she'd been telling since they'd met. Tried to forgive the fact that she'd been lying.

And he wondered...*what other lies had she told him? What other secrets was she keeping?*

The mail cart clattered down the hallway, jerking Jordan back to the present and the Franklin Group office.

Jordan pulled the amulet out of his pocket and set it on the cherry desktop, staring at the warm amber, picturing the last time she'd worn the ancient necklace. The eye of Horus stared back at him...a symbol of strength and wisdom in battle. And he wished she'd taken it with her.

In the span of half an hour he'd gone from thinking her dead to realizing she wasn't.

Weeks ago, he hadn't stopped her from leaving. And he hadn't gone after her when he first realized she might be in that prison. He could fill his office with the regrets of things he hadn't done.

He didn't want any more regrets. Jordan rubbed at the amulet. Strength and wisdom. And he knew two things. She was still missing. And he still couldn't claim her.

But maybe he could find her.

CHAPTER 6

September 13
   Nassau, Bahamas

NOT SO TOUGH ANYMORE, are you, bitch? I taunted.

The syringe needle lay near my vein and I tried not to wince. For courage, I leaned against the rusted tub sink and stared into the half-silvered, half-black mirror above the faucet spigot.

My face, yet...not, stared back at me.

I'd already injected the experimental drug twice and knew the cool liquid would burn as it spread through my veins like a clear poison.

Soon it would be darkening my skin, ramping up my pigment, transforming me from a white girl with an olive complexion to a light-skinned black woman.

I wasn't sure I could get out of the Bahamas any other way. I'd gotten into the Bahamas without detection from any one. I'd be damned if whoever wanted me dead caught me getting out.

Someone had set me up to be captured and possibly killed. There was no other explanation for what had happened to me in Afghanistan.

Afghanistan was no Central America with people getting kidnapped and ransomed regularly. However, the CIA has procedures in place in the event of being kidnapped while undercover. So when my jailors asked for next of kin, I gave them the proper case officer code name and contact info, supposedly a widowed aunt, exactly as instructed if ever kidnapped.

No one had come to ransom me out of the prison. I'd been tortured and beaten, and if it weren't for Fariya's sacrifice, I'd be dead.

The CIA had forsaken me.

Why? Various reasons ran through my mind.

Before I'd left for Afghanistan I'd filed the paperwork to officially report Jordan as a 'Close and Continuing' relationship. Paperwork to inform the CIA of our involvement. And then came the wait for a positive response regarding my association with Jordan and hope it was within parameters some pencil pusher deemed appropriate.

The whole idea of having to submit to the agency for approval of my boyfriend made me bristle. While I understood intellectually...in reality, the process sucked.

Anyway, I'd done my own background check on Jordan before we'd ever even had dinner. Nothing in his past raised any flags except for the mystery of his father's identity. But since the father wasn't in the picture, I had let the subject go.

I couldn't imagine anyone had even looked at the information yet. Admin was notorious for taking forever. Besides, the CIA should have a better reason to decommission me, or kill me, or refuse to save me, than because I got a boyfriend.

The syringe was cold and real in my hand as I contemplated the likely reason I'd been a target. Being with Jordan brought up all my old insecurities. I wasn't sure I had it in me to be the best for him. After my parents died and I went to live with my grandparents, life changed. Then when my grandparents were murdered, my life changed again.

I realized I needed closure about my grandparents' deaths. When I went back over what happened to them, the mugging and stabbing that had no witnesses, I started to wonder what really happened to them.

And when I'd been looking into my grandparents' deaths, I had discovered Department 5491. A super secret, National Security Agency, Department 5491.

Starting right after my grandparents were killed, every month I received a check. I'd been told it was insurance money and I'd never wondered about that money.

Until I went back over what happened when they died. Carson Black had come to me and professed his sympathy. A friend. A mentor. He was the reason I got into espionage work. He was the man who helped me after the rest of my family perished. And I'd never questioned his involvement. I'd been eighteen and shell-shocked.

But when I started asking questions a few months ago, I was shut down and shut out.

Firmly. Emphatically.

When my queries to Carson were unanswered and information about the mysterious department 5491 was stifled, my desire to know more rose.

And I realized it all tied into those monthly checks. The more resistance I encountered, the more determined I became to get to the bottom of Department 5491.

That's when I discovered there was a whole list of people receiving the same checks. Checks that started after someone in their family had been killed. All in October of 1995.

Same as my grandparents.

So now while I thought my troubles likely stemmed from my investigation into 5491, I didn't have a freaking clue where the threat came from. Who was behind Department 5491?

The NSA, the CIA and the DIA were all possibilities. All had employees on the list who were receiving checks. But none of the family members who were killed worked in espionage or for those agencies. So why were we receiving those checks?

And, I was stalling.

With a huge exhale of breath, I twisted the rubber tourniquet and waited patiently for the vein in my left elbow to pop. I ignored the slight wobble as I moved the needle into place. I splinted my left arm whenever I was alone, but the still knitting bone ached constantly. I didn't splint it in public. I had no idea if my captors had known my arm had been broken, but I couldn't afford to assume that they hadn't.

Outside the ramshackle and only door, the chickens clucked and squawked. The warm breeze as trade winds hit the island's shore shifted the ragged bit of fabric tacked over the window behind me. Sweat and the oily, sickly scent of my fear coated my grimy face.

No one was coming. I'd purposely tossed corn feed around my door and window to set up a warning system. The scrawny hens would squawk and screech if anyone bothered them while they tried to peck up the offering.

The simple measure was probably as effective as the fancy alarm system I had in Alexandria.

Nice stall, Stace.

I inhaled, trying unsuccessfully to ignore the odors of rotting garbage and refuse of the people too stoned or too tired to care where they defecated.

Afghanistan was hell.

The Bahamas were paradise...if you had enough money and influence.

If not, you were stuck in clusters of houses with amenities from the last century, bacteria-laden water, less-than-ideal refrigeration, and minimal electricity.

"And you're still stalling, dammit." My voice came out ill-used and harsh, and my words grated inside my throat like claws trying to tear out of me.

I'd hoped talking to myself would jolt me out of this funk long enough to get the job done. If I didn't shoot the damn drug, Fariya would have died in vain. That--I couldn't let happen.

I snatched the syringe and angled the sharp point of the needle at my blue, blood-engorged vein. With a sharp exhale, I jabbed the needle in, pressed the plunger down.

How the drug could be so freaking ice cold in the humid, languid heat of the Caribbean was beyond me.

But it was.

The liquid seared into my blood, working its magic. I pulled the needle out slowly and watched the blood pool into a drop at the crease of my elbow. I turned my hand over slowly. After two injections I already saw the difference in the color of my skin.

My once extremely light, olive skin was a coffee brown. The drug seemed to be working faster than expected, possibly because of my Arab heritage. Just a few more treatments of the pigment-producing drug and I would pass for a mulatto or maybe even a black woman.

Then whoever was looking for Staci Grant, white skin, blond hair with light brown streaks, and blue eyes would pass right over me. My skin would be dark enough, dark brown contacts would shield my blue eye color, and the mahogany brown dye and lack of conditioner would turn my hair into a much rougher and scraggly mop.

With the slight limp I'd acquired getting my butt from Afghanistan to Pakistan, no one should connect urbane, sophisticated, wealthy Staci Grant to the run down, ragged, beat-up woman in a cheap Bahamian cotton sundress.

The toe-popper I'd triggered had ripped off a piece of my right little toe. I know I should be grateful I hadn't blown up my whole foot, but shit, I'd already lost what felt like everything and right now I didn't have faith I was ever going to get it back.

A wave of nausea broke over my body, sheening my skin with sweat and rolling through my stomach.

The damn drug.

The nausea hit me at the oddest times. Most of the time it was minor, but every once in a while I'd have to choke the sensation back down.

I wrapped a bright orange, batik-patterned pareo around my head, turban style, and slid the brown contacts into my eyes. Then I rubbed self-tanning gel over my exposed skin to add to the already changing color.

I had one quick mission which couldn't be put off any longer.

I waded through the pecking chickens and hopped on a bicycle, heading for the other Bahamas. The one where people shelled out big bucks for a week in their own paradise. The difference between the shanty town and the pristine beach was a McDonald's Big Mac vs. Daniel Boulud's burger stuffed with foie gras.

I pedaled toward my 'house of record' in the Bahamas, ignoring the ache in my left arm, the burn in my right toe, and the ice cold flowing through my veins.

The ride from squalor to extravagance took less time than you might think.

My house was a white, modern triumph of architecture plopped down on the blindingly white sand beach, rimmed by the turquoise ocean, and capped by an Azure blue sky.

The last time I'd been here was with Jordan, in August, before I'd left for Afghanistan.

We'd had a perfect weekend. Peaceful, elegant and easy.

In the evening, the sun had bled pink and yellow across the simple, luxurious furniture, highlighted billowing sheer curtains, and carried the scents of vacation: the salty sea, charred wood from a bonfire, melted butter, savory grilled lobster, and the crisp aroma of a chilled Chardonnay with a hint of apple, pear, maybe a touch of cinnamon. Half-burned candles flickered with the ocean breeze. The staff murmured quietly as they cleared the kitchen for the night.

Even now, I could almost feel Jordan lying beside me, tucked against my back as he cradled me to his hard body, our heads pillowed on plump goose-down cushions as we enjoyed the romantic pleasure of the sunset.

The longing to recapture that one perfect moment unfurled within me.

Our easy camaraderie and heated passion had made me feel closer to him than ever. I'd yearned for our closeness to deepen and our relationship to strengthen.

A truck blew its horn and startled me out of my memory. I blinked against the stark, hot daylight.

I pedaled right past my house, not even looking at the

structure. As we planned, my housekeeper Neli should already be at the Pearsons'...my sometime neighbors.

I'd met them once or twice throughout the years I'd owned my house although we rarely spent the same weekends on island. We shared the same housekeeper, Neli, and she often helped me out on the side.

I pedaled up the Pearsons' grand circular driveway and around to the servant's side entrance, then knocked politely, in case anyone was watching.

Neli came to the door with a bucket of cleaning supplies in hand. "Come on den, let's get to work."

Just as I'd requested, she treated me like extra help, going so far as to speak to me in her native Bahamian Creole when I knew perfectly well she spoke excellent English.

But the look of horror on her face told me my appearance had shocked her. I wasn't real fond of looking in the mirror these days myself.

"Good God, look at yuh," she whispered as she dragged me to the Pearsons' living room.

"Just a little beat up."

I tried to grin, but she'd yanked on my bad arm and I really needed a moment to stop from spewing all over the highly-polished Brazilian cherry floors.

"Yuh look half dead."

"Better half than all."

"Yuh and yorn tings." Neli tut-tutted all the way through the expansive elaborate kitchen with gleaming stainless steel appliances and a river of black granite.

In the living room, with furnishings more suited to a manor on the East Coast of the U.S., she plopped down the bucket.

"Did you bring the bag?" I made the request softly, trying to act casual but not feeling it.

Neli handed me my emergency bolt bag.

The bag had i.d. and the key to a safe deposit box that held the information I'd collected on 5491. The last time I'd come I'd put the information in the bank. Information I thought just might be why someone wanted me dead.

Then she handed me the pair of binoculars I'd requested. Focusing on my beach house, I surveyed the damage through the lenses.

The curtains had been shredded...literally. I guess they'd been looking for a microchip hidden there, but I wouldn't have been so stupid as to put something so fragile in fabric the housekeeper could pull down and wash any day. The chip would be ruined.

"I never realized how unbelievably well the Pearsons' could see into my house," I murmured.

"Curtains. Dey used to hide everythin'." Neli stood with her hands balled and fisted at her rounded hips. "Dat's one big mess."

I peered through the binoculars. A thick layer of goose feathers covered the floor, concealing the tan bamboo. The sofas were turned upside down, violent slashes ripped apart the muslin under-upholstery, and tufts of cotton pouffed out like giant marshmallow vomit in a sea of feathers.

I could even see that all of the switch plates had been unscrewed and discarded, probably somewhere beneath the feathers.

Sea-scented candles had been dropped like matchsticks on the bamboo coffee table, their holders in pieces next to them.

Fury trembled through Neli's body with little indignant tremors. "Dis bad juju."

"Calm down. It's just stuff," I replied mildly. "And you can cut out the Creole. We're alone."

"Ruined stuff. They done ripped that beautiful paintin' right from the frame."

I took another look. She was right. The expensive beach scene lay on the fireplace hearth, the canvas stripped from the frame, the stretchers smashed.

"Yeah," I confirmed absently. The more Zen I channeled, the more Neli's ire rose.

"I have to clean." She grabbed a dust cloth and started intently cleaning the objets d'art the Pearsons' had scattered around the ornately furnished, immaculately clean room.

I raised the binoculars again and scanned the damage and looked for some clue as to who had ransacked my house, but nothing seemed clear or in focus.

The destruction of my serene retreat annoyed and disturbed me on some level I wasn't even aware of. Why would they be so stupid as to believe I would leave anything of importance in a house of record? That seemed naive.

The destruction was systematic and brutal, but I sensed no anger, no malicious intent--just a determination not to miss anything.

It looked like my instincts had been right.

When things started going to hell in Afghanistan, I'd called Neli on my Sat phone and told her to stay away from my house.

"You haven't been back there, have you?"

"No. I listened to your instructions, but it's killin' me to leave your beautiful house like that."

I heard a car pulling up to my driveway. They wouldn't be so bold as to come back to the house in broad daylight, would they? It seemed inconceivable, but everything about the last few weeks was skewed in a pattern I couldn't seem to intuit.

As if information had been coded in an unfamiliar key.

I trained the binoculars on my front door, wondering if they'd have the chutzpah to walk right in.

"Has anyone shown any interest in me lately?"

"Your man called my house and my cell 'bout every day since last Monday."

A few days after I escaped. Something to consider...why then?

Neli continued, "I always told him what you said. Told him I hadn't seen you since the last time you were here." Neli swiped over the wood floor, while gently chiding me. "He sounded near frantic yesterday."

Jordan. Regret poured through me. I'd left on uncertain terms. Our last night together had been the best and the worst of our relationship.

The fight was a relationship buster.

He'd been angry, I'd been angry.

We hadn't even really come to any resolution, and the next instant we were on the bed, ripping each others' clothes off, and the sex had been amazing and hot and surprisingly intense all at the same time.

And then...I'd left.

We'd emailed a few times, but the messages had been stilted and too formal. I'd known this secret, wonderful person I treasured was on the way out of my life. I couldn't blame him. Too many secrets, too many lies already between us, and too many yet to come.

We couldn't ever hope to achieve that sense of coupleness my grandparents had. But the sorrow, the loss had stunned me with its intensity. I had wanted our relationship to work.

I think, in his heart, so did he. But we wouldn't be able to move past the deceptions and the lies. Even if he had cared enough to check on me.

I sighed, heavy and despondent.

"You need to call him," she admonished again. "Let him know you're...."

"I'm...what?" A mess? Under some sort of death threat?

When I'd hit Pakistan, I'd thought about calling Jordan. Just to hear the sound of his voice. And then I realized...I had no idea who had engineered my capture, or my ransom. The CIA had chosen to leave me in that prison for a reason. I had no idea why.

I couldn't take the risk of contacting Jordan. I didn't want any link, any connection between us. I didn't want whatever was dogging me to spread to him.

It was the only way I could protect him.

I trained the binoculars on my house, waited for whoever was at my door to show themselves, and pushed Jordan to the back of my mind.

Assuming whoever set me up and wanted me dead didn't get their way, I would have years to analyze how our relationship went wrong.

The front door to my house swung open slowly. The angle of the sun backlit the figure, shadowing his face and casting his body in darkness.

But I didn't need light to identify the intruder. I'd recognize his form, his shape, his body anywhere. I jerked my head away from the binocs, with a stiff neck.

"What is it?" Neli asked.

I shook my head. That couldn't be right. Resolutely I put my eyes back to the binoculars.

My heart sped up and the sorrow I tried to keep buried welled up inside of me. The sharp prick of tears burned my eyes. I rapidly blinked the moisture away, hardened my heart.

I'd known I would see him again. After all, back in D.C., we lived next door to each other. I knew one day I would return to my life there. But I'd thought our next meet would be on my terms. When I was ready.

My only consolation: he couldn't see me. My real concern...what the hell was he doing here? "It's Jordan."

He took one more step into the light. The sun struck the side of his face, highlighted the stark lines of his cheekbones and poured down the rest of his body.

Greedily, I catalogued his broad shoulders, sculpted biceps, and muscled thighs. He'd dressed down in jeans and a black polo shirt. When he turned slightly, the sun glinted off the Franklin Group logo.

On the black interlock, the white kite embroidery shimmered in the sunlight.

I'd seen that logo before.

CHAPTER 7

Images freeze-framed in my mind.

Guard slumped in his chair.

Wine bottle lying drunkenly on the hard-packed dirt.

A blue logo on a white mug clasped loosely, fingers hiding most of the design.

The guards had been drinking out of Franklin Group mugs.

The Franklin Group. Where Jordan worked. Another connection flashed as my brain clicked into gear.

My final email to Jordan.

In the email, I'd referenced the area I was in. We'd gone off plan, shifted to the East because there'd been insurgent fighting to the South near the village we'd been scheduled to visit.

I'd been captured not long after that email.

I'd known he was keeping things from me. I'd hoped they were not similar omissions to my own, but as the pieces fell into place now I wondered. Had I been wrong? Could there be some more sinister explanation for his reticence?

I remember the first time I saw him at the podium in the

lecture hall. A study in contradictions; a warrior's body, muscled and sleek, encased in a scholar's garb, an unrelenting black suit of extremely fine wool gabardine. A collarless, fine linen shirt, black, of course, clung to a chest better suited to an action hero than a think tank geek.

The lecture had been...a whim. Something to do on a slow Wednesday night. Professional curiosity. He'd been speaking about non-violent alternatives to counteracting terrorism.

Our meeting couldn't have been engineered, could it?

To Neli, I said, "I need a favor. Go over there." I laid out specific instructions for what I wanted her to ask. "Keep him in the living room or on the patio and get him to face this way." I'd be able to read his lips through the scope on the rifle in my bag.

"What you doin'?" I could feel her start of surprise. "You don't think he did that to your house? Not your man."

No, I didn't think he'd trashed my house. But the question remained...what the hell was he doing in the Bahamas? The bag over my shoulder hung like a carcass on a hook, the old rifle inside weighing the bag down. I couldn't get the damn thing out until I got rid of Neli.

"He didn't trash my house. I just need to find out why he's here."

She licked her lips slowly. "He isn't dangerous, is he?"

To me, just maybe. "Not to you."

Jordan detested collateral damage. It was one of the reasons he'd left the FBI.

"After you're done with him, go on home. Don't linger in the house, don't contact me again."

"But...."

I patted her hand, willing her to leave so I could start assembling that weapon. "I'll be fine. I'll call you when I think it's safe to go back into the house. But don't go back until I tell you it's okay."

"You don't want to see him?" she asked slowly.

I never thought I was vain about my appearance. I appreciated luxury in my textiles, my clothing, my possessions, but I'd always thought myself above the narcissistic beauty of my own looks.

As I catalogued my injuries, the maimed toe, the hideous, still-healing scar on my leg, the various burns and cuts strewn over my body, I acknowledged I'd been fooling myself for a very long time.

I was a mess. Outside and inside. My emotions were all over the place and my body was not the one I'd left home with. We were over, and I'd rather he remembered me the way I was than be thankful he'd dodged a bullet.

That wasn't fair to him. He hadn't been with me because of my looks. But I sure didn't want to find out they mattered to him as much as they turned out to matter to me.

And if he did have something to do with my current predicament, I sure as hell didn't want him to know how well they'd succeeded in tearing me down.

If I ever saw him in person again, it would be when I was strong, whole, and invincible.

Ruthlessly I pushed down the wish to have a moment. Just a hug. A minute in his arms, wrapped around him, absorbing his warmth, his comfort, his sheer bulk.

"No. I don't want to see him," I lied.

"God spare life, be safe." Neli scurried out the door and jumped on her bicycle.

I reached into the drawstring bag slung across my shoulder and quickly pulled out the metal pieces, then began to assemble the ancient sniper rifle.

Jordan was here.

Through the last few weeks, I'd held him in my mind like a talisman. I didn't contact him so I could protect him, keep him safe.

I locked the bore into place.

Except, just maybe, he'd been the missing piece of the faction out to kill me. How could I even be thinking about a hug from him?

I shoved the clip into the magazine with a little more force than necessary. Had he set me up? Had he, all this time while I'd been protecting him, been searching for a way to destroy me?

My heart cried, no! But the more I thought about it, the more it seemed possible. As I ran through everything, I realized I was a fool not to have factored him into my suspicions. He had the connections, he had the tactical knowledge, and he'd been angry before I left.

I screwed the scope onto the top with quick jerks. Dammit.

Liquid splashed on my finger. *One. Two. Three.*

Shit. With the heel of my hand I wiped away the perspiration. I refused to be crying as I did this. I took a slow, deep inhale.

Since my imprisonment, I couldn't seem to apply the same detached, unemotional reasoning that was the cornerstone of my work and my life. I used to look at all the angles, calculate gains and losses in a way that made sense, and decide on a course of action.

But now, my empathy level had gotten skewed. I couldn't figure out if it was due to the torture...or the general loss of myself, but my decision-making process was off.

Clearly, I'd been remembering our interactions with a romanticized view.

At this point, I couldn't trust anyone. If Jordan was the

person who set me up, I'd have to deal with it, deal with him. I fingered the barrel slowly. The Springfield was for shorter range shooting than the Remington Jordan had used in the FBI.

But it would get the job done.

I wondered if he'd trained with one. Probably. I wondered if he would be able to feel the crosshairs along the nape of his neck.

If he'd played me, he'd played me well. The cold possibility of betrayal tore through me. All the longing, yearning I'd done. I felt a fool.

I lifted the weapon slowly to my shoulder and stared down the sight, keeping my finger away from the trigger while Neli made her way to my house.

The butt rested coldly against the bare skin of my shoulder. I steadied my hands, hoping my body could support the weight of the old weapon. Praying I wouldn't have to use it. If necessary, if it came down to him or me, I would kill him....

But I might hesitate.

CHAPTER 8

September 13
  Nassau, Bahamas

WHAT THE HELL was he doing here?

If he could just get one clue, one shred of proof Staci was alive and well, he'd let it go.

Go home and conclude their damn relationship had been slated to fail from the moment they met. Just because the woman in the picture wasn't Staci didn't mean she was still alive. After all, she hadn't contacted him since that last awkward email.

Maybe she really was dead.

Except, he'd found out someone was watching her townhouse in Virginia.

If only he could get rid of the feeling she was in grave danger, satisfy himself that his worries were irrational.

Staci could take care of herself. And obviously wanted to...if she was alive.

Her mother's amulet burned in his pocket. He fingered

61

the carved stone, as if rubbing the small memory of her would cause her to appear like a genie from a bottle, and he paused to let his eyes adjust from the bright Caribbean sunshine outside to the shaded cool interior.

Even before his vision cleared, Jordan knew his problems had just gotten a lot worse.

His heart stopped as he took in the destruction of her beautiful, peaceful retreat. He stepped cautiously into the open floor plan and surveyed the damage.

The house had the stale, stagnant air of a home closed up for some time, overlaid with the stench of decay in a humid tropical climate.

Please God, don't let it be rotting flesh.

Jordan tore through the house, the kitchen, the great room, the bedroom, the bathroom, frantic for any sign she was here.

Alive.

Anything else was unthinkable.

He returned to the entry-way, leaned against the fake stone pillar, his breath sawing through his chest, scraping at his insides like a dull Ka-Bar. Someone had completely trashed her house. Not in a 'I'm robbing you to get money' way but a 'Where the fuck is it?' way.

"She isn't here. She isn't dead." He repeated the mantra as if by saying the words over and over he could make them true.

The house was a study in neutrals. White, beige, cream, tan and wood tones. Before this violation, her home had been extremely soothing. Now, every item had been ripped apart and discarded like garbage.

He had to investigate, look for any clue as to what had happened. Finding anything was unlikely. He'd been part of enough search warrant teams to believe any evidence of significance was history.

No one had been here since the ransack. Which was odd. He knew from his visits here, that Neli usually came in once a week to clean and keep the place immaculate. He'd called Neli every day, hoping maybe Staci had made her way to the Bahamas. So why hadn't Neli mentioned she hadn't been to Staci's house?

Jordan began his search in the kitchen and noted details with a sense of calm he was far from feeling. The oven had been pulled from the walls, the ice maker disassembled, the refrigerator unplugged.

The rotting smell was worse in here. The refrigerator contents, the usual condiment jars, had been dumped into the sink and left, contributing to the stink.

The freezer held one package, plastic ripped open, of some indefinable meat, which had begun the decay process. That was the source of the awful stench.

Thank God.

He rested his forehead against the wall and waited for his heart to settle into an easier rhythm, listening to his breath as relief swept through him.

After a minute, Jordan kicked through the mass of goose feathers on the living room floor and made his way to the bedroom in a trail of white fluff.

In the bedroom, metal coils poked out from piles of mattress stuffing. The sheer curtains lay in shreds on the bedroom floor. Every single lamp had been taken completely apart, bulbs smashed.

Good thing the house was furnished in island spare.

Standing in the doorway, he gazed at the bamboo platform bed and tried not to let memories overwhelm him. They'd tangled in those sheets, wrestled and laughed and loved with a passion he had never imagined. But now the linens were slashed and ripped. He smoothed a rough finger along a strip of what was left of the pristine white cotton.

He and Staci had been here in August.

Before. Before everything turned to shit. When he'd really thought they had a future. He hadn't told her about his father, but he'd been thinking about it.

If only he could have let go of the nagging little niggle that something was wrong, something was off.

His instincts had been right.

In the bathroom, the lingering smell of gardenias assaulted his senses, taunting his memory.

She'd playfully lured him into the open glass shower, the floral scent on her body, in her hair. She lathered the soap and run her slick, teasing fingers over his body. They'd explored each other with murmured laughter, the rest of the world locked far away, unable to intrude.

Now, the fixtures lay in pieces on the cream granite floor; the showerhead, the jets from the tub, towel bars, toilet paper bar, all disassembled and strewn liked broken shells on the beach.

He flexed his arms, fisted his hands and thought he would welcome the chance to have a little one-on-one with the person responsible for this mess.

Deliberately, he unclenched his fists. Anger would get him nowhere. He needed to channel his rage into a cool, calm, analytical assessment of the facts.

He drew on his HRT training. No value judgments, no moral quandaries.

Emotions had no place in a sniper's world.

The search destruction was meticulous and all-encompassing. Professional all the way.

The devastation had only one good message: they didn't

have Staci. If they did, there would be no need for the complete annihilation of her property.

Jordan realized he couldn't let go of the idea that if he could only restore the house, then she would come back as well.

The thought was stupid and futile.

But he couldn't leave until the place was clean.

He started in the bedroom by pulling the rest of the batting from the mattress and stuffing a garbage bag with the cotton. His mind wandered as he did the menial work.

Gaining access to the house would have been easy. Half the houses on this tiny inlet were only occupied a few weekends a year and rarely at the same time.

He heard a noise at the front door. On instinct, he reached for his weapon. A year out of the field, and he still followed training.

But of course he wasn't carrying.

He knew that Staci kept a weapon in the bedside table. Based on the thoroughness of the destruction, odds were the small P229 was gone.

It wouldn't hurt to check.

Carefully, Jordan put down the garbage bag and eased toward the night-stand next to the bed. He slid the drawer open soundlessly. Empty, except for an open box of condoms and some outdated Vogue magazines.

No weapon. Which meant, the ransackers had stolen it. Through the crack in the door, Jordan had a clear line of sight.

"Oh, dear Lordy."

He heard the whispered epithet, recognized the voice of Staci's housekeeper, and relaxed his ready position.

"Neli?" he called softly, hovering in the shadows, peering though the slit, waiting until she showed herself.

In case she wasn't alone.

"Dat you, Mister Jordan?"

"Yeah."

Neli tentatively tread into the living room. There she stopped, pivoted around in a slow circle. "Did yuh make this mess?"

"What do you think?"

She shook her head slowly back and forth, as if she couldn't believe the devastation. "My poor beautiful house," she wailed.

He waited another beat before deciding she was alone and not guilty, then walked cautiously into the living room. "This the first time you've seen it?"

She stared at him, anguish in her gaze. "It's awful."

Jordan thought about possible surveillance measures on the house. Thought about the methodical precision with which every single item in the house had been stripped and destroyed.

The effort behind this search meant time, money, and training. With the resources already expended, the logical assumption would be they also planted a bug. He wasn't touching this conversation inside where anyone could be listening in.

"Outside," he barked.

He yanked open the floor-to-ceiling glass slider and stalked out onto the cream stone patio. Waves crashed against the shore while seagulls squawked lazily, dipping and swooping into the surf for their lunch.

Jordan studied the pergola.

They hadn't neglected the outside either.

Neli paced around the patio, her jerky movements irritating him on some subconscious level. Finally she twisted around to stand awkwardly to his left. He pivoted away from the interior of the house. Even if there was a camera or bug out here, the sound of the pounding waves should mask their words.

"Why haven't you been here before now?" He kept his voice low so she would have to lean in to hear.

"Miss Staci, she called me about a few weeks ago and said not to worry about cleaning the house for some little bit. Knew she wouldn't be back." Her gaze skittered away from him.

She was lying.

The question was--about Staci calling or about when she called?

"Really?" He crossed his arms over his chest, flexing his muscles and expanding his shoulders. At six foot three he could be pretty damn intimidating. "Have you seen her since?"

"I've been talking to you every day, haven't I?" She countered, fluttering around the patio like a dragonfly on speed, picking up chair cushions, trying to stuff batting back inside. "Just look at dis mess."

Her distress at the destruction was clearly real. However, she hadn't answered the question.

"What yuh doin' here?" She planted her hands on her hips and glared at him.

"Staci is...missing." He tried to keep the emotion out of his voice, but a tiny tremor rippled through. Ruthlessly, he suppressed the betraying quiver. "I'm looking for her, any place I can think of."

"She's missin'?"

He went for shock value. "Presumed dead."

"Dead?" Neli fell back a step, her head canting back to her right, then looking around again at the shredded remnants of Staci's patio.

Interesting. She hadn't considered Staci being dead. Why not?

"Her other house in Massachusetts was trashed as well." He analyzed her reaction. "Whoever did this may be after her."

Neli squeezed her hands together as if in prayer. "She in danger, yuh tink?"

"Yeah. Grave danger. I want to help her." She clearly needed help. "Has anyone else called you about Staci?"

She blinked, her lashes moving in slow motion. "No."

"You're sure? No one called with a seemingly benign inquiry, like the newspaper or utility company or...the phone company?"

"Well, the electric company called because my phone number is on record for emergencies, sayin' they wanted to put her on some monthly maintenance plan."

"What did you tell them?"

"They'd have to talk to her when she was in town."

"Did they ask when she would be here?"

"Why, they did."

They'd been pretexting Neli, fishing for information about Staci. "You didn't give them details, did you?"

"No. I know how to keep me mouth shut." She firmed her lips, making a locking motion with her long brown fingers.

"She's in danger," Jordan said urgently. "I want to help her."

Neli shifted again. "I never thought about that phone call. I hope I didn't mess up."

He interpreted her words, heard the worry. If she didn't give them information, why was she worried about messing up?

Suddenly he realized her appearance was awfully

convenient. How had she known to show up exactly when he was here?

He grabbed her by the shoulders, feeling the bony outline of her thin body through the worn cotton dress. "Where is she?"

Neli shook like a palm tree shivering in the aftermath of a hurricane. "Please don't hurt me, Mister Jordan. Please don't hurt me."

Fear, sweat, and lemon furniture polish rose from her skin.

The feeling of being watched trickled over him. He should know better. Hadn't he done surveillance on narcos from nine hundred feet away?

"How did you know to show up here, right now?"

"I didn't know you'd be here." She bent back, trying arch away from him. "Please, please don't hurt me. I got a child."

"Tell me what I want to know." Impatiently, he tightened his fingers on her shoulders and pulled her up, toward him. His voice was low and rough as he forced his face right up to hers. "How did you know I was here?"

"I...I...."

She tried to hunch away again, the whites of her eyes stark in her shiny black face. His grip was too strong and his will too fierce.

"Please, don't hurt me."

"I don't want to hurt you. I just want to know how you knew I was here."

Her breath jerked out of her body in great huge bursts. "I was," gasp,

"cleaning," gasp,

"Pearsons' house," gasp,

"heard," gasp,

"car." Her eyes rolled back in her head and her body went limp beneath his hands.

"Shit." Jordan lowered her carefully to the wicker chaise lounge. He put two fingers to her neck and felt the rapid fluttering of her pulse. She'd be okay in a second. Terrific. He'd scared a little housekeeper so badly, she'd passed out.

Jordan rubbed the back of his neck and from his crouch swept his gaze around the patio. He couldn't get rid of the feeling of being watched.

A camera could be hidden anywhere in this mess. If they'd wanted to make a move on him, they'd had ample time.

He stood, stretched.

Jordan bent down and checked on Neli again. Her breath was slow and deep, her eyelashes fluttered.

"The Pearsons' house," he repeated. Jordan pictured the layout of the street in his head, stared into the floor-to-ceiling plate glass window, and then toward the neighbor's house. Where Neli had been working, where she'd looked when he said Staci might be dead.

The neighbors.

Jordan pounded down the shell driveway, shoes crunching loudly as he sprinted toward the other house.

He ripped open the side door of the Pearsons' house and tore through the elaborate kitchen and ornate rooms.

But the house was empty.

A lone can of lemon furniture polish and a rag rested on an end table near the windows. Jordan lifted the rag and looked toward the window. From here, there was a clear view into Staci's house.

Maybe it really was that simple. Maybe Neli had been cleaning here, happened to see him walk in, and come to talk to him.

Shit. This had been a total waste of time.

But he wouldn't, couldn't give up on finding Staci.

He refused to believe the decapitated woman in the picture was Staci. It wasn't. It couldn't be. The scar was missing.

Staci was alive.

He felt the truth in his soul. He would know if she were dead, he thought fiercely. He wouldn't rest until he found her and made sure she was okay.

Jesus, he was a mess. His sniper's calm was completely trashed by worry. He needed to slow down and think.

Little things had started to add up after their fight, after she'd left, after he'd learned she worked for the CIA.

She had been more paranoid, more protective of her privacy and more cautious than he'd ever realized. As each detail stripped away his blinders, he acknowledged he'd been taking note subconsciously and ignoring signs from the beginning. Her requests to keep their relationship private, their almost clandestine meetings in places other than D.C.

What he'd intuited as a sense of adventure and travel had really been attempts for them to be together outside of her main home city, Washington.

Reviewing their conversations, discussions about how to deal with the threats against the United States, he had begun to piece together what she really did for the CIA and his suspicions weren't pretty.

If he was correct, she'd been a recruiter, recruiting on several different levels. One level for the CIA and on another level, she'd recruited potential terrorists. He figured the CIA tracked and turned those recruits later on, assuming they could catch them before they committed a grievous act against the US or their allies. Those recruits would be infiltrating groups who wished the U.S. harm, without realizing that the government was watching them and recording their contacts.

Where Jordan had been working to mitigate and eliminate terrorist threats, Staci had been actively developing new recruits.

Jordan and Staci's positions really had been polar opposites. He'd just ignored the clues. And while he actively disagreed with what she had been doing, in the end, her job didn't matter to him. What mattered was Staci was in trouble.

He was honor bound to help her, without tipping off the CIA that he knew she was alive. He'd go home. And start trying to dig into those private computer files he knew existed in her hidden office in the attic. He'd find the link, he'd find the leak, he'd find whoever was searching her houses. He'd find her.

He'd make amends for their final, bitter confrontation. Then they'd be done. He could move on.

If the process ripped a hole in his heart, so be it. He'd right the wrong.

As he left the Pearsons' house, Jordan could swear he smelled the faint scent of gun oil.

CHAPTER 9

S eptember 15
     Nassau, Bahamas

THE NASSAU AIRPORT hallway had an industrial feel, walls
either a soft, pale yellow or a warm cream, dingy from years
of incessant heat, dust from the field along the airstrip, and
the insidious dirt of thousands of travelers.

Security personnel inspected every bag with a languid,
inattentive sweep of the bomb detection cloth and less
interest in the luggage contents than a teenager listening to
their parents drone.

They waved me through, and I made my way to the
gate. My insides heaved but I kept down the bile rising in
my throat. Acid burned through my esophagus, igniting a
sharp pain. I rubbed my breastbone to soothe the ache.

I couldn't afford to throw up. If they thought I was sick,
they might not let me on that plane.

Sunlight streamed through intermittent windows.
Guards in pairs sat in metal folding chairs at regular

intervals, their burnished ebony skin gleamed with sweat as their gazes skimmed with a routine boredom over the passengers herding toward the gates.

Ceiling fans circled lazily, swishing the oppressive heat in new directions, doing little to cool off the long bare hallway. An occasional gust of wind, a precursor to the approaching tropical storm, would swirl through the windows and grant momentary relief.

I had my cover story in place. My passport was Bahamian, and I was a fifty-year-old black woman going to visit her sister in Philadelphia.

From Philly, D.C. is a short two hour drive.

The sheen of perspiration should be taken for perpetual sweating, not the uncharacteristic nervousness that gripped my stomach.

I'd planned for one more week of treatments to change the amount of pigment in my skin. Fortunately, I had turned even darker in the past twenty-four hours, because after Jordan's visit, I decided to step up my timetable and get out of the Bahamas now.

I'd told Neli to stay permanently away until I figured out what the hell was going on. She was happy to do so after her run-in with Jordan.

Poor thing. She'd barely recovered. Jordan continued to call Neli every day to check in. Every day he pressed harder.

He wouldn't hurt her and I told her so.

After their altercation, I wasn't sure whether he'd been involved in my capture, or not. His reaction to Neli, his desperation, had come through with every movement.

I wanted to hope the desperation was for my safety. Not for my harm.

I wanted to believe he'd come to the Bahamas to help me. Wanted to believe far more than was wise.

On one level I couldn't believe he had anything to do with my imprisonment and torture. On another I knew plenty of operatives before me had been exploited and betrayed and there would be plenty more afterward.

Any type of physical relationship left an agent vulnerable to undue influence and betrayal.

If he wasn't involved, he needed to shut up about me, or someone was going to notice him asking questions.

First things first, I had to figure out who was after me and why.

In the brightly woven canvas bag slung casually over my shoulder, a USB flash drive was sewn into a false lining. The information on the drive was the ticket to discovering why I'd been targeted.

Thank my paranoia for making a copy of the file I'd compiled on Department 5491 and putting the storage device in the bank on my last visit here.

The file consisted of details on me and eleven other people.

An unusually high percentage of people on the list were currently in government service. A few with the NSA and CIA. One with the DIA. One college student. One with very little information beyond a name. She'd dropped off the grid several years back.

And one final person identified only by the initials A.D.A.

That was all the information I had right now.

"Passengers may now begin boarding. Please have your passports and tickets ready."

I heaved up from the hard plastic chair and shuffled toward the line of passengers, trying to quell my thumping heart. I had two more gauntlets to pass before I was back in the States. Getting on the plane was first. Going through customs in Pennsylvania was second.

Gripping the cheap metal cane in my uninjured right hand, I dragged my sore leg behind me. My cane had been checked thoroughly by the swabber.

No explosives on this baby.

The deep contusions from the wrist manacles looked like age spots on my arms increasing my look of frailty and adding to the image of an older woman.

I waited patiently in line, pretending to stare out at the shimmering tarmac and watching the airport personnel inspect each passport and person cautiously. When my turn came, I presented the papers to the woman with a steady hand and smiled politely.

I readied my muscles to run if they challenged me. But I knew that with my damaged toe and scarred leg, I couldn't outrun even the fat security guards.

My five-minute mile had clearly suffered in the past month.

The woman nodded and reached for the next person's credentials.

As I walked down the gangway, I kept my pace sedate, almost leisurely, the thump of my cane and the rustle of cotton a steady rhythm. Inside I was singing.

One step closer.

One step closer to finding out who set me up.

One step closer to revenge for the condition of my body after suffering the indignity and agony of torture.

One step closer to discovering the real meaning of Department 5491.

One step closer to retribution for Fariya. For her death, for her sacrifice.

The gangway sweltered as the humid heat seeped

through the partial seal to the plane. I picked up my pace, eager to get settled in my seat and get home.

As the last of the ticket holders straggled onto the plane, I strapped in and observed the other passengers carefully.

The couple across from me, unabashedly making out, were either on their honeymoon or married to other people. I felt sorry for the guy in seat A who had to sit next to them for the next few hours.

Unable to bear watching the couple and yearning for something I would never get back, I lounged in my seat, tipped the straw hat down to cover my face, and closed my eyes.

The spurt of envy surprised me. Jordan and I had never made out in public. We'd never get the chance now. I'd been too cautious, too concerned about the CIA finding out about him.

Even though we'd conducted our entire relationship in secret, it had still felt damn real. I'd thought we were on the verge of something important, something scary.

He didn't understand how much I'd hated to deceive him.

I hadn't explained. There were rules to be followed, and I'd taken care to not break those rules while treasuring him as my own personal secret.

Maybe keeping him a secret and keeping secrets from him had been the wrong thing to do, but for once I'd wanted someone, something just for me. I'd been fighting the good damn fight for so long, and by the time I met Jordan, I wondered if I'd made the right choices.

I was so very tired.

The toll of the last few weeks had beaten down my natural energy. My left arm lay on the arm rest, the bone and muscle throbbing with the exertion I'd used to get my bag to the airport.

The murmur of passengers, the scuff and slide of luggage being moved in the overhead bins, people shifting in their upholstered seats lulled me into a slight doze.

A passenger rolled a carry-on down the aisle, one of the wheels squeaking in stops and starts. The passenger bumped into my seat, jarring my still-healing arm. I stifled a small scream.

"Bless my soul," the woman said in a soft, Southern drawl. "I'm so sorry."

I waved away her concern, but the pain kept my back jammed against the seat. I held in a hot ball of pain in my throat and pressed my lips into a thin, fake smile.

Suddenly I swore I could smell Jordan, and I looked out the little window, longing to see him. When I first met Jordan, I'd been attracted to the package. The very muscled body in the very personally-tailored GQ clothes and the very intelligent brain behind the very attractive face.

He'd been put together well enough I thought maybe he played for the other team. But as soon as I'd gotten close to him, the scent he put out was all hetero. The hint of sweat, the hint of spice, a touch of shaving cream, and the indefinable scent that made him...him.

I smelled that scent now. My heart ka-thunked in my chest. I was having an olfactory hallucination. It was the only explanation.

He had to have left by now. It had been two days since he'd been at my house. No way was he still in the Bahamas. We're talking the original workaholic. I'd had to practically sever him from the office a few hours early for our quick weekend trips down here.

"Let me help you with that, ma'am." The hand attached

to that husky voice reached into my line of vision through the tilted hat.

He effortlessly lifted the woman's carry-on into the overhead compartment with long elegant fingers, tendons in his wrist in sharp relief, and the dusky skin of a half-Hispanic, half-White, all male arm flexed in exertion.

I knew that hand, that voice.

Jordan.

As if my imagination had conjured him. I wanted to reach out, just touch his wrist, his hand. The urge was so strong, I forced myself to relax.

Instinctively, I tilted my head down just a little further, hiding the curve of my jaw as best I could. There was no way, no way he would recognize me.

I was black. I had a cane. A hideous scar on my right leg and another on my left arm.

I wanted him to notice me and I wanted him to walk past.

I wanted him to see me and wondered why he couldn't.

Torn between longing and practicality, I didn't know what I wanted.

CHAPTER 10

September 15
    Nassau, Bahamas

He was losing it.

On the fast train to Crazyville.

Jordan rubbed a hand over his breastbone, in the region of his heart, and slid into his seat. He saw Staci everywhere.

When he'd lifted the suitcase, he'd been distracted by the woman in the aisle seat. The slant of her head and the way she held her arms lightly against her body, right hand crossed over left, reminded him so much of Staci....

He'd been tempted to knock the woman's hat off so he could see her face. Totally illogical.

Staci was white.

The woman was clearly black. Not the true black of the islanders, definitely some mixed blood.

Even with a heavy tan, Staci wouldn't be that dark.

Also, she was far thinner than Staci. Staci prided herself on an athletic and fit body, but she wasn't a stick.

The woman on the plane was one step up from emaciated.

And...he was obsessing about a stranger. Anything to keep his mind off of his real problem.

Staci was gone. Missing. Believed dead.

He'd stuck around the Bahamas far longer than planned, watching, waiting, hoping, for a sign. Something to indicate Staci was here. In the end, he'd had nothing but a low-level feeling she was close.

If he could just see her, talk to her, hold her, breathe the same air...everything would be okay again.

Until the end, being with her had been easy. Maybe too easy.

They had both avoided the hard stuff, and their relationship stayed on the surface. They'd hovered on the precipice of something bigger than both of them. Better than both of them. But their link existed.

Silent, unspoken.

Damn, he missed her.

He missed their arguments, excuse him, discussions about government policy and world affairs and the best handgun for target shooting. Even though she hated shooting.

He missed sparring with her, their hot, sweaty martial arts practice frequently degenerating into a round of energetic sex on the mat.

He missed making up with her. He even freaking missed waking up with her.

Jordan recalled the last time he'd woken up with her....

He'd woken to an empty bed. After their fight, they'd had the most explosive sex ever, but the moment he opened his eyes he'd known.

She was still leaving.

A part of him, a big part, admired her. She had conviction. She had guts. She was tough. And she was doing something she believed in absolutely.

She was also vulnerable.

The protective part of him, the one nurtured by his mother and his aunt, wanted to pull her back into his house and keep her safe from the harm in the world.

Harm he knew intimately.

Jordan lay in the bed a moment longer, listening, testing the air for movement or sound. Where was she? This was her house so he knew she had to be here. Tactically he'd played it smart and spent the night in her bed.

If they'd been at his place next door, she'd have left in the middle of the night. The pattern had happened frequently enough for him to predict her behavior.

Especially when they connected so completely on a physical level.

Usually after the kind of sex they'd had last night, she pulled back for a few days. Since she was leaving the country this morning, the pull back could be permanent. So he shoved the tangled sheets off and headed toward the bathroom where he'd heard her moving about.

Steam coated the mirrors and potted ferns perched on the edge of her Jacuzzi. Her back to the door, she sat on the white porcelain one leg propped up on the ledge, rubbing cream into the satiny skin of her calf.

"Smells good." He opened with a non-argument starter, knowing the next few minutes were critical.

"Gardenia," she replied, seemingly engrossed in spreading the lotion evenly over her already moist skin.

He sat down, carefully, next to her. His bare shoulder rubbed against her back as he traced a rough finger along the curve of her neck and the soft terry of her robe.

She stiffened, rejecting the gentle caress and the intent behind the light touch.

The only thing left was surrender.

"What time does your flight leave?" Not what he wanted to say.

He wanted to say, Don't go.

Logically he knew she could protect herself. The absolute knowledge drew him.

But he had a horrible feeling in the pit of his stomach.

He wanted to explain that this urge to wrap her up and protect her was ingrained. From the time he was old enough to understand, he'd been raised with the responsibility of protecting the women in his life.

But explaining his upbringing would open up avenues of conversation he wasn't ready to deal with yet. Especially if this relationship was on its way out. So, he didn't really want to expose more of himself to her.

She relaxed infinitesimally. "About five hours."

She began rubbing cream into the skin of her thigh, and the short hem of her robe parted, hinting at the cluster of blond curls he knew were just beyond his sight.

Gardenia-scented steam hung in the air, still thick from her hot shower. The languid, almost sultry sweep of her fingers mesmerized him.

He brushed a feather light kiss over the curve of her bent neck. "You want a ride to the airport?" Don't go.

She softened a little more, her hand stilled. "You sure you want to take me?"

He dipped his fingers into the pot of cream and scooped some out. Then, slowly, tentatively, a little unsure of her response, he flicked aside her robe and began working the scented cream into the firm skin of her inner thigh. He swept his fingers closer and closer to those curls he still couldn't see.

Jordan shifted his body, slid one leg into the tub and planted the other firmly on the tile floor, inviting Staci to relax into the V he'd created.

"I want to take you." A lie, if he meant to the airport. Truth, if he skewed the meaning.

The graceful curve of her spine softened even more, and she leaned back into the hard cradle of his arms and chest as his fingers swept lightly over the concave hollow of her belly.

The brush of his fingers was like the spell to a magic kingdom, her legs drifted open, falling languidly apart to rest on the rock hard muscles of his thighs, granting him better access.

"Okay," she whispered into the hushed, expectant air.

He wrapped his other arm around her waist and slid his hand between the flaps of her loosened robe. Fingers spread wide, tips pointing down, his hand glided gently on the path between her belly button and pubic bone, massaging the sensitive area with the heel and at the same time urging her back toward his throbbing erection.

He licked at the warm skin of her neck and ignored all the reasons why this was a really bad idea.

"God, you get me so hot."

"Feeling is mutual." Staci arched against the press of his hands and fingers, urging him farther.

She brought one arm up and around to cup the back of his neck and insinuated her other hand between their bodies, arrowing down to rub the engorged head of his penis.

The movement pushed her ass into him, the combination of her hand stroking the head and her ass cheeks enveloping the thick staff of his erection caused more blood to rush south.

Her loosely tied robe gave up its fight to conceal and her breasts swung free of the soft terry to jut out, waiting, pouting as if impatient for his touch. Her nipples, rosy with arousal, enticed him.

They might be at odds over her leaving...but physically, they synced perfectly. He would make her think about this, about them. Not about leaving.

His middle finger just barely entered her slick passage, teasing her with a small circular caress.

He squeezed her breast firmly then plucked at her nipple as he pushed his middle finger in to the hilt and used his palm to press on her clitoris while the rest of his fingers stroked her aroused and swollen lips.

He continued to play with her nipples but left his other hand exactly where it was, feeling the muscles inside her swell and clutch at his finger.

"Oh, God." She panted.

"Call me Jordan."

She snickered, then gasped as the contractions from her laugh echoed throughout her body. "That feels...."

Her hand squeezed his cock, her thumb pressing on the extremely sensitive spot below the head.

And he moaned. "Back at you, babe."

They needed to move, needed to shift but he waited, in the back of his mind knowing this could be goodbye. As her hips pulsed in the tiny range of motion he allowed her, he wondered if maybe this was too good.

She wasn't thinking about goodbye.

She pulled her hands away from his body, and leaned forward to reach for the drawer where she kept the condoms. She whimpered as the movement pressed her pubic bone down toward the ledge of the tub, but his hands and fingers were there, pressing harder.

"Brilliant," he gutted out. Jerking his hand away from her breasts, he held his palm out. "Condom."

She shoved it into his hand and tried to lift off of his fingers, but the iron bar of his arm held her in place.

"Not until I say you can move."

The command stilled her. They were usually equal partners in their sexual exploration, but right now he wanted to dominate. She was leaving, and he'd damn well give her something to remember.

Using his fingers, hand, and arm, he lifted her body up from the tile ledge. The action causing her to whimper again. "Jordan."

"Minute." He shifted his lower body back from her ass and rolled on the condom with one swift jerk. "Put your weight on your feet."

For a second he thought she was going to disobey. But she must have reconsidered because she shifted her weight to stand and didn't try to pull away, then she balanced there waiting for his next directive.

He lifted her body off the tile by about six inches, gave her pubic area a small "good girl" squeeze and slid his finger out in a slick controlled move, rubbing hard along her clitoris.

"You are so fucking wet," he ground out. He'd never been so hard in his life. "For me."

He grasped her hips with both hands and impaled her on the jutting freaking sword of his penis.

"Yes," she hissed as the soft skin of her ass met the rough hairiness of his thighs.

The forced spread of both their legs as they straddled the side of the tub meant he controlled the friction and their movement. He moved her up and down, her hands gripping his as her cheeks slid along his penis then connected with the flat of his abdomen.

He wanted to suck on her nipples, he wanted to rub her clitoris as the rest of their bodies connected, but he couldn't reach anything.

With his mouth, he latched on to the soft skin where her neck met her shoulder and bit her gently as they moved together.

The position was perfect. Perfectly erotic.

In the end, she controlled their release. She reached down and squeezed his engorged balls and he swelled to bursting.

His orgasm exploded through his body, detonating like an unstable block of C4. Blowing his pseudo attempt to control their last encounter into the sky.

The powerful surge of adrenaline and blood and his orgasm sent her over the edge. She screamed. The sound filled him with a primitive and euphoric sense of power.

His vision blurred as he wrapped his arms around her waist, and she rested her head back against his shoulder. The soft soughing of their calming breaths the only sound in the quiet room as the tension that existed before slowly crept back in.

The glow of arousal faded. The remembrance of their argument and the reality that she was leaving flowed back in like the fog on a damp spring morning.

Thank God they weren't facing each other. He didn't want to look into her eyes, because he didn't want to see.

Post-coital glow aside, he didn't want to see regret or defiance.

As if she felt the same, she pushed off of him and reached for the toilet paper to clean up.

And he knew he'd only wished he'd felt the soft brush of her lips against his hair.

That was the end.

Later he'd dropped her at the airport without saying anything more. What was done was done, and talking to death wouldn't help anything.

He'd thought maybe they could work things out...when she came back.

Except she hadn't come home.

Regret, longing, futility. Now, weeks later, the situation was completely different, yet his emotions were exactly the same.

He was going crazy. Remembering their last encounter would get him nowhere. He needed to focus on the future not the past, to look to tomorrow, to influence events that hadn't happened yet.

The past was done. It couldn't be changed.

He could change what happened next. He would find her. He would do whatever it took to make sure she was safe.

She might not be the older woman three seats ahead of him, but she was alive. She had to be.

Jordan clutched the amulet in his pocket, holding tight, as if he held fast to the amulet he could keep her safe.

CHAPTER 11

One week later
September 21
San Francisco, CA

THERE'S JUST something about the smell of hospitals. Did anyone like it? Did anyone walk in, breathe deep, and exhale with a joyful sigh...Ah, eau d'hopital.

I hated it. Antiseptic, disinfectant, Betadyne, decay, and preservative-enhanced food permeated the floors, walls, counter-tops, clothes, everything. The smell was pervasive and unavoidable. How did the staff live with those odors day in and day out? Or were they just so inured they didn't notice anymore?

My freaking unstable stomach picked now to rear up again, a lingering nausea that struck at odd times or when certain smells hit my nose.

When I was out of this mess and got my life back, I'd be sure to let someone know a significant side effect of the experimental pigment drug was rather severe nausea.

I was done taking the drug. Thank God I'd only needed the pigment-altering drug to get back into the United States. Unfortunately the effects of the drug were lingering, my skin was still dark, and my stomach continued to be troubled.

As I strode toward the hospital room, I wondered if I was crazy to even be here. The reason for this hospital visit likely didn't have anything to do with my inability to go home or my personal problems.

When I got back in the States, I'd rented a car and driven to D.C. After checking out my neighborhood, I'd realized my townhouse was under surveillance.

I wasn't any closer to figuring out who wanted me dead. And I sure as hell wasn't going to make it easy for them to find me.

Instead, I accessed a hidden private bank account with a black credit card and holed up in a hotel. I didn't check in with the CIA. They hadn't bothered to rescue me in Afghanistan. Until I had a clear answer why, checking in wasn't a priority.

I liked to imagine the problem had gone away...and then I'd drive by my townhouse in Alexandria and check out the surveillance team just waiting for someone, presumably me to show up. Dammit.

I could get past them. No question.

Except every time I'd attempted it, Jordan had been around. Sometimes even in my house. Clearly he'd been accessing my living space. Jordan and I had put in a connecting door in our attics so we could go from one house to the other without going outside.

The biggest question was why was he in my house? I knew he'd been looking for me but I didn't know if he was worried about me. Because suspicion still lingered that perhaps he was somehow involved with my current problems.

I shoved away the longing, regret, and the spear of disappointment that colored my thoughts every time I remembered our time together.

And now was not the time to wallow.

I pushed open the door to the hospital room. John Michael Wishbone was the ticket to my peace of mind, then I could concentrate on figuring out the mystery of 5491 and why someone wanted me, possibly all of us, dead.

The door to a standard double hospital room squeaked open. The kid in the bed was eighteen, but Jesus, he looked young. The other bed was empty. The boy whipped his head around, eyes wide. "Who are you?"

I had to make a decision here. One I should have thought out ahead of time. I was tired of dicking around. I wanted action. And maybe, just maybe, I could kill two birds at once.

The CIA must know I wasn't dead. They would have typed Fariya's DNA and seen we weren't even a close match.

The USA Today tucked under my arm told the story. Every day I checked the classified section for a message from my contact. Every day there was nothing. Maybe it was time to shake things up a bit.

"My name is Staci Grant."

His gaze narrowed suspiciously. "And...."

"I'm here to offer you a proposition." I didn't have time to be subtle.

Usually when I recruited kids, I analyzed how to cultivate the relationship, gain their trust, and slowly reel them in to working for the CIA. Plus, I only laid the groundwork. Someone else executed the actual recruitment.

But I knew all the triggers. How hard could it be?

"Not interested."

"This is service to your government."

He turned his head away and closed his eyes.

"John. This is something that would make your father proud."

If I hadn't been watching closely, I'd have missed the little jerk of surprise when I mentioned his father. Considered a hero, his father had worked for the FBI and he'd died when the second tower had gone down.

The fact John had managed to conceal a quick jolt of reaction was a point in his favor. "I work for the CIA."

He snorted. "Right."

Walking to the aisle between the two beds, I ignored his disbelief. I'd be disappointed if he accepted my statement at face value. "I have a job for you."

"I don't think so." He closed his eyes, pretended I wasn't there.

I leaned down and whispered in his ear. "I've been watching you for a while." I wasn't lying. He fit my profile.

He stiffened slightly but still didn't open his eyes. I studied him, not wanting to acknowledge how damn young he was.

Perfectly ripe. Idealistic. Passionate.

He just needed someone to sculpt his attitudes while he was still naive and innocent.

"Your father was killed by terrorists." I glanced over to the stuffed bear with the small helium balloon on the window sill and catalogued his flinch.

I needed to remind him of his pain, his passion. Those qualities were key to his agreement for this little mission.

"I'm the good guy."

His eyes popped open and he frowned at me. "Look, if

this is about my friends, forget it. I'm not going to roll over on them just because they're Arabic."

"Loyalty is good. As long as it isn't misplaced."

His face reddened. "Fuck you."

"Not what I'm here for, Junior," I replied mildly. "Your current behavior could be construed as treasonous, associating with ME's, young men of Middle Eastern descent." So much for the whole no-profiling thing.

"They haven't done anything wrong." He closed his eyes again. "Neither have I."

"You're right." I paused a beat. "Unfortunately the same is not true of the father of your friend. He's got questionable ties to a mosque currently under investigation."

"I would have thought a woman of color such as yourself would have a little more sensitivity," he said hotly.

"Nice." Way to twist my argument. "Got a mouth on you, and you're protective."

I perched on the edge of the bed and pulled out the picture of Bella Holden: eighteen, blond, gorgeous, a freshman at Georgetown, and potentially in danger. I just didn't know. "I've got a situation, and I'm hoping you can help me out."

He turned his head away, stared hard at the television mounted near the ceiling.

I was convinced that my problems had something to do with the mysterious Department 5491. Of the twelve recipients of those monthly checks, nine were agents of the U.S. Government. Bella Holden, Sunshine Smith, and the mystery initials ADA were the exceptions.

The agents had the training to take care of themselves. But Bella and Sunshine were innocents.

A few incidents involving the people from the

Department 5491 list had me wondering. Was someone trying to get rid of the people from 5491?

In Afghanistan, suddenly I'm arrested and imprisoned.

A few days ago, agent Brad Johnson was killed by a suspected Russian double agent. That one made the papers.

Two incidents was more than coincidence.

On one level, I really didn't think Bella Holden was in any danger. On another, I wouldn't be able to forgive myself if something happened to her when I could have prevented it but didn't bother.

I dangled the picture in front of him, hoping the lure of a pretty girl and his curiosity would prompt him to ask questions.

"Want me to take her to the prom?"

There was something wrong with me because his smart ass remarks tickled. "I don't have time to waste romancing you into taking this assignment."

"What assignment?"

"Get to know her. Protect her."

"Just like that?"

"You've got weapons training, right?"

"Yeah." He swallowed, glanced away.

The faint squeak of wheels from a cart of some kind came through the closed door. I forced myself to hold still.

Must be meals. The odor of hospital food had preceded the squeak and my hyper-aware sense of smell had already communicated to my hyper-sensitive stomach that food was on the way.

I straightened, swallowed down bile as my stomach protested. "What about hand-to-hand?"

"Yeah." He pushed up and back against the puffy white pillow.

"Level?" Making my voice authoritative seemed to snap him to attention.

"Fifth degree black belt." Finally, he looked interested. "So I'm supposed to...what?"

"Just keep an eye on her. Make sure no one else is keeping an eye on her. Make sure she's safe."

"Do you really think she's in danger?"

"I can't afford not to think it's a possibility," I replied honestly.

"What's in it for me?"

"Money. Chance to travel. A chance to serve your country." Sort of.

"What's the catch?"

I saw the wariness in his gaze. Wariness I didn't have time for. A little pang hit my stomach. Not the nausea. Remorse? Regret?

Emotions I definitely shouldn't be feeling. Second guessing my moves and actions was not an option right now. I had places to go, puzzles to solve.

He'd been in the hospital for observation after a car accident. Concussion. But he was due to be released later today. He was fine.

"We leave now." I used my real name which meant that I couldn't linger in one place for too long.

"Now?"

"As in...get your clothes, leave a note for your mother, and we haul ass."

I could see him weighing the pros and cons.

"Your father would be proud of you." The final twist of the screw.

His gaze went to the television again. Obviously he had a deep-seated interest in Oprah. Not.

"Okay."

"I'll bust you out of here. Write a quick note. And I'll explain the entire situation on the way."

I had to hope protecting Bella Holden was precautionary. I really hoped I was wrong and she wasn't in any danger.

One checklist item checked.

Now if I could just figure out who was trying to eliminate the people from Department 5491. Specifically, who was trying to eliminate me...life would be peachy.

Right. Peachy.

CHAPTER 12

F our weeks later
       October 17
  11:00 am

THE GRAY, cloudy sky matched the tenor of Jordan's mood. A hint of wood smoke wafted in the air and a breeze blew frigidly across the exposed skin of his face. His new cashmere duster, specially tailored to accommodate his shoulders and arms, muted the brisk wind.

As Jordan passed by the monument to the soldiers who'd served in World War II, a cascade of multiple water sprays splashed into a circular pool, drowning out the murmurs of the tourists paying their respects.

The rectangular reflecting pool surrounded by the small wood fence was to his right. The Lincoln Monument rose in the distance.

Continuing on the paved path bordering the west basin, he strode toward the all but forgotten symbol of the First

World War. A discarded remnant of a time very few people alive could still remember.

The small domed structure, styled like an ancient Greek temple, perched in untrimmed foliage and grass that should have been cut weeks ago.

Unkempt and untended.

Jesus. That was how he felt...like this monument, still standing as a reminder, except no one was looking.

Just as he was the only one still searching for Staci.

Whatever agency was surveilling her house, their surveillance had tapered off to a single guy twenty-four/seven. For a long time, that surveillance detail gave him hope that he wasn't the only one searching for her. Now it looked like he was the only one who still believed she was alive.

In the meantime, he'd been shocked by the phone call from the chairman of the Senate Select Committee on Intelligence requesting a private meet in an obscure location. The guy wouldn't even discuss over the phone what the subject of the meeting was about. Jordan turned over possible reasons for this meeting.

Nothing good came to mind.

He'd been working on a few projects for the Franklin Group, but if the projects had anything to do with Congress, the senator probably knew as much about the details as he did. What the hell could the man want?

Traditionally if Jordan met with a member of Congress, the meet took place in their office. What was so damn secret it couldn't be discussed over a phone line? The senator had been adamant that the meeting must be done in person. Away from the office.

Jordan stepped into the old marble monument, and noted the inscription, "The war to end all wars."

"Mr. Ramirez." The senator was already seated, tucked away in the shadows, so no one would see him.

"Senator," he replied warily.

Jordan sat down several stained pillars over from the senator and waited. He'd learned plenty in the FBI about interrogations and he wasn't about to be the first to break the silence. He wanted to be able to analyze the lying sack of shit's face, but noticed other things instead.

The old goat looked damn good for a man in his late sixties.

His hair, brushed off his forehead and away from his face, gleamed from the skill of an excellent stylist and colorist. The gray was there but artfully layered with a deep, rich brunette to convey the appearance of a younger man.

His skin was buffed and moisturized to preserve his pale, patrician features. His clear hazel eyes were sharp from cataract and laser surgery.

No doubt. He was a handsome sack of shit.

His lanky build and white bread appearance was an exact opposite of Jordan's own burly shoulders, compact muscles, curly black hair and flat features of an Anglo/Hispanic mix.

But other details crowded in, amusing Jordan.

The navy pinstripes on their one hundred percent Egyptian cotton shirts were precisely the same width. The cuffs on their worsted wool suit pants were tacked and creased to the same length.

Jordan would bet three of his personally-measured, hand-sewn silk suits that if they compared stitching, they'd both have the distinctive monogram of one of the most exclusive tailors in Washington.

Working for a think tank paid a hell of a lot better than the FBI.

The senator's lips tightened, as if he'd noticed the same details. Boy, Jordan bet that really frosted the senator's ass.

As the silence lengthened, Jordan decided to eat his lunch and opened the bag. It would be a good cover in case anyone who was anyone happened to walk by and see them in the same out of the way monument, he thought mockingly.

The senator was known for walking through the Mall occasionally and playing king--at least that's how Jordan always saw it--treating everyone as a potential constituent, never forgetting maybe someday they might be.

Jordan opened the brown bag he'd brought with him and started to unwrap his turkey sandwich. He'd bet his butter-soft Italian leather loafers, the senator had never brown bagged lunch.

The rustling of the paper was loud in the pregnant silence. Jordan opened the little wax paper bag and tried with a pang not to think of Staci. She'd read somewhere that wax paper was more eco-friendly and suddenly a few days later a box had appeared in his cupboards.

The senator broke first.

"Your name appeared in a report I received this morning."

Jordan took a bite of the turkey on whole wheat. Another of Staci's contributions. Before they'd hooked up, he'd pretty much eaten white.

He chewed his sandwich and then swallowed carefully past the lump in his throat. "Seeing as writing reports is what I do nowadays, I'm not surprised."

"What can you tell me about the situation?"

"What 'situation' are you referring to?"

He'd been working on several reports that might have bearing on this senator's committees but based on their location and the clandestine manner of this meeting, Jordan had no idea what the man wanted.

"There was a shooting...."

Jordan's blood froze and he held extremely still.

The thud of his heartbeat reverberated in his ears. Birds chattered in the trees behind them. Exhaust from the cars zipping along Independence Avenue drifted over the concealing hedge into the suddenly close air.

Muffled shouts from an impromptu collegiate soccer match in Potomac Park were less than murmurs in the protected space of the old monument.

All faded as he remembered the shooting from last week.

In an off the books favor for an old friend, he'd hooked up with Lucas Goodman and Jamie Hunt. He'd also hoped to find out more information about Staci. When Lucas Goodman's search subject, Johnny Wishbone and his girlfriend were kidnapped, he'd helped rescue them. It turned out that Wishbone had seen Staci. And finally, Jordan had gotten a step closer to finding Staci.

Who was alive. Dammit.

Johnny Wishbone had seen Staci just a few weeks ago. There were some slight discrepancies in Johnny's account, he thought Staci was black, but he'd also identified a picture of Staci.

After the information Jordan had learned from the kidnappers, finding her was imperative. Staci had been injected with a mysterious drug and she needed the antidote.

But right now he had to get through this bizarre meeting with the senator.

"There are shootings all the time in our nation's capital, you'll have to be more specific."

The senator glanced at his Perpetual Oyster Rolex in

platinum, frowned and shifted closer. "I'm talking about the incident at the Presidential Suites hotel."

The 'incident' was the death of the kidnapper. He'd been shot during the rescue of Johnny and his girlfriend. Although Jordan hadn't killed him. An unknown assailant had fired the fatal rounds. The entire 'incident' was highly classified, so even Jordan didn't know the reasons why Johnny and his girlfriend were kidnapped. His only concern was that Staci had contact with Johnny earlier in the month.

The shooting had only happened last week. The media had not gotten wind of the kidnap or the rescue, so how could the senator possibly know about it?

Jordan ripped another bite of his sandwich off and chewed vigorously while analyzing this development, projecting indifference when what he wanted to do was shove the sandwich down the senator's throat.

"I'd like your report," the senator said testily.

Why would the senator be asking Jordan for information? Classified and highly sensitive information regarding a report, that if it existed, should have taken months to assemble, then sanitize, before being released to the Senate committee.

Because there was no report. At least, not yet.

"I know you were there," the senator hissed, obviously impatient with Jordan's delaying tactic.

"You should also know that even if I were there, I would be unable to answer your questions." His anger built as deep buried rage bubbled up. Jordan rarely lost his temper but when he did, it wasn't pretty. "You think you can circumvent the system? Go through me to gain classified information?"

"So you were there," the senator said triumphantly.

Jordan crumpled his lunch bag with one fist and stood. "What's your angle?"

Because, God knew, a man like the senator always had one. Some position he was working for his own advantage or defense.

Jordan took two menacing steps forward.

The senator tipped back his head but didn't stand. As if assuming a more defensive posture would somehow validate the threat.

Jordan took another step to loom over the senator. "To protect yourself? Did you have something to do with the incident?"

How could the senator know about the shooting? Unless he was involved with the unauthorized injection of the mysterious drug into unsuspecting espionage agents. The funding for the mysterious drug experiment had to come from somewhere. The thought that this asshole could have appropriated and approved funding for an experiment that fucked with the lives of people already serving their country made him sick.

The old man held his ground, not standing or giving credence to Jordan's anger. The senator glanced down at his watch impatiently. "That's neither here nor there, and I've got to get back to the Hill for testimony on the amount of heroin coming out of Afghanistan. What do you know about the shooting?"

In his peripheral vision, Jordan could see the senator's bodyguard hurrying toward them. Apparently the bodyguard was a little more concerned with Jordan's body language. "Why the hell would you think I would help you?"

"I need answers, dammit." The senator's face turned bright red, but as a contrast his lips were white with fury, and his eyes narrowed with frustration. "And I think you have them."

The bodyguard skidded to a stop a few feet away, his

hand on the weapon concealed by his suit jacket. "Everything okay here, Sir?"

Jordan slammed the remnants of his lunch into the metal garbage can and then stalked away. "Get your answers someplace else, Senator."

CHAPTER 13

Why was the senator asking him for information? The meeting had left Jordan extremely unsettled. He could count on two hands the number of times they'd met in person.

He tried to analyze in a dispassionate and detached manner, but everything came up jumbled and he couldn't make sense of it.

The senator was privy to most of the same information the Franklin Group reviewed when compiling their reports and recommendations. Probably frosted the old goat's ass to constantly see Jordan's name on the reports and recommendations used to make decisions influencing policy.

Only a handful of people even knew Jordan had helped out with the extremely off the books rescue of John Wishbone.

The only ones who knew were Jamie Hunt and Lucas Goodman, Zeke Hawthorne, Jamie's boss, Carson, no last name known at least by Jordan, and David Armbruster, the Assistant Deputy Director of the NSA. Oh yeah, and Susan

Chen, who was in a federal prison for her role in kidnapping espionage agents and injecting them with drugs.

An even smaller number of people actually knew what had transpired in that hotel room before someone shot Susan Chen's co-conspirator.

Susan Chen was in a highly guarded prison.

Jamie and Lucas were taking a well-deserved vacation. Besides, Jamie was more close-mouthed than Jordan. No way in hell had she talked to the senator.

There was pretty much only one person left.

Jordan dialed his cell and asked Zeke Hawthorne to meet him for a drink. Preferably now.

"What the hell," Zeke responded with a touch of bitterness. Jordan could almost see his shrug. "It's not like I have anything better to do. Give me half an hour."

Jordan rode the Metro to his regular haunt. The bar was mostly empty. For which Jordan was thankful.

Fuck. He needed a beer. "Two Guinnesses."

"Sure thing, Jay." The bartender, a petite blue-eyed blond named Delia, called everyone by their first initial. She began the delicate process of building the draft.

Zeke Hawthorne sauntered into the bar a little later, dressed in board shorts, a psychedelic t-shirt with Zoo York wrapped from front to back, and at least a two-day stubble on his jaw.

On a good day Zeke didn't dress up, but today he was pretty high on the grunge scale.

Jordan grabbed their beers, and jerked his head toward a table in the back, close to the jukebox, and far enough away from the other patrons they could talk without being overheard.

After they sat at the booth, Zeke slapped his palm against Jordan's. "Dude. How's it going?"

Zeke punched his fingers into a fist looking to knock against Jordan's clenched fingers.

Zeke looked like a surfer with his blond corkscrew curls going every which way. The guy was a total geek head, sounded like an extreme sports nut, and could probably do extreme quadratic equations in his sleep.

"Uh. It's not." Jordan had hit a dead end after tracking Staci's movements to California. She'd used her own name to get Johnny Wishbone out of the hospital and convince him to protect Bella Holden, then she'd dropped off the grid again.

"I had a really bizarre conversation today and I need to run it by someone who knows the situation."

Zeke rubbed a hand through his curls, grabbed onto the ends and pulled them over his eyes for a second. "You know I've been suspended pending investigation, right?"

"Shit. Sorry. I didn't."

Zeke shrugged casually as if it was no big deal. "No worries."

Which was a total freaking lie.

Jordan noted the lines of tension around Zeke's mouth and the misery in his ocean blue eyes. If Zeke wanted to pretend everything was fine, Jordan wasn't going to argue.

Their friendship was new and some places guys just didn't go.

"This has to do with our, uh, adventure."

"Nice way to put it." Zeke smirked into his beer. "Thanks. Haven't smiled in a few days."

"I just had a very weird meeting with the chairman of the Senate Select Committee on Intelligence."

Zeke's gaze shot to his. "That blowhard."

Jordan snorted. "Called that one." He took a slow draw on his beer.

Zeke studied him quietly for another moment. "So what did the esteemed senator from Virginia want?"

"Information about the incident at the Presidential Suites."

"Are you shitting me?" Zeke dropped his beer on the table, the dark, yeasty liquid sloshed over the side to dribble onto the scarred tabletop. Zeke leaned toward Jordan and lowered his voice. "No one, and I mean, no one knows about that."

"Yeah. So where is he getting his information?"

"I'm on leave. And not allowed any-frickin'-where near an agency computer or anyone who knows anything," Zeke bitched softly.

"Then what are you doing with me?"

"You work for a think tank. With the exception of Carson, who I'm pretty sure won't bust me, no one else knows you had anything to do with..." Zeke waved his hand dismissively, "...the adventure."

"Yeah. So how the fuck does the senator know I was there?"

"Dude. You didn't ask?"

Jordan closed his lips firmly and leaned back against the leather banquette. He'd been so on guard against the man, against giving him anything, it hadn't even occurred to him to come out and ask.

"The whole meeting was just short of a weird-fest. That was an off-the-books job. How could the senator even know about it?"

"Someone leaked the information," Zeke murmured. He took a big gulp of stout. "Shit. Had to be someone fairly high up."

"You have any ideas?"

"No idea. Haven't been in the office since. Ya know?"

Zeke took another large swallow of the dark beer. "I'm in a tenuous position as it is. The Assistant Director himself is handling and reviewing all aspects of this clusterfuck. I sure as hell don't want to come to his attention more than necessary."

"Okay. Fine. We can work around this." Jordan sipped at the brew. "What if I sort of speculate out loud and you can hand signal me if it seems like a logical solution."

"And later we can use our invisible ink to write messages on our napkins," Zeke responded in a singsong-y voice.

"I'm desperate here." Jordan inhaled sharply, then blew out a breath slowly. "I need to find Staci and...I need help."

"Hey, sorry, dude. You haven't been able to turn up anything else?"

"It's like she disappeared after 'hiring' Johnny Wishbone to look after Bella Holden."

"What about the cell phone number she gave the kid as a contact point?"

"Disconnected." Jordan clenched his fist around the glass, feeling the cool condensation against his palm. "But it's a pay-as-you-go phone anyway. No way to trace it."

"All known residences?"

"Checked and double-checked."

"All known bank accounts?"

"Haven't been accessed."

"Could she have an unregistered bank account?"

"I wouldn't be surprised."

Shit. When he'd found her bank statements, he'd been surprised by the amount of money she had.

She was loaded.

He should have known. The clues were there. A rowhouse in Alexandria, a house on the cape of Massachusetts, and another in the Bahamas.

But beyond certain extravagances, money wasn't important to him or her. So how would he know if she had a hidden bank account?

"But I haven't got any way to find a hidden bank account...or access it."

Zeke pursed his lips. "All known associates?"

"That's a little more difficult. I don't know anyone else."

"She didn't have any girlfriends?"

"She had some work acquaintances through Georgetown." It had been one of the things they'd had in common. They'd each been a little bit lonely. Work consumed them both to the point where outside relationships were almost nil.

"When I called to ask if they had heard from her," he said in disgust, "they asked to meet for drinks."

He'd learned after the second meeting they didn't have any info. The were just trolling for a date.

"Wow, dude. Must be nice."

"Not really. I don't want them." Shit. Did his voice just break? He drained his glass.

"You are crazy." Zeke joked, but Jordan heard the underlying note of truth. "I'd take some of that action."

Zeke stared hard at the jukebox, his attempt to avoid eye contact told Jordan he was being brutally honest.

"I don't do anything but work and all of the sudden, I've got nowhere to go. Nothing to do and no one to do it with." Zeke thumped his head into his hands. "Jesus, could I whine more? Don't listen to me. I'm feeling a little sorry for myself. I'll get over it."

"Help me find Staci."

"As long as it doesn't get me fired." Zeke tapped his fingers on the scarred wood table, like he was at a keyboard. "Or worse."

"I could really use your help." Jordan hesitated. "Clearly I'm not doing so well on my own."

The fact that the senator knew about the shooting in the Presidential Suites upped his pucker factor.

Jordan needed to get to Staci.

His need to find her had increased exponentially after learning she'd been injected with a mysterious drug. She needed the antidote. This wasn't just about his need to find her anymore. This was about his need to save her.

And maybe he needed to hold her in his arms for a minute or an hour or fantasy time, a night, and just be thankful she was okay.

"Can you tell me...."

Zeke waited with patience for Jordan to spit it out. "Can't tell if you don't ask."

"Did you feel different when you had that drug in you?"

Zeke was the only person he could ask. He had been injected with the unstable compound. He'd also gotten the antidote which should have rendered the original drug inactive and returned Zeke to 'normal'.

"Do you remember?"

"Shit. You don't ask easy stuff, do you?"

"If it isn't hard, it isn't worth it."

"I was a little more manic than normal about work. I'd check and re-check everything. As if...I was working at hyper-speed. And patterns. I could see patterns in everything. Not just work but everywhere I looked there were patterns I'd never noticed before."

"You liked what the drug did."

Zeke gazed at the jukebox as the lights on the display flickered and flashed, and his voice got softer and softer. "In some ways, it was amazing."

"Are you sorry you got the antidote?"

Zeke shifted his gaze back to Jordan, as if becoming aware of his surroundings and their conversation again.

"My grandfather was a little bit crazy," he said abruptly. "Mostly OCD, Obsessive Compulsive Disorder. You know. Little nightly rituals, lock the door three times, check that the stove is off four times, wash your hands five."

Jordan nodded, not wanting to interrupt.

"Sounds fairly harmless...until you're living with it," Zeke said wryly.

He slouched against the wood paneled booth. "And the drug Susan Chen gave me, without my permission," his mouth tightened belying his relaxed posture, "It made my slight tendencies extreme. So no, I wasn't sorry."

Jordan shifted, uncomfortable with having a glimpse into Zeke's private life. He liked the guy. Even though normally he took a while to warm up to people, he and Zeke had hit it off right away.

Probing Zeke for intimate details made Jordan feel as if he were asking too much, delving too deeply into Zeke's feelings without the requisite lapse of time while they got to know each other.

At the same time, he needed this information.

"Staci is alive."

"Based on Johnny's account, she is definitely alive," Zeke said slowly. "What you need to do is focus on how she acted after she had the drug. Go back and try to remember everything that happened right before she left for Afghanistan. Because whatever she was working on then, is most likely what she'll be concentrating on now."

"You're a genius."

"Why yes, yes, I am." Zeke smiled, baring his white, perfectly straight teeth. "Sometimes I forget."

"She was obsessing about her grandparents' death. And

about something at work. She had a spreadsheet, but she didn't tell me what it was for and I didn't ask."

Zeke leaned in close and glanced around to make sure they were isolated enough. "Fifty four ninety one," Zeke murmured. "Her grandparents' death was part of that. That's where you need to start."

5491? He had no idea what that meant. But her grandparents' death. Rightness settled in Jordan. Her grandparents mugging and murder was the key. He knew, he knew. "That's it."

"What?"

"It's almost October nineteenth."

A pained look crossed Zeke's face.

Jordan asked. "What about that date?"

"My grandfather died in a climbing accident." Zeke blinked. Once. Twice. "Patterns. Shit."

"That's when Staci's grandparents died. In a mugging."

Zeke tapped his fingers on the tabletop again, a faraway look in his eyes. "Yeah. I remember the information from my look at the file." So the file had something to do with both Staci and Zeke's grandparents' death. Jordan turned over the information, thinking and analyzing. "There's only one logical conclusion."

"You've got to go to New York."

"You're a genius."

"I thought we already established that." Zeke was starting to sound like his old self.

Jordan still needed more to go on. "If I gave you access to all of Staci's known accounts, could you possibly find an unregistered account?"

"I might be able to." Zeke pursed his lips. "If she set it up in the last few years and if I could access her travel records. Forensic accounting isn't exactly my thing but I know enough to start."

Jordan thought about travel records. Thought about the number of times they went to the Bahamas in the six months they were together. "Focus on the Bahamas."

Zeke tapped the tabletop. "She's got a house there, right?"

"Yeah. What's the maximum wire transfer that doesn't have to be reported to the Treasury Department?"

"Under the Bank Secrecy Act, under $10,000 and the transaction is exempt. Although if you have a steady stream of them, the bank has to report them." Zeke smiled. "If I can find that account, and get into her spending records, then you can find Staci."

"I still think New York is where she'll be."

"Probably right, but Manhattan is a fairly large borough." Zeke rubbed his hands together. "If she's there, maybe I'll be able to narrow it down to a few blocks based on her transactions."

"There's one catch."

"What's that?"

"When you find her, you have to let me know first."

"Done." Zeke thought about the request, then slumped back. "You know, I'm not supposed to have any contact with the NSA until they can verify I haven't given away state secrets."

"She's CIA, not NSA."

"Semantics," Zeke said.

"She was investigating her grandparents' deaths before she was imprisoned. Your grandfather is in that 5491 file too? What if her file on 5491 is what got her into trouble?"

"5491." Zeke said reverently, "Wish I had access to that

file. I'd really like to analyze the data, understand what happened."

Jordan hesitated. "I can get you a copy."

"Are you shitting me?" Zeke pushed the half-finished Guinness away.

Jordan wanted to make sure Staci wasn't penalized if the contents were discovered. "You have to promise to be discreet."

"My middle name, dude." Zeke's eyes lit up. "You really have access to that file?"

"Yeah."

"The whole thing?" As if Zeke still couldn't believe it.

"Yeah."

"The patterns in that file are just waiting to be discovered." Zeke said, "I only got a small glimpse of the contents. There were what, eleven people and their parents' or grandparents' deaths, right?"

"Twelve."

Jordan looked at Zeke and realized he couldn't hold the file hostage. Zeke had a right to the answers about his grandfather's death.

"I'll get the file for you."

"Do you know how incredible it will be to finally figure out the truth behind my grandpy's death?" Zeke put his palms flat on the table, spreading his fingers, staring at the white of his hand against the scarred wood. "I've been haunted by that accident for fifteen years."

"Why?"

"He was an expert climber. Taught me everything. He expounded on safety, so much so I could recite the rules in my sleep. Some people get comfortable with rules, get lax, but my grandfather didn't."

He paused, swallowed. "He was...obsessive. Compulsive.

He checked his ropes, his carabineers, his equipment all the time."

Zeke's intensity finally clicked with Jordan.

That was how Staci felt. She had an overwhelming need to understand every aspect, review every detail to make sense of her grandparents' deaths.

He should have tried harder to understand.

He needed to go to New York, follow her thought processes, if he could.

And fuck....

He needed to find her.

CHAPTER 14

O ctober 18
    4:00 pm
New York City, Broadway and 51st

I WAS at the end of my options.

I have been investigating and running for five weeks, and I'm still no freaking closer to figuring out why I was arrested and tortured in Afghanistan or who was behind it.

After researching every other person in the 5491 file, except for the one identified only by the initials ADA, I wasn't any closer to understanding why my family and eleven others were torn apart by death in October of 1995.

No one from the CIA had attempted to contact me.

Finally, I figured I had to go back to the very beginning. That's why I tucked the USA Today under my arm, entered Ellen's Stardust Diner, and prepared to open up the painful subject of my grandparents' death.

The diner was in a fifties time warp. Black and white linoleum tiles. Formica tables and leather booths. A counter with the requisite soda fountain. Every few booths, shiny metal poles extended upward, complete with coat hooks.

I sauntered over to a cherry-red booth then slid onto the worn, slick seat and slipped the gently-used cardigan, a vintage twinset sweater embellished with tulle flowers, off my shoulders.

The air in the diner felt close, or maybe it was me. A slight sweat sheened my skin, highlighting the blotchy areas on my forearms where the bruises lingered.

The between hour, too late for lunch and too early for dinner, guaranteed the diner was only minimally occupied.

A few minutes later, Sergeant Emilio Ravini plopped down across from me. "Staci Grant, right?"

I'd had no choice but to use my real name. Ravini wouldn't have spoken with me otherwise.

He had thick, black hair curling down to his shoulders, eyes the color of dark cocoa nibs, and a remote expression on his face. He'd just come off duty, dressed in a wool sport coat, the shoulder holster beneath curled around a wrinkled, white button-down shirt.

I nodded. "Thanks for agreeing to meet with me." Especially away from the precinct. I couldn't be sure whoever was after me hadn't put out a **BOLO**, or worse, on me.

If any kind of official bulletin existed, this detective would know. I'd spoken to him on the phone a few times, couldn't get him to release the case file on my grandparents' death. The only way to get answers was in person.

Though the diner was mostly empty, the sidewalks and streets were crowded. I'd already scoped out the back exit if I needed a quick getaway.

So far, I'd seen no evidence anyone other than Sergeant

Ravini had come to this meeting, but a girl couldn't be too prepared.

"No problem, Miss Grant."

Ravini shifted slightly in the booth, his discomfort only slightly discernible. The sergeant was only a few years older than my thirty-two. If I wasn't mistaken, his gaze held a sense of pity. Look at the crazy woman, she couldn't forget a fifteen-year-old murder.

Didn't help that I looked, and felt, like hell. My skin was nearly back to normal, the limp was gone, and my arm was mostly healed. But my complexion was sallow and drawn from the sickness that still plagued me.

He ordered coffee, I ordered tea, and we pretended to peruse the menu. I'd guess he was avoiding the conversation to come and I, I was trying not to heave.

The waitress popped back over to the table, all perky and young, in her Pepto Bismol pink fifties-style uniform and bright, shiny blond hair wrapped in a matching pink-sequined band.

"Piece of cherry pie, whip cream, no ice cream," he requested.

Her cotton candy, painted lips smiled encouragingly as I waited for my stomach to calm before ordering.

"Wheat toast, no butter. A hard boiled egg if you've got it." I smiled wanly. "Getting over the flu."

Her abnormally blue eyes, encased in sparkly false eyelashes, widened. She took an instinctive step back before scurrying away in her black and white saddle shoes and rolled bobby socks. Probably to put our ticket in and wash her hands, not necessarily in that order.

Ravini snickered. "You certainly have a way with people."

"It's a gift." I shrugged, then leaned my bony arms on

the silver-speckled Formica table, startled by how thin and fragile they looked. "You said on the phone you remembered my grandparents' case."

"Uh, yeah." He rubbed at a thick, dark mustache over his lips.

"Why do you still remember?"

"First week as a detective." His chocolate brown eyes held regret. "This is...off the record, right?"

"I'm just trying to understand about their deaths." I clasped my hands together, as if in prayer, and injected the most earnest tone into my voice I could muster. "I don't care about anything but figuring out what really happened to my grandparents."

"Okay. Sorry, it's just...."

Yeah. I'd dealt with enough political and legal issues to understand where he was coming from. "You don't need to worry about any repercussions."

I must have been convincing, because he started talking.

"Right." He closed his eyes, as if mentally reviewing the case file. "They were mugged, but seemed to me it was a little too professional of a stick. Perfect single stab wound on both victims. What are the odds?"

I clenched my fingers convulsively around the ceramic cup, trying to disassociate from the image. I'd seen enough death in my job. Even dissected and discussed the methodology and psychology behind the act. But disconnecting from something so personal was harder.

"Oh, hey. Sorry." His blunt fingers patted my wrist in comfort, then slid away as I didn't respond.

"No. It's okay. I asked." I deliberately loosened my fingers on the cup. "What about the perpetrator?"

"That was the other thing. Maybe even more than the manner of the stabbing." His gaze quartered the room subtly. "Two days later, we found a homeless guy, dead of a heart attack, with their wallets, jewelry, and the murder weapon."

"How was that odd?"

"Guy like that, he would have spent some of the money and pawned the jewelry right off. Not waited a few days."

"How did you know he hadn't spent any of the money?"

"His prints were only on the outside of the wallet. He hadn't even opened it to see how much money was inside." Ravini shook his head. "That doesn't make any sense."

"How'd you know about the prints?"

"One of my first cases. I did a lot of extras just to get a feel for things." He sipped at his coffee, a tired look in his eyes. "Took time to really understand everyone's job. Thought it would make me a better cop. One of the steps was brushing for prints even when the case seemed like a no-brainer."

"So why'd you close it?"

"My partner insisted. The case was cut and dried. We found the wallets, murder weapon, and the only person with a clear gain," he hesitated.

"Me." I willed the tears back into their ducts.

He nodded. "You had a rock solid alibi for the time of death."

I'd been in the hospital. I'd just gotten my tonsils out. "They'd had the tickets for months," I murmured. "After all, it was just one night. No big deal."

I'd told them to go. Insisted almost.

I knew why I remembered every detail about their deaths, but I had to double check his recollections.

"You seem pretty sure of all of this." I circled the lip of my tea cup with a bony finger. "How come you still remember?"

"It never felt right. I re-read that file a coupla times a year."

"Anything new pop out at you?"

"Look. I was young then. Green. Unsure of my instincts. Now," he paused then said grimly, "Now I would keep digging. The more I learned the more I thought we'd closed the case too soon."

The waitress set down our food. "Hope you enjoy the show."

The jukebox started, far louder than before, and two servers, a guy with hair slicked back and a girl dressed similarly to our waitress, began to sing. The music stopped the few patrons there, most people putting down their silverware.

I just wanted them to shut up.

A sultry lament from the latest Broadway show filled the diner as they sang for their keep and the potential of a professional gig.

Their expressions were full of hope, kept alive by a job that might be a stepping stone to their dreams. As the last note died out, I tried to ignore that hope.

For me, hope was all but dead. And watching them made me feel lost, sad and just the slightest bit lonely. "What else can you tell me?"

"You may not want to hear what I think." He bit into the cherry pie and waited.

"I need to know."

Ravini said, "It was a hit. I've always thought so."

"A hit?"

"Pretty complicated for one lone guy to manage. Although not impossible for a pro," Sergeant Ravini said matter-of-factly. "Take out two people without a sound.

Even if you take out the bigger threat first, the second target is going to make some noise."

I saw his point. I could feel my skin go white. A professional.

The connection between everyone receiving funds from Department 5491 was the death of either their parents or grandparents. Theoretically most of the deaths were accidents.

If they weren't connected by 5491 I would have assumed the conclusion was correct. But they'd all been on or about October Nineteenth.

Tomorrow.

"Anything else?" I asked through lips that suddenly felt bloodless.

"No one saw anything." He jabbed his fork at me. "They left the theatre the same time as everyone else, walked along a sidewalk easily half the theatre district uses to exit the area and no one saw a thing."

"I thought the Times Square area was pretty safe."

"You ever seen a show on Broadway?"

"Yeah." I'd gone with my grandparents many times. I hadn't been back since their deaths.

"It's packed. All the shows get out about the same time. Pedestrians, cabs, limos everywhere. Great time to get your pocket picked."

The detective added, "How the hell does this homeless guy, who would be noticed among all the suits, high heels and fancy dresses, manage to stab two people with single perfect aim and no one notices?"

He shook his head again, his mouth pursed in disbelief. "It just doesn't play for me."

I bit tentatively into the toast and chewed slowly, ever

hopeful I could keep the bread down. "So it was a hit, but why?"

"We never looked into the vics' background." He slurped at his coffee. "That would be where you come in. You really want to know, you've got to look at your grandparents' background. Who would want them dead and why and how did they profit from it?"

"That's where I'm stuck," I whispered. "I'm the only one and I sure didn't profit from it. I lost my whole family in one night."

He looked me over, sizing up my slightly worn twinset tank and faded jeans, the split ends and damaged condition of my hair pulled into a haphazard pony, the bruises and mottled discoloration of my skin, leftover from the remnants of the drug still leaving my system.

I didn't look like myself. Which was the whole point of dressing this way. Anyone who knew me would look right over me.

Staci Grant was always immaculate. Groomed and polished with a clear patina of money coating everything.

"I'm really sorry." He patted my hand again, the gesture in no way sexual. I hadn't been touched in so long, the skin on skin contact reminded me of Jordan.

And all that I'd lost.

"I know." The need to connect with another human being was strong. I thought about grabbing his hand and just holding onto his warmth for a minute. Just a minute.

I looked at my trimmed fingernails, my skin a dried husk of what it used to be, my arms stick thin, elbows scrawny, bones clearly visible underneath the little muscle left.

I was wasting away and couldn't seem to stop.

The waitress dropped off the check, topped his coffee and left quickly as if worried about contamination.

"Why don't you get a sandwich?" The cop's gaze was sympathetic. "My treat."

"I can't eat," I whispered. "Nothing stays down." I knew I'd given away too much.

"Is there someone I could call for you?"

Jordan. My heart wanted to call him. Touch base. My head said there were too many coincidences regarding Jordan. I had to stop thinking about him. About us.

I had no one. "No. Thanks."

"You're sure?"

Emotion welled up inside me, more overwhelming than the waves of pain I'd endured when I'd been beaten. I slid quickly from the booth and pulled a crumpled ten dollar bill from my jeans pocket, trying to ignore the trembling in my hand before dropping the money on the table.

"I'm good." The answer might have been believable if my voice hadn't wobbled. Ravini pulled out his wallet, while trying to get up and check on me.

I had to get out of there. I grabbed my cardigan. "Thanks for your time. I really appreciate it."

Talking about my grandparents' death brought it all back. They were gone. Jordan was gone. I was all alone.

I had to leave. Now.

As I rushed away, I glanced back and saw the concern in his eyes turn to suspicion. Hopefully I hadn't blown it. If he started investigating, my attempts to lay low would be shot to hell.

If he ran a check on me in the NYPD database, my cover as a college professor and sometime philanthropist should hold. Though he might not be able to reconcile those facts with the woman he'd met today, he'd let the discrepancy go.

The bigger issue: the check could raise a red flag. The people who were looking for me would be on my ass again.

Damage control.

Start acting like the freaking CIA officer you are.

I headed back toward Ravini and smiled with self-deprecation. "Sorry. My stomach still isn't recovered from this flu. Do you know where the bathroom is?"

His suspicion morphed back to sympathy.

"Over there." He gestured toward the rear, past the soda fountain and counter. "You want I should wait for you?"

"No, thanks. I'll be okay." The urge to back away from his touch was so compelling, I forced myself to hold out my hand. "I appreciate your help."

"One last thing," he said, in an almost offhand manner. "I found it interesting you weren't the only one to call me about this case."

"Someone else called you?" A desperate fear struck at me. Why would someone else be looking into their deaths? And why now?

"Yeah. He's from D.C. too. I'm meeting him tomorrow." He held my gaze. "It never sat right with me, what happened to them. I won't mention I saw you today."

Protecting me. That's what he was doing. And I did appreciate it.

"What was the person's name?"

He hesitated.

And I could tell he wasn't going to give me that information. The panic bubbled back inside my stomach. "Never mind. Did he say why he wanted to talk to you?"

He shook his head. "Investigating an old case was all he said."

He. At least that gave me a starting point. Super. I could eliminate half the population. "Thanks."

"Good luck," he said quietly. His fingers curled around mine with firmness as he shook my hand.

I hesitated, once again feeling awkward and not at all like myself.

Staci Grant was self-possessed, self-assured, and didn't lack for self-control.

Somehow I'd lost that Staci.

I had to get her back.

CHAPTER 15

October 18
4:45 pm
New York City, Times Square

JORDAN WANDERED AROUND TIMES SQUARE, figuring he'd gone totally over the edge. Yeah. Come to New York City and just walk around hoping to find your pretty much ex-girlfriend who happened to be with the CIA and could probably hide for years without being found.

Fuck.

He leaned against the cold brick siding of some store and let his gaze skim over the chaos of the streets. A bright multi-story panel projected the NASDAQ.

Further up the street, a layered sign stacked Hershey Bars on top of french fries on top of Cup of Noodles complete with steam rising from the giant cup, all glowing in bright 3-D neon. America's homage to commercialism in a few square blocks. Nike, NBA, Sephora, Element, Ann Taylor Loft, GAP, Roxy.

He fought the urge to check his six. He couldn't shake the feeling he was being followed. Jordan snorted. Right. Followed by the other twenty gazillion tourists in this little slice of Manhattan.

The aroma of boiled hot dogs, the tang of mustard, the smog from the constant chug of cars on the congested streets, and the grime of daily exhaust streams assaulted his senses. On the sidewalk, bags of garbage waited for pickup.

A crisp fall wind swept through the tunnel created by the buildings and blew out the scents for a moment.

Jordan let the honk of horns and the chatter, English, French, Spanish, German, Japanese, Hindu, Mandarin roll through his consciousness, not tracking any one conversation but filtering the snippets.

A massive stream of humanity in all colors and sizes flowed on the sidewalks. Intermittently a group of Japanese tourists would stop to snap pictures of the spectacle and foot traffic would break and flow around them.

A bicycle delivery guy with spiked black hair, studded belt, skin tight black pants, bulging black messenger bag, and a Bluetooth receiver clipped to his ear zipped by and turned the corner.

Through it all, Jordan watched. And waited.

For nothing.

He should probably go back to the hotel. He'd been insane to think coming to New York would work. This was a total goatfuck.

It had been six weeks since he'd seen the report of Staci's death.

She was alive.

She was clearly hiding from someone. She was in trouble. Yet, she hadn't contacted him, hadn't asked for his help. If she'd wanted to talk to him or see him, she would have.

If he could walk away, he would. There was just one little matter. She needed that damn antidote.

The scientist, Susan Chen, had been adamant that the drug injected into the espionage agents needed to be reversed. Jordan needed to find Staci and get her the antidote.

But she didn't know she'd had the drug and clearly didn't care that she was evading him.

Hope that wouldn't quite die came up with alternative scenarios for why she hadn't contacted him. Maybe the drug had skewed her thought process, maybe she wouldn't come to him because of the drug. Maybe she was trying to protect him.

And maybe he was insane.

She'd been with him before she left for Afghanistan. She'd had the drug in her then, even though he didn't know it and neither did she.

She'd re-appeared back in the U.S. at least four weeks ago, based on when she got John Wishbone out of the hospital. If she was in trouble, she sure as shit wasn't coming to him.

More than anything, that hurt.

He wanted to be the one she turned to for help. Dammit.

His mother and his aunt had raised him. But he'd known from age nine, he was the man of the house. The caretaker.

That was his role.

With Staci, she'd changed the rules by refusing to let him take care of her. In fact, that was one thing that had attracted him. She could take care of herself.

Wasn't that a fucked up reasoning? Did he want to take care of her or did he want her to take care of herself?

Jordan found himself in front of one of the glittery Broadway theatres. He had no idea which theatre Staci's grandparents had gone to on the night they died. He wondered if there was some way to find out which theatre they'd attended the night they died. Then he could just stake out that venue. Tomorrow when he met with Detective Ravini he could ask.

Jordan wandered along Broadway. Remembering the last time he'd been here with Staci, she'd been distant and melancholy throughout their trip. They had been strolling down Fifth Avenue, buying out the sales. She'd been teasing him, "I'm not sure I've ever met a man who likes to shop as much as you do."

He had more bags than Staci. "I was forced to endure hours of shopping with my mother and aunt."

"Really?" She laughed in pure delight. "Bet you hated every minute of it."

"Some of their...enjoyment must have rubbed off."

"Tell me more." She threaded her fingers with his.

"They used to dress up in their best clothes. Me too." Had to look like they were serious shoppers or the stores would have kicked them out. "My mom and my aunt would try on every fancy dress they could."

"Did they buy out the store?"

"Ah...no. We couldn't afford it." His Mama and Tía would be appalled at the amount of money he'd spent in the last two hours. "After spending all day at the mall, they'd buy one small thing, usually on super markdown clearance."

And frequently for him. Shit. Why had he never realized that?

"You didn't buy anything on super markdown clearance today," Staci teased.

"Yeah, and I've never seen anyone power shop the way you do." He gestured toward the bags she was swinging back and forth.

Staci stopped to check out the window display at Takashimaya. She glanced back from looking at the display of satin-covered hat boxes to throw him a provocative look.

"I know what I want and I go after it." Her eyes had sparkled with the most joy he'd seen since they'd gotten to New York.

He leaned down, his front crowded against her back, invading her personal space. He brushed his cheek against hers, then rubbed his nose in her hair and inhaled the scent of her deep inside.

The lotion she religiously smoothed into her skin surrounded him and he wanted to drown in scent. "How do you always smell so amazing?"

"Female stuff." She laughed again and twirled away from him, heading into the next store without even looking.

As soon as she got through the revolving door, Staci stopped dead. Right behind her, he saw the hesitation, the sudden dejection in her posture.

So he moved closer and did the only thing he could think of. "You know, few places strike fear into the heart of a happily single man, but a jewelry store does the trick."

She'd laughed, as he'd known she would and grabbed his hand. He let himself be dragged over to the display cases of silver, gold, platinum and precious stones.

Staci traced a finger over the glass case of delicate platinum bands with aquamarines. Once again her expression turned reflective.

"Everything okay?" He rested his hand on her shoulder, squeezing gently.

"My grandmother loved Tiffany's."

She fingered the anniversary band on her right ring finger. "Every time we came to the city, we'd come in here and my grandfather would bitch and complain. And every time we'd walk out with a blue box, and my grandfather would have the biggest...."

She paused, swallowed. "Smile. The biggest smile on his face."

The sadness on her face tore him apart. He'd give anything to get back that silly mood. So he leaned down and growled in her ear, "I know what would put a smile on my face...and it won't cost a thing."

She'd laughed again and they'd raced for the door. Their hotel, the Pierre, was only a block away....

Someone bumped Jordan's shoulder, bringing him back to the present. As Jordan looked around Times Square, he realized he'd seen the same bicycle delivery guy at least three times in the last hour.

Could be this was his delivery territory, but as Jordan mentally flipped through the times he'd seen the guy, he realized that the shape of the bag hadn't changed.

Suddenly the Bluetooth took on a totally different meaning. He was communicating with a partner.

After bicycle guy zipped by, he must hand surveillance off to someone else. That someone must still be around. Jordan slowed, then stopped to look in a store window with the ubiquitous 'I heart NY' t-shirts and mugs. Pretending to look over the merchandise, he checked the reflection in the glass for anyone paying too much attention to him.

Shit.

He strolled casually along until he came to a tiny noodle

shop. Wandering inside, as if he had all the time in the world, he looked over the menu, thought about his options, and wondered who the hell could be following him.

If the CIA had learned he'd been asking discreet questions about Staci, they could be doing surveillance on him.

The senator?

That reasoning made a twisted sense. If so, the man was certifiable. Following Jordan wouldn't get him the information he wanted. Our tax dollars at work.

Jordan gave the guy behind the counter a twenty, and asked for the back way out. Easing through the kitchen, he passed the chef, bent over a giant pot of steaming soup. The aroma of chicken broth, egg drops, and spicy peppers gnawed at his gut. He hadn't eaten since early this morning.

Jordan ignored his stomach's complaint, slid out the back, and crouched next to a dumpster.

No one followed.

Didn't mean they weren't behind him. If he didn't spook out of here soon, whoever watched the front would be inside and bribing the counter guy just like Jordan.

He came out the alley, hugged close to the buildings, and tried to make his silhouette smaller while keeping a lookout for bicycle guy.

He'd thought if he'd hung around Times Square he'd have a better chance of seeing Staci.

Jesus, what had he been thinking?

Too many possible routes, too many theaters to keep track of, too many people, too many options. Guess the manzana didn't fall too far from that tree. He was insane.

This endeavor was futile.

He'd have better luck staking out the lobby of the

Waldorf than wandering aimlessly around Times Square. Jordan headed back toward the hotel.

His heart stopped.

Staci.

Ba-bump. Ba-bump. His heartbeat double-timed. Babump-babump-babump.

Ridiculous. He couldn't possibly just run into her on the street, could he?

The woman wore faded jeans and a worn sweater in a shade of green Staci wouldn't be caught dead in.

Her shoes were dirty Converse high tops. Staci wore Italian leather.

The woman's hair was in a ragged, black pony tail, over-processed with split ends and streaks of wildly contrasting blond and red. Staci was always perfectly groomed, her hair a shiny, healthy mass.

Besides, the woman was thin to the point of starvation. Staci had at least fifteen pounds on her.

Yet Jordan couldn't shake the hope it was Staci.

You're losing it, man. He was so desperate, he was seeing her everywhere.

He wanted to run. But he wasn't sure if he wanted to run toward the woman or away. Unable to help himself, he sidled closer.

He checked his six constantly, looking for the tail. On the streets, bicycle guy was conspicuously absent. No one else raised suspicion.

Of course, he'd only spotted the first tail after forty-five minutes.

Jordan continued to follow the woman, moving at an even speed, slowly gaining.

Jesus, she was thin.

Within five feet of her, he knew he'd gone totally insane.

The closer he got, he could see the jeans practically hung off her frame. Her hair was wrong. Everything about her was wrong.

Except the gentle curve of her neck.

He stared at the curve and the feeling in his gut intensified. His heart pounded in his chest, a primal drumbeat. And right up there on the weird-o-meter, he caught the edge of the scent of gardenias.

The woman stumbled slightly, caught herself.

She was drunk.

She wove back and forth, nearly falling, until a crack in the sidewalk finished her off. Jordan lunged forward to catch her. He scooped his arms around her stomach, and she flopped forward like a rag doll then started to struggle.

"Leggo o' me." The woman's harsh curse echoed in his ear.

He pulled back to find his own balance before letting her go.

Alcohol fumes poured off her enveloping him in a suffocating cloud. Or maybe reality was suffocating him.

Not Staci.

Not even fucking close. The curve of her neck. Jesus, he really was losing it.

"Sorry, ma'am." He released her. "Just trying to save you from falling."

"Pervert." She stumbled away, muttering.

Save her.

That's what this trip was all about. Saving Staci.

But the truth was evident. She didn't want or need to be saved. She didn't want or need him. If she needed him, she would have contacted him.

What a total waste of time.

Jordan headed toward the Waldorf, his steps slow and

heavy. About two blocks from the hotel, he saw the sign. Murphy's Irish Pub in gold scrollwork across a small, cheerless window.

But the light behind the window was warm, and the place reminded him of Staci. When they'd been in New York, they'd stopped in at this exact pub for a drink. He remembered thinking the tavern, a little bit run down, an odd place for her.

But she'd insisted.

And been a little bit melancholy the entire time.

Jordan eased open the door. A blast of warm air hit him in the face. The cheery sound of the Corrs singing about the stars going blue washed over him.

What the hell.

He'd have a glass of Irish to remember her and then get out of New York.

If she wanted to see him...she'd be able to find him.

CHAPTER 16

Jordan headed for a booth in the back of the pub.

The stools at the bar were all occupied with what appeared to be regulars, arms akimbo on the lip of the polished mahogany counter and one hand never far from their pint.

The bartender, a burly, red-faced man, laughed at something one of the guys said, then went back to wiping the counter.

He lifted his chin at Jordan. "What can I get ya?"

"Club soda with a lime and a Guinness."

Bartender gave a short nod of approval. "I'll bring it over."

He slid into the booth at the back, giving himself an unobstructed view of the door. The window was at shoulder height so he'd only be able to see someone if they passed on the sidewalk, not in the street.

Let them follow him. Shit. He didn't have anything for them to find. He hoped his tail wandered around looking for their asses.

Conversation was muted, murmurs accompanied by

clinks of glass and silverware hitting ceramic. The bartender plopped the glass of club soda on the table, then gently set down the glass of Guinness.

"Anyt'ing else?" he asked, the lilt of Ireland in his voice.

Someone came through the door, the swift rush of cool air swirled over him.

His stomach growled. "Yeah. Burger medium rare, no cheese, steak fries."

Jordan rubbed his hands over his face and wondered how he'd come to this. Sitting in a bar in New York City, looking for a woman who didn't want to be found.

He'd let his work go.

He'd let everything go in the quest to find her.

By the time the bartender moved to the table in front of him, the woman had slid into the next booth. Her back to him.

Jordan surveyed the stick thin bones of the woman's shoulders and arms. She was almost as thin as the woman he'd accosted in the street.

She ordered, her soft tone clearly audible over the music, which had segued into a rousing rendition of the fiddle version of Joy of Life/Trout in the Bath.

She lifted a shaky hand to swipe at her hair, the grace of the movement at odds with her condition.

"Thank you," she said, her voice husky.

Jesus, now he was hearing her voice. He fingered the amulet in his pocket, taking comfort in the familiar carvings.

"You want anyt'ing else?"

"No, thank you." It was Staci.

He was afraid to believe. Thinking he was going to make a fool of himself. Again. "Staci?"

Her back stiffened but she didn't turn around. It was her!

Pure joy rushed through him. He instinctively moved out of the booth and kept his gaze on her.

If the bartender hadn't been unintentionally blocking her way, Jordan was pretty sure she would have bolted. As it was, she had no way to get out, or away.

"Jordan." She sank back against the booth. Her hand fluttered toward the scar on her left arm as if trying to hide the angry red slash from him, before she defiantly set her arm down in plain view.

"You two want to sit together?" The bartender was grinning, playing matchmaker.

"Yes."

"No."

"Yes," Jordan repeated more forcefully. "I'd like to catch up."

Jordan insinuated into her booth, on the same side of the table. The position was awkward but he wasn't giving her any chance to escape.

"What brings you to New York?" she asked politely. As if they were minor acquaintances, rather than lovers.

Former lovers.

"You."

She jerked back. He'd surprised her.

Jesus, she looked like hell.

She'd always had the softest skin. Now, the texture was rough and as he bent closer he could see fine spots, almost like liver spots, and that wicked scar, puckered and pink along her left forearm.

The need to touch her, to reassure himself she wasn't a figment of his over-taxed and over-stimulated imagination, steamrolled through him.

He opened his arms, ignoring her slight flinch, and pulled her into his embrace. He wrapped his arms around her shoulders, bony and sharp against his biceps. His big hand cupped the fragile curve of her head, as he pressed his cheek against hers and inhaled her unique scent.

God, he'd missed her.

He knew better than to voice that thought out loud. Mentally, she was further away from him than when she'd been in Afghanistan.

Jordan held on tight, even though she didn't feel right. The stiffness, the hesitation, the roughness of her skin, the scars that marked her. Staci's body language made it clear she wasn't his anymore.

Right. He'd known that. Really, he had. But seeing her had obliterated that knowledge.

"What are you doing here?" Her voice was muffled against his collar.

He'd have to let her go, but first he threaded his fingers through her raggedy hair and brushed the dark-colored bangs away from her face.

"Looking for you."

"Found me. I'm fine." Her tone a total dismissal.

He regarded her solemnly. "I can't leave just yet." He had to tell her about the agents and the injections and the antidote she needed. Jordan glanced around. "We can't talk here."

"Then I'll leave." She nudged her hip against his, and once again he was struck by how fragile she felt.

"What happened?" He fingered her skin, noting the blotchy blobs of color, darker than her normal skin tone, unlike any kind of tan he'd ever seen.

He recalled Johnny Wishbone's description of Staci. A black woman. Not real dark, but definitely black. What he was thinking was so preposterous except the evidence seemed to be right in front of him.

"You turned your skin black?"

She calmly took a sip of her Jamieson, her gaze averted.

He took in the other changes.

She'd lost a ton of weight. Not just weight, she'd lost muscle. They used to work out together every day. She'd had a solid build. Not heavy by any means, but definitely not skinny.

"You're half-starved."

Without meaning to, he ran a gentle finger over the scar on her arm.

She covered the scar self-consciously. "Just like a man to cut and run when the looks are gone."

He noted the hesitant, shaky brush of her fingers. No way would he fall for that. Jordan leaned in close. "I didn't cut and run. You did."

She pushed back stubbornly against the high back of the booth, face forward, lips compressed into a flat line, hands crossed over one another in her lap. So ladylike.

Something about the position of her hands, just so, nagged at him. Suddenly he put the pose together with the darker skin tone.

"That *was* you on the plane, when the lady bumped into you." He shouldn't have doubted his instincts. Dammit. "Wasn't it?"

She refused to answer.

"Just great. The silent treatment."

The bartender dropped his plate down onto the table, gave Jordan a look. *Better be good, boyo. I'm watching you.*

The odor of slightly charred beef hit his nose, and his stomach rebelled. Logically he'd known she hadn't wanted to see him. If she had, she'd have come home.

Come back to him.

But deep down inside, there'd been hope that something

had prevented her from contacting him. Some unknown force had kept them apart.

Instead, his own mind had refused to let go of what they'd shared.

A relationship built on lies. One that was over.

He had no appetite left.

She, on the other hand, was wasting away to nothing. He pushed the burger in front of her. "Eat. You look like hell."

Staci looked down at the burger. Her face blanched, and she swayed.

"You're fading away. You need to fucking eat." He shoved the hamburger in her face.

She did some sort of exorcist move with her head. "Let me out. I'm gonna be sick."

She pushed half up off the seat, her shoes scuffing on the floor as she frantically tried to get past him.

"Shit." Not kidding. She was gonna blow.

Her throat jerked convulsively as if she were trying to keep the contents of her stomach from spewing right there.

That shot him into action. He jammed out of the booth and she was gone, like a bullet from a sniper rifle, into the ladies' room.

Jordan threw forty bucks down on the table, called to the bartender, "Can we get that to go?"

He followed her. Just in case she was trying to pull a Houdini, he'd hang by the bathroom until she was done. Jordan leaned against the wall, hearing and trying not to listen to the sound of her being violently sick.

He took a step toward the bathroom. The bartender came up and handed him a styrofoam container. Jordan paused, weighed the wisdom of his next question carefully before deciding he had to ask. "Any other possible exit from the bathroom besides this hallway?"

The bartender assessed him coolly. "Nope. One window, too small and too high up to get out."

Jordan nodded his thanks. "Got any saltines?"

"I just might." Suddenly the man grinned. "Be right back."

He scurried toward the bar, reached underneath then headed to Jordan.

In the background, he heard the faucet running as the bartender gave him the small packages. "Always helped Mrs. Murphy."

Jordan registered that the water had been on too long. He lunged for the bathroom door and rattled the handle. "You got keys?"

Murphy grabbed the key ring clipped to his belt. "Right here."

Mr. Murphy unlocked the door and swung it open carefully. And there was Staci half-in, half-out the small window.

Her old self wouldn't have been able to fit. As it was, her new emaciated, heroin-chic, God he hoped not, self, was just barely squeezing out. "If she comes back in, don't let her leave."

Jordan didn't want to hurt her, but he was damned if she was getting away.

"She done something wrong?"

Thinking quickly, he made up the first thing that came to mind. "Nah. We had a fight, and I'm trying to make up but she won't talk to me."

"I've got her covered." Murphy called out to him as the screen door to the alley slapped closed.

Jordan hustled around into the narrow strip between

buildings. He picked up her messenger bag and slung it over his shoulder.

Staci was almost to the ground when he caught her around the waist, feeling her ribs beneath the fragile sweater.

"You're bones," he said helplessly.

After he eased her gently to the ground, she sagged against him. Her forehead rested on his collarbone, body shivering relentlessly, breath sawing in and out.

"Honey. We have got to talk. Come with me and we'll sort it out."

She nodded numbly, all the will sucked out of her. "'kay."

Jordan curled an arm around her shoulders and led her toward the street. About five feet from where the alley opened to the sidewalk, he paused to watch the traffic. Staci rested against him lethargically, as if once the fight was gone, it was all she could do to keep herself upright.

He wanted to make serious tracks for the hotel, but he needed to be patient. Wait.

He'd had to really cultivate that skill when he'd been on the Hostage Rescue Team in the FBI. The endless hours of waiting had been the hardest part of his training and the job. But he'd finally gotten it. He forced himself to hold, patient and calm.

A single light over the backdoor of the tavern provided meager light. The lid to Murphy's dumpster was open spreading the odor of decay and garbage.

"We've got to move soon, or I won't be able to make it," she whispered. Her body stiffened. "Unless you're waiting for a pickup."

He swallowed back a sharp comment. They could fight later.

"I was being followed earlier. Just making sure they aren't still out there, watching."

"Followed?"

She straightened, just as the bicycle messenger crossed the street in front of them.

Jordan saw the guy's gaze search the alley and widen as he found in his target.

"Shit. I hope you can run, 'cause we aren't home yet."

CHAPTER 17

I didn't have time to react.

Jordan grabbed my hand, did a one-eighty, and hauled ass down the alley. I'd barely gotten a look at the guy then we were flying.

The world whooshed into tunnel focus, everything receding, falling away.

Getting away, from the guy, from Jordan, ought to be my priority. But I could concentrate only on the hardness of his hand in mine. Such a simple thing, and yet the comforting solidness of him eased something within me.

"Pretty sure it was a team surveillance," he said softly. "So it's possible someone else is close. Depends how long it will take them to get in place."

The words dropped me back into the present with startling clarity. Instead of the surreal tunneling of a moment ago, I was bombarded with sensory details. The stench of the bagged up garbage, the overwhelming odor of cheap bourbon, the crunch of a broken bottle underneath the thin soles of my high tops. A pigeon swooped low and cooed at us.

My breath huffed in and out of my chest in great gasps, burning my throat. The most recent and humiliating bout of nausea wasn't helping. My legs trembled with the exertion, and we'd only covered the length of the alley.

Jesus, I was out of shape.

I mean, logically I knew it, but trying to outrun a team surveillance brought my out-of-shapeness home a little too clearly. And the moment was a little too important.

When we ran together a few months ago, I used to kick his ass. He was too bulky to be fast. He just powered through, but it wasn't pretty. Now he was much faster than me.

"You...should just...leave me." It would eliminate two problems. I could get away from both Jordan and the guy following him.

He didn't even pause, just scooped his left arm around my waist and half-lifted me off the ground as he continued to run.

Guess that was a no.

Jordan's gaze moved constantly, his right hand near his hip. And I realized he was carrying.

He held me up while I clung to him like a helpless little girl. "What are we looking for?"

"Never saw the second guy." We skidded to a stop at the end of the alley.

Sweat sheened over my entire body. Amazing really, I shouldn't have any extra hydration because of all the puking.

Jordan assimilated us into the flow of pedestrians at a seemingly leisurely pace, or as leisurely as foot traffic was in New York City. He hugged me close but kept his hand near his belt.

"First guy, bicycle messenger. Black clothes, black

helmet, messenger bag over his right shoulder, Bluetooth in his ear."

"You sure he wasn't just a messenger?"

He cocked his head at me.

"Okay, sorry. Why is someone tracking you?"

After all, his think tank job wasn't exactly espionage and he'd been out of the FBI for over a year.

We walked, me plastered against his side, his head bent down as if he were nuzzling my hair while he quartered the street in front of us and continuously glanced behind.

"Not sure."

My shoulder rubbed against his chest. The bulk of his body, the heat of his skin, the woodsy scent of his soap and shampoo, the familiarity of his heartbeat, overwhelmed me.

When I had allowed myself to imagine a reunion at all, hot sex had been my favorite fantasy.

I needed my brain to start working properly. Not focusing on things that didn't matter.

"Damn, you're bony," he blurted out.

My heart constricted.

I was a goddamn mess. I knew it. I also never realized how much my appearance mattered to me until taken away.

"Yeah." I wasn't going there. "So why is someone following you and why are you carrying?"

He had a permit to carry concealed, but when we were together, I'd only seen him with a weapon when getting some trigger time at the shooting range.

We dodged a slow-moving couple, man with a cane, woman with a blush-pink pillbox hat, playbill coming out of her matching pink purse.

"I was involved in a shooting last week."

My steps dragged for a minute. "What?"

"Not the place." He glanced around meaningfully and, really, I knew better.

But I couldn't wait. "Shooting...." I prompted.

"I helped an agent from the NSA and an old FBI friend recover two teenaged kids after they were kidnapped."

Startled, I glanced up into his face, set in a hard expression, mouth a thin line, gaze constantly roving.

"I believe you know the boy."

"I do?"

"John Wishbone."

I stumbled. John Wishbone. So I'd been right, and the girl had been in danger. "She okay?"

"Bella?" The light turned yellow.

Jordan sprinted across the street, dragging me along. As the light went red, taxis and cars jumped forward in a puff of exhaust.

"Yeah." Jordan kept his gaze on the traffic, the congestion around us. "She's fine."

I'm sure I imagined the censure in his voice.

I wracked my brain for a reason why he would have been involved with John Wishbone and Bella Holden and couldn't for the life of me figure out how or why he would know either one.

The suspicious part of my nature kicked in. I hadn't even begun to process that we'd run into each other at Murphy's. "How'd you hook up with them?"

The sidewalk narrowed under scaffolding covered with a canvas tarp. I didn't want to be confined. The flat, grim line of Jordan's mouth confirmed he felt the same.

He held fast to my hand and we hustled through the dark tunnel. "That's a pretty long story and the reason I've been looking for you."

We emerged from the darkened walkway under the

scaffolding and fell into an easy partnership. He checked right while I took left.

Everything appeared ordinary. I breathed a quick sigh of relief. We sprinted across 49th Street and I finally realized where he was dragging me.

The Waldorf.

Could be he was heading toward the W, but my luck wouldn't be that good.

I hadn't been to the Waldorf-Astoria since my grandparents' death fifteen years ago. I swallowed hard, this time from the memories.

"The Waldorf?" I didn't want to go inside.

"Yeah."

The doorman smiled as he pulled open the ornate brass doors for us, not even blinking at my attire or that we were both sweating.

Jordan hustled me up the intricate Persian runner. The light streaming from the elaborate crystal chandelier felt ultra bright after the onset of dusk outside.

We headed for the elevators. The piano tinkled from the lobby bar for the hotel guests seated on the curved sofa. A distinguished man in a tux and an older woman, perfectly coiffed, in a bronze beaded gown, sauntered around a large round mahogany table, laden with a flower arrangement so huge, the top almost touched the smaller crystal chandelier in the elevator lobby. But not everything was so formal. A couple of younger guys in jeans, sweatshirts, and tennis shoes hurried past us with Starbucks cups.

The elevator doors were sliding closed. Jordan took two long strides forward, and put his hand out to stop the doors from closing.

We stepped into the empty elevator. He punched the number for the fourth floor.

"Hate elevators. Ambush waiting to happen." His tension was contagious.

When the elevator dinged for our floor, we instinctively moved to separate sides, almost pressed up against the wood paneling of the wall where the doors opened.

If anyone was waiting, they'd think we'd gotten off earlier.

The doors slid open.

No one moved.

A vacuum cleaner droned nearby. I peered out, looking at the mirror across from the elevator bank as Jordan pressed the button to keep the doors open.

The foyer was empty.

As if choreographed, we exited quickly. "What room?"

"Service elevator."

He strode toward the center of the tower, clearly already having done reconnaissance. Expecting trouble?

Jordan glanced at his watch. "We've got two minutes before any of the other elevators could get back here, assuming they didn't stop along the way."

"Stairs?"

"That's why we're using the service elevator."

He stepped through a door marked 'private', and punched the elevator call button. We held perfectly still, listening for any kind of pursuit.

We jumped inside, and I jabbed the 'door closed' button. Jordan hit the button for the eighth floor, then pulled out his cell phone and pressed speed dial.

"Who are you calling?"

"A friend." Jordan spoke quickly and quietly into his phone. "I'm coming. I need you to be at the door, ready to let me in. Someone is following me."

We made it to the room without incident. The door swung open and Jordan jerked me inside.

"Dude. Can't believe you were followed."

As the door slammed shut behind us, a guy with a mop of curly blond hair stood in the suite's foyer and looked at me with total surprise.

"Holy shit, Staci Grant. You found her." A big smile lit his face showing a line of straight white teeth. "What, you just wandered around New York City until you ran into her?"

"Uh, sort of," Jordan replied.

He beamed at me. The whole situation felt surreal. We stood in a small foyer that reminded me more of the entry to an apartment than a hotel room.

I knew this little foyer. We'd always gotten a suite when we'd come to the Waldorf. My grandmother insisted we have a formal flower arrangement for the little key table so every time we walked into the room we saw and smelled roses.

A lump formed in my throat.

I hadn't been back here for a reason, dammit.

Jordan still had my right hand in his left. I used the distraction of the surfer guy to reach into Jordan's holster with my left hand and grab his weapon.

The weight of the gun in my weakened hands and arms was almost too much. "Who the hell are you?"

"Whoa." Surfer dude's hands went up.

Jordan released my right hand so I could steady the weapon.

"The safety's on. Let's keep it that way." He was calm as he stepped in front of the surfer guy. "Staci, meet Zeke Hawthorne."

Wait a minute. I knew that name. I'd studied every name

and situation in that damn file so many times I could recite the information in my sleep.

"Dude. You didn't tell me she was crazy."

Jordan said, "She's feeling off balance and threatened right now. Cut her a break."

"Maybe if she freakin' lowers that weapon."

Jordan spoke to Hawthorne but didn't take his gaze from mine. His hazel eyes, steady and confident, stared back at me, waiting for what I'd do next.

"Give her a second to process. She knows what she's doing. She won't shoot by accident."

They calmly sat there discussing whether or not I would shoot them. As I swayed slowly, I realized either one of them could disarm me without breaking a sweat. They were giving me control of the situation.

"Zeke Hawthorne. Grandfather killed in a climbing accident." My skin was slick with sweat and the weight of the Glock was starting to seriously affect my weak muscles.

"Yeah. That's me." Zeke peered over Jordan's shoulder, looking somber. "Staci Grant, grandparents killed in a mugging, homeless man found two days later with wallets, etc., case closed. Staci Grant. Presumed dead."

I glanced at Jordan, he didn't look surprised, or confused, by our conversation, which was something I'd have to explore later. I stated the obvious. "They weren't accidents."

"Yeah. I pretty much got that from the file you started." Zeke dropped his hands slightly.

I lowered the weapon cautiously. I couldn't figure out why they would be here or how he'd seen that file. "What are you doing here?"

"Looking for one Staci Grant, pronounced dead in an Afghan prison, according to an intel report complete with graphic photographs. Considered dead by everyone except this guy." He jerked his head toward Jordan.

I blinked. There was a weird rushing sound. The gun drooped. "Do you hear that?"

The lights flickered. A single trail of sweat trickled down the side of my face. The sound was getting louder. Suddenly my vision went white and then....

Nothing.

CHAPTER 18

"Shit. Catch her." Zeke went for the Glock.

Jordan twisted to scoop one arm around Staci's back and the other around her knees while Zeke carefully supported the weapon from a safe position if her finger accidentally pulled the trigger.

Jordan lifted her higher into his arms completely freaked by how light she felt. They'd done enough physical engagement through Krav Maga and some fairly energetic sex for him to recognize her condition had deteriorated significantly.

"Jesus, she's skin and bones."

Zeke pried her fingers from around the grip of the weapon very gingerly. "Got to give her snaps, she didn't let go."

Jordan strode into the living area of the suite and headed for the sofa. "She needs to eat."

"Judging by the condition of her skin, she's dehydrated," Zeke said analytically.

Jordan lay her down gently on the sofa, and with more

reluctance than he would like, let go. The urge to just sit and hold her jacked through him.

He situated her, propping her feet with the throw pillows, smoothing the hair away from her face. "She threw up at Murphy's and then I set a pretty hard pace to get here."

"Cut yourself a break."

Zeke paced behind him, around the coffee table, through the two chairs, in front of the business desk, and past the television that he had on low.

"I'll go get carry out from Oscars downstairs. I can assess if we've got any unusual activity in the lobby or lower level at the same time."

Jordan pressed his fingers to her neck, feeling for her pulse. "Slow and steady."

"Maybe she's just worn out."

"Yeah." She was more than worn out. She looked like life had kicked her in the ass.

"Wonder where the hell she's been for the past six weeks."

Jordan surveyed her, brushed the neckline of the wool away from her neck, and noticed the fresh scars. Small, raised circular marks marred her neck.

"Hell."

"Cigarette burns," Zeke said in a hushed voice.

"That would be my guess."

She'd been tortured. He should have been prepared for the possibility. She'd been in the prison where the woman had been beheaded. With excruciating clarity, all the marks on the unknown woman's body came back to him.

He pushed up her sleeve to find deep tissue bruises braceleting her bony wrists. Now the wicked scar and clear signs of an unset break on her left arm took on a more sinister meaning.

"Fuck."

Zeke pulled a Glock 17 from his suitcase, activated the internal locking system, and placed the weapon cautiously in an ankle holster above his Saucony's. "What do you want me to get from the restaurant?"

Probably to cover the sound of Jordan's harsh breathing.

He forced himself to focus on what he could do rather than on things he couldn't change. The past was over and done. Focus on the future.

"Bland food. Hot tea. And carbs. Lots and lots of carbs."

"Later."

"Watch your back."

"You know it, man." Zeke hesitated at the door, staring hard at the unconscious woman. "You gonna be okay?"

Jordan clenched his fists, knew what Zeke asked.

"She's fine." He deliberately opened his hands and gestured to her frail form. "She's harmless. Look at her."

"Dude. You don't know where she's been." With his hand on the doorknob, Zeke peered through the security viewer.

Jordan pushed back the anger, kept his mouth shut. As much as he wanted to argue, Zeke had a point.

"And she pulled a gun on us." With that parting shot, Zeke let himself out.

Jordan pulled her necklace from his pocket, dangling the carved stone from his fingers, staring at the eye of Horus, the ancient symbol of protection.

Jordan grieved for the ways he hadn't protected her and the ways she hadn't let him. His lungs seized, banding together refusing to allow in air. Grief wrapped like a boa constrictor around his heart, squeezing.

Her breath was soft and shallow, as if she had just run five miles. Or as if caught in a bad dream.

Using his thumb, Jordan gently lifted her eyelid to check the murky blue of Staci's eye, glazed with exhaustion, before letting her lid drift closed.

What could be dogging her so badly she would let herself go like this? Her body was a mess. While there was nothing wrong with the vintage clothes, her outfit definitely wasn't her.

And why, why, why hadn't she come to him? Maybe they'd left things very unresolved when she left, but she should know his personality well enough to use him and his expertise. Until she'd left for Afghanistan, it had felt like the beginning of something.

Something he'd never had before.

That alone should have scared the shit out of him. Because of his parents' situation, he was always careful about getting involved beyond a certain level.

"Stace?" He pressed a hand to her forehead, noting the sheen of sweat with a frown. "You okay, babe?"

Stupid question.

An unfamiliar anxiety pressed in on him as he watched her sleep.

Staci stirred, a soft soughing of her breath as her eyelids floated gently open. A little V creased her brow as she looked at him for a moment.

"Jordan?" she whispered. He stroked his hands over her arms, and aware of her bruises, brushed gently down to clasp her fingers lightly in his.

His weapon lay on the coffee table; he kept his body between her and the gun. And dammit, it pissed him off that he even had to be thinking that way.

She wasn't a criminal.

"I'm here, babe." His voice rumbled deep in his chest. Some people wake up right away and are perky, alert. Not Staci.

In the morning, she needed a good fifteen minutes before she was coherent and pleasant. Still in that place between asleep and awake, her smile was soft and welcoming, her gaze warm with dreamy affection. God, he wanted to brush his mouth against hers, wake her like he used to.

"Hey," she sighed. Her muscles bunched slightly under his hand, as if readying to move.

He leaned into her, inhaled the scent of her, a hint of gardenia on her skin, and surreptitiously brushed a kiss against her hair. "Take it easy. You passed out."

He could see exactly when reality returned. To prevent her from pulling her hands away, he tightened his grip.

"Let me go." Her tone was suspicious, harsh.

Sorrow bled through him, but he suppressed the emotion and kept his voice even. "You need to promise not to point a weapon at me again."

"Yeah, sure." Now that she was awake, her gaze was sharp, distrustful. "Where's surfer boy?"

Jordan snorted with amusement. "I sent Zeke to get food."

Her stomach growled.

"Not a minute too soon, sounds like." He teased, still holding onto her hands.

"Why were you trying to find me?"

Because they'd been on the brink of something big and he hadn't wanted to let it slip away. Because he thought he'd loved her.

But it was clear from her question and her actions that she hadn't felt the same. He shoved that thought into a tiny corner of his mind, someplace where he could examine his feelings later, maybe never.

Jordan kept the smile on his face as he debated how to answer.

She'd lied to him, evaded him, ignored him, crushed his heart and he still had this powerful need to care for her, to protect her.

The feelings were illogical and ill-advised.

He'd have been better off to just...forget about her after she cut him out of her life so completely. Yet here he was, after following her trail for the last four weeks and she didn't trust him.

He wasn't sure what that said about him. He wasn't a glutton for punishment. He wasn't a masochist. So why was he here?

Jordan's smile slowly faded. "Why didn't you contact me?"

My body reacted to the familiarity of his voice, unleashing a tension I didn't anticipate.

My throat constricted, freezing the muscles, making speech impossible. My chest was a solid block of concrete, taking in air a struggle. Pressure built in my head, my eyes, and I trembled on the brink of tears.

I couldn't let him see any weakness. I had to protect myself at all costs because Jordan's rejection had the ability to wound me far deeper than physical torture.

Involuntarily, I brushed my fingers against the hollow of my throat, seeking reassurance from my touchstone, my mother's necklace. But it wasn't there. Because I'd left it behind when I'd gone to Afghanistan.

I blinked back the moisture and took refuge in the attack. "You want to tell me what the hell is really going on?"

"Welcome home, honey." The tenderness he'd shown

when I awoke was gone, replaced with a cold sarcasm. "I was kinda hoping you were going to tell me."

"Why were you looking for me?" I couldn't reconcile it. We hadn't parted on the best of terms, and our last email had been stilted and distant.

I couldn't afford to trust anyone. Someone had betrayed me and set me up to die in that prison.

"I didn't believe you were dead."

"Why would you think I was dead?" Zeke had mentioned the same thing right before I passed out.

"Because of these." He grabbed a manila envelope and dumped the pictures out abruptly. Shock, horror froze me.

Fariya.

The stark picture zoomed me back to that place of cold, grit, hunger and pain. To that state of mind. To the sheer torture of existing.

I rubbed the skin around my wrists, still tender from the shackles. The yellow and purple contusions had faded from my skin, but not from my mind.

In some ways, I'd been lucky. Their methods of torture were old-fashioned and primitive.

"Did you ever go through SERE?" he asked quietly.

Survival, Evasion, Resistance, and Escape training. "Yeah." I'd had it. I truly believed the training had saved my life.

"You okay?"

"I handled it." No waterboarding, thank God.

He cleared his throat, as if wanting to ask but afraid of the answer. And he said brusquely, "I've read the reports on the Dark Prison and the Salt Pit in Kabul. It wasn't pretty." Jordan's gaze moved to the bricked-in fireplace.

"Those are our prisons." Except woops. Yeah. Those

prisons don't exist. My bad. "This was strictly local." My jailor's methods had been primitive but effective. Making me stand for over twenty-four hours, shackled to the wall. At least I'd had underwear, so I wasn't forced to stay naked for days on end. "Fortunately for me, their methods were not as sophisticated."

Through the small window, high up in my cave room, I had been able to measure and track day and night, see the passage of time. Which saved my sanity. Taking away sleep and a sense of time and place was the easiest way to make a prisoner lose their humanity.

Plenty of people broke with just that little bit of deprivation.

"They gave you food?"

I knew why he asked. I was skin and bones. Since the Bahamas, I was sick most of the day. Usually in the evening I could keep down some food.

I didn't know if it was a reaction to the pigment drug, or if I'd contracted some sort of bacteria in prison or escaping. "They fed me. But they varied the times and amounts of my food." Limited though the sustenance had been.

"Did they give you the drugs that turned your skin tone dark?"

Oh, no. I wasn't giving up what I'd done to get back into this country. Jordan had figured out I was still alive, tracked me to the Bahamas. Found me here in New York. He knew me too well to be trusted. And I still didn't know exactly why he'd tracked me down. Once I recovered and got that information, I was outta here.

"No drugs." At least...not that I remembered. I'd had some basic drug resistance training because of the places I traveled to occasionally. You don't want your first taste of heroin to be when you're in a stress-filled situation.

"What did they want?"

"Excuse me?"

"What kind of information. Usually when you're tortured, they want information. Names, dates, plans. What did they want?"

They hadn't really asked for any specific information. Maybe that's why I was spared the more intense and damaging forms of torture. They had just seemed to be playing with me.

"Nothing," I whispered. "They wanted nothing."

And that's what they had almost reduced me to. Nothing.

Some days I felt as insubstantial as a puff of dandelion seed on the wind, being whipped about, blown here and there, without any clear destination laid out for me and an inability to control where I would land.

Forcing myself, I looked at those pictures again. To see, catalog, and then forget what had happened to me.

However, I had to remember Fariya. Her death would not be in vain. She had given her life so I could make a difference.

I would find out who had set me up and why and expose them and their sins to the world.

Then I could continue to fundraise for de-mining, and use my contacts at UNOCHA to work toward eliminating the poppy fields and the unwilling mules.

Maybe I would campaign to stem illegal heroin production by starting a program like we'd done with Turkey in the 1970's, legalizing and managing the production of poppy crops for morphine and other legal opioids.

I noted the fine tremble in my scarred hand as I traced the lines of Fariya's tortured body.

I'm so sorry.

Unable to stand another moment without some sort of contact, knowing the move was unwise, I rested my hand against Jordan's chest in a bid for comfort.

The muscles underneath my hand felt solid, real, substantial. The steady thump of his heart against my fingertips was reassuring, reverberating through his muscles, his chest connecting my hand to his energy, vitality.

Jordan's heat buzzed through my hand, my arm, my heart infusing my body with electricity. Warming my frozen emotions and awakening longing.

The longing to recapture the incredible sense of completeness I'd experienced when we were together flowed over me.

I stared at my hand cupped protectively around his heart, unwilling to look in his eyes, wondering if my sudden fear was for what I wouldn't see.

Brutally I shoved back the tender sentiments. I had to get my head together and get out. I deliberately forced my gaze to the picture. "You thought this was me?"

"For a few minutes."

Jordan reached over to the coffee table, picked up his weapon carefully, and put the Glock in his holster.

Away from me. Smart move.

Finally he mentally eased away from me. I saw the distance widening, the subtle but definite way he moved into the chair on my right.

The distance hurt. The burn in my breastbone was psychological rather than physical.

I needed to get my head back into what was going on instead of remembering useless and obsolete emotions.

He'd thought that was me. Despair, sorrow flashed over his face, his hazel eyes serious.

I didn't want to deal with his emotion, so I redirected the

conversation and searched for information I needed. Such as...what a member of the 5491 list was doing with him.

"How does surfer boy fit in to this?"

Jordan didn't respond.

Zeke Hawthorne. Shit, more of what I'd discovered about Zeke Hawthorne came rushing back. He worked for the NSA. "Why is the NSA looking for me?"

"Because you were injected with an experimental drug and they have access to the antidote."

I shoved my feet into the cushions pushing up to glare at him. "What?"

"You were injected with a DNA-altering drug."

I shook my head back and forth while I verbally denied what was coming out of his mouth. "Are you crazy?"

"The NSA has access to an antidote. Which you need," he said firmly. "I've been helping them look for you. Sort of."

The 'sort of' gave me pause. What the hell does 'sort of' mean?

"How'd you hook up with the NSA?" Shouldn't I be more suspicious since all the people on my 5491 list were being paid with funds from an NSA department, even if they didn't work for the NSA?

"I was...looking for you. And so were they."

As I started to rise, Jordan walked to the foyer, and physically blocked my exit. "My investigation crossed with theirs."

"With the NSA?" I repeated slowly, my body tensing.

He hesitated. "I wouldn't exactly say I was with the NSA, more like I joined forces with a few of their agents."

"Zeke?"

He nodded.

"And?"

"Jamie Hunt," he said.

Another 5491 name.

"I was trying to figure out where you might be hiding."

"So what you thought you'd ride in and rescue me?"

He looked uncomfortably tense as if I'd nailed his motivation.

"Maybe I just wanted to find out why you didn't contact me after being captured and escaping an Afghani prison and having numerous people after you," he blurted with frustration. "We had that last weird email. And then you were gone."

The uncomfortable truth in his expression convinced me more than pleading or anything else would have. He hadn't necessarily wanted to discuss things when he tracked me down.

"I just...wanted to make sure you were okay."

His words hit me.

No one bothered to make sure I was okay. No one.

From what I knew of his childhood, he'd feel like he'd have to care for me because of our relationship.

But I could look out for myself. Had been, in fact, since I was eighteen. I'd been alone for fifteen long and lonely years.

When we'd been together, having someone watching my back had started as a foreign concept and grown into a welcome gift.

I knew Jordan was there for me.

I had even come to rely on the surety of his presence, knowing if I needed him, he'd be there.

A quick little knock at the door startled me. Jordan had his weapon out and safety off before I could blink.

Bump-bada-bump-bump.

"One assumes the bad guys wouldn't knock," I said drily. Especially with the rhythm of a joke punch line.

Jordan assumed a defensive position right next to the door jamb anyway, listening to the key card slide into the lock and the tumblers click into place.

I tried to ease off the sofa to take cover, but my legs gave out.

He frowned. "I've got you."

Maybe once but not anymore.

"Honey, I'm home." Zeke's voice carried into the living area. "And we've got problems."

He bustled in carrying multiple Styrofoam containers. The salty aroma of chicken noodle soup perfumed the air. My stomach gurgled.

"Sit rep?"

"Definitely a deuce in the lobby watching the elevators for this tower. There might have been a single at the elevators to the newer tower." He peeled the lid off of the container and set the steaming soup in front of me, careful to keep the coffee table between us.

I nodded at him, still uncomfortable with the fact that he worked for the NSA. "Thanks."

"Uh, yeah." Zeke popped open another container and dropped into the chair across from the sofa. "They might have been watching me."

"You're not sure?" I couldn't keep the incredulity out of my voice.

"I'm not a field agent," he grumped. "I'm a programmer."

"What are you doing here then?"

"You're the reason we're here."

"Don't look at me. I've been in New York for two days without any problems," I said sarcastically.

But I'd met with Sergeant Ravini just a few hours earlier.

I didn't have to share that information. I damn well wasn't sticking around if they had people following them. Of course, I wasn't sticking around period.

"The big question is why...and how?" Jordan said. "The bicycle surveillance took skill. And why would they be following me? I'm just an analyst for a think tank."

Big duh. The US government didn't need a reason, just a directive from someone. "Did you make any secret of the fact you were traveling together?"

Zeke's eyes widened, revealing a clear ocean blue, his pale lashes blinking slowly. "We booked separately but shared a taxi. Sat next to each other on the plane."

"We didn't think there was any need to hide," Jordan said calmly.

I snorted. "There's always a need for camouflaging your actions. You don't know who is watching or why. And you never know who is being paid to pass along information."

Jordan shot me a startled look.

Yeah, that was how I lived my life.

"Did you register under your real names?" They couldn't have been that naive–could they?

"Uh, yeah."

I thunked my forehead into the palm of my hand.

Zeke paused, a fork full of salad halfway to his lips. He was staring off to the left as if he were solving some complex math equation in his head. The fork dropped back into the styrofoam container. "We forgot an important fact."

"What?" Jordan asked.

Zeke jabbed the fork at us. "Susan Chen's accomplice had connections. Connections we never did uncover. Susan either doesn't know who he was working with...or she isn't saying."

"Or no one told you about it," Jordan completed.

Zeke blew out a breath. "Yeah. Dammit."

"What does this have to do with being followed? Or me?"

"At one point, they used the Secret Service, the FBI, and we think even the Defense Intelligence Agency to try and track Jamie Hunt down."

"Jesus, to have those kinds of connections...." I trailed off. You had to have a butt load of power. And the crowbar to wield it.

"What if they're following you?" I pointed at Zeke. "Maybe they picked up Jordan as a person of interest because he is traveling with you and the surveillance has nothing to do with him. Especially if you traveled together openly."

Zeke shoved a bite of salad into his mouth. "Maybe. Again, you're looking at multiple surveillance teams, which means manpower and money. Someone with a lot of cojones had to authorize the money and mobilize the agencies. Power."

Jordan looked perplexed. "To what purpose? Why would the government use so many resources? The only law enforcement subject currently getting that kind of coverage relates directly to terrorism."

"Holy shit." Zeke jabbed his fork at me. "You are linked to terrorists."

"Indirectly, yeah. But I'm dead." I smirked.

Jordan shoved his food container away, as if the flip comment soured his stomach. "Whoever's been surveilling your townhouse sure doesn't think so."

"And only certain people know that you aren't really linked indirectly or directly to terrorists." Then Zeke pointed his fork at Jordan. "Next. What about the fallout from your meeting with the Senator?"

Jordan stiffened imperceptibly. If I hadn't been observing closely I might have missed it.

"Doesn't seem likely." Jordan shrugged. "And why? Following me wouldn't get him information on the shooting."

"What Senator?" That's what caused him to tense up.

Waiting for his answer, I took a sip of the chicken noodle soup and nearly moaned. Warm and smooth, the salty broth exploded on my taste buds. "God, this is good."

"Anything tastes good when you're starving yourself to death," Jordan said acidly.

"It's all the rage in Africa."

Zeke's head swiveled back and forth between the two of us for a minute. "Children. Can we focus, please?" His mouth turned down, lines of tension bracketing his lips.

"Right. What Senator?"

"It's irrelevant." Jordan finally popped open his container.

"Senator Jordan," Zeke replied. "He tried to shake down our buddy here for information."

He didn't want to talk about Senator Jordan. I ran through what I knew of the man. Distinguished and established senator from Virginia. On the Senate Select Committee for Intelligence.

"He'd have the power."

"Again, to what purpose?" Jordan's question seemed more angry than defensive.

"We don't need to know his purpose. Right now, we just need to figure out the target." The edge in Zeke's voice was unmistakable now, drawing my attention back to him.

I suddenly wondered, again, what Zeke's angle was and why he was here.

"Why aren't you working?"

"I'm on administrative leave, pending an investigation to see whether I compromised National Security." Zeke looked pissed. "As if."

My brain started firing synapses I think had been in semi-permanent hibernation.

"If you are the target," I gestured at Zeke, "then I need to get out of this room."

"If I'm the target," he looked pointedly at me. "I'm fucked."

I poured a large gulp of the soup into my mouth, running through scenarios and possibilities until I came up with one that suited my needs.

"We need to separate. You need to start doing vacation stuff."

"I don't take vacations."

I ignored him. "Draw them off, whether they are looking for me or checking you two out. If you go do typical touristy things, then they'll be convinced you don't have anything going on."

"I'm going home. I accomplished my mission."

I tensed up again. "What mission?"

Jordan slathered butter on a still warm roll and handed it to me.

"Help this guy here find you. And look." Zeke lifted his hands up beside his face as if surprised. "You're found."

I took a bite and tried not to moan at how good the yeasty warm bread tasted.

They'd accomplished their mission.

They could go.

I could go.

We'd all go. They could go back to figuring out who was following them. And I would go back to figuring out who wanted me dead.

Alone.

I flicked the crumbs of the bread from my thighs and stood up. "Thanks for the information about...everything."

I tried to brush away heaviness in my chest and throat as easily as the crumbs.

I looked around for my cardigan, smiling benignly. Then I wrapped the warm sweater around my shoulders, grabbed my messenger bag, and headed for the door.

Shit. It was beyond hard to get my throat working properly. I had to use all of my acting skills so that good bye would come out nonchalantly and slightly cool.

"Jordan." I only half turned my head, hoping he'd let me leave without a confrontation, dimly noting the dropped jaw from Zeke as his gaze shifted back and forth between Jordan and me. For an infinitesimal moment, I thought my exit would be successful.

Then, Jordan barred the door, narrowed his gaze.

I took a step closer to the exit.

The subtle scent, uniquely his, drifted toward me, warm and musky as his temperature and blood pressure rose.

He didn't yell. Didn't chastise. Just shifted his shoulder to completely block the door. "I don't think so."

"You found me. You delivered the information." I didn't touch him, but the urge to reach out and just lightly skim over the hard, firm muscles of his shoulder tempted me.

Something about the position of our bodies, standing just a hair's breadth away, one small sway from our bodies melding and molding to each other, reminded me of a time when we'd have been making up and halfway to bed by now.

The longing to go back to that easier time struck at my heart.

Definitely not a memory to have while trying to leave.

"I need to get out of here."

"You need the antidote."

"I'd appreciate it if you wouldn't tell anyone you…located me."

"You need the antidote."

"I'm fine." I felt fine. Sort of.

"Yeah. You look great." He hadn't moved forward at all and yet his posture was stronger, bigger, and somehow more menacing.

"I don't want any more drugs." Why take an antidote when I didn't feel any different? Besides, until I figured out who wanted me dead, I couldn't trust anyone.

"You need the antidote," Zeke said.

Okay. Play this out and see what they were going for.

"And how would the antidote be delivered?"

At that, Zeke looked uncomfortable, looked to Jordan. "You want to take this one?"

Jordan straightened his shoulders. "I have to take you to the NSA."

No fucking way. So not happening.

I believed Jordan believed what he was saying but he wouldn't be the first to be manipulated by false information.

"Has it ever occurred to you that this is some elaborate scheme to get you to bring me in?" I directed my question to Jordan. "They've concocted this whole drug pretense to get your aid and bring me in."

"Why?"

The Department 5491 I'd been investigating had been top secret and hidden deep. Once I'd discovered the connection, it had taken months of painstaking research and dead ends to dig up more information to relate the twelve names on the list into a cohesive structure.

I still wasn't even sure what all the data meant.

"I'd been investigating a secret department within the NSA."

"5491." Jordan nodded.

I blinked. "You know about it?"

That was information I needed to think about.

"All of the people given the gene manipulation drug were from your 5491 list," Zeke blurted.

That information gave me pause. "All of them?"

"Yeah."

Jordan hesitated. "One of the...subjects died."

"Brad Johnson."

"Yeah."

The circumstances of his death had been unusual. Although the press had reported the sensationally public death, reading between the lines I'd known more had been going on.

"He'd been engaging in serious risk-taking behavior," Jordan said.

I laughed. Didn't we all?

"His addiction to adrenaline was magnified by the effects of this drug. He literally took outrageous chances outside the realm of even his previous danger level." Zeke paced around the room.

"Hello. Anyone who works in the espionage business is an adrenaline junkie."

We stood in the foyer, Zeke off to the side, Jordan trying to make his posture as intimidating as possible.

"What will it take to convince you that this is in your best interests?" Jordan asked softly.

"Nothing," I said. "If I go to the NSA my safety will be compromised."

"No."

"Yes," I said emphatically. "Besides. Who's to say they didn't set me up in the first place?"

The sound of Linkin' Park blared in the tiny alcove. We all jumped.

Zeke's cell. He checked the display. "It's Jamie."

He stepped away to take the call, and all I could think about was GPS locators and wonder if this was the set up and they would take me in against my will.

I wouldn't be able to fight them off.

"I need to go." I appealed to Jordan, hoping he could do this last thing for me. "You found me. You delivered the information. I'm okay."

"Fine."

I relaxed momentarily. He was letting me go. Except, this was Jordan. I needed to consider what other angle he might be working.

"No following me."

"No following." He agreed.

I should be pleased, but the wash of disappointment was stronger and more intense than I'd expected.

"We both go," he said.

The disappointment evaporated. "Alone."

"Either we go together or you don't get out of this hotel room."

Resolutely I stiffened my spine. "Alone."

"Not happening."

Stalemate.

I leaned in closer and the slight scent of his lunch and the smell of his shampoo suddenly overwhelmed me.

God. The citrus-y odor from his hair surged through my senses, knocking into me like a tidal wave.

I couldn't stand it.

Nausea welled uncontrollably. I ran for the tiny bathroom, arriving at the toilet just in time to expel the lovely soup I'd just consumed.

Over the sound of my vomiting, I heard Zeke say, "Are you fucking kidding me?"

CHAPTER 21

J ordan hovered behind Staci, watching her spew her guts out.

He brushed the hair back from her face with one hand and grabbed a dry wash cloth with the other, trying to quell his own stomach as she threw up.

Turning on the hot water, quickly he dampened the cloth, then squeezed out the excess water. A myriad of emotions swirled through him as he tried to objectively observe her on the floor.

She looked...fragile.

Unlike the warrior woman he'd known before.

This bundle of bones and bravado was so far removed from his Staci he had trouble reconciling the two as the same woman.

He gently rubbed the warm cloth over her face. Her lashes lay like dark blond crescents against her splotchy skin. Tenderly he wiped at her mouth. "Okay?"

She withdrew into herself, like a turtle easing its head back into his shell. "Fine."

She wasn't fine. "How long have you been like this?"

Staci shrugged. "A month?"

"Since your captivity?" he pressed. "Or longer?"

"Honestly a lot of the last few months is a blur."

"Are you keeping anything down?"

"Most days after about five o'clock I can eat and I'm okay. But that's about it."

He hadn't been privy to all of the information about the gene manipulation drug. Most of his knowledge was secondhand or through eavesdropping.

His main focus had been to find Staci and bring her in for the antidote. "I don't think anyone else has had that kind of reaction to the drug."

"I think I picked up a bug somewhere between Afghanistan and the Bahamas."

"You haven't been to the doctor?"

"Right."

She hated doctors. Hated them. Hated hospitals. Hated anything even remotely medical. She'd been a bear when she'd had to go for her physical. "I forgot."

"Yeah. Well, I haven't."

She'd told him once that they reminded her of her grandparents. She'd been in the hospital recovering from a tonsillectomy when the police had come to notify her of their deaths.

The antiseptic smell would forever remind her of the horror of that day.

A surge of tenderness came over him so suddenly, he wanted to soothe, to offer comfort.

God, wasn't that a weird vibe?

They hadn't really done tenderness. They'd been passionate and romantic and heated and intense. They shared a love of fine clothes and fine food and a passion for commercial fiction and obscure non-fiction.

But there hadn't been any real tenderness between them.

How could he have missed that? How was it that he never noticed the lack? And how could he feel this overwhelming need to soothe her when she opposed everything he tried to do for her?

Whatever he thought they'd had, whatever feelings and emotions he thought they'd shared, he had to accept that he'd been wrong.

The bond he'd thought they had didn't exist.

He could mourn that loss later. What he'd really been trying to keep alive was the romantic ideal of their relationship. That was foolish and futile.

"It's no big deal. It'll work its way through my system, and I'll be fine."

The tenderness evaporated in a puff of total disgust.

"You'll be dead." He wiped at her face again, a little more roughly than before. "You need to go to a doctor--or you need the antidote. Preferably sooner rather than later."

Zeke rushed over, pausing in the doorway to the tiny bathroom that could barely accommodate one and couldn't even begin to hold three people.

"Great, just what I want. An audience," she snarled.

Zeke ignored her. "We've got problems."

"More?" Jordan couldn't imagine things could get much worse, unless the guys following him, them, whoever, suddenly showed up at the suite's door.

"That was Jamie."

"Get on with it, surfer boy."

Zeke blinked at her, half lying across the toilet. "Susan Chen escaped."

"Knowing how difficult escaping is, I applaud her ingenuity." She rested her arm on the toilet rim and closed her eyes, either totally ignoring or not computing the implications.

"Dammit." Jordan swore.

"Who is Susan Chen and why do you care?"

"She's the one who developed the drug and the antidote."

"Again, why do you care?"

"Because she's the only one who can make the antidote."

"Doesn't matter." Staci yawned, her mouth wide open, jaw popping.

"You don't understand." Zeke said carefully. "Each antidote is tailored to the individual DNA of the person who received the original drug."

"So you're telling me I can't get this 'antidote' now?" Her attitude morphed into suspicion.

"I don't know." Zeke moved into the bedroom and began throwing clothes into a duffel bag.

Staci looked like she was thinking about getting up. "Did she really escape, or did they move her to a different facility?"

"The word from very high up is she escaped."

"How high?"

"Carson Black."

Staci froze at Carson's name, just a quick pause. After that small giveaway, she didn't acknowledge she knew Carson in any way.

"She had to have had help. No one escapes from federal detention without an inside contact."

"David Armbruster himself is handling the interrogation."

Staci processed the information slowly. "The Assistant Director of the NSA?"

Zeke nodded while he shoved toiletries into the bag. "We have to get out of here."

"Yeah." Jordan leaned against the doorjamb of the bathroom, appearing relaxed, arms crossed over his chest. But his muscles were bunched, his fists clenched.

Zeke stopped packing. "We can't just leave. We need an exit plan."

"Give the man a gold star." Staci pushed off the toilet seat into a crouch before slowly standing up. Her movements told the story of how bad she really felt. She used to move fluidly, even gracefully. "If you were watching for someone, what would you do?"

Jordan reasoned out a surveillance plan. "I'd have one person in the security room monitoring the cameras. The others stationed at exits. We have to hope the security room has a block of monitors and the images rotate through all the floors."

That would give them some wiggle room.

"Even if they have a photograph of you," he pointed at Staci, "you'd be difficult to i.d. in your...present condition."

That would work in their favor.

Jordan took her arm and led her into the little sitting room. "We need to split up."

"I'm on my way to the West Coast." Zeke headed for the door.

"Why the West Coast?"

"I've got to go see a chick named Sunshine. Since she's not officially affiliated with any agency, I'm safe in going to protect her."

"News, surfer boy, women don't appreciate being called chick."

"Yeah, well, I'm going to watch her not date her, so it doesn't matter."

"What does Sunshine have to do with any of this?" Staci's tone was belligerent.

"Not a damn thing, but in case we're wrong, Jamie thinks someone should keep an eye on the woman."

Staci shrugged, but Jordan noted the line between her eyebrows eased.

"I should leave with Zeke," Staci said.

"Over my dead body."

She grabbed the file with the pictures from the prison. "It just may be."

"Sorry, dude." Zeke zipped up his bag. "I can't be seen with Staci. If someone had physical evidence of me meeting with or being in the company of her, my life is over."

She took a tentative step. "Mr. Melodrama over here."

"Yeah. That's me." Zeke grimaced.

Jordan thought for a minute. "Okay. Before you go, we need to get into the room next door and order a wheelchair."

"Dude. My B & E skills are a little rusty. Programmer here. Not super spy."

"I can get you in," Staci piped up.

"You aren't going out the door until we're ready to leave."

"I can get you in without stepping out of this suite. No problem."

"Hurry then. We don't have much time." Jordan efficiently packed toiletries and tossed them into a small leather backpack. "Zeke, you cannot leave this room until the chair is delivered. If they're after you, one will follow and the other will search the room. We've all got to be gone."

Staci went into the foyer and opened the closet door. On the back wall of the closet was a cleverly hidden pocket door. "Look in my messenger bag."

Jordan dug through the pack on her back, and pulled out picks and handed them to her.

"Gotta love a woman who's prepared."

Staci grinned, and for a moment, the sparkle, the sheer life of her shone through her tired features.

Within a few minutes, she had opened the lock. Her hands were shaking as she silently put the picks back in their case.

Shit, just the effort to hold her arms up and steady had worn her out.

"Let me check it out before we go in." Jordan eased into the suite on the other side of the pocket door, to find a mirror image of theirs.

He came back through a few seconds later. "We're in luck. There are definitely people staying here, but it's empty right now."

He and Staci went into the other suite and closed the secret door.

Jordan picked up the phone and ordered a wheelchair from the housekeeping staff. He flipped open his cell and called Zeke. "We're waiting for the delivery. Should be here in a few minutes."

Zeke responded. "I'm wiping down any surface we touched. May not get everything, but if they decide to look for prints this will make the job a little more difficult."

"Good idea."

Jordan paced around the room, antsy to get gone.

"Where are you going?" Zeke asked.

"Not going to tell you."

"Yeah, yeah. 'Cause then you have to kill me." Zeke laughed. "Jeez, I really want to be back in my little office playing with my software."

Jordan heard the serious longing through the silly phrase. "Good luck."

"Yeah," Zeke replied soberly. "You too. Don't take your eyes off of her, and don't let her near your weapon."

Jordan eyed Staci, perched on the chair by the executive desk looking frail and totally done in. "Shouldn't be a problem."

A knock on the door interrupted.

"Showtime. Wait for my signal." Jordan pulled a twenty out of his pocket and headed for the door. "Get in the closet, just in case it isn't housekeeping."

She bobbed her head tiredly, went into the closet, and slid down the wall. He eased the door mostly closed.

Jordan settled his leather jacket over his belt holster and made sure he had unobstructed access.

The delivery of the chair turned out to be a non-event. The housekeeper was grateful for the twenty-buck tip, thanking Jordan profusely.

He slid the closet door open. Staci rested against the short wall, eyes closed, breathing slow and deep.

She was asleep.

He thought of all the times he'd woken her from sleep, early in the morning. Lying in bed together, savoring those few moments of total trust when she curled into him and rubbed her cheek gently against his bare shoulder. The longing for that closeness, that connection took him by surprise.

Jordan knelt down until his face was level with hers. For a moment, he just stared, taking in everything.

With an ache in his chest that wounded, he leaned over and brushed a soft kiss against her forehead. Goodbye.

"Time to wake up."

He watched her eyelids lift slowly then stood before he could see her draw away again.

His heart couldn't take the rejection.

CHAPTER 22

Our exit plan went off without a hitch.

We took a cab to Grand Central Station using the camouflage of the wheelchair.

At the station, I pretended to be helpless, which totally grated on my nerves. Fuck. Even worse--I was somewhat helpless.

I wouldn't admit the truth, but riding in the chair instead of putting one foot in front of the other had been a welcome respite.

I was a mess.

I could barely hold lock picks.

Couldn't keep more than a minimum of food down, and when I placed my hand in Jordan's, the clearly visible bones in my fingers shocked me.

I used to be a vibrant vital woman, and now I was a mere husk of my former self.

Jordan rolled me through the station quickly and with purpose. The historic building had gone through a major renovation, restoring the bustling transit center to its former glory.

As soon as we approached the doors on the other side, he rolled me down the hallway toward the bathrooms.

He pulled a black shirt out of his backpack and handed it to me. The material was silky and sensual. He also handed me a black Yankees ball cap. "Put this on, and meet me right back out here."

I nodded, too tired to do more than acquiesce.

"I have a friend who's a doctor," he stated abruptly. "I'll set it up. She should have the basics at her apartment. You should go to a hospital but...."

"Thanks," I said, my voice raspy and raw.

I went into the dirty, dingy white-tiled bathroom. Guess the renovations didn't extend in here...they probably ran out of money. I quickly shed my sweater, slipping the silk over my plain white tank top and knotting the tails at my waist.

The action reminded me of weekend mornings when I'd worn Jordan's cotton dress shirts, tying the tails over my naked body, reveling in the soft material against my bare skin. The cheeks of my ass hanging out the back gave Jordan a peek-a-boo show while we cooked a leisurely breakfast, or lunch if we'd stayed in bed extra long.

Then I'd felt sexy and invincible.

Now I was slowly fading away to nothing, becoming invisible.

He was right. I did need a doctor.

I threaded my hair through the back of the cap. Time to go. Grasping the door handle, I held myself still for a moment, listening to the creaks of my body, feeling as if I'd aged a hundred years. I took a deep breath and opened the door.

He was right where I'd left him, propped against the wall.

"I got a hold of my friend, Thea." He snapped his cell

shut quickly, his gaze shifting for a moment. "She's going to come get us."

We took another taxi to Rockefeller Center, stood beneath the flags and waited for his doctor friend. Jordan bought a pretzel for me from a street vendor.

The taste of salt burst on my tongue. God, it tasted good.

"Can you keep it down?"

"It's usually better later in the day."

His friend came roaring up in a Porsche 911. My impression was of dark, thick beautiful hair and radiant luminous skin before she turned her attention back to the crowded New York streets.

Jordan introduced us briefly. "Thea, Staci."

They caught up on mutual friends while I huddled in the miniscule back seat like a recalcitrant child and hoped that I wouldn't puke all over the pristine, butterscotch leather.

I hadn't allowed myself to think about the material things I'd left behind on my quest to find out who was after me. And I knew it was silly, but I missed my car and my soft, soft six hundred thread count cotton sheets and my gardenia-scented Jacuzzi.

I knew in my heart those objects were just symbols. What I'd really lost was myself. I knew I was more than a collection of things, more than bank accounts and assets, but inside...I was lost.

I was floundering like a newborn colt, lurching around trying to find balance, find me again. Most days every step took me further away from myself. Maybe it was time to become someone new.

But how...when every move was dictated in response to some unknown threat from an unknown source.

I went over the details again, thinking something would

jump out at me. I considered the other people on the 5491 list and how we could all be connected. I suppose someone could be targeting all of the survivors receiving those payments, but so far Brad Johnson was the only dead recipient of that money.

Thea pulled her car into the garage in her building, across from Central Park.

"Right, Staci?" Jordan asked.

I blinked. I'd lost complete track of their conversation and mutual admiration society. "What?"

"I described your symptoms for Thea. Extreme nausea, inability to keep food down."

"You're not having any trouble right now, are you?" Only smooth professionalism coated her voice, but I heard the little tremor.

Worried about your car, honey?

I couldn't help it. I hesitated, making her squirm for a second, then smiled cheerfully. "Nope. Actually I'm starving right now."

"Exhaustion. Lack of energy."

We got out of her car and headed for the bank of elevators. "Hmm. Let's go inside where I can take a closer look."

Thea even freaking walked gracefully. I shuffled along like an old lady, my gait awkward.

Of course, her apartment was perfect.

Beautiful, elegant, bright art with fluid lines reminiscent of Diego Rivera subtly lit with accent lights and sleek modern furniture in a minimalist style.

"Why don't we go into the bathroom for some privacy." Thea waved casually toward the kitchen. "Jordan help yourself to something to drink. I've got a lovely Cab on the counter just waiting to be opened."

I wanted to tell her Jordan wasn't really a wine guy. He preferred a hearty stout to wine, but he answered first. "Thanks. Your wine is always *bueno*." Jordan smiled easily, sincerely as they fell into a sort of Spanglish.

As I watched their easy interaction, I had to remind myself again...whatever I'd thought we had, wasn't, anymore. It was amazing really how much that hurt. How much I wanted to focus on that sad fact rather than the more immediate problem of my health and safety.

As Thea and I walked into the bathroom, I tried for simple curiosity. "So, how do you two know each other?"

"We went to the same church growing up. My mama and Jordan's are *amigas*."

She pulled a doctor bag out from underneath the sink. Fitting the stethoscope to her ears, she listened to my heartbeat and lungs. Then she checked my mouth, nasal passages and ears.

"Hmmm."

She used the light to check my eyes. Hit my knees with her little hammer. Did all the innocuous things that doctors do. All the while, hmmm-ing at each part of my body she checked.

She used her hands and pressed on the sides of my neck. She moved down to the spot where neck and shoulder met. As of yet, she hadn't asked me to take off my clothes which I was dreading.

My scars disgusted even me.

I hated to look at them. No one besides my captors, and me, had seen them.

She pushed back the cuffs of the sleeves and involuntarily took a step back. "Jesus. What happened to you?"

"Classified." I didn't want to talk about it.

I certainly wasn't going to spill any of my secrets to her. She pressed gently on the yellowing bruises, hesitating when I winced.

"These are deep tissue. They're going to take a long time to heal."

"Guess I won't be doing any modeling next week," I replied flippantly.

She pushed the cuff all the way up my left arm, taking a quick breath when she saw evidence of the break. "This wasn't set properly."

"I know." I shrugged the sleeve back down and said mildly, "Can we move on to something new, like any suggestions on how to keep food down?"

She hesitated for a moment. "Can I run my hands over your ribcage and abdomen?"

"Ribs are fine." Apparently I'd won the torture sweepstakes and missed broken ribs. I'd had them before and they sucked.

"Please," she asked tightly.

"Go ahead."

She ran her hands slowly over my ribcage and down my stomach, stopping at the evidence of my hipbones sticking out and the concave valley of my abdomen.

"I'd like you to give me a urine sample."

"You can run tests here?"

"I can do a few simple ones, then I'll take the rest in to the office tomorrow."

She handed me a plastic cup, and turned around while I took care of business.

"You have any idea what's wrong?"

"I have some suspicions. Let me run the tests, and we'll go from there."

So at least she'd seen whatever was dogging me before.

As I turned around to give back the cup, we both noticed that my urine was a dark yellow.

"You have to drink more liquids."

"Yeah. I know I'm dehydrated, but I can't keep anything down."

"As soon as the time of day comes when you can keep food down, you really need to drink as much as you can." She puttered around the bathroom. "I'd really like to set you up on an IV drip."

"Not happening."

"Okay. Go on out to the living room. I'll be out in two minutes."

Wow. The tests must be fast. "Okay."

Jordan stood staring out at the lights of Central Park, a glass of blood red wine in his hand. His long fingers clasped the glass tensely, the strength in his hands, his wrists standing out in the healthy veins.

"How'd it go?"

"She thinks she might have an idea."

Thea was back out two minutes later, her face pale and set. Shit. That didn't look good.

"What's wrong?" Jordan asked before I could even open my mouth.

"I need to talk to Staci. Alone."

"It's okay." I was so tired I wanted a second pair of ears to listen to what she had to say.

"I really think you'd prefer to do this alone."

"Just do it."

"When you were...tortured." Thea paused.

Give the girl a gold medal for figuring out that one.

"Did they...rape you?"

"What?" Rape. Why would she think that?

"Jesus," Jordan said.

"Did they...."

"I heard you the first time, and no. They didn't rape me."

"Thank God," Jordan whispered.

"Why would you think that?"

"You're pregnant."

In the minimalist room, the loud roar of silence was heavy.

No one moved. I was frozen, as if someone had impaled a giant spike through the middle of my body and literally nailed me to the floor.

No one spoke. We all just stood there as if struck mute.

Really. I had heard her. I knew what she said. She hadn't been speaking in tongues, except, except....

"*Madre de Dios*," Jordan whispered.

"Fuck," was my more succinct reply.

"I would say that is what got you this way," Thea said briskly.

Ha, ha. Suddenly she's a comedienne?

I couldn't be pregnant. I was on the pill. And we used condoms.

"You weren't raped?" Jordan asked again with just a little too much urgency for me. Was he looking for a way out? A 'Get Out of Jail Free' card. And then I stopped that thought. Of course he didn't want me to be raped.

But the horrified look on his face spurred me on. "No luck for you, huh?"

"What!?"

"Maybe you're hoping I've miraculously had sex with someone else between leaving you in D.C., getting thrown in an Afghan prison, escaping, and being on the run. Yeah, it's been a regular sex-fest." I grabbed his leather backpack. I knew I was being unfair but the words just kept spewing out.

Thea's eyes widened as she looked at Jordan. I knew what she was thinking. You had sex with *her*?

"Yes. He had sex with me. Apparently one too many times. Right, *amigo*?"

I opened the flap and started rifling through the contents looking for his wallet.

"I...I'm going to write you a prescription for some pre-natal vitamins. Which you should start taking right away."

I pulled out his wallet, opened up the shiny crocodile skin and grabbed a few Benjamins.

I ignored her. I couldn't fill a prescription under my name.

"What's the best over-the-counter vitamin?" I worked on keeping my cool as the reality of her diagnosis sunk in.

"You need to see an obstetrician, to come up with your due date or...a cut off date." She cast a worried glance at Jordan as she scribbled on a prescription pad.

I knew exactly when the baby was conceived. Even being on the pill, we always used condoms too. Except for that one time.

I could probably narrow the conception down to a fifteen minute window. The night before I left the U.S. and my world shifted on its axis.

My world was shifting again.

"I'd appreciate it if you forgot you ever met me," I

addressed Thea, although Jordan would probably benefit from that advice too.

He just watched me stuff the bills into my jeans pocket.

Even knowing I'd planned to leave him, I found that his lack of protest burned a hole through my gut. Or maybe that was just the acid churning in my stomach.

Usually by this time of night I could keep stuff down, but it had been a hell of a day.

"And forget about the capture, prison, escape thing." I couldn't believe I'd been so off-balance I'd revealed that information.

Jordan said, "Thea, can we borrow your bedroom?"

"Uh, sure." She glanced back and forth between the two of us waiting to see what would happen next.

Jordan grabbed my forearm with far less gentleness than I'd expected. But I let him. We had to have this out, and then I could blow this pop stand.

He led me into her bedroom. The mood in here was similar to the rest of the apartment, luxurious and minimalist all at the same time. More Rivera-like art graced her walls.

Over the bed two lovers twined together in an embrace that was frankly sensual.

I glanced away, unwilling to bring up memories of other times we'd been together in other bedrooms.

"You don't really think you're taking off, do you?"

I consciously avoided thinking about the last ten minutes. "I'll pay you back."

"You think I'll let you walk out of here when you have my baby growing inside of you?"

Baby. Didn't want to go there. Wasn't touching that one.

His voice had risen spectacularly which was, on one hand, totally fascinating.

Forget the whole stereotypical Latino hothead image, Jordan was impossibly calm and serene. Nothing ever made him blow his cool, and he never, ever raised his voice.

On the other hand, did he really think he was going to order me around?

I watched him pull back his temper, tuck it away, and fall back into the cool, collected front he normally presented to the world.

"You are not leaving without me."

The steel in his voice was unmistakable.

Every once in awhile I underestimated him. He could be such a teddy bear I tended to forget about his sniper training with the FBI. They didn't take just anyone for HRT. You had to be patient, focused, and deadly accurate.

And live with the surety of your decisions. He once told me he never regretted anything.

Bet he'd changed his mind on that one.

"Guess we should have used a condom," I jabbed.

"Shut. Up." Jordan stared at the picture over the bed. "We've got to figure out what to do next."

"Nothing. We do nothing."

He looked down at his hands, realized he was still clenching the glass and took a large gulp of red wine. "Jesus."

"No, I'd say if it's a boy we name him...Paul. Look. This is not your problem."

"You are right," he said fiercely. "A baby is not a problem."

Suddenly the reality of everything hit me.

Pregnant was only one piece but I couldn't seem to focus on anything else. Oh shit. Oh, shit. A baby.

A baby.

How the hell could there be a baby inside me?

And oh my god, I'd injected the pigment drug to turn my skin dark. That drug couldn't possibly be good for a baby, as it wasn't very good for an adult.

"We've got to find Susan Chen," he said desperately.

"What?"

Now that certainly wasn't first on my list of things to do--since I had people after me and just figured out I was cooking a baby.

"I'm gestating. Find Susan Chen? What the hell is that?"

"She's the only one who will have any idea what the DNA drug in your body will do to a baby."

Shit. I'd forgotten about the supposed DNA drug.

Great. Barely out of the zygote stage, and my baby was a drug addict.

I sank down onto the plush duvet of the bed. I was already a failure as a mother.

The scent of corn tortillas and some sort of spicy pepper wafted into the bedroom where we'd both fallen silent.

Really. What was there to say?

"I need to figure out who is after me. Otherwise the drug is the least of this baby's problems. If I'm dead...."

"I will protect you." Jordan straightened, squaring his shoulders.

The odor from the food grew stronger. And it smelled really, really good. Suddenly I was ravenous.

I needed food. Now.

"I need to eat." We hadn't solved anything and right at this minute I didn't care.

"We need to settle this."

"I need to eat." Just in case he wasn't getting it. "Now."

"That's Thea's mama's Chile Rellenos. It's probably too spicy."

"It smells great, and I want it." I was already out the door and headed for the kitchen.

"Okay." I could hear him following me. "But this isn't over."

We had about seven more months. Assuming I could stay alive that long.

We walked into the kitchen silently.

Thea slid a platter on the black lacquer table. "I just got paged. I have to go."

"What kind of doctor are you?"

"Cardiologist." She put a container of salsa on the table. "My father had a massive heart attack in front of me when I was eight."

Wow. Then her specialty sunk in. Ha. Cardiologist. Not an obstetrician. For a moment, I had hope. She'd made a mistake.

"*Chica*, those home pregnancy tests are ninety-nine percent accurate. It wasn't a mistake."

Apparently she was a mind reader too.

"You two are welcome to spend the night in my guestroom. It's a little on the small side, but will work for a night or two."

I was too busy shoveling the stuffed peppers into my mouth. I'd never tasted anything so good in my life. "Oh my god, these are great."

"Go easy on those or you'll end up with heartburn," she cautioned. "And drink lots of milk or water tonight. You really need to--"

"Hydrate. I know. I know."

She swung a Prada bag over her shoulder and headed for the door. "*Adios*."

The door closed. Whirlwind Thea was gone and suddenly we were all alone.

Totally alone. Just the two of us.

With no catastrophe to rescue me from having to deal with him. I took a large swallow of water, put my head down and kept eating.

Jordan ate slowly, contemplatively. I really didn't want to know what he was thinking with such a somber look on his face.

"We need a plan."

We? "Seriously, I can figure this out."

"I would never abandon my child."

"No one said anything about abandonment. But really, it's not like we planned this." I'd figure something out. At least I had plenty of money. Once I could come out in the open and access the funds again.

I couldn't think about a baby. I'd never even let myself believe I would have children. I'd have to let someone close to me. Until Jordan, the possibility had seemed remote.

He just looked at me. "I never told you about my father."

Okay. Right there was a start to a conversation I'd prefer not to have. Not now. Perhaps not ever. "Uh, no. Just, he wasn't in the picture."

"My mother worked in his house."

It appeared I wasn't going to get a vote. Clearly he needed to get this out.

"Logically, morally she knew having an affair with her employer was wrong. But he was rich and powerful and paying attention to a lowly maid. She said she was so enthralled."

Okay. His father was a pig.

"When she got pregnant, he gave her money to get an abortion."

A big pig.

"She didn't have one. Obviously adultery was one thing but killing a baby...she couldn't do it."

I swallowed away the lump from the emotion in his voice.

We wouldn't be having this conversation if she had. "I promise you, I would talk to you before I made the decision to abort the baby." Except just the thought of an abortion had me placing my hand protectively over my stomach.

"I want you to keep the baby," Jordan said fiercely. "His wife fired my mother when she found out Mama was pregnant. I'm not sure if she ever knew the baby was his, but she wouldn't have an unmarried, pregnant maid in her house."

That sucked.

"They were both unprincipled pigs."

"No argument from me."

Jordan rested his elbows on the table, hands gripped tightly together. "My mother is an amazing woman."

"No question." She'd raised Jordan into a decent, caring man, alone. "However, I'm not sure what this has to do with me."

"I refuse to abandon you or the baby."

Okay. New scenario. So we're going to spend the rest of our lives, however short that might be, on the run and raising a baby together?

"Let's take it one step at a time." First I had to figure out who wanted me dead.

A swell of exhaustion overtook me so completely I nearly fell over. The lethargy was so encompassing, my body felt surrounded by jello.

"Go sit on the sofa." He jerked his head toward Thea's ultra-modern, sleek and probably completely uncomfortable, couch. "I'll clean this up."

As I sank down, the sofa was amazingly soft and welcoming.

"I think someone has been watching my house lately as well as yours," he said as he scraped dishes and put the plates in the dishwasher. "Or they're watching both. But that doesn't make any sense. No one knew about us."

There was something in his voice I hadn't heard before. Had I hurt his feelings by keeping our relationship a secret?

"Any ideas?" Jordan interrupted my musings.

I'd filed the paperwork to declare him a 'Close and Continuing' relationship right before I left. I didn't really want to address this subject, but I should probably let him know.

"I, uh, might have an idea."

Jordan started the dishwasher and came over to the sofa with his half-full glass of wine and a glass of milk for me. Settling on the other end, he propped his feet up on the kidney-shaped cocktail table.

The normalcy of sitting together struck a weird chord, bringing back memories of making out in my living room.

"It's probably nothing."

"Spit it out, Stace."

"I filed the paperwork to officially register you as my boyfriend."

He plunked his glass on the coffee table and angled his body to face me. "You have to file paperwork?"

"Uh, yeah. If you start dating regularly, you're supposed to give the CIA the information so they can check out the significant other and make sure you aren't putting yourself in a compromising situation. They do a comprehensive background check. I just hadn't filed the paperwork earlier...."

Because I'd wanted to keep him to myself. Just a little bit

longer. Once your significant other has official status, quarterly reports have to be filed.

The invasiveness of the process seemed annoying and stupid.

He was mine.

"I'd heard that their investigations take forever. Half the people I knew weren't even dating the person anymore by the time the background check was completed."

"You'd heard?"

Damn. He'd picked up on that. "Uh, yeah. I've never actually filed paperwork before."

He processed that information carefully, his lips curving as he recognized the significance of my answer. "So we need to assume the CIA has connected us?"

"Yeah." And dammit, I didn't want to bring my shit down on him.

"We'll just have to travel carefully." Jordan's cell phone rang. He looked at the display. "It's Thea."

I could hear her voice on the other end of the line. She seemed pretty upset or excited or something.

"Calm down. It's okay. I'll explain when you get home." Jordan never raised his voice, didn't panic. "It's fine. What channel?"

He flipped his phone closed, grabbed the remote and pushed the power button.

"What's wrong?"

The plasma screen on the wall flared to life.

"That." He pointed to Thea's 42-inch, wide-angle screen.

A larger than life-size picture of me was displayed prominently, and *Wanted, Armed and Dangerous* scrolled across the bottom of the screen, along with a phone number in case I was spotted.

Someone had just changed the rules. The private hunt for me had just gone public. They'd given every law enforcement officer in the country permission to shoot me on sight.

I was marked for death.

CHAPTER 24

"Who the fuck is after me?"

Thea's modern apartment was silent but for my labored breathing. I looked at the serious faces in the press conference on the television. A White House press secretary spoke at a podium, U.S. Flags hanging on poles behind him.

Two men flanked the press guy. A military official, in full dress uniform decorated out the wazoo with fruit salad and...Senator Jordan.

The same man Jordan had met with earlier in the week.

My stomach roiled from a sense of ultimate betrayal.

"It's your buddy."

"Shhh," Jordan shushed.

"How do I rate a White House press conference?"

The press secretary continued to disseminate information. "Former professor, philanthropist, Staci Grant is being sought in connection with various terrorist networks." After he asked for the entire freaking country to be on the lookout for me, he said, "We believe she used her position of authority as a professor to find and recruit trainees for terrorist camps."

Jordan's lips tightened--he didn't approve. "You really did recruit kids?"

Deep down I'd always known if I told him about my work for the CIA he wouldn't approve. Even though I knew I shouldn't, I was compelled to explain.

"In actuality, the people I referred approached me. I just steered them toward organizations the CIA thought might be recruiting. We tagged them and then were able to identify more members of militant factions. Later we turned them into assets promising them immunity from prosecution for gathering evidence."

Dates, times, leaders, methods of communication, key people.

"The CIA isn't supposed to operate on U.S. soil."

"Yeah. Well, what you don't know can't hurt you." Actually we just couldn't recruit Foreign Nationals on U.S. soil or spy on American citizens. These kids were actually U.S. citizens.

"You really thought this was okay?"

I was proud of my work, of my service to my country. My grandparents had raised me to honor and respect the government. To do my duty to the greatest nation on earth.

"Wait a minute, Mr. High and Mighty. You used to kill people for the U.S. government. I don't think you have a lot of high ground here."

We both stood, facing off like combatants, the cocktail table in the gulf between us, while the press secretary droned on and on.

"Those kids were going to find a way to support a perceived injustice whether I helped them or not. What I do, did," I caught myself, "ultimately saved lives. We've been able to shut down or deport hundreds of potential terrorists based on the information they obtained. And we stopped attacks on several targets."

"And what about those kids?" Jordan said, "You used their idealism to put them in danger."

I knew I shouldn't do it, but I couldn't help it. "They chose that path. They could have gone into the freakin' Peace Corps and changed injustices that way. These are kids who wanted to fight."

Jordan blew out a breath in disgust.

"I redirected far more kids than I ever recruited. Most of the time I tried to channel their idealism into something else." It really pissed me off that I had to explain. "Some of the kids were recruited to work directly for the CIA."

"They should be giving you a medal instead of hunting you." Sarcasm was heavy in his voice.

My heart cracked. There was no other word for the sensation. His words wounded me with a physical pain as he dismissed my work.

"You know me."

Jordan was stoic in the face of my near desperation. He retreated without moving an inch, his face expressionless, closed, remote. "I thought I did."

He'd known me better than anyone else in my life. His total shut out exploded in my face more effectively than the toe popper that had almost taken off my foot.

I had a desperate need to pull him back toward me, emotionally, physically, any way I could.

Thinking if I could just touch him, connect with him physically, he would accept me again, I lunged toward him. I banged my shin on the coffee table, hitting my already damaged leg, sensitive nerves screeching in protest.

My vision dimmed as pain zinged through me.

Jordan steadied me before I could gasp. Here was the contact I'd wanted, but in a completely different, impersonal manner.

Rather than retreat, I leaned on him, into him. The warmth of his body soothed me, comforting me, familiar and right.

I had thought I loved him.

That was the reason I filed the paperwork. I thought we'd been moving toward something permanent. But I should have known a relationship based on lies would never succeed. Maybe it was time to start using the truth.

My cell phone rang. I ignored it.

This was more important.

"Look. My main job was to track and analyze potential Agency employees for the CIA using a set of criteria I developed based on my own recruitment."

The CIA didn't make value judgments on race or religion or politics, and their targets were strictly expedient. They just wanted people who could be of use in the espionage war.

He removed his arm from around my waist. I mourned the loss of affection even as he lashed out at me.

"Wasn't it dangerous for you to be working both sides, so to speak?"

"I was never the direct contact person for recruitment of CIA personnel or the terrorist trainees. I just identified their names and information."

Jordan crossed his arms over his chest, withholding his touch and sending out clear defensive signals. "Explain."

"For the kids they are accusing me of recruiting for terrorism, I never hooked them up. I suggested clubs or religious organizations we thought might be fronts for more sinister groups."

"They couldn't prosecute you?"

"Not under normal law." Although with the expanded power of the Patriot Act, they might be able to get me for recruiting terrorists. The arrest and detainment guidelines were fairly loose.

"For the CIA recruits...they were told they'd been identified as potential recruits. Because the CIA is so secretive, even within the organization, with the exception of a direct superior and a few other higher ups, no one knows exactly what anyone else does."

"Which brings up an interesting question. Why haven't you reported in?"

"The CIA didn't get me out. They left me in that prison."

And I checked the USA Today classifieds every day. No contact.

"You told me your trip wasn't CIA," he accused.

"I wasn't in Afghanistan for CIA business. It was personal. However, if the CIA was going to set up a...situation, my imprisonment would be perfect."

"They knew you were there?"

"Of course, but I wasn't connected with the Agency officially."

"So you assumed since they didn't get you out that they wanted you there?"

"Yes." I couldn't afford not to assume my death would be expedient for someone, somewhere at the Agency.

I just wasn't sure why.

The only thing I could come up with was my file on Department 5491. Someone didn't want that information made public. Although I would never have exposed the file.

"Department 5491 is from the NSA but included CIA

agents as well as NSA and DIA. I don't know who to trust. Someone set me up."

Jordan sighed and gazed steadily at me. His anger still burned below the surface but in his hazel eyes I saw his support. "You can trust me."

I knew him. Knew his core decency. Knew his protective instincts would encompass me and the baby. At this point, likely the *only* person I could trust was Jordan. He wouldn't let anything happen to the baby even if he was still mad at me.

"When I was arrested in Afghanistan...they specifically came for me."

"How do you know?"

"Because the other people in the UNOCHA group I was traveling with were allowed to leave. They only wanted me."

"What was the charge?"

"Funny thing about foreign prisons. They don't have the same laws regarding incarceration. They don't have to tell you why you're in prison."

"Why did your group leave you behind?"

"I told them to go." That may or may not have been a mistake on my part. "I assumed the CIA would quietly get me out. But that didn't happen, and I spent two weeks in hell." My voice broke, which pissed me off. I'm tougher than that.

Thankfully the military guy on the television, identified as Major Tony Vandenburg, interrupted my little breakdown. "We have reason to believe she is in New York City and traveling alone."

This press conference could be a ploy by the CIA to get me back, to find out what had happened to me. Maybe they'd gotten tired of doing surveillance on my house and just wanted to know what information I had and why I had never reported in after escaping.

Jordan was still watching the flat screen. "How would they know you are in New York?"

I'd only spoken with Ravini, Zeke, Jordan and Thea. Four people. Obviously one too many.

Even if Thea wanted to turn me in, she wasn't going to risk putting Jordan into a difficult situation. Was she?

I edged away from Jordan. "Did Zeke turn me in?"

"He wouldn't have done that. His ass is in trouble already."

"Maybe he thought it would gain him some points if he turned in a known terrorist recruiter."

"He wouldn't turn you in." Jordan paced around the room, stopping to stare out at the view of Central Park at night.

The trust I thought I felt vanished as I stared at the senator flanking the press secretary in the press conference. "Maybe you did. It would certainly eliminate your problem."

That pissed him off. "I don't have a problem."

"It would get you off the hook if I'm in federal prison." Or worse.

"I don't want to be off the hook, dammit." He grabbed my upper arms, pulling me close. "Don't make assumptions."

"You met with the Senator," I gestured to the television screen, "just a few days ago." All the doubts that had been crowding my head suddenly coalesced.

What if I'd been wrong about being able to trust him? What if in my mind I'd built our entire relationship into something it wasn't just to get me through all the other shit?

"Don't do this. Don't throw up walls." Jordan's heart

thudded against his chest as his desperate hazel gaze bored into me. His fingers curled around my biceps, not letting me back away. "If you know nothing else, you know that you can trust me."

The sharp sting of pain was nothing compared to the ping in my heart. I wanted to trust him. I did. Maybe too much.

My shoulders slumped as I finally gave in. "Okay."

"Good." Jordan squeezed me against his chest, his relief palpable.

My cell phone rang from inside my bag. The phone was a throwaway I'd bought to contact Ravini. Suddenly I put it together. Ravini was the only one who had the number. I could trust Jordan. "Shit."

I grabbed my backpack and rummaged for the phone. After I dug it out, I glanced at the screen. I had one other missed call. Hurriedly I turned the phone off and shoved it away from me. "This needs to be thrown in the trash compactor or even better an incinerator if this building has one."

The GPS locator in the phone was off. But for all I knew, we were experimenting with new technology that would work as long as the phone was equipped.

Jordan grabbed the phone. "I'll take care of it."

But before he could dispose of it, the sound of a key in the lock had us both diving for cover.

Thea stomped back into her apartment, muttering in Spanish.

I tried to get up in a dignified manner but it wasn't easy. My muscles and bones protested, creaking and whining, as I lifted my head over the back of the sofa.

"Are you still here?"

I wasn't sure if the question was supposed to be rhetorical so I answered. "Yeah."

As Jordan walked toward her, she went off on him, with a torrent of Spanish, a lot of finger jabbing, and hair tossing.

I couldn't blame her for being upset. A known fugitive in your living room wouldn't make anyone's day.

"And you," she rounded on me. I held my hands up as if in surrender. "What are you thinking to drag *miho* into your disgusting and depraved activities."

I couldn't tell her I worked for the CIA. But just maybe I could calm her down a little. "Thea."

"What?"

"Do you always believe everything you see on television?"

"Of course not."

"Things are not what they appear, *mi hermana*." Jordan patted her shoulder gently.

I certainly couldn't fault her for being upset with me.

"We need your help."

"You need to leave my apartment."

"We will. First thing in the morning, after you rent us a car."

"I'm not renting you a car." Thea stomped her Donald J. Pliner shoe. "I want you out. Rent your own damn car."

"We can't take the chance Jordan is being tracked too." I pressed.

"You dragged him into your," she waved her hands wildly, "illegal activities!"

"There's no official link between the two of you, is there?" I clarified, ignoring her theatrics. "No way for you to be listed in Jordan's file as someone to watch if they are looking for him?"

"They're looking for Jordan too?" Her eyes widened in horror.

"It's not as it seems," Jordan said consolingly. "I, we, will be okay."

"This is bad." She paced back and forth in front of the window, one hand to her mouth, the other on her hip, her eyes wide and trouble. "I don't want anything to happen to you."

"It will be fine." Of course, I was lying. What I really wanted to do was shake her and tell her to snap out of the hysterics. But for the time being we needed her cooperation.

I took her arm gently.

She snatched it away. "If you weren't pregnant, I would punch you."

"Fine. When I'm not pregnant anymore, you can punch me."

"A baby," she wailed. "What kind of mother will you be?"

That barb hit home.

What kind of mother? The kind who stole other babies away and sent them into dangerous situations for a government who was now throwing me under a bus.

My throat tightened. I couldn't swallow, couldn't even breathe. I didn't know anything about being a mother.

"Thea. That's enough," Jordan said calmly.

I found my voice and pushed my defensiveness deep down inside me where it could hide forever. "We won't ever find out if you don't help me. Us."

I could be the pushiest bitch on the planet when I needed something, and we needed her on board right now. Or we were going nowhere. "You with us or against us?"

Thea didn't say anything. I started reviewing ways to incapacitate her for an extended period of time.

We could steal her car. At least that would get us out of the city, and then we'd need to dump it, in a river preferably, and get a new one.

Just the effort needed to plan the minor op had me dragging. I was so freaking tired.

Thea continued to hesitate.

I readied my body, thinking about strike points and carefully calculating so I would only render her unconscious but not kill her.

Jordan stepped in front of me, his gaze boring into mine. "No."

Shit.

Now it was both of them against me. Worse case scenario, I bet she had some drugs around. I could put them both to sleep long enough to get out of Dodge. But dosing sleeping pills was always dicey.

Jordan hadn't moved. "Thea. We need your help."

Finally, she sighed. "What do I have to do?"

CHAPTER 25

October 18th
9:45 pm
New York City

SHE WAS HAVING A BABY.

They were having a baby.

Jordan was smiling. A great big grin energized him. Every molecule of his body was filled with joy. A baby.

He'd envisioned this part of his life happening differently. He'd thought taking the step to becoming a father would involve long bouts of careful consideration before the actual deciding. But everything had changed with a few significant words. Staci was pregnant.

He shouldn't be quite so happy yet. He knew it but couldn't help the smile on his face. He wanted to be a great father.

Determination blossomed through him. He would be a great father. The best father a kid could ever have.

Shit. He didn't know anything about being a dad. He'd

been raised by his mother and his aunt. Thea's father had been around, but he'd died young. Besides, Jordan wasn't going to be any kind of father unless he could get them out of this situation.

Staci lay on the sofa, sound asleep. Intending to gently nudge her awake, he leaned down, but she shifted in her sleep, making room for him to slide in behind her.

Just for a second.

Just a second to hold onto her and forget about their problems. Which were legion.

Deliberately he eased in behind her. His head fitted beside hers on the pillow, and his arm automatically went around her waist to pull her snug against his chest. He brushed a light kiss against her hair.

The familiar weight of her breasts was soft against his forearm. But the ridges of her ribs, so slight under his shirt, and the roughness of her once silky hair against his cheek were unfamiliar. Different.

She was different. They both were. Different wasn't bad...it just was.

He should focus on other, more crucial things, but his mind kept going back to Staci, and the baby.

Jordan knew the moment she drifted awake. Her body tensed slightly, and then relaxed into the cradle of his embrace.

He squeezed her gently, somehow needing to say it out loud. "You're having a baby," he whispered.

"Oh my God," she shuddered. "I didn't do this by myself. You were there too."

He waited, refusing to get mad before he heard where she was going with it.

"You know when it happened." Staci continued.

He knew exactly when she'd gotten pregnant. He even wondered if he'd subconsciously invoked this situation.

He'd known he wasn't using birth control. Instinctively, he'd wanted to claim her.

He held her firm against him, just in case she planned to get up. This was important. "That night—you were right there with me."

"I know." She rubbed her palm over his forearm, her hard callouses catching on the hair. "I could have stopped, insisted you put on a condom, and I didn't."

She was quiet.

He'd gone back to that night over and over again, after she left, after she was imprisoned, and after she'd been listed as dead.

"We're both very careful about protection," he stated deliberately.

"I was on the pill." She shrugged. "I guess it didn't work."

He'd wanted to bind her to him. In an act of pure insanity, pure possession he'd wanted to mark her, make her his in a way that couldn't be undone.

Some might think he'd been caught in the heat of the moment. But he wouldn't lie to her. Not about this. "I remember a calm, clear decision to...not use a condom."

"Why?"

He knew why, but putting the emotions, the feelings into words would make him sound crazy. He'd embraced the primitive and totally anti-modern feeling. "You were mine."

"You Tarzan, me Jane?" She snorted. "A little caveman of you, wasn't it?"

But she was laughing not angry.

"Yeah." He still wasn't sorry.

Even after she'd gone, all he'd felt was satisfaction. He'd

marked her in a way he'd marked no one else. He'd wanted to believe with total conviction they'd stay together, even if it hadn't felt like it at the time.

"I was committed to working things out."

"Really? You could have given me some clue."

"Just because I thought we'd work it out doesn't mean I wasn't upset about the whole CIA thing." More about the lies than the CIA, although frankly he hadn't told her everything about himself either. "Because I was."

"Yeah. I got that," she said drily.

So he had to be truthful, to himself at least, and give her a little leeway. Wasn't that what you did when you loved someone? Compromise. Understanding.

So he said, "I just needed a little time to deal with the information. It was a shock."

He'd worked enough covert ops to understand you were never sure of your friends and associates. The only life important to them was their own and occasionally a spouse or child.

You never knew what another person's triggers were, sometimes even if you'd known them for years. So how could he, in good conscience, stay angry with her?

Especially since he was keeping a few secrets of his own. "I forgave you before you'd even cleared the Atlantic."

"Might have been nice if you'd shared that with me."

They hadn't been able to discuss any of this while she'd been thousands of miles away.

"I was hyper-aware of every single word we exchanged over that damn Sat phone."

"You just sounded...."

He'd sounded stilted and mad and dissatisfied because she was thousands of miles away and they'd had a bunch of issues to talk about.

That right there should have told him how he truly felt about her. In the past, if a woman had issues she wanted to talk about he was heading for the door...not anxious to have a conversation about it.

"Yeah. I'm sorry." He should have been more truthful.

She sighed. The breath pushed out of her forcibly, and he could feel the contraction of her diaphragm against his arm. "What a mess."

"Yeah."

Except he couldn't view her pregnancy as a problem.

A complication, perhaps. Mostly he was worried about the drug in her system and how it was affecting her and the baby.

He had to bring it up. Until now, she'd been blowing him off, but this was important. "I'm worried about this DNA drug in your system."

"You really believe I was injected with something?"

"I know you were." He'd heard Susan Chen talk about the drug and its side effects. He knew Staci needed the antidote.

"I don't want more drugs," she said almost plaintively.

"I know." She didn't like drugs. Almost as much as she didn't like hospitals. "But you may have to give in. Have you noticed anything different?"

She slowly grew more stiff, tension tightened her muscles. "Everything is different," she whispered.

Jordan knew what she was thinking. Everything was different after being tortured and on the run. How the hell was she, were they, going to get out of this situation?

Staci looked back at the now silent television. "I've just got to find out what someone thinks I know that's so important they'd release my name and face to the media."

Jordan's stomach knotted. She was in serious danger.

"They're trying to destroy my credibility."

"I'm pretty sure they succeeded."

"Why?" Staci asked. "I wasn't bothering anyone. The Afghanistan trip was personal. I wasn't exposing Department 5491."

"It's too coincidental. Everyone who received the DNA drug is also on that list. What's the correlation?" Jordan asked.

Staci shifted to look back at him. "I don't know."

His senses had slowly awakened from their dormancy, and details were registering. The swell of her breast against his arm. The curve of her butt nestled against his hard on. Like a trained reaction, his body had responded to arousal stimulus. He shifted slightly trying to put some distance between her body and his.

But she followed, rubbed her ass against his granite cock. "Is that a cell phone in your pocket or are you happy to see me?"

He laughed. "Smart ass."

But then Jordan's cell phone vibrated...and his amusement disappeared. Things were going to get tense again soon.

"It's better than thinking about how much trouble I'm in."

Yeah. And the trouble wasn't just going to go away. They needed help. He'd made a call. He just hoped Staci would understand.

"You shouldn't just assume the reason for them calling the press conference is related to your investigation of Department 5491."

"It's the only thing I can think of."

"What about your trip? Maybe they didn't like where a private citizen was going in the Afghan country. Maybe they didn't want you criticizing the efforts of the military projects there."

"I didn't see anything. Just a bunch of poppy fields and villages clearly engaged in the Commander's Emergency Relief Program, or Operation: Rebuild. Both programs aid the villagers with infrastructure, building schools with running water, building roads, medical supplies, all in exchange for helping the military secure the areas and keep the Taliban from encroaching."

"What about the local people?"

"Many of the natives are happy we're there. Since we changed the aid program and are trying to emancipate them from the prior government and get them started on a new path, they welcome us."

She was silent for a moment. Then she said, "The villages I saw, the warlords got along with the army and vice versa." Staci frowned. "They take advantage of the negotiations to destroy their poppy fields and earn the money back from the US government. The U.N. gives them new crops to plant and supplies."

"What about your activities for the CIA? Maybe someone else in the government doesn't like what you are doing so they decided to out you."

"Yeah but I can't do a Valerie Plame and have my day in court. I'll be dead before that happens."

"Assuming they even take you to court. They could just ship your ass to Guantanamo."

Staci rested her hand on her belly. "It's a possibility."

Jordan's cell vibrated again. He checked the display, but he already knew who it was.

He got up from the sofa. "Let me get Thea on her way."

"What?"

The gurgle of the coffeepot covered his footsteps. "She needs to go rent the car."

"True."

Jordan hustled Thea out of her apartment before she could do more than give Staci the evil eye and threaten her. "Don't fuck up, or I will find you."

Staci rolled her eyes.

Jordan walked Thea to the elevator, checking the hallway, worrying about what to do about Staci.

He had to figure out what was going on before Staci bolted.

She was going to. If she got the chance. He'd seen the intent in every gesture she'd made, every glance she'd given him. She was out of here.

The truth was like a Ka-bar to the heart.

She'd be gone unless he found a way to stop her from leaving. He'd been wracking his brain for any lever, any hammer he could use to keep her here. Because if she walked, he'd never see her again.

He'd do anything to keep her. Anything to make sure she stayed with him.

Anything.

As they came to a stop at the elevator, Thea brought him back to the present. "Are you sure this is such a good idea?"

"It will be fine, miha."

"I don't think so."

"It has to be," Jordan said fiercely. "Leave the keys under the front seat. Don't come back until we're gone. I don't want anyone to see us with you."

The elevator doors slid open. "You hear what you are saying?" Thea accused.

"It will be fine," he soothed. Jordan ran a finger over Staci's scarab, still in his pocket. He should have returned it to her, but he didn't want to let go of the amulet. As if he held onto the necklace, he could hold onto her.

Thea bussed his cheek gently and then stepped into the elevator. "I hope you are right. Be safe." She stared at him with a worried frown as the elevator doors closed.

Jordan's phone buzzed again. Safe. He'd make sure of it, assuming Staci didn't kill him when she discovered what he'd done.

CHAPTER 26

October 18
        11:30 pm
New York City

WHILE JORDAN WALKED Thea to the elevator, I rifled through Jordan's bag, wanting to be armed for whatever came next. Both times when his cell buzzed, he'd tensed. That behavior hit the top of my suspicion meter.

Pulling out his Glock, I chambered a round, then assessed the apartment's exit strategies. The front door was the only way out.

No balcony, no terrace, just windows that looked out over Central Park and didn't open.

While Jordan was still outside the apartment with Thea, I used the sink in the kitchen, rubbed some water through my hair and over my face. I had to be alert, ready for whatever came through that door. I positioned myself on the sofa, facing the door, weapon at the ready, using the arm of the sofa to prop up the gun.

Someone knocked.

"It's me," Jordan called softly.

He could get back in, so I assumed he gave me the heads up for a reason.

"I brought friends." Jordan walked in slowly, hands out in front of him. There were two people behind him. A man, very short blond hair, sculpted features, good body, carried himself like a fighter, intense gray eyes. A woman, streaked short blonde hair spiked every which way, well-dressed, clearly in excellent condition, and a scowl on her face.

Were they here to take me in? Had Jordan betrayed me?

Pain wrapped around my ribs and threatened my air. I thought about those coffee mugs in the prison which I'd conveniently, for him anyway, forgotten.

Shit.

I had to stay calm if I wanted to get out of this alive. I was fairly sure Jordan wouldn't let me get killed. He wanted the baby too much, I thought mockingly. And tried not to let that truth hurt.

"Jesus, look at you." The woman's eyebrows rose, her mouth a round o of shock.

I lifted the Glock.

"What the fuck?" she snarled.

I stared at the three. "Why the ambush?"

"It's not an ambush," Jordan said calmly, slowly, holding still, hands up and out. As if he would catch the bullets if I started firing. "Unarmed here, Stace. Put the weapon away."

"We're trying to help you." Ungrateful bitch. I could almost hear the woman tack on.

Something about her was vaguely familiar. Her hair was glossy and artfully streaked with blond. She wore cream wide-bottomed linen pants, a wrap-around black linen top tied at the waist, and low-heeled black shoes.

I realized why she looked familiar. I had an outfit just like hers. My hair used to be the same colors. Our facial features were different but otherwise it was like looking in a mirror. Or looking in a mirror before I'd become a human toothpick.

"Yeah. They're your clothes. I didn't give them back."

What the hell was she talking about?

"Jamie," the other man put a restraining hand on her arm. He said to Jordan wryly, "I take it you didn't tell her we were coming."

Jordan flushed. "Better not to."

"Yeah, it's working out so well right now."

The woman just stood there, her face a serene mask, but I knew better. She was pissed. Which frankly, I didn't get. I was the one who'd been ambushed.

"Let's discuss this rationally," Jordan continued in that low, calm voice as if we were discussing whether to have beer or wine with dinner. "Staci, this is Lucas Goodman."

The handsome man tipped his chin at me, his gaze trained on, and never leaving, my weapon. Smart man.

"And Jamie Hunt."

From the list. From 5491. The other NSA person he'd hooked up with.

No one rushed me. They all just…waited. I didn't know what they wanted from me.

All three stood, legs apart, hands visible, and looking like a unit, while I sat on the sofa…alone.

"Give me one good reason why I shouldn't just shoot now," I asked curiously.

Jamie Hunt stepped slightly in front of Lucas. "'Cause I'll kick your skinny ass back to Afghanistan if you do."

"You and what army?" Of course, all she'd have to do was blow on me and I'd float away on the wind.

She snorted.

We all waited. No one looked at their watch, no one twitched, or fidgeted. Their gazes were solidly trained on the Glock resting on the pillow, while I decided what to do.

I suppose someone could be waiting downstairs, or in the hallway, or in the parking garage, but Jordan seemed to be trying to protect the two behind him from me, rather than the other way around.

And I knew in my heart, he wouldn't let anything happen to the baby.

I moved the weapon into my lap, pointing the barrel toward the side of the sofa and away from the trio.

"'Bout time."

I was tempted to aim at her again, but frankly I wasn't too sure I could hold the damn thing up.

"As much as I'd like a catfight...." Lucas Goodman trailed off, his lips curling up in a little half-smile, his fingers squeezing Jamie Hunt's forearm.

"In your dreams," Jamie said.

He gave her a look that said, oh yeah. "Perhaps we can move on to business."

"I'm listening." I didn't let my attention shift to Jordan. Didn't want to focus on the intimate betrayal. I'd told him I couldn't go in until I figured out who was after me. Instead of respecting me, he'd brought the NSA right to me.

I saw the way Jamie Hunt and Lucas Goodman looked at each other. The way they'd both taken steps to protect one another.

They were a unit. A couple.

They moved together with a grace, a connection clear to even my inexperienced eye. Their closeness evoked an unfamiliar longing, reminding me of my grandparents. Of what I'd hoped to have with Jordan. Dammit.

"We're only here to...deliver something you might find useful."

"They have the information on the DNA gene manipulation drug." Jordan commented softly, "I thought we might be able to get analysis on how the drug changed you if we could get the original files."

So he hadn't betrayed me. At least, not completely. I directed my question to her. "How did you get it?"

"Classified."

"How come you still have it?"

If she really had gotten the data and it really was classified, she shouldn't be carrying it on her person and she shouldn't be about to give it up to me.

"I'm not about to turn this research over so someone else can start up the project again," Jamie hissed. "They fucked with enough lives already."

"Why give it to me?" I couldn't figure that out. She didn't like me, although I had no idea why. I'd never met her.

"I asked her to," Jordan said.

"I'd still rather kick your ass," Jamie grudgingly said. "But I owe Jordan."

"Just give them the flash key," Lucas said, "The sooner we leave, the happier Ms. Grant will be."

Jamie Hunt reached into her big black leather tote.

My weapon went back up.

"I'm not going to shoot you." She pulled out a flash key, holding the storage device with a tissue, and handed it to Jordan. "If I attack you, it will be the old-fashioned way and you'll see me coming."

I aimed the gun at the sofa again.

She directed her comments to Jordan. "This has the data for all ten people who were given the drug. You'll be able to access her file with the original DNA analysis. According to Susan Chen, she," Jamie jerked her head toward me, "is File #3."

Lucas Goodman reached out to grasp Jamie Hunt's fingers with his. I noted he made sure to keep his gun hand free.

Jordan nodded once. "Thanks."

"No one knows I had that data. Be very careful about where you go for help." Jamie's lip curled derisively. "You try to turn me in to curry favor, I'll deny I ever had the information."

I understood her perfectly. She'd done exactly what I would have in the same situation.

"Fine."

"You have any idea where to take the information for analysis?" Lucas asked slowly.

I waited for Jordan. Did he have an idea? Had he planned that far ahead or was he winging it?

"No."

"You need to get out of New York," Jamie said. "Pronto."

"We've got that covered." Jordan was more taciturn than usual.

"Where are you going?"

"Don't tell her." I didn't want her knowing anything more than she already did. I still couldn't figure out why she didn't like me or why she had my clothes.

"A friend of mine, Barb, is already familiar with the project." Lucas ignored my animosity. "And would likely be willing to help you."

I eyed Jamie and wondered what was really going on

here. "You're awfully free with handing out data on experiments you supposedly don't want continued."

Jamie didn't respond, but she wanted to go for me. I could see the desire in her stance. Why the hell didn't she like me?

"I believe she's at a conference in D.C. this week." Lucas rattled off her cell number as Jamie's scowl deepened. "She's extremely discreet."

"Thanks." Jordan's voice was deep and choked. "Where are you going?"

Jamie didn't say a word. Cautious.

"Seattle," Lucas answered.

"Why there?"

"Susan Chen has family in the area watching her daughter."

And they took time to drop this flash drive off in NYC? "How did you have time to stop here?" I asked suspiciously.

"Chen can't travel by air, rail or bus. She's got to steal a car or hitch across the country. Even taking the extra hours to drive here," Lucas slanted a slow, heated look at Jamie. "And catch a flight out of JFK, we'll still get there well ahead of her."

"She could have an accomplice." Would almost have to if she'd escaped a federal prison.

"Possibly." Lucas frowned.

"Why would she go to Seattle?" I wondered aloud.

"To protect her daughter."

I still wasn't getting it. She should stay far away from her daughter, especially if she had family taking care of the child. "It doesn't make sense."

"It does if you have a heart," Jamie sniped. "Maybe you lost yours when you were recruiting terrorists."

"Not you too." I was totally disgusted. "What is your deal?"

"You were going to recruit my sister."

Admittedly I had a lot of names in my databases, but I thought I would remember a connection to Jamie Hunt.

"Who the hell is your sister?"

Then it clicked. Jordan helped rescue John Wishbone and the girl I'd asked him to watch over. So that meant...Bella Holden was Jamie Hunt's sister?

"How is that possible?"

Jamie pressed her lips together. What so now she wasn't talking? Fine.

"It's time for us to go." Lucas Goodman smiled at me easily. Then he grabbed Jordan in a bear hug, slapped him on the back. "Glad you found her, man."

I could hear the 'even if I think you're crazy' in his voice.

Fuck him.

"Thanks." Jordan pounded Lucas with equal enthusiasm, the flash key still gripped tightly in his fist. "For everything."

Jordan aimed a look at Jamie. "Thank you," he said, his voice thick with an underlying emotion.

"I won't ever forget." Jamie stared hard at me.

I got the impression she meant more than just Jordan's favor.

Jamie finished, "You need anything, call."

CHAPTER 27

Octubre... October 19
        10:00 am
Washington, D.C.

Fuck the government. Fuck the CIA.

I had a Canadian passport and a date with a country without a strong extradition policy with the U.S.

Cuba, here I come.

Shit. Beach, sand. Again.

I'd managed to avoid any number of touchy subjects-- say those Franklin Group mugs in the prison, the ambush, yeah, I'm still calling it that, with Jamie and Lucas, Jordan's refusal to let me go--by sleeping most of the way south.

I should have been planning my escape. Instead I'd avoided everything by crashing. Except I really did feel better now.

I'd just woken up and the interior of the rental car had that new car smell which wasn't sitting too well with my stomach. So I nibbled on a vanilla scone, hoping the pastry would stay down.

We'd arrived in D.C. a few minutes ago and were on our way to meet Barb, the scientist, at her hotel.

Lucas Goodman's name must be a magic password. When we called, she'd asked when and where. Didn't bother with what or who. So I'd let Jordan 'convince' me to go to D.C.

In reality, my plan was to retrieve a bolt bag I had stashed for just such an occasion. I'd gone back and forth, examining possibilities, and any way I sliced it I needed to get out of the country.

Maybe I could just straight out convince him to go away. I didn't want to hurt his feelings, and I'd really like to get him set before I left. Maybe it was sentimental of me, but Jordan had, in his own way, been looking out for me. It was time for me to return the favor. A wash of melancholy flowed over me.

This was for the best. Separate now while it would be painful but not impossible. I had a feeling the longer I hung out with him the harder the break would be.

"I've been thinking." I hesitated. I wasn't sure how receptive he was going to be.

Lie. I was pretty sure when I told him what I was thinking he'd blow a gasket.

He drove easily and competently, staying in the middle lanes, never going above the speed limit. "Go ahead."

"I think you should take a hike."

"Excuse me?"

"Take off. Just...go home."

"You want me to leave you to face this by yourself." It wasn't a question.

"I was actually thinking more along the lines of...."

He shifted his gaze from the road to frown at me. His macho side didn't come out very often but it did make an appearance every now and then. And now I knew this time would be one of them. Somehow I couldn't phrase my request any other way.

"Protect yourself from the shitstorm coming my way."

His biceps flexed as he tightened his hands on the steering wheel. "And you think I'll just what, say 'sure, go on with your life, see you around, I'll pay you and the baby visits in prison'?"

"I know it's not ideal."

"Not ideal…" His voice got lower and deeper, his body got stiffer and harder, as if you'd need a sculptor's chisel to change any facet of his muscles. "…is being unmarried when the baby is born. What you are suggesting is a disaster, like having only a sniper rifle for close quarters combat."

I opened my mouth.

"Don't even say it." As if he were still part of a team, he made the spec ops hand signal for freeze, a closed fist at head level, without looking at me.

"Fuck," he whispered.

I was going to try one more time. But he kept going.

"I have a responsibility. One I will not forego because you think you should do this alone. And damn you for thinking I would do that to you and the baby."

"Yeah." Way to hit my hot button. I'd been a responsibility for my grandparents too. "Maybe I don't want to be a responsibility."

"That's not what I meant."

"It sure sounded like it." And what the fuck were we doing arguing about something so far in the future it was fantasy?

"I will take care of you and the baby."

"Forget it. I need to get out of my current mess before we concentrate on your responsibilities." I stressed the word snidely, just to piss him off.

"Fine. Let's just get through this meeting with Barb." He jammed his back against the leather seat. "We can argue about the meaning of responsibility later."

Okay. I tried. I'd ditch him as soon as I could.

The Sofitel was located at 15th and K Streets. Only a block from the White House. Was I thumbing my nose at the assholes in that damn press conference? Or exhibiting plain stupidity?

Take your pick.

Barb had told us that she was staying at this hotel. Logically, meeting there in private versus a more public venue made sense. But as we got closer, trepidation edged in. What did we know about this woman?

Not even her last name.

"You should be wearing more of a disguise," Jordan said as we walked toward the small lobby.

The Yankees cap wasn't much.

On the other hand, I sure didn't look like the picture they'd flashed during the press conference.

"Jamie Hunt looks more like me than I do."

Jordan sounded thoughtful. "Yeah."

"Maybe there'll be a case of mistaken identity." Heh, heh. Wish I'd written down that tip line number.

I subtly catalogued the elegant lobby, checking out the doorman, the desk clerks. Looking for anyone suspicious, anyone paying more attention to us than appropriate.

The patrons in the Le Bar were the most likely to recognize me. The suits taking their power coffee here wouldn't have the chops to go after me, but they could easily alert their federal law enforcement buddies.

I had to be wary. D.C. was a virtual hive of security. Every federal building had guards inside and out. I didn't want to bring that wrath down on Jordan.

I didn't want to spend a long time here, as I was very aware of the danger. We didn't know this woman. We had only Lucas Goodman's assurance she was safe.

Barb had no idea who we were. However, after she saw me, it was possible she might turn me in. Suddenly the whole meeting seemed like an exercise in disaster.

And me without a weapon.

"You trust this guy Lucas, right?"

"Absolutely," Jordan replied. "Don't worry."

We exited on the third floor into the blandly elegant elevator lobby and headed to Barb's room.

Jordan and I jockeyed for position in front.

"I'll be first, since I talked to her," he said.

"Fine."

Within seconds of his knock, the door swung open to reveal an absolutely gorgeous black woman. "Come in."

We both hustled inside, unwilling to be the focus of any security camera for too long.

Watching to make sure she didn't recognize me, I positioned myself in case she leaped for the phone.

"Have a seat." She gestured toward the sofa, while she sank down into an edgy modern chair of chrome and upholstery.

I'm not often struck dumb by the beauty of a woman, but I was now. She had beautiful deep brown eyes and high cheekbones accented by her super short hair.

The cut emphasized the shape of her head and the graceful curve of her neck. If she and Halle Berry went head-to-head in a beauty contest, Barb would kick Halle's ass.

"You're friends of Lucas?" When she smiled, her focus on Jordan was warm and friendly, but impersonal.

"We go back aways."

"Me too." She fiddled with the button on her exquisitely tailored gray and white pinstripe suit. "What have you got for me?"

Since this was his gig, I let Jordan speak and just observed her. She had an earnest cant to her body, legs crossed but leaning slightly forward into the space between us.

"Lucas indicated you're familiar with the data from a certain...experiment."

"The gene manipulation." Her eyes were bright with curiosity, and her fingers twitched.

We needed to get this over with and get out of here. I didn't like being trapped in this hotel room so I cut to the chase.

"We need an updated DNA analysis on a person and then a comparison of the results to the original data."

"Okay." Some of her enthusiasm dimmed. "But I don't have access to the data."

Jordan shifted in his chair. "We've got it."

"Do you have a syringe so I can take a blood sample?"

Shit. Hadn't thought of that. We'd have to improvise. I strode into the ultra modern, granite-tiled bath and scrabbled through the tray of toiletries looking for some q-tips. "Will this work?"

"In a pinch."

We were pinched.

"So will you be able to analyze what the drug changed?"

Barb blinked, her eyes wide, as she pondered Jordan's question.

"I can give you specific chromosomes that were

changed, but most likely can't tell you how the drug would impact the person." She hesitated for a moment, then continued. "If possible, you might want to talk to the other people who had the drug."

Jordan huffed out a breath.

Like that was going to happen.

"Which one of you had the original drug?"

I wagged my hand in the air like a little kid. The silk cuff fell from my wrist, exposing the deep tissue contusions.

I ignored her indrawn gasp. "Can you compare a current sample to the baseline data?"

"It will take a few days but sure." Barb looked anxious to get started.

"So you need the original information?"

"Oh, yes." Barb's gaze shifted to the blank television screen. "I destroyed the files after my analysis was finished. I didn't want to get...anyone in trouble."

Good. I hoped that sentiment extended to when she saw my picture plastered all over the news.

I handed her the q-tips in their plastic sleeves. She carefully ripped open the package and leaned toward me.

"Open wide."

My mouth yawned open and she swiped the q-tip along the inside of my cheek.

Jordan chose that moment to ask the question bothering him. "Can you tell what the impact of the drug would be on a baby?"

"You're pregnant?" She bobbled the q-tip.

I brought my hand up to steady her wrist before she lost the damn thing in my throat.

Jordan answered for me. "Yes."

She tilted her head, blinked again as she processed he

was the father. And then carefully slid the q-tip back in the little package. The wheels in her head were turning, turning.

Yes, he slept with me. I wanted to snarl. I knew I looked like something that had been dragged through the desert but really was it so hard to believe?

"We should take two, just to be safe." She avoided my gaze, studiously checking out and swabbing the inside tissue of my mouth again.

When she was done, I sighed.

I couldn't wait to get out of here. Away from all these people who were shocked Jordan had lowered himself to sleep with me, look for me, find me.

I bet they all wished I'd just disappeared.

Jordan persisted, unaware or unfazed by her shock. "Do you still have the data on the antidote?"

Her gaze slid to the window. "Uh, no. I destroyed everything once Lucas gave me the go-ahead." She was lying. She still had that data. I had to wonder why she kept it.

I knew why she didn't tell us, but still it made me wonder what other secrets Barb was keeping.

While Jordan transferred the data on the flash key to Barb's laptop, I picked up the USA Today sitting on the coffee table.

The press conference must have been after the paper was put to bed, because thankfully there was no mention of my 'wanted' status. I only partially listened as Jordan and Barb worked out particulars regarding the timing of the results. It was all stuff I didn't care about since I wasn't going to be around.

Idly, I flipped to the Marketplace section.

Jordan and Barb exchanged cell phone numbers. "I'll be

in touch." Their conversation muted to a murmur as I zeroed in on a new problem.

There, in black and white, was the message I'd been waiting for since I returned. A short advertisement about a castle for sale in Virginia.

A powerful cold whooshed through me, my fingers clutched the newsprint so tightly the paper crinkled in the suddenly quiet room. I tried to take in air but as if the cold had frozen my ability to breathe, nothing came in.

"What's wrong?"

Jordan had leaned closer, placed his hand on my elbow. The simple impact of his touch flared through me, and finally I could gasp in air.

"I need to go."

We needed damage control, to make sure Barb didn't talk, if we were going to get out of here.

I stood, leaned into her personal space. My heart bumped against my breastbone and flooded my body with adrenaline, as fear coursed through me.

The ad in the paper was nothing but trouble.

"If anyone asks you about this meeting, he wasn't here. Are we clear?"

"Ignore her." Jordan tried to tug on my arm.

Barb pulled her chin back, gave me a penetrating stare, then propped her hands on her hips. "I'm getting damned tired of being threatened by you women."

You women?

"First, her. Now, you." Barb wagged her finger in my face. "I'm doing this as a favor to Lucas."

"Then protect him and his friend." I jabbed back. "Otherwise you're an accessory."

"Accessory?" Her voice rose in alarm.

"Shit." Jordan sighed. "Way to win friends and influence people."

My heart still bumped in my chest. Get out. Get out. Get out, the rhythm warned.

I warned Barb. "Leave your cell on the table and go in the bathroom. Count to fifty." I folded the paper carefully, leaving it open to the classified section.

She threw her hands up in the air as if throwing confetti. "Who am I going to tell? I don't even know your name."

I thought about the press conference. I thought about the ad in the paper tucked under my arm. They were closing in. "You will."

Eyeing me cautiously, she spoke to Jordan. "One last thing, do you know what subject number she is?"

"According to," Jordan paused, "our friends...she is subject three."

Barb nodded, slightly distracted as I continued to glare at her. "Wait. Three?"

What now? Could we absolutely not catch a fucking break? "Yeah."

"You're sure it's three?" she asked.

Jordan shifted closer to me as if to shield me from whatever was coming next. "What's wrong?"

"Nothing, if she is three." Barb twisted her hands together. "I may not have been completely truthful about destroying the data."

"And?"

"I studied it exhaustively." She blinked, her arms crossed defensively across her stomach.

We didn't have time for this. "And what?"

"Three was given a placebo."

CHAPTER 28

A placebo. A fake. No drug.

Susan Chen had lied to them. Or she hadn't known that I had gotten a placebo.

"Good news, huh?" I could cross one worry off my list.

Jordan grabbed me by the shoulders. "You're going to leave." He was asking, demanding the answer.

"Yeah."

"Just give up? Let whoever is doing this win?"

I hated to put it in win-lose terms but.... "Yeah."

"What about us? What about the baby?"

I couldn't answer, couldn't even think about that right now.

"If you were really going to leave, you'd be gone already. You're a super agent. It's not like I've had you handcuffed to me."

He was right. I'd been putting it off, delaying in the inevitable, because in truth, I didn't want to leave. Not here. Not him.

Not...us.

If there was such a thing. I wanted that chance to
find out.

"Stay. Fight for yourself. Fight for us. Fight for
the baby."

Barb's eyes were wide with alarm and fascination.

Jordan had me by the biceps, holding on. Not so tightly I
couldn't break his hold if I really wanted to, but tight
enough I knew he was serious.

I didn't say anything. My throat was too taut with all the
things whipping through my head, clamoring to get out, to
get said.

I wanted to stay with him. I really did. But I didn't want
him hurt. In any way. I shook my head, unable to express
my thoughts.

Jordan moved his fingers to my shoulders, squeezed to
the point of pain. "If you try to leave, I'll turn you in
myself."

What? If he'd wanted to stab me physically he couldn't
done a better job of cleaving my heart in two.

My hands gripped his wrists. My knees buckled and my
heart literally stopped beating. "You're going to turn
me in?"

"Only if you try to leave."

What kind of sense did that make?

"If I turn you in, I can do it under my terms, where I
know you'll be safe, with someone I know will protect you.
Otherwise you risk being hunted down and shot like a rabid
animal," he hissed.

"You'd turn me in."

"For your own safety."

"You want me in prison."

"No! I want you safe." Jordan shook me gently. "I need
you. We need you."

But at what cost?

"I don't want you to get hurt." The words finally burst out of me in a rush.

"And I don't want you to get any more hurt than you already are but I can't guarantee that. I can't guarantee anything. Except you have more of a chance, we have more of a chance--together."

He was right. I knew he was right.

I wanted to believe with everything in me we really did have a chance.

First we had to find out who was out to get me. Because if they got me, they might get him. And I couldn't allow that to happen.

We hung suspended in this moment, an unbelievably personal significant decision, witnessed by a stranger.

The stranger was still watching with a growing sense of alarm. I growled at Barb. "Don't talk."

Jordan took my answer as a yes. "Give her a break."

I didn't know if he was addressing me or Barb.

Jordan grabbed me around the ribcage, forcing my arms around his shoulders, cradling me against him in the sweetest hug on the planet.

"Thank you for helping us," he said to Barb.

She nodded, blinked once, her whole body stock still as her gaze took us in.

"Please don't turn us in," Jordan said. "Or if you have to turn us in, wait a few hours."

"I wouldn't want to stand in the way of...that." Barb finally broke out of her trance, her smile luminescent and just a little bit melancholy. "Good luck."

"WHAT UPSET YOU?"

He'd waited to ask until we were outside on our way to the parking garage.

My messenger bag, slung across my chest bandolier-style, thumped against my hip with every long stride.

I tried to ignore Jordan. Perspiration slimed the back of my neck and my forehead. The day was middling cool, but the heat building inside me came flowing out of my pores.

I tried to ignore the message in the USA Today Marketplace. Wanted: Buyer for 10,000 sq. ft. castle in Virginia. Be your own queen. ph. 800-555-2708.

I knew that ad.

If I'd seen it three weeks ago, I'd have called right away. Now, the timing was suspicious. Could they be setting me up?

And just to up the cluster factor, suddenly, I had to eat. Had to.

I grabbed him by his black Polo shirt and gestured. "Food."

We were in front of Bread Line on Pennsylvania between 17th and 18th. The place was so busy no matter what time of day, we would be just another customer in the throng.

No one had followed us.

"I'm starving."

Jordan curved his arm around my waist, pulling me close. For a moment, I savored the strength of his body, supporting me, sheltering me. I subtly inhaled the familiarity of his scent. The temptation to just hold on tantalized.

"You're going to tell me."

"After I eat." Suddenly seriously starving, I yanked open the door, interrupting the conversation.

He stopped me, his hand around my bicep, his words a breath in my ear. "You're going to tell me all of it."

We stood half-in, half-out of the restaurant. If we didn't move, we'd start to draw attention. I nodded. And the tension broke.

"Okay." He surveyed the packed restaurant, but everyone was minding their own business intent only on getting their food and getting out.

"Pulled pork sandwich and coleslaw." Sounded fantastic. My stomach growled loudly, and my mouth watered.

I hadn't thrown up in over twelve hours. A freaking world record for me lately.

"You sit, I'll order." He gave me one more quick look, as if double checking to make sure I wasn't going to bolt.

I jammed into a miraculously empty seat in a corner while Jordan headed for the counter. After interminable minutes, he was back with everything in a to-go bag.

He said quietly, "Let's get going. Someplace where if you have to throw up it won't be so noticeable."

Lovely. He's worrying about whether I'll blow chow in the restaurant.

He was right. Yet in that moment, I would have gladly surrendered for one freaking bite. One bite of that soft, chewy white bread, with the flavors of simmered pork and sauce exploding in my mouth.

"You can eat while we walk."

I unwrapped the sandwich and took a huge mouthful, feeling like an alcoholic taking that first hit of vodka. I closed my eyes, my mouth curved.

I knew exactly what he was thinking. "Get your mind out of the gutter."

"Been awhile."

It was likely to be a lot longer.

I thought about what I looked like right now. In a word, terrible.

My body hadn't recovered from the abuse of the past few months, and the morning sickness had ravaged my already stressed skin and bones until I looked more like a refugee than a debutante.

"You have a thing for emaciated, scarred women?" I asked through a mouthful of food, chewing as I walked and talked. I'm sure that was attractive.

He leaned over and whispered, "I have a thing for you."

I'd had a thing for him too. Somehow it had all gone so wrong.

We both suddenly realized we'd fallen into the old habit of teasing each other, that sort of verbal foreplay that we'd engaged in...before.

I may have agreed to stay and fight, but we were still a long way from our previous relationship.

I eased slightly away from him.

"Tell me why you turned white as a sheet in that hotel room."

I chewed slowly, debating how to structure the truth.

"You promised."

Actually I hadn't quite promised.

"Tell me what was in the paper."

"If I ever need to reach my contact through unofficial means, I put an ad in the paper."

"The ad was there?"

"We have a reciprocal agreement in case he's been unable to contact me through normal channels."

"Why isn't this a good thing?"

"Because the agency didn't get me out of that prison." He still didn't say anything. "Think about it. The timing is suspicious."

"I suppose." Jordan walked alongside me. "The ad would have been placed before the press conference was scheduled."

"I've been checking this paper every day since I got back to the States and nothing." I finished inhaling my sandwich and popped open the top on the coleslaw. With a plastic spork, I shoveled the cabbage and dressing into my mouth as if I hadn't eaten in months.

Oh wait, I hadn't.

"I can't take the chance they aren't somehow trying to bring me in."

Jordan walked silently beside me. "I think we should set up a meet."

I slurped down some cool ice tea. "We'd need to work out logistics." And just because I set up the meeting with my contact didn't mean I needed to show.

I could feel the blood pulsing through my body, as if I'd woken from a long sleep and were suddenly experiencing life again. The air smelled crisp and clean with a hint of traffic exhaust. Birds chirped along with the honking horns, cell phones trilled, scattered conversations jumbled around us.

"I'm not risking your safety," he said adamantly.

I wouldn't risk his either.

Walking back to the car, we haggled over details until we came up with a plan that suited us both. My biggest concern was keeping Jordan safe.

He said, "Technically I'm off the grid right now. My boss thinks I'm in upstate New York for a little break. And I turned off the transponder in my phone."

"So you should be safe."

"Yeah."

"The Franklin Group." Those mugs still nagged at me,

and I had to resolve this once and for all. "There were logo mugs in the prison."

"Franklin Group mugs?"

"Yep."

"Huh." He didn't prevaricate, didn't make excuses. "Apparently we consulted on that region, so I guess it's possible they would have mugs."

"Could they have had something to do with my capture?"

"Not as far as I know."

"What about our email transmissions?"

"I always used my personal email from home."

Okay. At some point I had to trust him. I still hadn't forgotten the CIA could be tracking him...all because I filed that damn form. I refused to feel guilty. We'd been together. So maybe I should have told him about the CIA sooner. But as soon as I'd revealed my true profession to him, I exposed him to danger and to scrutiny. "Unless somehow the CIA got ahold of those emails."

"Why'd you wait?"

"What?" But, I knew what he was asking.

"Why did you wait to tell them about us?"

"I hate paperwork." I flipped back at him, unwilling to bare my soul.

He stopped, stared at me.

"Okay. Sorry." I tossed the garbage from Breadline in a can. "I'd wanted to keep you to myself. Until I filed that form, until I told you about the CIA, you were all mine." In a way no one ever had been.

I'd cherished that sense of us. That sense of 'we' that I might never be able to get back. But I wanted it back.

As if I'd surprised him, he blinked. Unspoken feelings stretched between us and like a giant rubber band, we could only pull so far apart before boinging back together. Then, Jordan threaded his fingers through mine and started walking again.

Once we arrived at the car, the plan to meet with my contact at the CIA needed to be put into action.

"I'll need to change my appearance."

"Yeah."

In the car, I did a quick change into a black stretchy turtleneck and a black stretchy skirt, courtesy of Thea, and wrapped a vivid scarf in hot pink, purple and black around my neck.

No self-respecting agent would ever wear a piece of clothing that could trap them or potentially injure them. I hoped even if someone had a whiff of recognition they would discount it.

To alter my appearance, I sprayed more gray over my black dye job, smoothed it back into a crisp bun, and added an inflatable prosthetic I'd had in my backpack to make my stomach look as if I had a roll of fat. The clingy top only accented my new tummy.

I tucked some cotton balls into my cheeks to add fullness to my face. We didn't have time for anything more sophisticated.

I was ready. Hopefully this move would give us some answers.

"Let's do it."

CHAPTER 29

October 19
11:15 am
The Mall, Washington D.C.

The meet was set.

I'd used an extra disposable cell phone I'd had in my messenger bag and followed the instructions I'd been given long ago.

The recording had come on and said the castle was sold. I punched in the requisite code and left the meeting time and place Jordan and I had agreed on.

So here we were at the Smithsonian Air and Space Museum.

Jordan went in first and purchased his ticket for the show on the Cosmos in the Albert Einstein Planetarium.

After he entered, I waited five minutes, watching the doors, watching for any surveillance.

I hunched my shoulders, carrying a giant handbag with all of my belongings tucked inside.

No weapons, as they frowned on that sort of thing at the Smithsonian. The museum was predictably busy, although not as packed as a Spring Break day.

I'd hoped by picking a tourist destination we'd avoid security details looking for glory.

These guards weren't focused on finding a fugitive from justice. What sort of person on the Most Wanted list would take time off to check out the Apollo 11 memorabilia?

At least that was my theory.

After five minutes passed, I'd seen no one suspicious. I also hadn't seen my boss arrive.

I got in line, shuffling my feet as I progressed toward the entrance. At the door, I grabbed a brochure and sat on a bench near the planetarium and pretended to read, but the big glasses perched on my nose made the print blurry.

Watching the crowd, I studied the people, looking for anyone who was paying more attention to the people than the exhibits.

The crowd was boisterous. Children running and screaming with delight. Dads and grandfathers staring in wonder at the older airplanes suspended from the ceiling. The shiny hull of the space shuttle jutted up to the second story. The chatter of several different languages swirled around me.

I let my eyes go unfocused and centered into the Zen of waiting, listening without a specific target, letting my ear pick up words or phrases that caught my attention.

"...ai faim...let the baby touch...Heinrich, stop running..Jesus, it's hot in here...remember watching on the television...."

Nothing jumped out at me.

Jordan waited in line, hands clasped in front, shoulders

back, as he occasionally stared at the plane suspended near his position.

He didn't fidget or look around or glance at his watch, as if waiting for someone. He was in character, completely absorbed, and didn't break.

The other people waiting were hanging over the railing pointing to the various objects.

Out of the periphery of my vision, I noted someone rush up to the end of the line, polished Cordovan wing tips clicking on the floor, tan raincoat flying out behind them. Carefully I slouched against the wall, while my heart pounded in my chest so hard I thought it would bust right out of my ribs and bounce across the floor.

Carson Black, Director of Field Operations for the NSA, waited to hand in his ticket. This was not good news. Carson wasn't my CIA contact.

The belt loops loosely tied in back left the coat hanging perpetually open, and showed only glimpses of his perfectly pressed gabardine suit. His dark bald head gleamed under the heavy industrial lights hanging from the ceiling.

The unnatural florescent highlighted the sheen on the top of his head, as if he'd run to get there in time. True we hadn't given him a big window. Except he shouldn't have been at the other end of that phone line.

As I pretended to study my brochure, I ignored the funny twist in my stomach. Not morning sickness. But the little lump of affection and stress all rolled into one.

For all intents, Carson had been a surrogate father to me. I didn't know how he'd react to my current change in status. I didn't have so many people in my life that I could afford to lose one.

And I had to be suspicious.

My boss wasn't here, but Carson was?

Why and how would Carson have access to my contact information? What was he doing here?

If he had backup coming or if he had a wire, he didn't show it. That kind of relaxed body language took years to cultivate. He had no little tells to indicate a stiffness or itch from the tape. No hitch in his step. No roll in his shoulder.

Oddly enough, he'd been the one to steady me after my grandparents' death. He'd taken me under his wing, so to speak, and even had me over to his home for Easter in what had become a tradition.

He'd counseled me, mentored me, given me advice on an investment advisor, and generally been a sounding board. He'd birthed my entrance into the espionage world. Could he be here now to end it?

I hadn't seen him much recently. Since I'd taken up with Jordan, really.

Carson had a wife. He seemed to make their relationship work with his job, but I didn't want to know if he thought my relationship with Jordan was a bad idea.

So, I'd begged off the last time he'd called to get together for a drink.

I continued to observe the area around me. No one had taken undue interest in either Carson or Jordan.

I couldn't take the chance that somehow Carson had identified Jordan. Couldn't leave Jordan without a defense. The plan had been for Jordan to observe from inside the auditorium and watch for my contact to see what he would do. But I was changing the plan.

With one minute left to enter the auditorium, I shuffled up to the ticket taker, clutched a wadded up tissue in my right hand, and smiled at the rotund lady taking the computer-generated, time-stamped ticket.

I ambled into the auditorium, took a moment to orient myself and find both Jordan and Carson.

The circular room had a pit in the center where the images of the 360 degree film would be projected onto the domed ceiling.

The lights were, thankfully, already low.

We'd agreed I would wait in the lobby. Screw that. I wanted to be close. For backup and observation. I couldn't protect Jordan from the lobby.

The theater was about three quarters full.

I wandered into the room to find a seat in the back row, right by the exit.

I eased down slowly, wiggled the amplification device into my ear, then rolled my thumb over the little wheel to turn the device on. The ear bud fitted uncomfortably into my left ear, but hopefully the device was unobtrusive. I plopped the giant purse on my lap and dialed up the sound.

The background noise from the other occupants blasted in my ear as a woman in front of me let out a monster sneeze. Jeez, it's a wonder she hadn't blown herself halfway to Baltimore with that one.

A little kid halfway down the other side kicked at the row of seats in front of him until I wanted to scream. The lady sneezed again.

I surreptitiously quartered the circular room searching for both Carson and Jordan. I found Jordan immediately, his broad shoulders easily identified even in the dim light.

And then I found Carson.

My heart stopped.

They were sitting together. And it was clear they knew each other.

I must have jerked, because for a split second, Jordan's

attention was focused on me. His body stiffened and his mouth tightened as recognition dawned.

He'd made me.

Now the question was...had Carson?

Even more important. Had I been set up?

It was hard to say who was more surprised...him or Carson.

Jordan had seen Carson as soon as he walked in, of course. The last time Jordan had seen this man, they'd been working clean up on the shooting of Susan Chen's associate.

Carson made a circuit of the room before settling in next to Jordan.

Carson said softly, "I'm assuming this is not a coincidence."

"You wired?" Jordan asked Carson through clenched teeth, and hoped the answer was a solid no.

"Who had time?" Carson returned.

That wasn't a no.

If Carson had brought any backup, Staci had placed herself right in the line of apprehension.

Since he'd spotted her he'd studiously avoided looking at her. Dammit. This wasn't what they had agreed on.

Didn't she trust him at all?

And what was the deal? Carson Black worked for the

NSA, not the CIA. He was Jamie Hunt's boss. Not Staci's. So what was he doing here?

He didn't know Carson well enough to figure out if the guy was nervous. He seemed relaxed if a bit winded from getting here so quickly. Clearly Carson had come to meet with Staci. Maybe they could get some information out of him.

"Let's make this quick." Jordan surreptitiously activated the record button on his cell phone. "Can you help?"

"After you turn off that device." Carson crossed his arms over his chest and leaned back in his seat as if getting situated before the movie short began.

Jordan nodded once and flicked the button off. It had been worth a try. He consciously slowed his heart rate, concentrating on the flow and ebb of the blood through the ventricles.

He was more used to covert stakeouts than up close and personal meetings but he had to get his head back in this game. This guy was a master of espionage.

"You see the news?" Jordan asked as music piped into the room.

"Ah, yes." Carson rubbed a finger along the bridge of his nose. "Nasty business."

Jordan knew he had to be careful what he said. Just in case. "Why was that information released?"

"I'm as much in the dark as...you," Carson responded. "I tried to do some checking, but suddenly that file is extremely high clearance."

"Is it possible they don't realize what they've unleashed?"

"Probable." Carson relaxed back into the plush seat, one leg crossed over the other. "This has all the earmarks of a CF."

"Yeah."

Jordan wasn't sure how to ask the next question without revealing he had more knowledge than he should.

"Could this have anything to do with a certain file?"

"I don't know of any file that would be relevant," Carson answered calmly.

That was a lie, and Jordan knew it. "Let me refresh, a numerical file."

"What do you know about that?"

Shit. He'd hit a nerve. He could feel it.

Maybe Staci was right. Maybe her troubles did stem from her investigation into the mysterious Department 5491.

The music crescendoed to a climax and the theater went completely dark.

Jordan waited until the soundtrack began again before he answered slowly. "It exists."

"It should be irrelevant."

"You're sure?"

Even with peripheral vision, Jordan could see the pulse in Carson's neck pick up. "I don't see why or how." But his voice was faint and lacking conviction.

"Since she was accumulating data...perhaps someone wasn't happy with the contents."

"That's something I shall have to explore." Carson pursed his mouth, lips tightening as if he'd swallowed a sour grape.

He reached into his jacket pocket, the movement had Jordan tensing. All Carson did was pull out a roll of antacids. With a buffed, manicured finger he thumbed one disc into his palm. In an almost delicate move, he slid the antacid onto his tongue and closed his eyes for one brief second.

"I think it's the key to finding why all of this is happening."

Carson blanched. "It's a dead issue."

The lights from a meteorite exploding on the ceiling showered over Carson's face.

Jordan hesitated unsure about broaching this next subject. He was not even sure there was any connection to Staci, but unable to shake the possibility they were missing something.

"Was there a report filed regarding the events from last week?" He knew Carson would get the reference to the shooting at the Presidential Suites and the capture of Susan Chen. Carson had been there.

"Of course."

"Would it have been released to members of the Senate?"

"Most definitely not." Carson pretended to watch the stars float across the 'sky'. "Why?"

"Someone attempted to question me about those events, and he referenced a report."

Carson raised one brow. "Who?"

Rather than say Senator Jordan's name or the state of Virginia aloud, he gave the nickname. "Old Dominion."

"He is known for being a hardliner but also a friend to our," *the espionage*, "community." Carson lolled his head back against the seat and whispered, "I'll check into how he got access."

"How come you placed the ad?"

"I've been...concerned."

"How did you know what to say?"

"Because I'm the one who set up the process years ago."

Jordan didn't say anything but glanced around. They'd

been together too long. They needed to get the hell out of here.

"There's a lot of nasty refuse coming her way," Carson said. "Why not just get out?"

"I protect what's mine." Jordan decided to go for broke. She'd only reluctantly agreed to stay and with the slightest incentive, she'd be gone. "And she's mine."

"She's very lucky," Carson commented softly.

I'm the lucky one.

"Is she...okay?"

Jordan would bet Carson had seen the report from the prison as well. "As well as can be expected."

Carson's face tightened. "Let her know I'm available to help in any way I can."

"You mean that?" Jordan clearly heard the sincerity in Carson's voice. There had also been an element of affection and tenderness which surprised him.

"Of course," Carson replied.

"Thanks," Jordan said.

"Be careful. And watch your back." Carson clapped him on the shoulder. His gaze shot briefly to Staci and then back to Jordan. "Both of them."

Without another word, he was gone.

THEY MADE it back to the car without incident. Jordan hadn't bothered to talk on the way there. He was too worried that if he opened his mouth, he'd start shouting.

"How do you know Carson?" she asked after she slid into the front seat of the car.

When she ripped the stomach prosthetic from around

her waist and pressed to deflate the air, he caught a tantalizing glimpse of the soft skin of her stomach.

Not the right time. He took a deep breath and prepared to be calm and reasonable. "Carson? I met him when I helped rescue John Wishbone and Bella Holden."

"Carson Black, Director of Field Operations for the NSA was on an op with you. Right," she snapped, or tried to, her words coming out garbled. She spit out the cotton.

"The NSA doesn't have Field Ops." His denial was automatic.

She snorted. "Yes they do."

He sat thinking about that for a minute. "Okay. My turn."

She sat stubbornly in the passenger seat, arms crossed over her chest mutinously. A small piece of cotton fuzz was trapped on the curve of her chin.

"You know Carson."

"Obviously."

"So when you saw him, why the hell didn't you get out of the museum?" Jordan gripped the steering wheel with both hands. "What if he'd been there to bring you in?"

"If I left, I certainly wouldn't have seen you two getting all friendly."

They spoke at the same time.

"I was trying to get information to protect you."

"I was trying to protect you."

Emotions swirled around the interior of the car, turning the air heavy with their pent up aggression and frustration.

Without volition, Jordan reached out to brush the piece of cotton from her face, rubbing his thumb tenderly along her mouth to clear the final wisp. "My heart stopped when I saw you."

"It was unexpected, seeing him." She relented, for a

moment turning her cheek into his palm. "I just wanted to make sure you were okay."

"I'm fine."

Staci sighed. "It was a waste of time."

"Maybe not. He was adamant that 5491 had nothing to do with your problems."

A little too adamant?

They were both silent.

Finally, she said, "I think we should talk to Katerina Wolfe."

"Who?"

"She's another person on the 5491 list."

"Why would you want to get anywhere near her?"

"The idea's been brewing in the back of my mind."

He was more surprised than if she'd said she was hoping for twins.

"Both Zeke and Jamie are out of town. But Wolfe lives in the area."

He blinked once, slowly then his eyebrow rose. "And you don't think she'll turn you in?"

"Think about it. Barb said we should talk to the other people who had the drug. Katerina is connected." Staci argued. "She's part of 5491."

Jordan finished. "She also works for the Defense Intelligence Agency. Like Zeke, she's probably still on leave which means she has a vested interest in figuring this out."

The more he considered the idea, he could see the merit. But he had to remind her. "Or she could get back in their good graces by turning you in."

"So we're careful."

He had conditions to be met before he'd agree. "I cover your back and listen in."

"Deal."

Jordan continued, "If I sense any kind of trap or set up, we abort."

"Fine."

"If she's being followed, we abort."

"Fine."

CHAPTER 31

October 19
      12:00 noon
International Spy Museum, Washington D.C.

WHAT KIND of espionage agent arranges a meeting in the Spy Museum? Located on F Street, the museum was either a brilliant spot or a disaster waiting to happen.

Rather than take the elevator to the beginning tour room, we slipped passed the exhibit exit door and made our way through the museum backwards. We strolled up the corrugated steel flooring ramp, ignoring the lighted glass cases featuring spy memorabilia, until we arrived at the agreed upon meeting room which chronicled the escapades of Mata Hari, Harriet Tubman, and others, The Sisterhood of Spies.

The irony did not escape me.

Katerina Wolfe had taken the bait nicely. We'd agreed to meet in twenty minutes, which gave us just enough time to get here. Luckily we'd been able to buy tickets for the right time.

For this meeting I felt I needed to be recognizable. I had combed out most of the gray and hoped the average tourist wouldn't take notice of my face or recognize me, assuming they even watched television on vacation.

But Katerina would know who I was.

If I was making a mistake, so be it. But I truly believed the only way to move forward was to collect information from Human Intelligence. I'd used all my resources for CommInt. Katerina Wolfe was perfect.

"Professor." Someone hailed me from behind. My brain clicked quickly seeking target recognition through voice pattern.

Jordan tensed. I heard his huff of breath through our simplistic communication system, courtesy of the gift shop downstairs.

He led point, five feet in front of me, in case we had any trouble. Because we'd gone the reverse of regular foot traffic, neither one of us had anticipated a threat from behind.

I hushed Jordan softly. "He may not have seen the press conference." And truly, how many students would purposely make contact with a professor that hadn't seen them? Unless they were being used as--

"Bait," Jordan murmured.

I ran through the possibilities. "I'm considered armed and dangerous. I don't think so. They'd catch a rash of shit if I hurt a student." Or a tourist.

Jordan's fingers brushed the side of his coat hiding his firearm. "I'm still ready."

"Professor," the kid called again as he sprinted up the metal floor.

I pivoted slowly.

Six feet of lanky bones, the pale Asian kid was clad in designer jeans and a pink Izod. "Matthew." His last name escaped me.

"Hey, Professor." Matt's chest heaved, his breath bellowing in and out, bony shoulders lifting and falling, as he tried to catch his breath. "I thought that was you."

As if he'd just realized I was a physical mess, his eyes widened.

Matt had been a particularly enthusiastic student. I had never been able to figure out if his enthusiasm was for the subject matter or me.

"You too." I lied through my teeth and willed Jordan to act calm and cool. "How's this semester going?"

"Pretty good." His big brown eyes stared at me with hopeful intensity through his funky wire-rimmed glasses. "I was hoping you'd be teaching again this semester."

"I usually just teach in the spring."

His face lit up. "So you'll be teaching again next spring?"

Assuming I wasn't in prison or dead. "I'm contracted."

"Sweet." He just stood there staring at me with a slightly goofy expression on his face as if he didn't realize his crush was there for the world to see.

Jordan cleared his throat softly. But I already knew. I'd stood in one place for far too long. No way was this kid a lure or bait.

"Hey, nice to see you, Matt." I glanced apologetically down at the watch on my wrist.

"Oh, uh, yeah." Matt's grin faded.

Jordan had paused at a display, watching our interaction in the reflection of the glass case. I had to get moving before the kid noticed Jordan was spending an inordinate amount of time there.

When Matt saw the news and reported to the authorities that he'd seen me, and he would, I didn't want them having any idea I had a companion. That was assuming that Carson kept his mouth shut.

"Nice to see you too, Professor."

"Hope to see you next semester."

His gaze brightened. "Yeah. Me too."

"Take care, Matt." I waved casually, not wanting to turn my back on him in case my instincts were totally off and he really was bait.

"See anything or anyone suspicious?" I asked softly doing my best to scan for surveillance without being obvious.

"We're good." His voice was clipped, his mouth a flat line.

"What's wrong then?"

"Matthew Cho."

Cho. That was his name. Except...I hadn't mentioned Matt's last name.

"Yes."

I waited for the anger I could see Jordan holding inside.

"Mother killed in World Trade Center bombings. Father works for the State Department. No siblings. At this time, not a candidate but should be watched. He has the potential for recruitment," he recited.

My heart iced. "That's my file on Matt."

"Verbatim."

"You memorized the file on Matt?" Inside I was freaking. That meant he'd seen my files. "How?" Why?

"I memorized your files on all your recent 'students'".

That hadn't answered my question, and he knew it.

I started walking, slowly, deliberately as if I had no cares in the world and had no specific place to be. Inside I was running around like the road runner with my tail on fire. I couldn't afford to panic, and I couldn't afford to make any mistakes.

And I had a meeting with Katerina in just a few minutes.

"How?"

"After you disappeared and everyone presumed you were dead--I knew you weren't--so I decided to look for you."

By breaking into top secret, encrypted, and password protected files? "Look for me how?"

"I had to be discreet, by this time someone had surveillance on your house 24/7." Jordan took a deep breath. "So I broke into your private files and read them."

There were so many points in that sentence that needed to be addressed.

"I guess my password was easy enough." I'd used his initials and the day we'd met. Usually I change my password once a month but for sentimental, sappy,...stupid reasons I'd kept his initials and the date we met, far, far longer than a week. I'd thought since the computer was in a hidden room in my house and not connected to the internet, the information in my files was safe.

Clearly, I'd been wrong.

"My initials." He was silent, the only sound the ping of our heels echoing against metal floor.

The best way to interrogate is to drop a bomb and then wait. The longer you wait, the more nervous the interrogee gets.

"Never in a million years did I think that you would use my initials."

It was so high school, like doodling his name in cursive all over paper. I'd known when I'd done it and still hadn't been able to resist the temptation. I'd gotten a secret little thrill every time I'd logged on.

But at some point he must have figured it out.

Next point.

"You read my files."

"Yeah."

He'd read my work. Was he intrigued? Disgusted?

"All of them?"

"Yeah."

"And then...."

"I checked them out." Jordan's breath was coming faster. I knew it wasn't from exertion, so it must be from emotion.

The question remained, which one?

"You...."

"Checked them out."

I wasn't sure what to say. I'd known he wouldn't approve of my work. It was the main reason I hadn't explained what I do. He wouldn't understand and in my heart I was afraid if I told him, then he'd leave.

What did I say to that revelation?

I had no idea.

My mind wouldn't work. I didn't know what direction to go next. My head swirled with the implications that he'd looked into my files. Those files were extremely incriminating.

And extremely classified.

But not all of them. "Then you know Matthew did a stint for kiva.org?"

"Yeah."

"Where I sent him." I was compelled to add, just so he

would understand that I didn't send every kid off to be a terrorist or to work for the CIA.

But I also realized that Jordan Ramirez now had information about a significant number of terrorist and CIA recruits for the past several years.

And yet he'd still come looking for me. Hope unfurled within me. If he didn't approve, why didn't he just walk away? And why was he still here?

I walked into the Mata Hari room. The rest of the conversation would have to wait. I needed to concentrate on my surroundings and this meeting.

Katerina shouldn't have had enough time to set up any sort of trap, but I couldn't make any assumptions.

Any mistake now could get me killed.

CHAPTER 32

Jordan assessed the specs for the Secret History of History room, shutting down the emotion he'd let bleed through at seeing one of Staci's possible recruits in the museum.

The room had variables he didn't like.

Open.

Accessible. Anyone could walk in.

Plenty of security cameras so they'd be easy targets.

On the plus side, the lighting was dim and the museum difficult to police with a warren of walkways and timed entry tickets to control crowd and traffic flow. He was pretty sure the hourly security guys were more worried about kids vandalizing the James Bond toys than looking for Federal "Wanted" fugitives meeting with Defense Intelligence Agency employees.

Just in case, he had their exit strategy mapped out.

Partially hidden behind a Chinese screen, he stood ten feet away from the small movie room.

When he'd worked HRT, surveillance points were set up a thousand feet away. They'd watched drug dealers in the jungle or guarded rebel compounds waiting for a clear shot. Pretty much everyone was guilty of something.

Here pretty much everyone was innocent.

Katerina Wolfe approached the meeting place cautiously. She was five four tops, her figure bordering on petite.

He warned Staci through their comm system. "Don't underestimate her because of her size." Some of the meanest guys were the little ones.

"Roger," Staci said softly.

Katerina walked into the screening room, clearly unsure what to expect. Jordan couldn't blame her. He'd called her on her cell and been short and succinct and cryptic as hell: *I have information about your suspension.*

They had been right about Katerina. She was on suspension. Just like Zeke. All the espionage agents who had been given the gene manipulation drug and been kidnapped were on suspension until their agencies could ascertain if they'd compromised national security during their abductions.

When he was on the phone with her and indicated he might have information about why she'd been kidnapped, she'd jumped on it.

Jordan quartered the surrounding area looking for anyone showing undue interest in Katerina.

Everything appeared normal.

Everything sounded normal, the clang of feet, the shouts of children, the admonishments of parents to slow down.

Staci stayed concealed in the shadows. He'd wanted to be the front man, but Staci didn't want him linked with her in any way and while it chafed, he understood.

He was her ace.

"Ms. Wolfe."

Only the two women occupied the small movie room.

Katerina looked over at Staci in the shadows. "A man called me. Who are you?"

"No threat," Staci responded.

Jordan marveled at her body language which was as non-threatening as she could make it.

"I'm not susceptible to blackmail," Katerina said abruptly.

Katerina's black checked blazer barely hid the straps of a shoulder holster. In her late thirties, her white blond hair was regulation short and spiked, her nails unpainted and trimmed, her hands strong. The defined lines of her face gave her a hard edge.

Staci said, "I want to ask you some questions."

Katerina narrowed her gaze. "Nope. I'm not getting in any more trouble than I already am." She executed a military sharp pivot.

"Wait." Staci stayed in the shadows, keeping her face hidden. "I wanted to ask you about 5491."

"Never heard of it." Katerina started walking to the exit of the room, no falter in her stride, no stiffening in her shoulders.

Staci said softly, "Everyone on suspension, all the kidnap victims, receive monthly payments from a department in the NSA--5491. We believe they are reparations for the deaths of their parents or grandparents."

Katerina froze. "Insurance."

"Come on. How many insurance companies pay every month for over fifteen years?"

Katerina didn't say a word, her back still to Staci.

In the background, whoops from a particularly boisterous group of young children echoed in the corridor. Parents ambled by at a slower pace, laughing.

Jordan could see her weighing her words carefully. She pivoted back around to face Staci. "I was kidnapped and compromised because of those insurance payments?"

"Not as far as we can tell, but everyone kidnapped has been receiving those payments."

"So...what?"

"Something disturbing is going on."

Katerina's gaze flicked to the lighted alcove holding a picture of Harriet Tubman then back to the shadow of Staci. "I'm already in enough trouble. I can't help you." But she hadn't moved.

"This concerns your family."

"I don't have any family," Katerina snapped. "Just my little boy, and I need a job to take care of him."

"Why'd you come today?"

"I thought if there was any way, any information that you had that could get me cleared for active duty sooner, I would grab at it."

"I believe we can help each other."

Katerina paced around the display podium holding a copy of a communique from Mata Hari. "What the hell did you expect to accomplish here?"

They'd lost her. Jordan knew it would be impossible to get any more information, especially without giving anything away. As if Staci realized that too, the air shifted. Shit. Too late to stop her. Staci stepped out in front Katerina, revealing her face.

Jordan's heart double-timed in his chest. A hot ball of worry lodged in his throat. This was not part of the plan. Dammit.

"How much do you know about me?"

Jordan could see the moment Staci's identity hit Katerina. He pulled out his Glock and held the weapon at his side, seconds before Katerina's hand moved to her holster.

"Holy shit. You are alive." Katerina blinked once, twice.

Staci held her hand up in the classic gesture of stop. "Calm down."

"You're...."

"Not armed or dangerous." Staci paused.

Jordan kept his weapon at the ready. He wouldn't miss, not from this distance.

"Put the guns away. It's counter-productive," Staci commented, her voice full of reason.

"I'm in such trouble." Katerina Wolfe took a step backwards. "They're already vetting me all the way back to kindergarten. I am so fucked."

"I'm not going to tell anyone we met," Staci said.

"Right." Katerina laughed bitterly. "My career is already halfway down the shitter. This just totally caps it off."

"I need to ask you some questions," Staci said calmly.

The wheels were turning behind Katerina's cornflower blues. "Why are you here? Shouldn't you be OUTCONUS?"

"Outside the Continental U.S. would be a lot safer for me now. Unfortunately, my business is here in D.C."

"Business," Katerina dropped her hand from her holster.

"I'm being set up." Staci wiped a stray hair from her cheek.

"I read your file." Katerina's voice was scornful. "You recruit terror trainees."

CHAPTER 33

Katerina believed my press. After being outted on national television, my career was pretty much over. Any loyalty I might have had was gone. Maybe it was all supposed to shake out this way. Now I'd have more time to devote to de-mining and making a difference for women, for families in Afghanistan. What the hell.

I decided right then, I needed to defend myself. "For the CIA."

You've heard that expression jaw dropped, but until now I don't think I'd ever actually seen it happen.

I could see her processing at rapid speed while I continued.

"I started looking into Department 5491, and a month later I was imprisoned in Afghanistan, declared dead by the U.S. Government, and then as soon as I resurfaced in the U.S. someone outted me in a national press conference." I hammered home my points.

"I think it has to do with Department 5491 from which you are receiving payments, and connected to why you were kidnapped, and resulted in your suspension."

Katerina Wolfe shook her head in denial, stepping back slowly one at a time. "I can't get involved with you, with this."

"You are involved." I thought of the only lever that would twist her. I placed a hand over my belly and hoped I wouldn't have to threaten her son. "Where did the information about me come from? Do you know?"

"I've been suspended for the past two weeks." Her gaze flickered away from mine.

"But your office knew about me before you were suspended."

We needed her to confirm this. "Yeah."

"Who is the military guy at the press conference, Major Vandenburg?"

"Major Tony Vandenburg."

"What's he in charge of?"

"He runs the Civil Affairs Division."

Why would that guy care that I was in Afghanistan? The Civil Affairs Division had multiple programs run by the military to facilitate aid to the countries we occupied. But every village I'd visited seemed to be benefitting from his programs.

Familiar bile rose up in my throat. Dammit, not now.

"I was captured in Afghanistan eight weeks ago." My voice was rough with effort to keep the contents of my stomach in my stomach, instead of all over the Spy Museum. "Someone set me up. The region is friendly to Americans. And yet, I was imprisoned. Then once I escaped, there were American soldiers at the village near the prison looking to recapture me."

Knowledge bloomed in Katerina's eyes.

I continued, "They aren't about to piss off Americans. We're paying them to destroy their poppy fields, protecting them from the Taliban forces, we're giving them money and supplies through Operation: Rebuild."

The facts were clicking through her brain, I could see her putting them all together and coming up with the same conclusion I had.

"They aren't going to piss off Americans," I deliberately used the phrase again, "unless someone with high-level connections got to them." Perhaps offered them a better deal with the government than they already had.

"Maybe your imprisonment was a mistake."

Mistake my ass. "For two whole weeks?"

"Communiqués get lost. Slow military time." A fine sheen of perspiration coated her face as Katerina put the pieces together. Fear coalesced in her eyes. "I can't help you."

"Someone wanted me to stop investigating 5491. Your grandparents were murdered. And the government is making reparations. Doesn't that tell you that something stinks?"

"I have to protect my son." She said bitterly, "You picked a hell of a day to bring this up."

Well, shit. The anniversary of the death of my grandparents and hers was today.

Grief hit me in the chest, gripping my muscles in a hold so complete I could only lock my knees and hope I didn't fall down. Fifteen years ago today, I became an orphan.

A child alone.

Until Carson had offered me a way out of the grief and malaise I'd been mired in.

Something suddenly occurred to me. If all of our relatives had died on the same day...when had we all been recruited? Right then? Right after their deaths? Like I was? That question was worth considering.

"Did Carson recruit you too?"

Her eyes were wild now. "I don't know anyone named Carson."

But she did. I could see the truth.

Katerina's gaze flicked away to the screen showing footage from the OSS and World War II. "My grandparents are gone. Nothing I do now will bring them back."

"Just tell me why you looked scared when I mentioned the region in Afghanistan." Jesus, I wasn't sure if the lurch in my stomach this time was from the baby in my body or the remembrance of my stay in that prison.

"This is public record, or relatively public. I'm not telling you anything you couldn't find out without a little bit of digging." She took a step back and then another getting ready to bolt. "Major Vandy was in Afghanistan that week."

The major in the press conference that announced my status as a terrorist recruiter was in Afghanistan when I'd been captured? A chill wiggled down my spine. Major Vandenburg again. "Who is this guy?"

"That's all. I'm gone."

I put on my best menacing face. "Don't tell anyone about this meeting."

She snorted. "Right."

My stomach lurched. "I'm trusting you. I'll turn around, you have ten seconds to get out."

I turned around, leaning against the wall, swallowed down the nausea, and listened to the slight scuff of Katerina's shoes. Jordan's touch against my back was the first indication that she was gone. She was hiding something. It was possible we weren't done with Katerina Wolfe.

"We need to get out of here," Jordan said.

No shit. Except every time I took a step my body told me how badly I was feeling.

"Come on." He hustled me out. "We need to get gone, in case Katerina or Carson turned you in."

"Could go either way," I theorized. If I'd been her, I wouldn't admit to even having heard of Staci Grant. But as of late, I'd become a poor predictor of human behavior.

And Carson, I had no idea.

"I'm betting not," he commented.

I snorted.

Except the effect was lost when I tried to brush the extra long bangs from my eyes and my hand and arm shook so badly I couldn't connect with the small strands of hair.

"We need to...." Do something. A wave of exhaustion swept over me. I could see the car, parked maybe twenty feet away.

Suddenly as if I were stuck in a vat of viscous liquid, fatigue sucked at my legs, slowing my movements to a crawl.

My head hurt with the effort of trying to move...some sort of disconnect between brain and body.

In theory, Jordan was only curling his arm protectively around me, but if he let go I would sink to the ground in a puddle of bones and muscle.

Even the effort to speak was too much. I slumped into his grasp. The rounded curve of his shoulder pressed against my cheek, his bicep supported my back, curving against my deltoids, and his left elbow and forearm held me upright as he half-carried me to our car.

"I don't feel so good."

"You're a goddamn mess." Except he didn't sound angry. I blinked up at him trying to figure out his expression. Lines crinkled around his eyes, not happy laugh lines, more like 'how did I wind up here?' lines.

"You could just drop me at a hotel," I offered. Part of

me hoped he'd take me up on the suggestion. The other part screamed a fast denial.

"Right."

He got me to the car and shoved me in the passenger seat.

My skull lolled back against the headrest. I knew I should buckle my belt but really what was the point?

The meeting with Katerina, her unwillingness to talk, Carson's warning, the man-hunt. It was all too much. "I'm dead."

I couldn't dredge up the emotion to care.

"You are not dead," he said fiercely. But he hadn't had as much time as I had to assimilate everything against me.

"Look at me," I countered, even my voice was a shaky trembling mess. Figuratively I was already dead. I wasn't myself, would never be that woman again. I'd lost the essence of me.

The government, with all their resources, was after me.

Jordan pulled the seat belt across my middle and clicked it shut. Then he put the car into gear.

We rolled into traffic. And I wondered if we were being followed even now.

I wouldn't care, except....

I had to consider Jordan. "You need to dump me off somewhere."

"Right." His lips tightened. "You really think I would leave you?"

"You need to protect yourself." I rubbed shaky hands up and down my biceps.

He ignored me.

"Really this is for the best." I had i.d. and credit cards in my new name. If I managed to retrieve my bolt bag, I could be in Cuba tomorrow.

"Whose best?" He drove without looking at me.

I kept my gaze on him as if by lasering him with my eyes, I could get him to agree. I took in his broad shoulders, the long, lean strength of his forearms muscles bunched as he gripped the steering wheel. "Yours."

The silence in the car built. "What about the baby?"

The baby? Oops. I'd forgotten. Sort of.

He flinched at my instinctive reaction. "Yeah. That's kind of what I thought."

I opened my mouth to defend myself and then wondered if this was the way to get rid of him. If I acted cavalierly about the baby, he'd leave.

"With throwing up every five minutes, I thought perhaps the baby would be a little more present in your mind." His tone was even, neutral but the disapproval was there. Below the surface.

"I guess I hadn't really equated my physical problems with the baby." This didn't seem like a baby but more of an extended, and particularly ugly, flu bug. It'd been going on so long I'd just sort of resigned myself to the discomfort, rolled with it if you will.

Jordan didn't say a word, just drove.

"Where are we going?"

Jordan just kept driving.

Fatigue smothered my thoughts, pulling me down into an abyss. My eyelids pressed down over my eyeballs. With almost physical effort, I pried them back open. My chin tipped down. I jerked.

"Rest. I'll take care of you."

Longing pulsed through me. Wouldn't that be nice for a change? That wasn't right. I was supposed to take care of him. I must have dozed because when he turned onto gravel, the sudden grating noise startled me awake.

Panic flashed through me. My arms curled around my stomach as my fingers fumbled for the seat belt. I forced a calm I was far from feeling and assessed our surroundings. He'd pulled the car up to an old clapboard house.

Big hydrangea bushes with flower balls in pale blue and white edged the house. A whimsical mailbox, painted to look like a birdhouse with a bluebird as the flag, sat on a post.

A huge American flag hung from the flagpole on the column supporting the overhang of the front porch. Two rockers and a tiny table with a pair of reading glasses and a paperback welcomed visitors.

"Relax." His voice rumbled in my ear. "We're at my mother and aunt's house."

I blinked. His mother and his aunt?

Oh no. I shook my head vehemently.

I wasn't ready to meet his family. Shit. I looked down at myself. The sleeves of the black top were pushed up, revealing the yellowed bruises around my wrists. Angry red spots and black pigment splotches mottled my skin. I had no makeup on and my hair was rough from the hair dye. I looked terrible.

"*Tía Lupe* may be able to help you with your morning sickness." His voice was flat in response to my obvious horror. He'd misunderstood.

"I can't." I tried to keep the hysteria out of my response, but based on his face I hadn't come close.

A parody of a smile touched his mouth. "Yeah. Not exactly how I'd planned it either."

Vulnerability curled through me. Two months ago, I would have been thrilled and apprehensive at the news that he'd planned for me to meet his family. Now I was flat out terrified. He needed to be getting further away from me, not drawing his family into more danger.

"You need to drop me somewhere anonymous and get far away from me." My panic came through with a vehemence that surprised even him.

"I can't do that." Jordan slid out of the car and came around to open my door. Fluffy honeysuckle bushes surrounded the yard, enclosing the space and offering a serene privacy.

An old Pontiac le Baron boat was parked in the ruts, worn down to dirt, in the grass driveway. The garage door was closed.

"Garage door must be broken again," Jordan murmured.

When we'd pulled in only a single lamp burned in the front living room. "It doesn't look like anyone is home." I couldn't keep the hope out of my voice.

"Parlor light. No one ever uses the room, but it is always ready for company." His affection for the tradition and his family was clear.

The back of the house was all lit up. That was where his mother and aunt lived.

"Is this where you grew up?"

He laughed, but it wasn't a happy sound. "Uh, no."

Jordan faltered for a moment. I watched him visibly brace his shoulders. That little hesitation tore at my heart. He was ashamed of me.

"Come on. We need to get inside."

Now it was my turn to hesitate. He'd been raised by his aunt and his mother. No father in the picture. No real role model, and yet he'd turned into one of the most honorable men I knew.

Initially, I'd been drawn by his looks. Who wouldn't have

been? But what had kept me with him for longer than any other man was his core sense of decency and moral compass. Those values had to come from these women.

They couldn't possibly have anything positive to say about me. I'd rather spend another day in prison than hurt his family.

"I don't think this is such a good idea."

"I know it's a bad idea, but I'm fresh out of better ones." His fingers held mine in an iron grip, yet his clasp was gentle. He rubbed his thumb over the pulse beating in my wrist and a long slow shiver shimmied up my spine, a sliver of desire I hadn't felt in forever.

We headed for the back steps. At the top of the stairs, Jordan punched the back doorbell. The melody of an old Linda Ronstadt song chimed in the air.

"Who's there?"

"It's Jordan," he said softly.

"*Mi sobrino*." She flung the screen door open and wrapped her arms tightly around him, eyes squeezed shut, a wide smile on her mouth.

His aunt. The woman in his arms was younger than I'd expected. She didn't look a day over forty-five, but I knew she had to be older than that. His mother had been eighteen when she'd had Jordan. He'd been raised by his mother and her younger sister.

His aunt was dressed casually in a velour sweat suit in bright coral, her shiny pitch hair pulled back in a perky pony tail, her lips splashed with coral gloss that matched her sweat suit perfectly.

As she stepped back to let him in, she registered my presence. I clutched the wrought iron railing, my fingernails, ridged and bare, a sad contrast to the sparkly coat of coral polish on hers.

He quickly introduced me to his Aunt Guadalupe. "This is Staci," he said as if he'd spoken of me before.

"Staci?" She blinked at me, for a moment her reaction clear. Oh, no, no, no.

Then she reached out and pulled me into the warmth of her kitchen. Sautéing beef, chilies, and onions simmered on the stove top, scenting the air.

"You poor thing," she fussed, squeezing my hand in a strong grip, holding on longer than normal while her gaze held mine. I must have passed the first test. "Come in, come in."

With a sense of relief, I said, "Nice to meet you." In any other circumstance, meeting his aunt would be a thrill but I didn't like bringing my troubles near this friendly woman.

"Where's Mama?"

"At work."

Jordan turned to Staci. "My mother and aunt built a multi-branch cleaning service from the ground up." His pride in their accomplishment was evident by the smile beaming on his face.

"His mother, she always tells him, you can be anything you want, do anything you want, you have the blood of kings in you."

Aunt Lupe had a melancholy look in her eyes as she rested her hand on Jordan's forearm. "One day he says, mama, why can't you be anything *you* want?"

"The rest is history." Jordan clearly embarrassed by his aunt's affection, sniffed appreciatively. "Something smells good."

Overlaying dinner was the scent of drying herbs. They hung from a copper pot rack over the island counter, large bunches and small.

A huge smile converted her face from merely pretty to

beautiful. "It's been too long," she admonished as she led us through the kitchen, passing an oval table with six chairs and a bay window alcove with cheery striped valances. A little television sat on the counter, the sound muted as the news was reported.

I had an impression of corner cabinets stuffed with china and candles. Pictures of saints and handcrafted folk art in tin staggered across walls painted a deep, chili pepper red.

She dragged me into what must be their main gathering place. A futon in eggplant, tossed with throw pillows in bright colors and geometric designs, faced an altar covered with a crudely woven serape, stacked with candles, a bowl with lemons, apples and scattered flowers, and a shallow bowl with incense. An 8 x 10 picture of Guadalupe, the dark-skinned Mary, presumably Aunt Lupe's namesake, again in a tin frame, and a large tin crucifix held places of honor.

"I know, *mi Tía. Apesadumbrado.*" Jordan looked like a little boy who'd stolen cookies before dinner.

"English," she said sharply. "We are American."

He nodded.

Aunt Lupe settled me on the sofa. "Drinks? *Agua fresca,* perhaps? I have some strawberry, just made."

He looked at the green cast of my skin and took a deep breath, preparing, I thought, for the eruption to follow. "Can you make her a tea? She needs something for nausea."

The wide smile slipped significantly from his aunt's face. She eyed me again more closely, her expression hopeful. "Nausea? Like a flu?"

Jordan hesitated. "Pregnancy, *Tía.*"

"She's pregnant?" Her mouth flattened, and her eyes narrowed. Coral tipped fingers gripped her generous hips.

Jordan didn't make any excuses. In truth, there weren't any excuses to make. We'd known what we were doing.

Except admitting the truth to your mother and aunt, the women who'd raised you, who'd instilled their values and morals in you, was a lot more difficult than actually making the decision to eighty-six the condom.

Oops.

"Why didn't you tell us?"

He replied somberly, "We just found out."

Aunt Lupe bustled into the kitchen, as if the task could take her mind off the reason for her services. First she put the kettle on the burner and lit the flame.

"Let's get you fixed up." Aunt Lupe went to her cupboard and pulled out an oversize fishing tackle box. In each of the drawers were loose dried herbs, little tags on the drawers carefully marked and labeled in her neat print.

She pulled out a mortar and pestle, scooping herbs from several of the drawers into the marble bowl. She replaced the fishing tackle box in the cabinet. Making the sign of the cross, she hummed softly and ground the herbs. Using a small plastic scoop, she tipped the herb mixture into empty, open tea bags then stapled them shut.

After pouring the steaming water over one of the tea bags, she eased down on the futon next to me. After dipping her thumb in the oil in the brass brazier, she gently swabbed my forehead and behind my ears, the scented oil a little slimy on my skin.

Then Lupe handed me a delicate ceramic tea cup. "Drink this three times a day until you have passed your twelfth week. It should help you keep the food down."

I smiled tentatively. "Thank you."

"If you have any *antojos*, cravings, satisfy them." She wagged her finger at me.

"Yes, ma'am."

Aunt Lupe handed me the rest of the tea bags in a brown paper lunch bag, and kept her eagle eye on me while she made sure I actually drank the tea.

As she watched, a frown crinkled her brows as if she was trying to place how she knew me. Suddenly, her eyes widened as my identity hit her.

"You," she pointed at me. "Rest. In about half an hour, you can have some food."

I nodded sleepily and sank back against the futon's pillows.

"You," she pointed at Jordan. "Come set the table."

That was aunt speak for 'grilling time', but Jordan didn't object. Obviously it was futile.

CHAPTER 34

"She is the one."

Jordan hesitated.

"The one you were keeping from us." His aunt paced around the kitchen, her Nike cross trainers squeaking against the worn linoleum.

"*Sí*." He fell back into the language his mother and aunt had always used when he was in trouble.

"English," she snapped again.

"Sorry."

His aunt waved toward the little old 13" that was always on. "She is also the one on the television."

Shit. "Yes."

"Did she do those things?"

That was his aunt. She never assumed. He'd gotten in trouble for fighting at school. A lot. Being the son and only man, therefore head of the house at an early age, in a primarily Hispanic neighborhood, he'd defended the honor of their unorthodox family frequently and effectively.

Tía Lupe had always been the voice of reason, the soul of

neutrality waiting for all the facts and his version of events before she judged.

But what did he say?

In some respects, Staci was guilty of the things reported.

How did he justify to his aunt with her innate sense of right and wrong an issue even he had problems dealing with?

"It's complicated."

"No, it isn't," she said gently. *Tia Lupe* opened a can of tomatoes and dumped them into the sauté pan.

"She's being falsely accused of some things. Others...." he trailed off. He really didn't want to detail Staci's activities. Especially since she would be a part of his family. Assuming they could get this current situation behind them. And assuming he could convince her to stay with him.

Tia peered over his shoulder into the other room. She bit her bottom lip, whispered, "You are sure...the child is yours?"

Jordan could feel his face reddening. This woman had raised him, as much as his mother. His sex life wasn't something he discussed with them. Ever. "Yes."

"Positive? Because sometimes the women, they use methods unknown to the men." She was virtually tapping her toe against the linoleum.

A hint of amusement curled through him, even at this late date, she was still being his second mother.

"I'm sure."

"Then you must uphold your honor."

"I will." Jordan shifted to hide Staci from his aunt, symbolically protecting her from Lupe's knowing eye. He had been raised with a core of unshakeable values. Even without those, he would still want Staci, still want this baby.

"This will upset your mama."

She was right. His mother's reaction wouldn't be pretty. Fortunately he had bigger worries right now, so he'd just put that particular funfest out of his mind. History was not going to repeat itself. He wasn't going to desert his child like his own father had done. "The circumstances are very different."

"This woman, she has money, yes?" She meant like his father.

"It's not the same."

"I hope for your sake it is not." She cupped her palm against the stubble of his jaw. "You were a gift. A gift."

His mother and aunt had survived hardship to bring him into this world. Disowned by their family, his mother had been fired by his father's wife when she learned Mama was pregnant. With no family, in a strange country, they had made a family with just the three of them. His mother and aunt had raised him to believe he could do anything, be anyone.

And he was.

His child would know the same love, have the same solid foundation and values as he did. And God help anyone who tried to get in his way.

From the other room, Staci snored softly.

"She needs to sleep. Give us shelter for a few hours, please," he asked.

"Of course," she replied. "Use the guest room at the top of the stairs."

Jordan moved to the futon and lifted Staci gently in his arms. She snuggled against him, rubbing her check against his bicep as he carried her toward the guest room.

She needed to sleep. And he needed to think.

His palm wrapped around her waist, his fingertips brushed against the concave hollow of her abdomen.

His baby. Their baby, he thought fiercely.

Jordan carried Staci up the stairs carefully, the creaks and groans of the old house familiar.

As he nudged open the paneled door, she shifted in his arms and her breath huffed gently over his neck, giving him goosebumps.

Jordan lay her down on the frilly white duvet. When he tried to leave, she pulled him closer into her embrace.

"Don't go," she murmured.

He decided he could think just as well propped against the white wicker headboard. So he eased off his shoes, stuffed a pillow behind his back and contemplated what to do next.

Staci lay curled up next to him, her body drawing heat from his. He rested his cheek against the top of her head, his arm curled protectively around her shoulders, and he was disturbed at how bony her body felt.

When she was awake, the force of her personality kept the worry at bay, pushing her frailty to the back of his mind. But now, as she slept, he couldn't ignore her weakened state.

Jesus. He crossed himself and said a little prayer to the crude wooden crucifix on the frilly night stand.

After all she'd been through, she was lucky to be alive.

In the chaotic midst of the last few days, since he'd found her, in fact, there had been no time for gratitude. No time for sheer relief that she still inhabited this world. No time to embrace her and hold onto her life force.

As if she'd let him.

The only time she let him get close was when she was unconscious. If that wasn't a sign of a fucked up relationship, he sure didn't know what the hell was.

He brushed a soft kiss across her forehead.

Staci let out of a sigh, a tiny sough of breath that could

be mistaken for relief, except that her arms tightened around his waist, just for a moment.

His cell phone chimed a warning at him.

The little trill startled Staci awake. "What?"

"Shhh. Go back to sleep." He shifted, pulled his phone out of his back pocket, then thumbed to his calendar.

"Forgot an appointment." In New York. He'd been slated to meet with a Sergeant Ravini.

Her eyelashes fluttered against the bare skin of his bicep. She skimmed her hand up his stomach and over his pectoral muscles until her palm rested over his heart. Staci stretched, shifting her knee up over his thigh, trapping them against the duvet and then settling back into slumber.

How many times had they lain in bed this way?

Not enough.

The thump of his heart was steady and true under her hand. He set his cell down on the bed and threaded his fingers with hers.

Thankful to have the real woman back instead of a stolen token, he rubbed his thumb over her fingers like he'd rubbed the scarab of her necklace so many times.

It was amazing how that one simple act could bring peace.

Then other details filtered through his consciousness. The heavy weight of her breast against his forearm.

The press of her pubic bone against his hip and a heat rising from her feminine core. Her lips brushed softly against the curve of his neck.

The combination of her gentle, unconscious touches and the lack of physical contact in the last two months bowled him over. His body responded as if she'd stripped naked and done a pole dance.

The reaction was inappropriate. And in just a second he would extricate himself from the sensuous bondage.

Except, a second later, she rubbed her hot core against the curve of his hip and shifted her knee just a bit higher. The little arch in her back uplifted her breast closer to the hand that held hers and the temptation was irresistible.

The backs of his fingers strummed over her hardening nipple drawing a soft moan. The scent of her arousal drifted through the air. God, he knew that scent, was tormented by the bouquet of her desire.

She was asleep. This was probably a bad idea.

Scratch that. This was a train wreck. Nothing critical had been resolved between them. He leaned over to lick her lips with his tongue.

As she strained her mouth toward his, he surrendered.

Their hands still entwined, she tugged his fingers down and trapped them between her body and his thigh.

Her hand skimmed over his burgeoning erection and traced the outline with just the right amount of pressure.

He knew her, knew her body, knew what do to do to take her to the next level. He curled his fingers, rubbing her through her panties but avoiding her sweet spot.

She retaliated by unzipping his pants and sliding her hot greedy fingers into his boxers. Her fingernails scraped at his balls, circling, squeezing, taunting him with the possibility of her touch against his cock.

He shifted slightly, easing her on top of him and lifting her so the pouting bud of her nipple was even with his mouth. He sucked the hard berry as he brought his other hand up to squeeze and pluck at the other nipple.

Her breath came faster as she pushed at the waistband of his pants. She shifted to straddle his hips, the stretchy black skirt bunched around her waist. Jordan held her just above his hard on, so the tip of his cock teased her clitoris with the merest brush of heat before slipping away.

Her eyes slitted open, and her hands came up to fist at his shoulders. He wondered if she would stop.

He'd have the biggest case of blue balls in the country.

She didn't stop. Instead, she brushed a kiss against his neck.

"Take your top off," he growled.

She ripped the clingy black fabric over her head as he reared up and feasted on her breasts. The action shoved her panty-clad bottom down on his erection. Her whimpers filled him with a fierce sense of satisfaction.

Here, here they had always been compatible.

Staci ground her pelvis against him. Using one hand he shoved the panties to one side and impaled her.

The slick wet heat of her enveloped him.

He swallowed her cry with his mouth as he pushed up into her velvet heat, holding her hips, rocking against her so he stroked her g-spot.

Her breath panted out in little bursts as she looked down at him. Her gaze held his as he suckled her breast while she thudded down on him, shaking the bed with the force of her thrusts.

It was wild and pagan and erotic as hell as she gripped his shoulders, then broke away from his mouth and threw her head back.

Her body convulsed, and he came in a blinding flash of light and heat and power as they continued to pump against each other.

The bed shook, the headboard squeaking from the fierceness of their joining.

Aftershocks buzzed through his body like little jolts of electric current. Staci breathed soft little hiccups, trembling in his embrace. He curled his arms around her back, her heart beat thundering in his ear, even as the languid curve of her spine stiffened into remorse.

He held tighter, refusing to regret the last few minutes. He'd missed her.

Not just the sex. Everything about her. Their intimate dinners, their spirited discussions about religion and politics and sex, their physical sparring on the mats, even the way she looked after him.

"God, I missed you," he said hoarsely.

She didn't answer, but her arms stayed soft and loose around his body.

It was the best he'd get from her, he knew.

A strong breeze set the lace curtains billowing, ushering in the sweet scent of honeysuckle. Beyond the window, children shrieked in a rousing game of tag and traffic rushed by a few streets over.

This interlude would be over in a second. He could tell by the gradual tightening of her muscles and the tenseness of her thighs caging his hips.

She pushed off of him. "Better get cleaned up."

Silently, he showed her the little bath adjoining the room. He handed her tissue and fixed his pants.

She wouldn't discuss this unless he pushed, and unfortunately they had other more pressing things to discuss. But one day soon, they would have to talk.

He'd make sure of it.

CHAPTER 35

Who said ignoring problems wouldn't make them go away?

Standing in the small bathroom, I tugged at the stretchy clothes and wished I could pull my emotions into line with similar ease.

The endorphins had faded, the fleeting euphoria of arousal was gone, although my blood still tingled with the aftermath of our explosive sex. Leaving his body, so hard and solid beneath mine, had been more difficult, more wrenching than I expected.

I wanted to wrap our intimacy around me like a warm blanket and snuggle in, close out the rest of the world and shelter in his hard, capable arms forever.

Unfortunately that wouldn't solve our problems.

White Shoulders, heavy and redolent, perfumed the cool air. My grandmother had worn White Shoulders. Her bathroom always smelled as if she'd slathered the lotion everywhere.

It was the only thing our relatives had in common.

After meeting his aunt, I realized his life would be better

without me. I'd seen the easy affection, the ingrained love, expressed so easily. My grandparents were not demonstrative. I knew they loved me in their own way, but it wasn't spoken of. Ever. I didn't know if I could ever give that much of myself, and he deserved more.

If my chest hurt and it was hard to breathe, well, I'd get over it.

Refusing to hide in the little bathroom any longer, I took a deep breath and opened the door.

Jordan sat at the end of the bed.

I headed to the dressing table with the ornate three-section mirror and dropped onto the wrought iron bistro chair, which was bound to be uncomfortable but a better alternative than sitting on the bed we'd just shared so intimately.

I said, "We need to figure out why someone is after me and possibly you."

We. Jordan lifted his eyebrows, his face impassive as he waited for me to finish.

I really didn't want him involved. For too many reasons to count. His future. My issues with intimacy. The previous twenty minutes aside, nothing had been resolved.

In some ways we were further apart now than when I was in Afghanistan.

But I needed another pair of eyes.

Jordan finally replied, "We need to figure out more than that."

Sex was easy. What he wanted was hard. I'd be perfectly happy never talking about our relationship again, but I had a feeling my previously stoic, taciturn boyfriend was about to turn into someone who wanted to share his feelings.

I was pregnant. Wasn't I supposed to be the sentimental one?

A glimmer of shame touched me. He shouldn't have to put up with my insecurities. "We get out of this, and then we'll discuss what just happened."

He held his hands up in the air. "Okay."

"We've got to focus on whoever is after me...us."

"Fine." Jordan rubbed the short black curls on his head, his bicep flexing with the movement, distracting me with the realization he'd carried me to bed.

Jesus, he was strong. Even half-starved, I was no lightweight.

Focus, Staci. Focus.

Jordan said, "Let's start with 5491, since you're convinced your problems began with that investigation."

I opened my mouth to reply, but he talked right over my fledgling attempt.

"But we're going to look at everything, including your recent recruits, and your trip to Afghanistan."

I sighed. He was right. "You're right."

"Maybe we're approaching this from the wrong angle."

I leaned against the metal scrollwork of the chair, the iron digging into the bones of my back. "How so?"

"Why were the family members of the people on the 5491 list killed?" Jordan asked.

I didn't know if my brain was fuzzy from the tea, the post-coital glow, or the baby but I didn't know where he was going. "I don't know."

"What was happening in the world?"

Finally, I got it. "Let's do a search."

Jordan booted up the laptop on the little desk and leaned closer to the screen. His shoulder brushed against mine. The scent of us swamped me. The subtle musk of our sexes mingled suffusing the air with the scented memory of his body slick against mine.

Had I leaned toward him?

I straightened guiltily. "1995."

"World or just U.S.?"

"Let's start with the U.S."

He played with the search engine for a few minutes. "Here's the big stuff."

As he recited aloud the major events, I read the data and tried to ignore the heat emanating from his body.

"Clinton was President; bombing of the Edward R. Murrah Building in Oklahoma City; the CIA releases cables from the Soviet Union deciphered in the 1940's including names and cover names of 200 U.S. spies in a public ceremony...."

The CIA.

We both paused. Department 5491 was NSA, so the subjects had no clear affiliation with the CIA. That meant nothing as none of the original people killed had worked in espionage, although Bella Holden's mother had been a diplomat.

This was probably all irrelevant. However, I mentally filed the information regarding the release of the cables.

Jordan kept reading, "Bosnia/Serbia/Herzigovina fighting still going on, UN sent peacekeeping troops including Americans and Russians; Yeltsin-Clinton relations strained, Clinton turns down an invite to Russia in May, Yeltsin agrees to come to the US in October—according to this October 23rd...."

So that was a period of a lot of unrest between Russia and the U.S., but I hadn't found anything to connect the people killed in 1995 to Russia. I kept reading, a little bit behind Jordan's oral recitation.

"Senator Richard Jordan appointed to the Senate Select Committee on Intelligence; Million Man March on

Washington had 400,000 participants; an influenza outbreak nearly shut down Congress in October."

"Hey, your senator buddy."

"He is not my buddy," Jordan snapped.

"Okay." Whoa. Sensitive much?

"Let's get back to the subject." Jordan, ever the inscrutable, sighed. "Another Ebola outbreak in Zaire; World Trade Organization replaces the GATT Treaty...."

"We could search forever and still have no idea." I said, "Instead of just trying to figure out why...maybe we focus on who. Who had the power? Who had the contacts? And who had the motive to have these people killed?"

Jordan leaned forward again. The little hairs on my arms and neck stood up in appreciation for the heat he was throwing off.

"We'd need to look at who was in the business then, and still is now, to find the connection between the people on that hit list."

"All the descendants on the list receive money from the NSA, correct?"

"Yeah."

"But were any of the victims from 1995 involved in the NSA?"

"Ah...no." I frowned. At least not as far as I knew. God, this was going nowhere. "Did Carson seem evasive on the subject?"

"His job description is evasiveness," Jordan said drily.

"Good point."

"He was awfully quick to dismiss the possibility." Jordan said, "Just like you dismiss anything other than this file."

"You're right." I made the admission grudgingly.

Jordan asked again, "Have you considered that your

work for the CIA prompted the attack against you and caused your imprisonment in Afghanistan?"

Of course I'd examined the possibility when I'd first been captured. "Except why there and why now? I've been recruiting for about ten years."

"Maybe information about your activities was released to the Afghans."

"Even then, someone here would have had to give them that information. I was there strictly on a de-mining mission."

"You really weren't working for the CIA in Afghanistan?"

"No." I hesitated. "I didn't start having problems until I investigated 5491. It's so classified, I'm pretty sure that it's the reason why I'm suddenly under a death sentence."

Even if I managed to come out of this situation intact, my career with the CIA was effectively over. Continuing with my recruitment work after my "profession" had been announced on national television was impossible.

He looked away from the screen. "There has to be something we're missing."

"I researched my grandparents all the way back until 1946," I blurted out.

"And?"

"There is no historical information prior to 1946."

He understood the implications as well as I did. "What about microfilm or microfiche? Maybe the information just isn't computerized or online yet."

That was a giant red flag for anyone, even someone who didn't make their living investigating other people for possible recruitment for the U.S. Government. I looked at backgrounds, vetting potential recruits and their families all the time.

The information about my grandparents wasn't just not online.

It didn't exist.

When I looked at the census information, my grandfather and grandmother's supposed Country of Origin was listed as Poland.

But they didn't speak Polish.

And if my grandparents didn't come from Poland...where did they come from?

Somehow my ancestors were an incomplete piece of a present day cover up. The recipients of money from Department 5491 were being targeted. Maybe there was some sort of conspiracy to eliminate those recipients.

Jordan had the thought at the same moment I did. "What about the others? Where did their family members come from?"

I could log on to my search program. All my internet accounts were registered under a false name with a black credit card. Completely untraceable. Except....

"Not here. If someone wanted to reverse trace the IP address from the targets I researched--it would be possible for them to backtrack to this house."

"Okay. Later."

Jamie Hunt and Zeke Hawthorne were potential sources. Katerina Wolfe too. Maybe they knew where their ancestors had been born.

I kept turning that number 5491 around in my head.

"So why is Department 5491 the connector?"

"The inverse of 5491 is 1945." It couldn't possibly be that easy, could it? Usually missions, cases, had no relevance or meaning. Their names remained purposefully obscure.

"Even if that were the case, what is the significance of

1945? Besides the obvious: the end of the Second World War."

"Carson would know."

"He knew 5491." Jordan confirmed. "He also got upset when I indicated your problems had something to do with the file."

Could Carson be in this mess up to his eyeballs? Was that why he'd put the ad in the paper?

Jordan cursed. "I should have pressed harder."

"Don't beat yourself up about it. He's good." I recalled a time or two when I'd pressed him for answers. And somehow he'd never quite given them to me.

I didn't necessarily want to bring up my thoughts with Jordan, seeing as he objected rather strenuously to my profession. But just maybe we were onto something.

"It was through his efforts I became a recruiter. He'd said they'd had their eye on me for awhile."

His lips tightened, but he managed to hold back the negatives. And he understood that I had more to reveal. "What?"

"The timing seemed so fast. He approached me, set me up and I was on my way to the Farm for training."

"What about the life you left behind?"

"Easy to do," I said.

"Boyfriend?"

"No one serious."

"Friends?"

"Besides my college roommates, I was alone in the world." Like now. "After I joined the CIA, even those relationships fell away."

No matter what anyone says, the truth is that being a woman in the field of espionage is trickier.

The standards are different. If you mess up, you're far

more likely to be out. The physical requirements are brutal. I'd been in pretty good shape before I went through the training program, and then afterward I'd been even tougher.

I kept in peak physical condition now. Or I had. Until I'd been beaten and tortured in prison.

I thought about the trembling of my muscles and shuddered. God, I had to get back in shape. Too much was at stake here.

Jordan shifted closer, placing his hand on the back of the chair. His nearness, the heat rolling off of his body, enticed me, tantalized me, until I wanted to crawl in his lap.

"Another possibility is: your imprisonment was the result of something you did or saw in Afghanistan."

I scooted my chair away from him.

"What about Major Vandenburg?" Jordan asked. "All we have is the information Katerina gave us."

We did a search on the internet and came up with thousands of hits. I clicked on a few articles about commendations for bravery. There were a whole slew of articles regarding the Civil Affairs Division project, Operation: Rebuild.

I couldn't for the life of me figure out any connection. "I saw firsthand the progress and positive outcomes of this project."

"We need more personal information than what we'll get from press releases." Jordan's knee brushed mine.

"Katerina would know," I said.

"She won't want to talk to you again."

"True." I rubbed my stomach. I knew ways to make her comply. "But we've got the leverage."

"Her son," Jordan said flatly.

"You saw her response. It will work." I was defensive.

"I know."

Jesus, I could hear the reprimand. I should want to protect the child. Of course I didn't want to threaten the boy. But I had to protect my own child, didn't I?

My baby. The thought was so frightening, so huge, I couldn't even imagine it. How could I be a mother?

The emotion unfurling through me right now wasn't regret or fear. I recognized it now. It was hope.

Hope showered over me, through my head and stomach, twirling gently along my arms and legs. Possibility floated in my heart.

And for a moment I let myself imagine a baby, a child. Someone who was all mine. To love me for me.

Unconditionally.

This baby was going to be the most loved baby on the planet and we were going to have the best relationship in the universe.

Assuming I lived past today.

"*Mi sobrino*," his aunt's voice was soft.

"Yes." Jordan's face reddened, and I knew he must be thinking about squeaking bed. This house was old and the construction solid. Chances are his aunt had heard us anyway.

Aunt Lupe said, "You need to go."

I raised my eyebrows. Huh, a little unmarried sex, and we were out the door.

The grimace on Jordan's face pierced my heart. Already I was shifting his relationship with his family. It would likely get worse before it got better.

I wanted to protect him from this disapproval. If he'd let me.

"Your Mama called."

Jordan yanked open the door, his broad shoulders blocked my view of his aunt. "What's wrong?"

I moved so I could see her face, draw her censure if need be.

"There were people asking after you." Aunt Lupe twisted her hands together. "They could come here next."

Shit. That wasn't good.

She held up a brown bag with the scents of the food simmering in the kitchen when we'd arrived. "I made you a care package."

He accepted the bag and kissed his aunt on the cheek. "Don't tell anyone she was here."

Lupe nodded. Her gaze never even shifted to me, her concern, her worry was all for Jordan. I saw the worry, concern I had brought down on this family.

Jordan grabbed a green and black camouflage duffel from the closet.

"What's that?"

"Supplies." Jordan reached for my hand. "Time to go."

CHAPTER 36

O ctober 19
        5:30 pm
Suburban Washington D.C.

THEY WERE CLOSING in on me, us.

We'd tried unsuccessfully to contact Jamie Hunt or Zeke to find out what they knew about their ancestors' past.

Katerina Wolfe was the only other person on the list in the Washington D.C. area.

In addition to information about her grandparents, she had knowledge regarding Major Vandenburg. Assuming we could convince her to talk.

I didn't want to approach her in her home, so we waited outside her house, and watched.

Finally she left her house in a Yellow cab. Something was definitely up. She could have driven her own car, but she was taking a cab.

We followed a few car lengths behind. I kept glancing in

the side mirror. I wasn't sure, but I thought I'd seen that blue American sedan more than once.

"You see that dark Chevy Impala?"

"Noted," he replied tersely.

The cab dropped Katerina off at the Giant.

I wondered if she was planning on catching another cab, instead she headed toward the grocery store.

The dark car sped off as we pulled into the parking lot. "Gone."

"Yeah." But, a worry line creased his forehead. He had the same hinky feeling I did. "Keep your eyes open."

Jordan parked close to the front, giving us a clear view of the automatic door.

At the entrance/exit, Katerina pulled a hot pink flyer and mini-stapler out of a tiny purse and attached the paper to a message board.

Then she went inside.

We agreed Jordan would be the one to follow her into the store. She would freak if she saw me miles from our initial rendezvous point and hours later. As far as we knew, she hadn't seen Jordan in the museum.

"You'll be okay?" Jordan twisted, his hazel eyes serious. His broad shoulders and hard arms enveloped me in a cage of protection and heat.

I freaking hated the vulnerability his question evoked. I'd be fine. I had to be. But the simple question made me want to cling.

"Go."

His gaze intense, he leaned forward and brushed his lips against mine. "Be safe."

The contact lasted mere seconds, but my lips buzzed and my pulse jumped as he left the car. He strode toward the store, the shift and play of his deltoids rippling against his tight cotton polo. Those shoulders could bear a lot of weight.

And the temptation to lean on him was strong.

Jordan stopped at the bulletin board and with his cell phone snapped a quick picture of the flyer, then sent it to me while he followed her inside.

"Can you hear me?" He touched a finger to the small transmitter in his ear. I didn't remember this fascination with gadgets when we'd been dating. I guess that just proved that we didn't know each other as well as I'd thought.

"Affirmative."

I stayed in the car and watched the flyer and the exit.

The picture of the flyer didn't give me any clues. Found Dog, a picture of a German shepherd and tag with no name, just a phone number. That was it.

A young staffer hustled into the market, his pinstripe suit impeccable, hair combed perfectly, but with no requisite laptop carrying case hanging from his shoulder, just a small leather case. Something about the guy bothered me.

I straightened, flipping through other scenarios. An FBI agent carrying his weapon in the man purse. A husband picking up dinner. A guy getting snacks for a late night meeting or even a date.

"Watch the pinstripe." I couldn't help but caution, my senses were tingling.

Jordan's cell phone beeped as he dialed a number. I'd given Katerina my cell number, so I couldn't call the phone number listed on the flyer, in case she recognized my number. "You checking out the dog angle?"

"Yeah. Disconnected. No forwarding phone number."

"Huh." I pondered that while I watched the market.

This particular store did a brisk business as it was mostly

a quick stop, 'pick up a few things for dinner and head on home' place.

Full plate glass windows displayed brightly lit checkout lanes; three Express '15 items or less' lanes were always busy while one full service lane remained conspicuously empty. The patrons seemed to be young staffers from the Hill, ethnic service sector workers still in their uniforms, a few obviously working second shift and on their way to work, or college students grabbing a quick sandwich or a microwave-able frozen entree.

The clientele trended between twenties and fifties, the older generation clearly already at home for the night.

In the twenty minutes since I started watching, ten cars had pulled into the lot. The shoppers bustled inside, wasting no time, and within a few minutes were back out and driving away.

Katerina, Jordan and the pinstripe were the only ones who hadn't come back out. Dammit.

"You see pinstripe?"

I waited.

News radio murmured in the background, the volume set low, as talking heads discussed the latest political snafu over the escalating number of heroin busts and record amount of heroin coming into the United States and Mexico.

"Heroin production worldwide is at an all time high," the reporter said somberly. "Even with the anti-drug programs the U.S. has in place, heroin distribution is increasing at an alarming rate."

I thought of Fariya's village and how her husband had disappeared after being forced to be a mule and carry opium across the border.

Sadly their plight was common.

Remorse prodded me. I hadn't thought of Fariya or her plea all day. I had yet to work out a way to honor her memory and bring justice for her sacrifice.

Jordan still hadn't answered. My heart quickened. A band wrapped around my chest, and the breath snagged in my throat, as worry built with every second of silence.

I couldn't see any of the three people I was trying to track. This waiting behind sucked. How had Jordan worked HRT and spent days on a stakeout?

"How the hell did you stand this?" I muttered, hoping I wasn't distracting him. "I could really use some reassurance right now."

"Looks good," he said in my ear.

A little of my tension eased.

Someone replied, too softly for me to make out the words. What the hell?

"Have you had that kind before?" Jordan said.

Again the reply was indistinct but feminine. The cadence of her voice struck me. He had approached the surveillance subject? What was he thinking?

One professional woman in the plate glass window caught my eye. She had a frozen macaroni and cheese dinner in her hand. My stomach turned. All of the sudden, I knew what I wanted.

"Hey. Are you near the bakery aisle?" I was desperate. "I need a cinnamon roll."

"Thanks for the tip."

I still couldn't get a visual on any of the three people I needed to see, and the giant pit that was my stomach suddenly threatened to swallow me whole.

"Cinnamon rolls," I snarled softly. It baffled me how my body could go from ripping my intestines out through my diaphragm to needing to eat so badly I wanted to gnaw off my own hand. "You owe me."

"Excuse me," Jordan said.

His clothing rustled and his shoe squeaked against the floor, and I prayed Katerina was heading toward the bakery so he could follow.

An older model, dark blue Ford Taurus pulled into the parking lot. The guy behind the wheel was the first shopper clearly in the elderly column. Best guess, he was in his eighties.

Could that be the car I'd seen earlier? Maybe it hadn't been a Chevy. Or was I just being paranoid?

And what about the pinstripe suit--who still hadn't come out of the damn store?

"Getting crowded here," I said to Jordan.

The old man didn't go inside. Instead he went straight to the message board, spent a few minutes scanning all of the papers--ads for used skateboards, skis, and bicycles; an advertisement for Battle of the Bands at the local dive; flyers with lost pets and cell phones--before he ripped down the hot pink flyer.

"We've got contact."

Using my cell phone, I took a picture of the license plate on his car and then another picture of the old man as he sauntered back toward the Taurus. The resolution on the cell would be next to worthless, and I didn't have access to any sort of recognition software, but evidence was evidence.

He got back into the sedan, slunk down in the seat, and pulled out a cell phone. I did a visual quick check of the hand holding the phone. Looked to be as old as his face. Unless he had a fantastic makeup artist, chances were excellent he really was an older gentleman. I wished I had a zoom lens.

I realized I hadn't heard anything for at least a minute. The range on our transmission equipment was limited, so Jordan could be out of contact in certain areas of the store.

He hadn't passed the big plate glass window since he'd gone inside. I wondered what Katerina was waiting for. She'd been in the store far longer than the average customer.

The old man put down his phone and started the car.

I thought about the flyer. Our only lead was the disconnected phone--a virtual dead end.

The flyer itself was basically a bust.

Unless we could figure out the significance of the message. Without any context we were screwed.

Suddenly the sound filtered in, Jordan must be in range again.

"Contact is leaving. I'm going to follow." Worry wrapped around my lungs like Houdini's straight jacket. "Keep your eye open for pinstripe. I don't like that he still hasn't reappeared."

It was really starting to bother me. Maybe the guy just couldn't decide what to have for dinner. But maybe the reason was something more sinister. I had to hope he wasn't following us.

Jordan was six three of brawny muscles and hard attitude...he could handle any situation that came his way. Except the situation was most likely my fault. And that didn't stop the guilt.

I still hadn't seen Jordan. I had to trust that he was still following Katerina. He'd been warned about pinstripe. I scooted over to the driver's seat. I'd put the fake stomach padding back, which seemed silly, but even a little change could throw off surveillance for a much needed few seconds. I twisted the key. The engine coughed and then turned over.

I called Jordan's cell, but the call went straight to voice mail, so I left a message about the car of the old man who took the flyer.

"Older car, Ford Taurus, dark blue, again, four door, Maryland license plate, can't get a read on the plate number." Something dark obscured the last two characters on the plate, upping my suspicion factor and sending my senses buzzing.

Not the car from earlier...at least, I didn't think so.

I tried to put it together: The old man takes down her flyer, doesn't go inside, and his license plate is obscured. The clues were adding up, except...to what?

I dialed his cell again and finally connected with Jordan. He'd heard my dialogue. He just hadn't been in a position to answer. "Guy's old enough to be Katerina's grandfather."

"Maybe it is her grandfather."

I shook my head in denial. "Nope. I have pictures of the grandparents. He was a big bull of a man with a neck as thick as my thigh."

"As people age, they get smaller."

"No way. Too big of a difference. Anyway, her grandfather is dead."

"Okay." Jordan thought for a minute. "How did her grandparents die?"

"Drowned, boat lost, bodies never recovered."

"Dead end."

The radio switched to local news.

I shifted in the seat, waiting for the guy to move.

The stretchy waistband, pressing at my waist, shouldn't have bothered my stomach, but somehow the material felt constricting. I'd been wearing the fake rolls of fat when I'd put the garment on and then the skirt fit fine.

Suddenly I had to get the elastic off my belly button. I

shoved the waistband down around my hips, and the feeling of relief was instantaneous.

The old man left, driving slowly, car rumbling softly. He tooled through the parking lot, not glancing left or right. In the dusk, his car became like fog, wispy and insubstantial.

I held back, waiting until he stopped at the light before moving toward the exit of the parking lot, trying to stay off his radar.

But our white rental car--thank you, Thea, who'd clearly never been trained in how to be unobtrusive--with New York plates was definitely noticeable.

At the traffic light, he flipped on his left turn signal. When the arrow turned green, he puttered along turning left onto the main road. I followed, keeping one car between us, hoping I was wrong about his next move.

Shit. Sure enough, at the first main road, he went left again. The car between us went straight, and suddenly I was even more visible. If he went left again, I was so screwed.

I glanced in the rear view mirror. Okay, make that doubly screwed.

Two cars back was a dark sedan.

CHAPTER 37

Dusk had disappeared into full on dark, so I couldn't positively identify the sedan behind me as the car that followed us earlier.

But I sure didn't like the coincidence.

The dark sedan hadn't been in the Giant parking lot. If they were following us, they'd picked me up on the first turn. The old man went left again, two streets past the grocery store. I had to go right. I had no choice, as the old man would make me otherwise.

The pattern was standard vehicle surveillance detection, a series of lefts, or rights, to check for followers.

At the next street, I zipped right and zoomed away from the old man. In my rear view mirror, I picked up visual again, watching him drive the opposite way and turn left again. The dark sedan behind me had gone straight, but if I was correct, and he was following me, he would turn right one more street down, and pick me up again.

I turned right, and then right again, hoping I'd come out on the same street as the old man and be heading toward him.

I was hoping the dark sedan in my rear view for a second time tonight had been a coincidence.

A whole lot of hope going on.

Of course my luck wasn't that good. I wouldn't be buying a lottery ticket this week.

One thing went my way as the old man and I came out on the same street, heading toward each other. The multi-turns had delivered us to the road behind the Giant. I assumed, with some trepidation, he intended to stop there. I drove sedately by him as he turned into the loading dock area of the adjacent drug store.

I checked my six, three, then nine, but no dark sedan caught my eye. Maybe my luck was turning.

But I didn't think so.

I glanced back at the loading dock. Katerina Wolfe hovered in the shadows beside a set of steps leading up to a back entrance. The old guy was going to pick her up.

I pulled alongside the curb across the street and turned off my lights.

Suddenly, in my earpiece, the static crackled and surprised me.

Jordan was back. "I see you. Circle around and pick me up in front."

"Not a good idea." I briefly filled him in on the sedan. "You ever see pinstripe?"

"No."

"Maybe they were following Katerina, not us." Had to throw that out there, except....

"If they were following Katerina, they'd found us too. Dammit." Jordan swore.

"Or they were following you," I said softly.

Silence greeted that statement.

I tightened my hands on the cold polymer steering

wheel, fisting my fingers as if I could keep the worry clenched inside. Jordan was holding back, but I didn't know if it had anything to do with me and this current situation, or if it was none of my business.

I needed to know.

"It's possible," he said finally as if saying it out loud gave the idea some cred.

The why of it would have to wait.

"The key is to hang back and see if the sedan follows them…or waits for us." The sedan had one person in the car, the driver.

"I'll drive around the block one more time." But I waited, observing Katerina's movements.

She headed toward the old guy's car, staying to the shadows. She'd put on a ball cap embroidered with 'Life is Good' and pulled the bill low enough to conceal most of her face.

"What the hell is Katerina Wolfe doing?" Had our meeting earlier spooked her…or was something else happening?

We couldn't take the chance the sedan was following her and that the driver would notice us. Rock meet hard place. That whole 'Wanted' thing hanging over my head sure cramped our options.

If the sedan was hanging back, waiting for us, they'd be able to pick up our white car at the next intersection.

"We don't need to follow them. I've got her covered."

"How?" We'd been out of contact off and on since he went into the store.

"Put a tracker on her purse."

"You had a tracker with you?" I said skeptically. He worked for a think tank, he didn't do field work anymore. At least, not as far as I knew.

An uncomfortable silence blanketed the sound waves. "I've been looking for you. It seemed as if you didn't want to be found. So if I did find you...I didn't want to lose you again."

No wonder the silence was uncomfortable.

Jordan's cell rang.

"Let me take this." He diverted his attention to whomever was on the other end of his call.

I went back to watching the car and Katerina. She ducked into the old man's car quickly, and he did a three point turn. They were going to come out the back lot, right by my car. I could duck down, but now I wasn't sure I wanted to.

Katerina Wolfe knew something.

Her behavior in the last half hour was textbook clandestine.

I was tired of lurking in the shadows. I wanted action. I wanted resolution. Wanted some movement.

Vaguely I could hear Jordan trying to calm someone down.

The radio switched to local news.

"And now in an important update," the announcer paused for dramatic effect, "Staci Grant, local woman and alleged terrorist sympathizer has been spotted in the District of Columbia by a former student."

Shit. Knew it was coming, hoped I had a little more time.

"Our station was able to speak exclusively with the witness whose name we are withholding for his protection."

The reported asked, "How did Staci Grant seem?"

"Yeah, uh, she looked a little, uh, beat up." It was Matthew Cho.

No shit. I was a little beat up. I'd be a hell of a lot more beat up if the 'authorities' got a hold of me.

"Did she threaten you in any way?"

"Uh, no." Matthew stumbled through his answer. "She, uh, said she'd be teaching in the spring."

"What kind of a teacher was she?"

This is the kind of question they always ask, and the neighbor always says, they were quiet and kept to themselves... except for those dead bodies in the basement.

"She was...is a great teacher," Matthew responded to the leading question fiercely.

"Did she seem agitated or menacing?"

"No, she just seemed like she had someplace to be. She looked at her watch a few times."

"What made you come forward?"

"Well, I saw the news," Matthew said. "Ms. Grant would have told me to go for it. I'm sure they've made some sort of mistake. She would never do the things they're accusing her of."

The reporter cut Matthew off, probably hustling him away from the microphone. Matthew's viewpoint didn't make for sensational sound bites.

"Authorities are actively searching airports, bus and train stations, any transportation exits out of the city, but with the few hours between when she was seen and when the contact was reported, she could be anywhere. Authorities would not answer speculation about why she would still be in the D.C. area. She has no strong ties here and allegedly has far reaching and unlimited resources.

For a picture of the fugitive, check out our website."

I thunked my head on the steering wheel. Ow.

"If you see her, you are advised to call this number

immediately but do not, repeat, do not approach her. She is still considered armed and dangerous."

Great. Now I'm freaking public enemy number one?

The adrenaline that had kept me upright and jazzed since we left Jordan's mother and aunt's house suddenly drop kicked me. Exhaustion so extreme I could barely keep my eyes open swept over me, drowning me in sheer fatigue. I yawned so hard and wide, I could have swallowed our entire rental car.

Jordan clicked his attention back to me. "Get out of the car."

"What?"

The airwaves buzzed with his impatience. "Get out of that car."

His sense of urgency finally penetrated the hazy fog of my brain.

"What's wrong?" I fumbled with the seat belt, my reflexes sluggish.

"That was Thea."

Had she had a crisis of conscience? "She turned me in?"

"No. They came to her."

My brain started firing on all pistons.

There was no way to connect Thea and me. But if you connected Thea to Jordan, then Jordan to me, suddenly that degree of separation was gone. It also meant Jordan's name was no longer a secret.

"They were following you."

"Yeah."

"Do you know who it was?"

"I've got a pretty good idea." His voice was grim.

"And they know about your relationship with Thea."

"Apparently so."

"And examined her credit card charges." Dammit.

Jordan shot out the back of the Giant, a small paper bag in his hand, and headed for me.

I dragged my body out of the car, grabbing Jordan's duffel and my backpack bag as I went. No time to wipe down the car.

Katerina and the old man had just turned out of the parking lot onto the street where I was parked.

Jordan loped down the stairs of the loading dock as another car turned into the parking lot at the far end.

I'm not sure what made me look. Instinct. Survival.

Shit. The dark sedan was back.

Staying in one place too long had cost us, and the sedan had come searching.

The car's headlights speared through the evening, highlighting Jordan's face. Panic thundered through my body, adrenaline ramping up my heartbeat. Suddenly I was wide awake.

The car with Katerina slowed down as they drove toward me and our rental, the bill of her cap swiveling back and forth as she processed Jordan on one side of the street and me coming out of the car on the other.

I pulled my weapon out and stepped in front of their car, and prayed they wouldn't mow me down. Fortunately they weren't going fast, and fortunately the old man had a conscience.

Through the windshield, I could see Katerina's mouth moving rapidly, telling the old man to keep going.

The old man shook his head violently and slowed to a creep.

Jordan interpreted immediately and went for the back door handle, yanking open their car door as I rounded the side. He slid in and jerked me inside.

My impulse was to curl my arms over my stomach. "Drive."

"What makes you think we're taking you anywhere?" Katerina snarled.

I started to wave my weapon, but the threat was unnecessary.

"You want to be seen with us?" Jordan asked calmly.

"No!"

Jordan gestured to the car in the parking lot, where the driver had slowed down to watch our drama unfold. Pinstripe came running out the back door of the grocery store.

Knew I'd been right about him being in the damn store too long. Wished I'd been wrong.

"Then get the hell out of here." Jordan snapped. "Or we're all fucked."

Katerina said, "You're going to regret this."

She had no idea.

CHAPTER 38

The old man took off with a peal worthy of a NASCAR driver coming out of pit row and gunning for first place.

He took the corner at fifty. Jordan slammed into me as I hit the car door.

I grunted. The pain from my still sensitive left arm zinged through my body. Stars waterfalled, blurring my vision, and reality faded into a dizzy whir.

Jordan steadied me. "You okay?" The solid heat of his body, the hard flex of his bicep against my back anchored me firmly back to him.

I nodded, swallowing a groan.

Jordan handed me a crumpled bag, a grease spot already blossoming on the brown paper. The scent of a smashed cinnamon roll hit my nose. My mouth watered as I ripped open the bag.

We barreled down the mostly residential street with no headlights in the rearview mirror. At least not yet.

The sedan had to pick up pinstripe and maneuver out of

the parking lot. They could also have a team surveillance set up. In that case we should be looking for the other car.

After eating half the pastry, I stopped, licked my fingers and figured we should get down to it. "Why the prearranged signal?"

"None of your business," she snapped.

"Aren't you going to introduce us?" I wanted to know who the old man was. I still wasn't sure we shouldn't have bolted in our own car. But chances were a BOLO was already in place.

"Fuck. You."

Succinctly put.

"Why not try for civility?" the old man spoke.

"Yeah." I mocked. "Try being civil."

"Do you have any idea what will happen to me if I'm connected with you in any way?" She jammed the heels of her hands against her eye sockets, like a little kid who doesn't want to see.

"Hmmm. You'll be put on the news as Public Enemy number Twelve. Spots One through Ten are covered by the FBI and I've pretty much locked up Eleven."

"I won't be able to protect my son," she gritted out. "Total FUBAR."

The old man swerved right again. I stifled a groan as I slid into Jordan, banging my shin with another sharp jab of pain.

"Buckle up," Jordan said calmly, ignoring us both as he stared out the back window. "We need to pool resources and talk."

He was right. But I'd admit it only grudgingly.

"Can they run your plate?" I asked the old man since Katerina hadn't done more than growl at me.

"Most common sedan purchased in the United States,

and it's possible the license plate might be obscured a bit."
The old man rubbed a hand over his whiskered smile.

"I'll keep watch while you talk," Jordan said, his voice a
deep rumble.

Katerina whipped around to glare at Jordan. "You were
following me in the store?"

He shrugged a sorry.

I peered out the back window, helping search for the tail
or any kind of surveillance as we roared down the street. No
one seemed to be following.

Houses transitioned to industrial warehouses and
factories. The streets were pretty much deserted, as first shift
had gone home or to the bars, and second was not quite
ready for lunchtime.

Hitting a pothole, the car bounced as we turned onto a
more main thoroughfare. So far, no lights behind us. Could
they have let us go?

The old man performed another series of turns, pulled
into a packed parking lot, trolled to the middle of a row and
pulled in between an SUV and a Prius. After he shut off the
headlights and turned off the engine, the car became
invisible.

No one said a word.

We all held still, like prey trying to outwit a predator.

"You're sure we lost them?"

"I don't make mistakes."

He was old. Older than I'd originally thought. But he
knew his stuff. "Who are you?"

I had a feeling I would get more out of him than I
would Katerina. That might be the way to play it. That way
she could honestly deny she gave out information if her
supervisors asked.

"Leave him alone," she growled again like a mama bear protecting her cub.

"Deniability, babe." If you won't answer someone else has to. "Let's try this. We'll exchange information until one or the other of us is...uneasy."

Katerina started to object, but the old man shook his head, patted her hand. His love for her was plain. "It's okay, Rina."

As he reassured her again before answering me, a pang of loss hit me. Their relationship was definitely close and clearly affectionate.

"I'm a friend of the family."

Evasive driving expertise and a highly developed sense of impending danger made me think he was more. "Anything else?"

Katerina opened her mouth, and the old man ran a quick hand over her hair stilling her objections. Discounting the manner in which they set up their meeting, these were two people with a long-standing personal relationship. Not a working relationship.

Suddenly something occurred to me. "Bodies were never found."

"Excuse me?" Stalactites dripped from her words.

"The bodies of your grandparents were never found." I met the rheumy gaze of the old man in the rear view mirror.

"Is there a point to your rambling?" Katerina's gaze shifted to the old man.

"Lost at sea. Never recovered." I let that settle for a minute.

The old man answered my insinuation. "I'm not her grandfather."

Yeah. I already knew that. But just who the hell was he?

"Never recovered." I took a shot in the dark. "Never killed?"

No one spoke.

"I was supposed to kill them," the old man finally piped up.

Okay. That one threw me. "You were...." Supposed to kill the grandparents. That meant, he hadn't? Or had he?

"A sleeper."

Wow. Hadn't seen that one coming.

I wondered why he'd told me. Just offered up that shocking revelation as if we were at a cocktail party making small talk.

My heart sped up, thumping rapidly in my chest. The spit in my mouth dried, and for a second, I wasn't sure I could speak as another thought occurred to me. Could he have been the one who killed my grandparents?

I finally croaked out, "Did you have more than one target?"

"No."

Relief flooded me. Jordan's hand was solid and strong in mine, my fingers aching with the force of my grip. I was supposed to be a big, tough agent, but the thought of sitting calmly in a car with my grandparents' killer was beyond my emotional capabilities.

I focused on the old man. "Why were you activated?"

I waited for his answer, possibilities roiling through me. Taken alone the deaths were accidents. Together they formed a pattern impossible to ignore, but we hadn't come up with any common denominators.

"I don't know." He shook his head. "I've had my suspicions but nothing concrete."

"Did you notice anything about the dates of the murders?" Jordan finally spoke, the soft rumble of his voice comforting and just a little bit welcome.

He'd been solid and stalwart beside me, not taking over but listening and thinking until he had something relevant to impart.

"Some are October 19th and some are October 20th."

Today. Grief clawed at my heart. I couldn't let myself think about the significance of the date.

"If you convert all the dates into Greenwich Mean Time, all the people were killed within six hours of each other."

"That indicates some sort of blanket order," I said.

"I didn't know the other people involved. All I knew were my orders." The old man tipped his head toward Katerina in apology.

"What were your orders?"

"If I got the call, I had a limited amount of time to make the hit."

Katerina flinched.

"Why those people? And if they were hits, why did they go to so much trouble to cover them up and make them look like accidents?"

I ran through the 'accidents', climbing accident, mugging, car bomb--although that made sense it was the preferred hit of the times--, car accident, drowning.

"Every sleeper tailored the hit to the individual people," Jordan posited.

I winced, disconcerted to discuss the most devastating moment of my life so casually even if it was necessary. "Required advanced planning and knowledge of your targets."

"Yes." The old man didn't elaborate.

"Why?"

"I was given this job as a way to fulfill a...debt to the U.S. government."

"But you didn't do it?" I commented.

"I couldn't." The old man clasped Katerina's fingers with his. "The Wolfes were...are my friends. And I'd known them long enough to know that whatever they'd done, they had clearly been model citizens since that time."

"So what did you do?" I was fascinated, even though I was pretty sure their non-death was irrelevant to my investigation.

"I told them what my orders were, helped them scuttle their boat. They'd had contingencies, bank accounts, identifications, escape plans, in place for years," he paused. "The hardest part for them was leaving Rina and her brother."

"Have you ever talked to them?"

"Defeats the purpose of letting them go," he said sadly.

I blew out a breath. Dead end. Unless....

"Do you know where they are?"

"We know nothing." Katerina said wearily. "I have no idea where they are."

"I've given you information of staggering value. Now it's your turn." The old man's voice was hard. Old didn't mean harmless. I should have remembered that.

"What do you want?"

"Leave Rina alone."

I waited, knowing I needed to say this right or I'd get nothing from them.

"I'm not trying to bother her," I said carefully. "I just need to understand why Major Vandenburg and the DIA released my name to the media. What do they think they have on me? If I have some context, maybe I can figure out who is behind this."

The old man continued to speak for Katerina. "She doesn't have anything to do with your problems."

"You have to give up something of equal value," she demanded, her pulse fluttering visibly against her throat.

If I was going to get any answers, I needed to fill them in. And frankly, I knew Katerina wasn't going to reveal whatever I told her. She was rabidly trying to protect her son.

However, after an adulthood of sharing nothing, and working in a culture of absolute secrecy, starting to trust was difficult.

Jordan squeezed my fingers lightly with his hard callused hand, strong and resolute beside me.

"I was...investigating 5491, a department of the NSA, and then I was in prison." I said roughly, "I believe my imprisonment and subsequent 'Armed and Dangerous' status has something to do with my research. Except as far as I know I didn't uncover much."

"I've never heard of 5491," she said. Her face and posture conveyed her earnestness. She really hadn't.

"Me either." The old man appeared to be telling the truth. His body had stayed relaxed, his demeanor alert and watchful.

"Katerina's name is in the Department 5491 file. You get money from the NSA every month since your grandparents disappeared." I hesitated. "Somewhere in there is a connection that we're missing."

"So?" Her tone said, why do I care?

"All the people receiving money are related or connected in some way. Brad Johnson is dead. Someone set me up to be killed. Just like my grandparents. For all we know someone is targeting the recipients of that money for assassination."

"You're assuming someone is systematically eliminating the 5491 recipients," Katerina dismissed.

Brad Johnson was dead. I'd been captured in Afghanistan. If I hadn't escaped I'd be dead now.

"I can't afford not to assume that."

"Okay. I'll give you this much--I receive money." She rubbed her hands over her arms, trying to warm herself or sweep away the dirt that seemed to be following the 5491 people around. "But Brad Johnson isn't dead because of 5491. He's dead because he took stupid chances."

The fact remained he was dead. I'd been targeted. All the recipients of money who were also in espionage had been given a drug and then an antidote. "We have to figure out how it all relates."

The old man said, "Why did you follow Rina?"

"She lives here in D.C. and my other sources are unavailable." I thought about how phrase this next question. "Were your grandparents born here in the U.S.?"

Katerina stared at me, the parking lot light streaming through the passenger window, bisecting her features diagonally, illuminating the flat, even line of her mouth. "Ask me something else."

"How is Major Vandenburg is connected to this?"

"He isn't," she insisted. "Look, word in the office is he's gone a little around the bend."

"Why?"

"His son was killed in an IED attack in Iraq." Katerina hesitated. "He hasn't been the same since."

"Can you find out who in the DIA is gunning for me?" Please. Jesus, couldn't I catch just one freaking break?

A car turned down our row, instinctively we all froze.

"I've got to protect my son," she shot back.

Instinctively my fingers brushed my belly. And I had to protect the life growing inside of me. Even if I wasn't sure I wanted a baby, I felt compelled to nurture the nascent life.

"My life is on the line unless I figure out why I'm being targeted." I pushed. "Yours could be too."

"Every second I spend with you puts me in more danger." She vibrated with nerves, her breath coming in shorter and shorter intervals, the acrid scent of fear sharp in the car.

"Yeah. You can't protect your son if you're dead."

"I'm giving you this information and then AMF," she said.

"What?"

Adios Mother Fucker, Jordan mouthed.

"Those are my conditions. Agree or get out."

"Fine." Wow. Hard ass Katerina was back.

Reluctantly, she said, "Major Vandenburg had a meeting with Senator Jordan right before the press conference."

In my peripheral vision, Jordan slowly turned to granite. His body tensing, muscle by muscle, until his face resembled a Greek statue, the sharp planes of his cheekbones, and the rock hard curve of his jaw, cast into shadow and light. I had to find out what connected him and the senator. Preferably yesterday.

Katerina said, "The press conference was literally scheduled within an hour."

"We have to find out what they talked about." But how?

Jordan sighed heavily. "I have a way to get to the Senator."

"How?"

Finally, I'd find out what made Jordan tense up every time the man's name popped up.

Shit. Suddenly I put it together. And I wondered why I didn't see it before.

"He's my father."

CHAPTER 39

Fuck. He knew how to drop a bomb.

He'd never spoken those words aloud. Of course it was possible he was in cardiac arrest as his heart slammed against his ribs.

As he'd sat in this car, Jordan realized withholding information from the team had put everyone at risk.

"Holy...." Staci trailed off, her eyes wide in the gloom of the backseat.

"Yeah." He clenched his teeth, knowing his expression did not encourage questions.

"Not your buddy."

"No."

She processed rapidly, understanding and some other emotion dawning in her gaze. He'd thought about all the things he'd told her about his father. Now Staci knew where he came from.

"We need to talk to him," Staci said reluctantly.

Denial reverberated through him, but Jordan had already concluded a face-to-face was necessary.

"I know." Whatever the senator and Vandenburg

discussed led to the press conference that changed Staci's status. They needed to know what happened during that meeting.

"How?" Staci tapped a long finger against her mouth. Her face had started to regaining color. She'd kept down the cinnamon roll and the food *Tía Lupe* had given them.

Silence smothered the interior as all three waited. "Blackmail."

The old man jerked.

"Only four people in the world know he's my father. Possibly five," Jordan amended, "if his wife knows."

He glanced around the interior of the nondescript sedan. An innocuous setting for proposing an action guaranteed to have long lasting repercussions. "Seven now."

He had to tell the old man and Katerina. He and Staci needed someone else to know and understand what was really going on, but damn, talking about his parentage was difficult. Sweat beaded on his face, and rolled down his temple to glide behind his ear. Adrenaline shifted his focus to higher alert, blocking unimportant sounds yet still filtering in possible threats. Physiological reactions he'd trained long and hard to ignore overwhelmed him.

"I'll threaten to go to the media unless he talks to me," he stressed.

As a set-up it was near perfect. Unless the bastard said no. Acid gurgled in his stomach.

If the senator refused, Jordan would have to make good on the blackmail threat and take the secret of his parentage to the press. The publicity for Jordan and for his mother would be horrible. His entire life would be under scrutiny.

But it was past time Jordan stood up to the man who had fathered him. All these years he'd protected his mother's secret. Now protecting Staci and their baby was imperative.

"You'd do that for...me?" Surprise, horror filled her slate blue eyes.

"And the baby."

The baby they wouldn't have, unless they figured out who was after Staci and why. There were so many complications and problems with his scenario, details he couldn't control, emotions and reactions he couldn't predict. Dammit.

"You're pregnant?" Katerina gasped.

"Yeah." Staci's tone made it clear she didn't want any comments.

He just had to hope the senator was too rattled by the threat to take evasive measures.

"Every time we turn around, his name comes up." Jordan ignored the people in the front seat, speaking directly to Staci. "Every time."

"Are you sure?"

"Too many secrets are what brought us to this point," Jordan said tightly. "We need someone else to know what is really going on."

"This is between you two," Katerina protested. "I can't be anywhere near this mess."

Staci held up her cell phone and took a picture of Katerina.

"What was that for?"

"When they get me, they'll find your picture on my cell phone."

"You bitch!" Katerina lurched toward the back seat, grabbing for the cell phone even as the old man tried to restrain her.

Staci flipped the phone closed and tucked it in Jordan's back pocket.

"We need you to document this," Staci reprimanded

sharply. "And now we know you have no motive for wanting us captured."

They were desperate. And finally, finally Katerina got it.

Jordan was quiet, calm, resolved. "He has the resources and the power to have me followed."

He thought back to the surveillance team in New York City. They had never approached him or Staci. Followed, yes. Reported, probably. But they didn't apprehend him. Same with the sedan earlier tonight. They followed but never made contact.

"Could it be while I thought they were after me, all this time they were after you? The surveillance we'd assumed on my townhouse. The ransacking of my house in the Bahamas."

"Not all of it. The Senator had information about a situation," he responded. He hadn't picked up a tail until after the senator grilled him about the shooting in the Presidential Suites. Jordan fisted his hand, ignoring the strong urge to punch something, someone, in particular. "He wanted to know what I knew."

Why? Could the senator be connected to the events at the Presidential Suites? Connected to whoever authorized Susan Chen and her accomplice's experiment? And if he was–did that mean he'd had something to do with scientists who had administered a DNA drug to unsuspecting agents?

From the moment of conception his father had been fucking up his life and he was tired of it.

"He is connected to me and you." Staci rubbed her stomach, drawing him back to their more immediate problems.

"We need to get this resolved," he said fiercely.

Staci turned away from the people in the front seat, to

face him, her gaze earnest and intense. "I don't want you compromised."

He placed a hand over her stomach, feeling the pulse of blood through her body.

"Let's use Carson to get to the Senator." Staci shot Katerina a look. "I know you know him so don't try to con me."

Katerina pressed her lips together.

"We'll keep a record." The old man negotiated, "With the understanding that you leave Rina alone after it's done."

"Agreed," Staci said.

Staci didn't like it, he could tell. Then she looked at him and understood he wouldn't change his mind. He wasn't going to back down.

He was trying to prevent her death. Trying to prevent the mess of her life from spiraling any more out of control. Trying to protect her.

"I hate the idea of you confronting him," Staci said softly.

"I'm not real crazy about it myself."

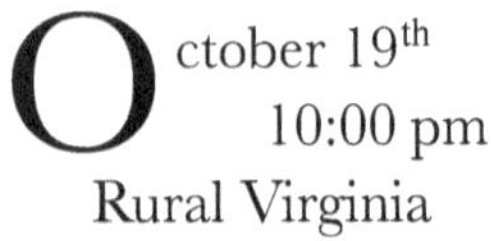

CHAPTER 40

October 19th
10:00 pm
Rural Virginia

CARSON BLACK'S house was an access nightmare.

No way were they ascending that driveway. The house, the final stop, was a good, wide open, half mile from the security gate.

If Carson called in a retrieval team while they were in the house, Jordan and Staci would be effectively trapped. The ranch style house had no cover. Bushes were trimmed. Trees were cut back, making access from the upper branches impossible. Much care had been expended to give the house a normal appearance when in reality the structure was a defensible and almost unbreachable fortress.

Jordan carefully examined potential access points. Finally he decided the best approach was from the neighbor's yard.

He was betting they had no perimeter alarm. Situated

on a rolling hill, surrounded by a lake of grass, the house position was so open, getting in close without detection was impossible.

Motion detectors were most likely only inside the house. There were too many critters in the country to make outdoor sensors a viable security option.

If he was wrong, they were fucked.

Their best hope was to cammy up and crawl in.

What fun.

"How are you feeling?" Jordan was worried about Staci. Her face was pale, her mouth lined white, her skin glistening with sweat.

It wasn't hot out.

"Fine," she said shortly.

He wanted to rub his hand across her shoulder, the comfort as much for him as for her, but she'd shrug it off. Jordan leaned closer, breathed the scent of gardenias and Staci, and then held the air in his lungs, wishing he could hold onto her as easily.

He exhaled softly, let the wish go, and scooped out a bit of greasepaint from the jar. Her legs and arms were covered by green army-issue pants and a long sleeve shirt in green and tan camouflage.

A camo cap perched on her ponytail.

All that was left was skin. He smeared the goop across her cheekbones, around her mouth, the tops of her ears. As he spread the paint he was struck by how gaunt her face appeared, how finely the skin stretched across her cheekbones.

She was so thin.

Staci hunched her shoulders as if aware of his concern, closing in on herself, shutting him out.

Jordan efficiently coated his own face, dismayed at how

the rote actions came back to him easily. He tucked the jar back in the knapsack and shrugged into the small pack.

The past year at the Franklin Group disappeared in the face of a threat, and he was a warrior again. That was a job he thought he'd given up for good.

Lately he'd done a lot of things he thought he'd given up.

He looked away from Staci and focused on their mission objective. Utilizing the binoculars, Jordan assessed the house and grounds one last time.

The layout hadn't changed in the hour they'd been watching. No one had approached or left the premises. He'd scanned the surrounding vegetation cautiously, looking intently for any kind of sniper blind, anything to suggest Carson Black was expecting company of the wrong sort.

"Let me look." Staci held out her hand.

Jordan gave the binoculars to her silently.

She competently scoured the area around the house and the few trees on the sloping hills.

"You see anything I didn't?" Jordan respected her ability and sometimes you needed that second pair of eyes.

"His wife, Antoinette," her voice faltered for a moment, "just walked back into the living room area again. She looks to be carrying a tray or something. CSI is on the plasma screen."

"You know the house?"

"Yeah. Carson was my...mentor after my grandparents died. He and Antoinette had me to dinner on Easter Sunday." She kept the binoculars pressed tightly to her face, fingers white on the stock. "Spent every Easter here from age nineteen on."

Every year, she'd been invited to his home for Easter dinner? "Why Easter?"

"Don't know." She shrugged. "But it was a tradition."

Even after Jordan had met with Carson, she hadn't mentioned how close their relationship was. Just one more example of how she hadn't really let him in to her life.

He'd examine the implications of her involvement with Carson and his wife later, when he had time to take things out and dissect their relationship.

"I haven't seen much of him in the last few years, except in a more official capacity." Staci hesitated.

Jesus, he knew that hesitation. Something bad was coming.

"Occasionally the CIA and the NSA...collaborate on projects."

"Collaborate how?" He thought he probably needed to know before he belly-crawled across a half acre of exposed open space.

"The Joint Special Collection Service does cross-over intelligence work. Like in a situation where the NSA can't approach without blowing cover but perhaps the CIA operative isn't known."

He heard what she was not saying. On U.S. soil. Where technically the CIA was prohibited from conducting operations.

Shit.

"Sometimes...there are certain non-official cover personas whose identity can be utilized by more than one agency."

A light bulb went on in Jordan's head.

Carson used Staci. Suddenly, appealing to Carson for help was more risky. "You sure we can trust him?"

"I'm sure."

Her whole life was a cover. Jordan couldn't focus on the hurt penetrating the shell of his emotions. The past was over. He could only control the future. To do that they had to get through this crisis.

"Let's go. It will take us at least an hour to reach the house, possibly longer." He lifted the flap to check the matte black watch on his wrist.

He'd have preferred another few hours of surveillance before attempting to gain access, but they didn't have the luxury of time on their hands. Every minute they spent in the D.C. area was another minute Staci could be recognized and captured. Especially if the guys following him found them again.

"It would be better if we could wait until the wife goes to bed."

"Antoinette is a night owl." She pursed her mouth, drawing his gaze to the perfect moue of her lips. "Good news, Carson is home tonight."

"Then let's get to it."

Jordan knew they hadn't been followed.

Staci had a car stashed in a parking garage in Alexandria. Jordan realized then she could have left at any time. Instead they had driven to the rural farm in Virginia. The closer they had gotten to Carson's farm, the more distant her attitude.

They'd taken indirect and rambling routes to finally arrive at the farm in rural Virginia. Just because they weren't followed didn't guarantee Carson's house wasn't under surveillance. After all, someone had connected Jordan and Thea.

"Did anyone know you came here for Easter?"

"Carson might have told someone. Every aspect of CIA life is secretive, so I never said a word."

"Except Jamie figured it out," Jordan commented.

A flutter of her eyelashes was her only response, but he could tell she was unsettled. "How?"

"She came for Thanksgiving." Jordan said, "You came for Easter. I wonder when Katerina came?"

"I wonder who else came."

Jordan put the binocs away. He picked up a few twigs and tucked them into the elastic straps on the camo hat, giving her a little gilly decoration. He tried one more time, figuring he'd get no further in the argument than he had while they were driving here.

"Why don't you wait here?"

"Nope."

He felt the compulsive need to go over the directions one more time. "The key to moving in on a surveillance target is to go extremely slow. No starts and stops, just slow flow as if you're crawling through jello. Sudden movements draw the eye whereas consistent movement is overlooked."

She nodded jerkily.

"If they have long-range snipers, we're dead." He placed his hand over the slightly rounded curve of her belly. The little bulge wouldn't normally be obvious but she was so thin everywhere else that he'd zeroed in on the change in her body when she'd been naked, on top of him.

Not the place to go right now.

"If I don't get these monkeys off my back, I'm dead anyway." Her hands went to his shoulders. "Maybe you should stay here."

He snorted. "Right."

"Then we go together."

"Together." He curved his arm around her waist, yanked her flush against his body. If anything happened to either one of them, he was going to make this final kiss count.

Jordan cupped her grease-smeared jaw, held her worried gaze with his, then dropped his gaze to stare at her mouth. Her breath came in little pants, warm against the evening chill.

The first brush of their lips was soft, tentative, barely clinging before separating.

Staci brought her arms up around his neck, slanted her head and nipped at his mouth.

Everything tightened, his muscles grew harder, his arms clenched her closer. She held his face in her palms, pulling his mouth to hers in a tactical assault.

She stabbed her tongue inside of his mouth, then he refused to let her retreat, sucking, dueling, devouring.

He kept his eyes open. Not wanting to be taken off guard by anything around them, but all he could see was Staci, her desperate grab for him and the near violence with which she attacked their kiss.

The scent of gardenias rose in the steamy heat they'd generated, puffs of white air surrounding their heads like a halo.

Jordan broke away, thinking she would only kiss him like that if she thought they might not make it.

"Let's go."

They dropped to the dark ground underneath the split rail fence and began the slow crawl toward the main house.

Jordan buried his face in the inches high grass, cool, damp, and fragrant as he crawled so slowly his muscles protested at the exaggerated, deliberate movement.

At least once a minute he surreptitiously checked his three to see how Staci was doing. His Glock was in a web holster at the small of his back. The range and accuracy were limited, but the small protection was better than nothing. They were still way too exposed for his comfort.

So far she was holding up pretty well. Especially since he knew she'd been half-dead only days ago. Crickets chirped and sang in the cool fall evening. Somewhere close by a cow mooed.

They got down the first slope with no incident.

Jordan wanted to pause at the little dip in the land, but it was better to continue moving than to start and stop even in this relatively sheltered spot.

"Keep moving," he murmured.

"Yeah." Staci huffed in the chill air.

They eased up the larger hill. The cow mooed again. Jordan was pretty sure the cow was just a cow. He was also pretty sure he hadn't spent much time around farm animals.

They crested the hill in forty minutes.

Staci shivered, trembling visibly, obviously working to control her body as best as she could. The dew had soaked through his clothes, making the crawl cold and wet. He hadn't really noticed his own discomfort, but Staci's shaking emphasized her vulnerability.

They were about a hundred yards from the house, near a grouping of wrought iron furniture set on a little stone patio. Staci pulled her cell phone out of her pocket, very, very slowly. "Time to make the call."

"Yeah." Jordan quartered the area again. His senses were telling him they weren't in any danger, but he still didn't like being so exposed. He calculated the distance between them, formulating his plan to cover her body with his if anyone started shooting.

Of course, if there were snipers, he'd be dead before the sound reverberated. On that cheery note, he listened to the soft clicks of the buttons on her phone as she dialed.

"Carson?"

Jordan could hear a response, just not the specifics.

"We need to talk."

She waited.

"As a show of good faith, walk out into your yard to the stone patio, sit in the loveseat," she said softly. "When you get there, I'll give you additional directions."

The front door thunked loudly and then Carson started down the path towards them. His shoes clicked on the Connecticut blue stone as he strolled confidently toward the furniture. Jordan thought Carson would be hesitant if snipers were in the vicinity. He wouldn't want to get caught in any kind of crossfire.

He hated this part of her plan. Once Carson sat, Staci was supposed to come up behind him, and immobilize him. Her rationale was Carson would not attack her, but if Jordan were the immobilizer, Carson could perceive Jordan as a threat.

But if Carson had watchers, Staci would be perceived as a threat.

Carson wiped the dew wet furniture with a handkerchief then shook out his trousers before settling on the metal loveseat.

It was time for her to rise up behind Carson. But Jordan saw the exact moment when her muscles failed. The low to the ground position of the last hour had trained her muscles in a set pattern. When she tried to shift, her body had seized.

If she'd been healthy and in her normal peak shape, the move would have been no problem. But her muscles, mineral and vitamin deprived from morning sickness, had frozen. And she was stone still on the ground.

Carson flipped his cell phone shut. "Would it be possible to take this inside?"

"Sure." Staci still hadn't moved.

Jordan said, "Give us a guarantee that you don't have shooters in place."

"Of course not." Carson brushed a fallen leaf from his pants. "I told you I'd help."

"How can we be sure you won't turn Staci in?" Jordan questioned.

The tap-tap, tap-tap-tap of Staci's chattering teeth overlay the buzz of insects and that lone moo-ing cow.

"Let's take this inside. No betrayal. No shooters. Just Antoinette, but if it will make you feel better I can send her to our bedroom without her seeing you."

"Works for me." Jordan had already shifted to a squat. He curled a hand under her elbow and eased her into a standing position.

She stifled a groan, barely audible. His body snugged up against hers, supporting her weight until she got the feeling back in her legs, and the vibration ran through her body and into his.

Taking advantage of her momentary inability to move, he brushed a hand over her shoulder, the way he'd wanted to earlier but had known she wouldn't welcome.

The past few hours had to have been shock after shock but she'd held. Rallied even.

His right hand was free and his weapon out as Carson turned around. The glow from the porch light only touched on Carson's forehead, nose, and mouth. His eyes were hidden in the backlit shadows, but his concern was evident. "Okay?"

"Just get us inside." Being this exposed was making him itchy.

Carson strode toward the front door without any furtive glances or hesitation. But Jordan's itchy feeling refused to go away. Maybe Carson didn't have shooters, but that didn't mean that no one was watching and waiting for them to show up.

Their footfalls were soft on the blue stone barely making a scuffle in the still night air. When they got to the porch, Carson held a hand up, gesturing them to wait.

The front door burst open.

A black woman came rushing out the door, her brown eyes wide. "Oh my God."

Jordan's weapon swung up to cover the threat.

Carson grabbed the woman with one arm and drew his weapon with the other, holding it steady on Jordan, not blinking as he held the woman tightly.

"My wife." Carson's gaze never wavered from Jordan's weapon, his own hand steady, weapon still aimed at Jordan's chest. "My wife."

The standoff, Jordan supporting Staci, and Carson restraining his wife, only lasted mere seconds, but in that time Antoinette Black registered both guns and the danger.

Her wide brown eyes met Jordan's gaze. "Don't hurt her."

CHAPTER 41

I had to diffuse this situation. Fast.

"It's okay." My voice came out weak, thready. "I'm okay."

Jordan and Carson nodded to each other. By silent agreement, both lowered their weapons. Neither put them away.

"Oh, sugar. You don't look it." Antoinette ignored both men, reaching her fine-boned hand out to stroke my hair, triggering the memory of the first time we met.

Carson had brought me to this house after my grandparents died. Antoinette was only four years older but I'd been so lost and she'd tried to comfort me.

She'd let me stay here and mourn; even though she had no idea what she was doing, she'd taken care of me. She'd stroked my hair, just like now. With compassion and gentleness.

"Inside," Carson said calmly.

We filed into the house. Jordan went last, keeping alert until the front door was closed and locked.

He wasn't letting me go.

He had his arm curved around my waist, even though I was finally steady and could walk without him. Probably. A shiver wracked my body, dew had soaked my clothes. The raw heat of him radiated at my side.

Weapon still ready, Jordan examined the house with the door at his back, looking left toward the kitchen, then right with a line of sight down a hallway with doors leading to bedrooms.

Straight ahead, the great room exuded welcome, a fire crackled in the massive stone fireplace, the television murmured, and a single glass of red wine sat on a Mission-style table next to a plush sofa.

The decor was spare, no hiding places. Carson strode to the giant windows and closed the white Plantation shutters with a snap.

Jordan tested Carson. "I'm surprised you have such open views."

"Bulletproof glass."

Jordan nodded, examining the room, checking for threats, searching for hidden combatants, anticipating attack.

It was a side of him I'd rarely seen.

He worked for a think tank, assessing threat levels, examining data, and making recommendations to prevent situations from materializing or escalating.

This camo-painted warrior in skintight, black Under Armour, eyes serious, muscles flexed, ready to do violence for me was exciting a visceral way.

He turned his danger analysis to the Blacks.

I could almost see his eyes pop.

Antoinette was gorgeous. Frappuccino skin, black silky ringlets in a simple bob, French manicured nails. She wore silk lounging pajamas in a pale yellow, which only she could get away with. She dripped with jewelry, large diamond studs at her ears, a trio of thin bands set with diamonds on her right hand and a platinum and diamond ring set with three large stones on her left. She was just the type of woman who would appeal to him.

Sophisticated, elegant, polished.

Everything I used to be. And wasn't anymore.

I couldn't help a surge of possessiveness. It was totally stupid. Antoinette was devoted to Carson and we weren't here for a social call.

I curled my fingers through his belt loop anyway, hanging on tightly.

Jordan shifted his gaze to me, instantly dismissing Antoinette. "You okay."

I nodded, a flush of pleasure flooding my face.

He transferred his attention back to Carson and inclined his head toward Antoinette. "Is this going to be a problem? Is she going to turn Staci in?"

Antoinette was a civilian. My picture had been plastered all over the media. I hadn't quite made the FBI's top ten but close enough. A regular, law-abiding citizen would already be on the phone to the authorities.

Antoinette answered before Carson could open his mouth. "Of course not." Her stance was pure indignance, hip cocked, hands fisted and planted on her slim waist, elbows canted. "I can't believe you have to ask. Staci is practically family."

On that note, she ignored Jordan and zeroed in on me.

"Come on, sugar, let's get you something warm to drink." She held out her hand, but Jordan still had a firm grip on my waist.

"She needs to sit."

I wanted to be annoyed at his high-handed treatment, except, he was right.

Antoinette stared hard at Jordan's arm, then nodded. "How about some coffee?"

The thought made me want to hurl. "Tea?" I croaked. "You want tea?"

The package with the herbs from Jordan's aunt was in Jordan's small backpack. I slipped behind Jordan and unsnapped the pack. Removing clip after clip, I held them tightly in my left hand while I dug around in the bottom.

Antoinette's eyes grew rounder and rounder at the amount of firepower I continued to extract from the backpack.

I wiggled my fingers until I closed over the paper bag, then pulled out a tea bag triumphantly. "Here."

She shot a wide-eyed glance at Carson. "I'll put the kettle on."

Jordan escorted me to the sectional sofa, got me settled into a corner of plump cushions, then returned to lounge against the front door, arms crossed over his chest, weapon held loosely in his shooting hand and at the ready.

I sank into the sofa and Carson stood with his back to the fire making it impossible to look at him for too long without the firelight affecting our vision.

Deliberately, I'm sure.

"I'm assuming you want something from me," Carson said softly.

Already we'd gambled with the facts and his offer to help, and we had agreed to come here. We'd laid out a specific strategy for requesting his help. But before we could move into the next phase of our plan, Jordan asked abruptly, "Why were the sleepers activated?"

He'd deviated from our plan and yet, the question was perfect.

Carson was shocked, but he hid his surprise behind a bemused, benign expression. He kept his gaze steady on Jordan and if I hadn't seen that split second of dismay I would have been fooled.

"Isn't that out of left field?" A small half-smile played over his thin lips. "You think there are sleepers after you?"

As an evasive answer, his response was perfect. A denial on several levels. "In October of 1995, sleepers killed people from ten families. Their descendants are listed in Department 5491," I said.

His face a serene mask, Carson shifted his attention to me. "I oversee Field Ops."

Not a denial, a misdirection.

"Someone ordered a hit on my grandparents."

The muscles around his eyes tightened. I'd touched a nerve there.

"I need to know."

Carson had to have the answers. He was the goddamn Director of Field Ops now. He'd been working for the NSA then. I'd asked him about 5491 before, when I'd first started investigating, and he'd brushed me off. I wouldn't be brushed off now. "I think that's why someone is after me now."

"Extremely unlikely." Carson was firm. "No one knows about the Department."

"You've got leaks all over the place," I said thinking of Jordan and the senator. "How can you be sure no one knows?"

"I can't discuss it. It was, and still is, a matter of national security."

I blinked. My whole adult life had been given to service

for a country that had betrayed me, and betrayed my family. "Screw national security. Why were they killed?"

If I knew why, then maybe I could figure out who.

"Carson, someone is after me. It started after I began investigating Department 5491." I paused. "I've been imprisoned, beaten, tortured, starved, followed, chased, and vilified by the media."

Jordan flinched at each escalation. Carson just listened.

"I'm considered armed and dangerous, which you know means any law enforcement officer in the freaking country who identifies me has the option to shoot to kill without any input from me."

"She has a right to know," Jordan said.

I wanted to throw up my hands in disgust. "Maybe the only way to get answers is to go public, expose Department 5491." Disclose the information to the media and see where the clues led. If someone was after me because of that information, I would take away the benefit of silencing me.

"You're playing hardball." Sports analogies. Never a good sign where Carson was involved. "Would you really go to the media?"

Assuming we could get out of here, yeah. "I have no choice."

Carson waited another beat.

"You need to understand the background. Relations with Russia were very tense back then." Carson rubbed his hand over his breastbone. "Boris Yeltsin was coming in late October for a summit meeting with President Clinton, but things were strained. Clinton had refused to go to Russia earlier in the year."

"What does that have to do with my grandparents?" I glanced toward Jordan, his face impassive, his gaze constantly moving.

"Your grandfather was a German codebreaker in World War II."

"German?" Not Polish, like the census indicated.

"Yes." Carson nodded. "Have you heard of TICOM?"

Jordan perked up, shot me an unreadable look. "Lucas Goodman once asked me about a connection between Staci and TICOM but I thought they were reaching."

"During the World War II, Britain and the United States formed the Target Intelligence Committee specifically to find and capture German codebreakers. We wanted the Russian code the German's had deciphered."

"Again. Why my family?"

"In 1945 we invaded a castle in Saxony, Germany, and confiscated their cipher machines and personnel. Before the Russians could get there, we hid the codebreakers."

"1945?" I made the jump. "So all of the people killed in 1995 were...."

"German codebreakers plus one Russian double agent."

I sank further into the fluffy, plump cushions, the soft down pillows enfolding me like a giant pair of welcoming arms. I processed information that finally gave me some clue as to why my grandparents had a hard time showing me affection. Their reticence and reserve were more understandable. The ability to open their hearts to anyone had been shunted by the reality that they could be gone in an instant, suddenly snatched away.

"I still don't understand why the hits were ordered."

"We had sleepers in place in case the codebreakers ever decided to talk about TICOM or return to Germany. These people had information about the U.S. and U.K. intelligence that, to this day, we cannot allow the Russians to get their hands on. The information is still classified."

"But October of 1995 was fifty years later," I argued as if I could change the outcome.

"In July of 1995, the CIA released cable transcripts of Soviet cables that we had intercepted and translated in the 1940's. The cables included names and cover names of over two hundred people who spied against U.S., some of whom were double agents and spied for us against Russia. In the documents released there was one code name, a Russian agent who was undercover in Germany. When we captured the Germans, we captured him and he chose to defect to the United States. According to our intel, the Russians had never discovered that he was a double agent."

I aimed a look at Jordan. He remembered reading about that information.

"What was the name?"

"Even I don't know which person was the double agent. He was only listed by his code name in the cable transcripts."

"Then why kill everyone?" I asked again.

"Because we didn't know which codebreaker was the spy. My guess is keeping his true name out of the records was done to protect him but all we knew was that one of the codebreakers was a double agent. We couldn't take the chance that the Russians would realize the double agent was alive and go after him." Carson said tightly, "Our relations would have become even more strained."

"Still the transcripts were released in July."

"The irony is that many critics actually questioned the credibility of the cables." Carson sighed, his mouth an unhappy line. "We tried, secretly using the media, to foster the idea that the information was false."

"What was the point of eliminating all of those people?"

"The point was nothing. An over-reaction." Carson

started pacing. "But by the time I realized it, the damage was done."

I. Had he just said, I?

Jordan shifted, pushing off the door to stand at attention.

"I?" I repeated softly.

Carson stopped, straightened, shoulders back, like a soldier awaiting punishment. His gaze was tortured as he met mine. "I carried out orders. But I didn't know anything about who the hits were on. I just knew there were sleepers in place."

My brain couldn't process, my body immobile, held in place by an invisible force field of disbelief, denial. Was he telling me that he ordered the hit on my grandparents?

"I was a junior director. I ignored my instincts. Ignored my gut and followed orders." Carson reached toward me. "I should have asked more questions."

I shrank away from his hand, forcing myself to ask the next question, forcing the images, the pain out of my body, into a tiny little box in my mind where I could take it out later and feel the hurt cut into my heart. Right now I needed to finish this.

"Where did the order come from?" I asked through bloodless lips. I couldn't imagine he could tell me anything worse.

Carson's gaze cut to Jordan. And I knew I'd been wrong. Something worse was coming. "The Senate Select Committee on Intelligence."

Shit. I recalled our research.

"I shouldn't tell you. But in light of the current circumstances...I'm sorry." Carson sighed. "Senator Jordan gave the order."

CHAPTER 42

Jordan lounged against the six-paneled, steel-reinforced door. His face unbelievably still and smooth like polished marble. Nothing to indicate Carson had just gutted him.

But I knew. Underneath that serene, calm exterior he seethed with pent up emotion. His father's legacy of deceit and betrayal continued to grow. The more I learned about Senator Jordan, the more I despised him.

I couldn't imagine Jordan's feelings. I wanted to reach out, stroke his shoulder, offer him comfort in some small measurable gesture.

But his face forbade any discussion or acknowledgment of the blow Carson had just dealt.

"Could the senator be after me because I'd been researching 5491?"

"Negative. He might have given the kill order but he doesn't know anything about Department 5491."

"Anyone else?" I asked.

"I did some quiet inquiries," Carson started slowly. "I

told the CIA weeks ago I didn't believe that was you in the prison photos. They were disinclined to listen."

"They wanted me dead?"

"I don't know." Carson hesitated. "They blocked certain information even from us. Usually we can access Intelink and get updates on unfolding situations, but any information about you was above my security level."

Above Carson's level? He was Director of Field Operations for the NSA. A division so secret many people didn't even know the NSA had field operations. His mere existence was highly classified.

"Why?"

"Best guess, they're trolling for a reaction from someone," Carson said. "They've got continuous surveillance on your place in Alexandria."

"Someone trashed my Bahamas house."

"I don't believe it was the CIA. Not their style," Carson said.

He was right.

"We came here to ask for help. I need to set up a meet with the Senator to find out why he was in that press conference." No sense of the rage boiling inside of Jordan was evident. "We think he may have answers."

"Is that wise?"

"It's necessary." Jordan's voice was low, controlled. "I need to strike now."

I? No way in hell was he going alone.

"We." I amended. "We need to set up a meeting."

"I don't want you anywhere near him." Jordan sat down next to me on the sofa.

I asked Carson curiously, "How well do you know him?"

"We've had a working association for the past fifteen

years." Carson didn't like him. Nothing in his voice gave him away, but the distaste for Senator Jordan came through loud and clear. "I can set up a meeting with your father."

Silence.

Apparently more people than Jordan realized knew about Jordan's parentage. I placed my hand over Jordan's and linked our fingers.

"Sperm donor," Jordan responded tightly. "He is nothing but a means to clear Staci."

He would never be like his own father. I could hear him as clearly as if he'd spoken.

Our baby.

Without thought I put my hand to my belly and gazed at Jordan.

I could feel the tiny pulse of blood through my fingertips, resting on the bump I'd tried to ignore ever since Thea told me why I couldn't keep down food.

A baby.

Emotion so tender, so breathtaking unfurled slowly inside of me.

Carson looked at my hand on my stomach, Jordan's fingers meshed with mine, and the protective way we both curled in slightly. "You're pregnant?"

I couldn't miss the surprise on his face.

Jordan gazed into my eyes. We were both cammied up, he had twigs in his hair, and black and green camouflage paint smeared over his face, his beautiful hazel eyes almost invisible.

One hand rested on my stomach, the other still held his Glock carefully pointed at the floor.

We would certainly be non-traditional.

"Congratulations," Carson said, appearing to be genuinely happy.

A swell of pure joy spread through me. "We're going to be parents." Nothing and no-one was going to hurt my family. Not if I had anything to say about it.

Pictures freeze-framed through my head. Katerina vowing to protect her son. Susan Chen running away to protect her daughter. Fariya protecting future generations as she'd failed to protect her own children. Suddenly, without a doubt, I understood why.

Their child was far more important to them than anything else...including their own survival.

And I knew what I had to do.

THEY PLANNED THE OP.

Sitting at the round game table, Jordan solidified details with Carson and Staci. Antoinette Black had gone to bed after fussing over Staci for half an hour or so.

All they had to do now was wait.

They would wait until the senator would be home for the night, wait until the meeting area would be empty, wait until the last minute to schedule the meeting--so there was no time for the senator to arrange for backup.

"What about backup for us?" Staci wasn't convinced the senator was harmless.

Us? He didn't want her anywhere near the bastard. And told her so.

"You're crazy if you think I'll let you go in alone," she said, flexing then fisting her fingers.

His mouth settled into a grim line. He needed to know what his father had done and why. And he needed to make sure Staci and the baby were protected.

Jordan laced his fingers with Staci's. For the first time

since he'd found her in New York, he felt as if they connected. In the same way as when they'd first met, when from across the room the intensity of their attraction had sizzled.

"I don't want you to get hurt."

"I know you're worried about the baby."

"*You*. I don't want *you* to get hurt."

As much as he agreed backup would be nice, he didn't think it was an option.

"Back up is necessary." Carson frowned. "Jamie and Lucas are in Seattle."

Jordan wondered which part he didn't like, Jamie and Lucas together or the fact that they were in Seattle going after Susan Chen.

"Zeke?" Staci asked.

Good thought. Even though the guy wasn't too fond of Staci, he'd be better than nothing. Hopefully he hadn't left town yet.

Carson's eyebrows rose. "You know Ezekiel?"

Uh...hopefully that wasn't a bad thing. For Zeke or Staci.

"We've met." Staci handed Jordan her cell. "Call him."

"Won't work in here," Carson said calmly. "It's shielded."

Carson picked up a landline and gave the phone to Jordan.

"Go ahead."

Technically Zeke was suspended, but this wasn't official NSA business, right?

Jordan dialed and listened to the ring tone, Jay Z and Linkin Park rocked the phone lines with Numb/Encore.

Zeke finally picked up. "Carson?"

"Hey, it's Jordan."

There was a pause as Zeke assimilated that Jordan was calling from Carson's home.

"Dude, how's it hanging?" His tone was light, but Jordan had gotten to know Zeke well enough to hear the underlying concern in his irreverent question.

"We're all fine." We. Just so Zeke knew he and Staci were still together. "We're about to take a meeting with the Senator and thought maybe you'd like to join in."

Jordan tried to keep the conversation as generic as possible since Zeke was on a cell which was not secure.

"I'd freaking love to, except I'm stuck in Nowheresville, California, doing a worthless surveillance detail on Granola Girl."

Jordan winced. Either Zeke didn't care or hadn't realized giving out details was a mistake.

"Uh, not secure."

"Shit. You're right." Zeke huffed. "I should not be here. I am not cut out for this. And nothing is happening."

"So you're out of the area."

"Yeah. Sorry." Zeke was silent again. "I'm no help."

The disgust in his voice bothered Jordan. "There's a reason you're there. Maybe it just isn't apparent yet."

"My, my, when did we become so philosophical?" Zeke mocked, then relented. "Never mind. Ignore me. I'm feeling sorry for myself. Again."

Jamie had sent Zeke there because of a hunch that Sunshine was in danger. "Do you think she's wrong?"

"Yes. Nothing happens here." Through the phone lines, the ocean crashed against the shoreline sweeping away some of Zeke's words. "No. Maybe. I don't know. I've got a weird vibe, but everything appears fine."

"Eyes open," Jordan said.

"You know it." Zeke paused again, then asked softly, "You got any backup?"

"Not exactly."

"Take Carson," Zeke recommended. "He's tougher than he looks."

Jordan hadn't even considered using Carson Black, but as Zeke's idea settled in, he realized the advice was perfect.

"Great idea. Thanks." Jordan signed off quickly. "Take care of yourself, pal."

"Keep safe," Zeke said softly.

Jordan carefully pressed the off button. "He suggested I take you."

Assuming Carson would agree, the idea was brilliant. Jordan was expendable. Life would actually be easier for the senator if Jordan was out of the picture. But the senator wouldn't and couldn't harm Carson. Not without serious repercussions.

Jesus, Zeke was smart.

"Excellent idea." Carson brushed an imaginary piece of lint off his wool pants. "Of course I'll go."

Suspicion fluttered in the back of Jordan's mind. He got the feeling they had just been maneuvered.

More was going on here than just saving Staci's life. Before they ever requested Carson's help, they should have factored in that he would have his own agenda.

Staci yawned, the muscles in her jaw stretching wide.

"Why not get some sleep before we go?" Carson offered the guest room.

They were safe here. This house was a fortress. They had almost three hours before they needed to leave for D.C. A quick combat nap would refresh him. Maybe Jordan could even get Staci to fall asleep. Then leaving her here would be a non-argument, and he could just sneak out.

"You aren't leaving without me," Staci said firmly.

"Sleep sounds good. Maybe a shower." Jordan's nose itched, but he didn't want to rub any of the camo paint onto his hands.

Staci groaned. "A shower sounds heavenly."

Carson showed them to a guest room, grabbed a stack of pristine white towels from the closet. He looked them over, and smiled. "Don't worry about getting the towels dirty. We've got bleach."

With that non sequitur, he looked at his watch. "Two and a half hours. I'll be in the kitchen, if you need anything."

Jordan closed the door. They were alone. He felt he and Staci had come to a tentative understanding, some place where they were in accordance with each other, and with the baby.

Maybe they weren't in agreement about confronting the senator, but two out of three was pretty good.

Jesus, what a crazy two days.

Jordan tugged gently, and Staci came into his arms without resistance. He rested his cheek against her forehead, wrapped his arms around her too thin body, and pulled her tight against his chest.

She was still cold. The heat from his body would warm her. And the comfort from their embrace would warm him. Win-win.

Staci sighed and melted into his arms. Her breasts pillowed against his chest, and the hard points of her nipples rubbed against his pectorals.

Suddenly, his body flared into an inferno. Great. One platonic embrace and his hormones acted like a hound dog in heat.

"You want first dibs on the shower?" His voice came out

husky and soft.

She sighed again, squeezed his waist, and let go. "You go on ahead."

"Yeah." If he got away from her, he could get his randy body under control with a really cold shower.

CHAPTER 43

I watched Jordan hustle into the bathroom. My former lover, lover, father of my baby, whatever, was running away. Away from me? Or away from the churning feelings and emotions that ran underneath every interaction we had?

Wrapped in the protective embrace of his arms, I'd finally felt as if I'd come home. As if I could rest my weary body along the rock of his and we could just...be. Our connection, our bond had strengthened challenge by challenge. But could we withstand what was coming?

I listened to the roar of the water and snuck out to the kitchen where I knew Carson would be waiting for me.

My request took less than a minute.

"Are you sure?" Carson asked.

"It's the only way to be free."

He nodded. "Okay."

I snuck back into the guest room, reviewing our relationship, the ups and downs, our time together...and gave thanks Jordan was still here, still with me. What a miracle.

Still by my side.

Still primed to fight for me, for us, for the baby.

Could I be sure that all of that fight wasn't strictly for the baby?

No.

On the other hand, I didn't see anyone else around. Anyone else believing in me, believing in my innocence.

Suddenly I wasn't willing to let that miracle slip away.

I had a limited window to let him know how much his support meant to me, how much he meant to me.

Glancing in the mirror, I looked at the train wreck of my reflection. I was too thin, too brittle. But Jordan didn't care. That was the truth, the beauty of his affection for me.

Somehow he didn't see me as I did. Instead he saw through to the warrior that lived beneath my fragile skin, to the woman who refused to give up and refused to give in.

I shoved open the louvered doors to the guest bathroom.

The noise startled Jordan, and he turned defensively, his face almost clear of the paint.

"Sorry."

"Everything okay?" He stopped, completely oblivious to his nudity, and completely focused on me.

"Fine." Water sluiced over his sculpted muscles, rolling down his shoulders, pecs, and six-pack, with an ease I envied.

How weird was that...to envy water?

I stared at him, unable to vocalize all the thoughts jumbling in my mind, emotions tumbling through my body.

He just stood there, staring at me, wanting me to leave...or wanting me to come closer?

I didn't know.

There was only one thing left to do. I pulled the soft cotton camouflage shirt over my head. Unbelting the pants,

I let them slide off my hips to puddle around my ankles, then stepped out of the pile. Reaching around, I unhooked my bra and let the serviceable white cotton drop to the floor.

His gaze dropped to my pert nipples, and my breasts full, heavy, and so sensitive from the pregnancy hormones just the lick of his regard flushed my body rosy.

I shimmied out of the white cotton panties and walked purposefully toward the shower, anxious to trace the path of the water down his body with my mouth.

At the clear shower door, I hesitated, prepping myself for rejection, hoping the reality of my beaten and scarred body wouldn't send him screaming into the night.

I didn't think he'd scare so easily. If the past two days had revealed one thing about Jordan, it was his innate capacity to persevere whatever the circumstances.

He popped open the glass shower door, his expression vulnerable. "You coming in?"

I stepped over the threshold and into his arms.

Home. I'd come home.

The surprisingly warm water cascaded over our intertwined bodies. His sculpted biceps cradled my smaller, thinner frame with care. The hard muscles and wiry hair of his thighs rubbed at my softer skin creating a delicious friction. His burgeoning erection pressed insistently at the juncture to my feminine core. He hugged me tightly, the flex of his muscles against my heavy breasts increased my rising tension.

I knew I should move, get to it. Sex was why I'd come in here, bared my scarred abused body to his. It was the only thing I could think to give him.

And if I was honest, I wanted this one last moment for myself.

Instead of taking us to the next level, he shifted me in his arms, holding me under the spray and apart from his body. "Close your eyes and tilt your head back."

I complied and he cleansed my face of the greasepaint, his fingers following the same path he'd used to smear it on, gently, gently, washing away the evidence of our crawl here, his thumbs tender as he wiped at my mouth. My lips tingled with each subtle stroke.

I started to open my eyes.

"Keep them closed." Starting at the fingertips of my right hand, he kissed each one as if giving thanks. With his tongue, he gently licked the wicked bruises along my wrist. He traced his fingers up the length of my arm, stopping at each mark, each burn, and pressing a soft, open-mouthed kiss on each badge of torture.

His hands and mouth catalogued then swept away each hideous moment of that two weeks, washing me clean, absolving me with his ministrations.

I wanted to thank him. Wanted to show him my gratitude. But I was afraid to open my eyes as the pressure built behind my lids, and threatened to come pouring out if I didn't hold myself together.

His fingers slid into my hair. With a firm circular motion, he massaged an evergreen-scented shampoo into my scalp and through the rough strands of my hair, washing out the temporary gray.

The touch of his hands was surprisingly erotic. He'd eased closer to rinse out the shampoo, and I took advantage of his nearness.

I slid my hands down the flat plane of his stomach, noting the weight he'd lost. My knuckles rubbed against the ridges of his muscles until I smoothed my palm down to his rock-hard erection.

There was a time for finesse, for long sensuous hours of exploring and tantalizing, and now wasn't it.

Now was the time for hard, pounding, life-affirming sex.

I wanted to get lost in the pleasure of him, of us, and forget everything else. Burn away my memories, burn away my tears.

His body still slick with soap, I took the length of him in my palm and rubbed along his pulsing, engorged erection, using my thumb to firmly swipe back and forth over the sensitive tip.

Jordan threaded his fingers through my hair, pulled my head back, and plundered my mouth.

He leaned back against the tile wall and pulled me flush against his hard body, his chest flattening my breasts as he slid his hot, callused hand down my back and over the curve of my butt. His fingers closed over the globes of my ass as he lifted me up.

He stopped, with my fist on his cock, priming him, his fingers digging into my ass as he braced to take my weight. "Open your eyes."

I waited for a second, the pulse of desire, thick and insistent in my body. The raging heat emanating from him, the water pounding against my back, the liquid pouring over my shoulders and caressing my breasts. "Can't I do that later?" I asked with impatience.

"Now."

I opened my eyes and stared into his intense hazel gaze. As soon as we connected, my body re-sensitized all over again. Every place we touched, my skin was on fire, every spot where our flesh and muscles parted was bereft.

"Let go." Somehow I knew he was talking about more than just letting go of his cock. Our gazes still knit together, I freed him.

He lifted me, my pubic bone pressing against his erection, my thighs scraping the soft skin of his underbelly until he held me poised above him.

Instead of the down, dirty, and fast I expected, Jordan carefully, gently, almost reverently joined his body with mine. My slick channel welcomed him with a rain of desire.

We moved together, slipping and sliding into a drowsy, sensuous rhythm, each glide stroking, arousing.

His sex swelled, the rigid length rocking inside me, hitting that hidden treasure spot. Pleasure swirled higher and higher with each stroke.

Jordan stiffened as he arched his body into mine and pulled my sex tight against his. The hot jet of his orgasm, and the hard pulse of his penis shattered me. Together, falling, falling into a euphoric rush. I trembled and shook with aftershocks, as his arms supported me, held me.

I brushed a soft kiss against the muscles of his shoulder.

That tenderness was just what I expected of him, the unexpected.

"Do you ever do what you're supposed to?"

He reached behind me and turned off the water. "Only when I want to."

My laugh was quiet. "Yeah." I rested my head in the curve of his neck. "What do you want to do now?"

"Go to bed."

I notice he didn't say sleep.

As he straightened, pushing off against the tile, his cock pulsed inside me, sending a trill of sensation through me.

He nuzzled my neck, then blew into my exposed ear, as he opened the shower door. I tightened my thighs around his waist and locked my ankles over the taut curve of his butt. "You don't have to carry me."

His mouth curved into a wicked grin. "I don't mind."

He grabbed a towel, drying us both randomly, and then headed into the bedroom.

Jordan held me tight against him, his hands sliding down to support my butt. At least that was what I thought until I felt the firm pressure of his fingers sliding along the crease of my buttocks, stroking my still-flush folds, and curling toward my clitoris.

I whimpered as he expertly plied his fingers in rhythm to the stride of his legs. By the time we made it to the bed, my whole body quivered on the brink of release.

He had swelled inside me, primed again.

Gently, gently he lay me down on the bed.

Oh no. We were not going this way again.

I wanted his last memory of this, of us to be wild, erotic, and unforgettable.

I arched up, using my ankles, restricting his ability to move away.

Jordan's control broke.

Our bodies collided. He slammed into me, hips pistoning, muscles straining and here was the roughness, the intensity I'd expected.

I gripped his biceps, his skin slick with sweat as we hammered together. My nerve endings were raw, sensitized, nearly bursting from more erotic stimulation. I bowed back, and his mouth latched onto my breast.

My orgasm exploded outward like a bomb detonating, I felt as if I'd lost all substance, all form, and shattered into a thousand tiny pieces from which there would be no recovery.

Jordan arched, groaned and poured himself into me.

And I knew I was never going to be the same. He'd given me everything.

I sighed, shivering in the chill air.

Jordan pulled the duvet over our still joined bodies. The solid hardness of his body lay between my thighs, a welcome comfort.

We lay there, savoring. Neither of us spoke, not wanting to destroy the fragile calm of this moment.

But it couldn't last. He propped on his elbows to stare down at me.

Emotion began to cloud his eyes.

Jordan twirled a damp curl around his finger. "Carson has an agenda. We need to know that we can trust him to watch our backs."

"Carson will do what's right." I only hoped Jordan could forgive him, forgive me.

"How do you know?" Jordan asked.

I'd rarely talked about my family. I knew why I'd avoided the subject. Nothing like a buzz kill to explain why you had intimacy issues. Of course, for most guys, women having intimacy issues was probably a pleasant change.

I'd gone through enough psych evals to know that I tended to keep people at an emotional distance. Friendly, yet remote. No best friends.

Until Jordan.

I had to explain, had to prepare him, even if he wouldn't understand until later. "After my grandparents' deaths, I was," I paused, "Devastated."

"You were close to them."

"Not exactly."

"How not exactly?"

I didn't say anything.

"There are a thousand other things we should be talking about, working 'what if' scenarios--"

"This is important." Jordan traced his finger lightly over

the scar on the under curve of my breast. "I know all about these. What I need to understand are the ones here."

He lay his palm over my heart.

And I was lost.

Was it any wonder I was willing to give up everything for him...for our baby?

"It's funny because they raised me, groomed me, and guided me." And yeah, I know they loved me but it had been a very distant love. Their love for each other was so encompassing...they'd had an epic story.

They were a Christian and a Jew married in a time when they still had segregated beaches, one for Christians, one for Jews. Now that I knew they'd come from Germany where religious tension was far worse, it only underscored the difficult reality of their relationship. They'd been completely solid.

"They were a unit, and I changed their lifestyle."

"What does that have to do with Carson?"

"He saved me." And he'd set the foundation for who I was today. The feeling in my gut was unshakeable. "Trust me."

He rolled onto his back, curving his arm to prop up his head. "I do trust you."

And I knew he was giving me a gift. "You promise? No matter what?" Reflexively, I brushed my fingers against my throat. But of course, the amulet was gone.

"Wait here." He vaulted out of bed, and I was thankful for the reprieve. I watched the play of muscle in his butt as he retrieved something from his pants pocket.

Jordan walked back toward me, his sex swaying with each step. But that isn't what held my attention, it was the look shining from his eyes.

He leaned over to tie the leather around my neck. The

familiar weight of my mother's amber settled on my throat. I curled my fingers around the carved scarab, my heart thudding in my chest.

"I...stole this from your dresser after you left. Carried it with me, everywhere." Jordan admitted as he slid back in beside me. "I kept thinking that if I kept it safe, I could keep you safe."

Moisture pooled in my eyes, and love gripped my throat.

"Hey, it worked." I blinked.

Jordan rolled on top of me, caging my body with his, covering me, his expression fierce. "Know this. I will not let him hurt you."

"Ditto."

And I prayed he'd understand.

October 20th
        2:18 AM
Lincoln Memorial, Washington D.C.

The Lincoln Memorial was deserted.

They were in place at the base of Lincoln's statue, waiting for the senator to arrive.

They'd let the senator think he was meeting only with Carson. Jordan flicked a glance at his watch, and wondered if the old goat would be on time. Would he be curious enough to arrive as soon as possible, or would he execute a power play and make the peon wait?

Carson had enticed the senator with information about Staci, indicating he didn't want to share with the authorities until after talking to the senator. He intimated the intel was something the senator needed to hear first before the knowledge went on the record.

Carson specifically told the senator to come alone, but Jordan was sure the senator would have at least one bodyguard with him. Cynically, Jordan wondered what the esteemed senator's wife thought about him taking a meeting at two o'clock in the morning.

She probably thought he was diddling an aide.

Jordan knew the old goat didn't have any other illegitimate kids because right after Jordan's birth, the senator had a vasectomy.

The dick.

All his life, Jordan tried to forget about his father, and most of the time he succeeded. He had little contact with the man over the years. Contact was always initiated by the senator, except for the first disastrous time Jordan had wanted to meet his father and tracked him down in his congressional office after hours.

Since then Jordan avoided him at all costs.

His distaste for everything the man stood for was absolute. If he could eradicate his father's DNA from his body he would be happy.

Fortunately he had his mother and aunt to counteract the poison of his father's legacy.

"You can be anything you want," his mother used to say fiercely. So fiercely, he'd always believed it.

Jordan was unbelievably proud of her. She'd had a hard life, come from Mexico to work in the United States, and when she'd gotten pregnant, she'd been disowned by her family, frowned upon by the church, and still managed to succeed.

If anyone had asked Jordan a week ago if he'd ever want to confront his father about anything, he'd have said absolutely not.

But as he stood in the shadow of Abraham Lincoln's marble throne, a surety of purpose blanketed him. Justice would finally be served.

And he would be the one to deliver it.

They heard the clicking of his father's heels. Staci tightened subtly. Carson relaxed. And Jordan knew what he had to do.

"Change of plan," he said softly. "I'll do the talking."

"Are you sure that's wise?" Carson whispered.

Jordan held up his palm before Staci could speak. "I have to do this."

She threaded her fingers through his and brushed his knuckles with her lips before letting go and fading into the shadows.

A solid lump of dread settled in his stomach. But using his HRT training, he settled into his zone.

This moment was his cold zero. The point at which your zero target and the cold bore of your rifle meet. That first perfect shot. And he wasn't going to miss.

Jordan stepped closer to the edge of the shadows just as his father walked up the final step. Standing underneath the mural representing angels and truth, Jordan's body would be visible but not his face.

Jordan searched behind the senator looking for his backup.

But no one was there.

They had set up the meet after they arrived at the monument. Since then, no one else had approached, so unless the senator had brought along snipers--doubtful--they were safe.

Jordan didn't want to take any chances with Staci's safety. But she had a right to her own answers and her own justice.

"Really, Black, was this necessary?"

"It was." Jordan stepped out into the light, revealing his face.

"Ramirez?" His father never called Jordan by his first name, as if he could distance himself from the truth of Jordan's existence.

"Yes."

"What are you doing here? I thought you were--" The senator shifted gears quickly, understanding he'd given something away, and put facts together. "I didn't realize you were acquainted with Black."

"Didn't realize you were keeping track of me that closely."

"Why are you here?" The senator stiffened. "And where is Carson Black?"

"I have questions and I want answers," Jordan ordered, using a hard voice.

"This conversation is over."

When he was younger, Jordan had a sort of sick fascination with his father. He'd studied him: His schooling, his career path, his social moves, even his way of dress.

"Why were you in the press conference regarding Staci Grant?"

"That traitor?"

Jordan knew exactly how to stick it to the senator. All those hours of analyzing him, dissecting his behavior were going to pay off spectacularly. "She's no traitor. She works for the CIA."

The senator snorted. "She doesn't work for the CIA. She recruits terrorists."

"Perhaps you should have done your homework, Dick." Jordan contradicted him, "She's a NOC officer for the CIA."

The senator paled, actually fell back a step as if by retreating he could deny Jordan's words. "You...you're serious."

"Oh yeah." A combination of triumph and fury bubbled through him. "Who authorized the release of her information? Intel of that magnitude is vetted high up."

"Your information is flawed," the senator said resolutely. "I saw the documentation on her activities. She's been recruiting--"

"For our government." Unbelievable. The old man was still trying to defend his position. "Who authorized the press conference?"

"I was just there for effect."

Trying to snag some of the publicity for his own gain. "Who?"

The senator blustered, "Major Vandenburg took care of everything. He had the appropriate paperwork and approvals."

Major Vandenburg again. "Why would he have it in for Staci?"

The senator frowned, his face barely moving. He must have had a recent Botox injection. "You're mistaken."

"Face facts. You've been used." Either that or he was one hell of an actor.

The senator shook his head, firm in his beliefs. "She was recruiting in Afghanistan."

"She was working for UNOCHA. They facilitate the de-mining of rural areas in countries like Afghanistan." Jordan hammered. "A cause you purportedly support."

"This is ridiculous." The senator pivoted on his five-hundred-dollar Cole Haan's. "I'll get this straightened out. I'd suggest if you are associating with this woman you disentangle immediately."

Jordan was as entangled as it got.

His anger built, his heart pounding, pulse beating.

As if she knew, he was at his breaking point, Staci

stepped out of the shadows. "We can't let you leave just yet, Senator."

Senator Jordan whirled around. "You!" The weapon in her hands made him falter.

"You won't shoot me," he said imperiously.

"I have nothing left to lose," Staci said calmly, her hand steady and her eyes serious. "You made sure of that. I'm as good as dead. Frankly unless I get this mess straightened out, I don't care who I take with me."

She smiled then and Jordan was thankful she wasn't pissed at him anymore.

The senator paled but held his ground. His hand in his pocket, he fiddled nervously with change.

"Hands out of your pockets, sir," she sneered.

She cocked the trigger and the senator complied, quickly.

"Do you know who you talking to? I'm the chairman of the Senate Select Committee on Intelligence. You can't touch me."

"It's like our own personal town hall meeting." She derided. "Would that be the same committee who ordered the execution of innocent war refugees in 1995?"

The senator ignored her question, his gaze focused on the weapon. "If you shoot me, they'll go after your family."

"I don't have any family, you bastard." Staci took a menacing step forward. "You killed them."

"That's utterly ridiculous. I didn't kill anyone."

Carson stepped out of the shadows on the other side of Lincoln. "Actually, you did."

"Black. You are here."

"I told you I needed to talk to you," Carson said calmly.

The senator put on a smarmy smile usually reserved for the press. "Can you take care of these people?"

"I'd be happy to," Carson said easily. "But first, go ahead and answer their questions."

"Fine. What do you want to know?"

Jordan's temper was starting to roil. The senator didn't give a rat's ass about what he'd done. "Why'd you order the deaths of those people?"

The senator paused. "It was a security risk we couldn't afford."

"In 1995, you were just appointed. So how did you make the decision?" Staci asked.

"Most of our committee was down with the flu," the senator said slowly, finally realizing how truly tenuous his position was. "There were only three of us in session, and we needed to act quickly. So we decided to err on the side of caution."

And he thought nothing of it?

"You destroyed ten families." Staci's aim was rock-steady as she held the weapon pointed straight at his rotten heart.

He took a step back toward the eighty small steps leading down and away. But he was trapped. There was no way to go down quickly without breaking his neck.

"Why did you have me followed?" Jordan bit out.

The senator tightened his lips, and his head canted to the side for an instant. "I didn't."

Jordan knew he was lying. He didn't like the way the senator kept looking behind him. He cautiously eased his weapon from the holster so that he would not jeopardize Staci. Thinking carefully, moving slowly, he thumbed off the safety and started shifting towards his future.

A cold calm reason settled in his mind. "How can we clear up this mess? Why did Vandenburg call the press conference about Staci?"

"National Security." The senator blinked, looked at the gun in Jordan's hand. "You won't shoot me."

"I trained with weapons every day for fifteen years. I have a near perfect kill shot, I rarely miss, and I am really, really pissed off."

"What do you want?" The senator demanded.

The only sound in the still air of the night was the harsh rasp of Jordan's breath. "Call off the dogs on Staci."

"I can't do that." He dismissed the order with a flick of his hand.

"Do it."

The senator said, "You're wasting your breath."

Time seemed to slow. The rush of the wind along the deserted monument, the skitter of leaves across the white marble floor, the frozen tableau of the four of them, stuck in a pattern without a way out, unless Jordan changed the rules.

"Do it or I'll go to the press." Jordan breathed in the frigid Fall air letting the cold cleanse his lungs. "The senator who runs on a campaign of family values tried to kill his own son, his own illegitimate son?"

"I never...." But the senator trailed off.

"You gave my mother money to have an abortion, another strike against that whole family values platform you pride yourself on, and your wife dismissed my mother from your household."

Jordan took a step closer to look into the senator's eyes. To let the man who'd been nothing more than a sperm donor see his contempt and disgust. "And despite the hardship your family caused her, she still managed to triumph."

Every word was a vindication of the distress and anguish this man had wreaked on Jordan's family.

"I'll be goddamned if I let you sorry excuse for a man destroy Staci Grant's life because of your fucking ego and inefficiencies."

The senator opened and closed his mouth like lobbyist caught with a bribe in his hand.

"The life of a good woman, a woman with values and honor and integrity."

Jordan realized Staci had all of those qualities in abundance. Perhaps he didn't always approve of her methods. But her motives and objectives were just. Unlike his father, whose only motivation was self-serving. He would not let the senator ruin her life.

"All the qualities that you should have and don't. Fix it."

"There's no way to do that without coming off like a total fool."

"It won't be the first time."

"I...."

"Don't worry, Richard." Major Vandenburg stepped into the light, a small pistol in his hands. It looked suspiciously like the missing Sig Sauer P229 from Staci's Bahamas house.

Fuck.

The senator, damn him, relaxed. This was what he'd been waiting for.

Vandenburg took a step closer. "I'll take care of this. Go on home."

CHAPTER 45

"Major!" The senator feigned surprise, eyebrows raised in polite inquiry. "What are you doing here?"

Scumbag. Clearly, Senator Jordan had called the major.

"He's going to try kill me," I said.

That wiped the smile off the senator's face.

Major Vandenburg sneered. "I'm going to succeed."

"I'd really like to know why," I asked pleasantly as if inquiring about the high cost of Army toilet seats rather than speaking about my death.

"You're a public danger." The major bared his teeth. "Don't you watch television?"

We were in a V pattern, Carson on my left, me in the middle, Jordan on my right. I was directly across from the senator. Major Vandenburg was behind and a little to the right of the senator, closer to Jordan than Carson.

I was the furthest away, but the Major had a clear line of sight to me. He was also only three feet away from the steps.

Jordan had the best angle of trajectory for hitting the

major, but first dammit, I really wanted to know why this guy wanted to kill me.

"Why?"

"You were in Zaman Khalili's village."

"Yeah."

"What did you see?"

"Poverty, evidence of U.S. dollars coming in, the kids had pencils and the adults had boxes of supplies."

"When you escaped from prison?"

"A lot of landmines."

"Jesus, after all this, all the worry, stress and extra work you caused me and you didn't even notice."

I scrolled through my memories of the village.

Then it hit me. I'd seen poppy fields. With harvested plants. Not destroyed.

"So you had me put in prison?"

"You were the only American on that team." The major spit a giant glob of mucus onto the floor, reminding me of Fariya, when she showed her contempt for Zaman Khalili.

And I suddenly realized, she had known.

She had known the U.S. military was using her village, using her family. That's why she'd freed me. She wanted it stopped. Wanted the drug harvesting and trafficking to stop.

Jordan glanced down at the puddle of spit and smiled wickedly. I knew exactly what he was thinking. DNA evidence to tie the major to this meeting.

"And then it all went to shit when I found out you worked for the CIA. Dammit."

"The CIA?" the senator looked horrified. "She, you, oh, my dear Lord. You knew?"

Yeah. Idiot. You fucked up. I smirked. "So what exactly are you doing in Afghanistan?"

Vandenburg replied, "We give the villages the army money from CERP, the Commanders' Emergency Relief Program, we give them supplies through the Civil Affairs Division, and then instead of destroying the poppy fields, they harvest the poppies and we split the profits."

"What about the Taliban?"

"We protect them from the Taliban." He paused. "They're happy to work with us because they get money, supplies and half the profits."

Not everyone was happy, I thought.

"What are you doing with the money? Got a nice bank account somewhere in the Bahamas, you piece of horseshit?"

"Bitch." The major took a menacing step toward me.

In the periphery, the senator had watched our exchange, his head shifting back and forth. "Now see here."

"Shut up, Dick." Vandenburg pulled an AK-47 from behind his waistband and handed the Sig Sauer to the senator. "Hold this."

Thankfully, the senator knew what to do with a weapon, and he kept the P229 pointed toward the floor.

"We use the money to outfit the troops," the Major ground out. "Do you know how much body armor costs? And the right kind of bullets? Our troops are dying," his voice broke, "because those blowhards," he jerked his chin toward the senator, "Can't give us enough money to protect our soldiers."

I said, "What about the heroin that's making its way all over the world?"

"That's not my problem." The major dismissed the increase in heroin traffic, the increase in opioid-related deaths with a shake of his head. "My charge is to protect the men and women who work for me-at any cost."

The major lifted his assault rifle.

"You can't mean to kill them," the senator bluffed.

"You're implicated, asshole," the major said. "It's either kill her, or your career is history."

I only had one choice.

I wanted to fight. I wanted to defend myself, defend the rights of the women and children in that village.

I had a responsibility to make sure Fariya's sacrifice was just. I was the only one now who could confirm to the authorities that those fields hadn't been destroyed until after the poppies had been harvested.

But I had to protect my baby too.

I felt the heavy weight of my body. My legs substantial and strong were rooted to the cold marble beneath my feet. I was here. I wasn't going anywhere. Like the stubborn dandelion, tough and hard to get rid of, culling life from any source.

"Now see here, I'm sure we can come to some sort of negotiation." The senator tried reasoning. "That's the Director of Field Operations for the NSA. You can't shoot him."

"The NSA doesn't have field ops," the major rebutted.

Surprise. Looks like Major Vandenburg didn't know everything.

Deliberately, I looked at the senator and the major. Very slowly I engaged the safety and turned the weapon to give to Carson. "Let it be noted that I am remanding myself into custody."

"Gentlemen, the fugitive has surrendered. Your work is done."

"What?" Jordan said.

"You promised to trust me." It was the only way to keep everyone safe. To keep Jordan from bearing the burden of transgressions of everyone around him. To keep the baby safe. I looked steadily at him as Carson put plastic restraint cuffs on my wrists.

"Shit," Jordan said softly, realizing he was trapped.

"You gave me the idea. This way I'm, we're, protected until we can get everything straightened out."

"You stupid bastard," the major barked at Jordan.

"That's me," Jordan snarled.

"You couldn't just leave well enough alone. Kept getting in the way," he ranted. Vandenburg gestured to me. "Why the hell would you go after her?"

The major hadn't taken his eyes off me.

"He's right." I was more trouble than I was worth. Yet Jordan had come after me, and kept coming even when it was apparent I was avoiding him.

Emotion unfurled in my chest, strong and bright and unchallenged. He loved me.

"You're mine," Jordan said.

"Well, isn't that romantic?" the Major sneered. "But it doesn't matter."

"You can't kill Carson Black," the senator said desperately, as if finally realizing all hell was about to break loose.

"Wait a minute. Carson Black?" The major blurted.

"Yes." Carson nodded once.

"You authorized the press release on her," the major said gleefully.

Fuck.

Betrayal sharp and hot, burned under my breastbone. Jordan had been worried Carson had an agenda. He'd been right. And I'd played right into Carson's hands.

I certainly would never have believed he would be the

one to engineer my death. But it made a logical sense. Fifty four ninety one was his mistake. His snafu.

And I'd been trying to open it up.

"I did." Carson's voice was neutral. Was he confirming or asking? "Major, you really don't want to shoot anyone." He stepped so that he was blocking Vandenburg's line of sight to me.

"You can't argue about shooting them." The major kept his gaze trained on us, never once looking at Carson.

I looked at Jordan. "I'm sorry," I mouthed.

We were outnumbered. "Shooting us isn't a good idea. Other people know we're here."

Carson himself had suggested we call Zeke. Wait. That didn't make sense. But I'd have to figure that out later, assuming there was a later.

We'd war-gamed the possibility of a gunfight. But we hadn't factored in Carson as a traitor.

"Negotiation's over." The major lifted his weapon and roared at Carson, "Get out of the way."

"Drop!" Jordan yelled.

I dropped to the cold marble floor as Jordan fired at the major. Taking in priority of targets, Major Vandenburg had to be first. He was the overt threat to both me and Jordan.

And if Jordan had time, he could shoot Carson too. But the repercussions of shooting a high-ranking intelligence officer were huge.

The senator didn't think well on his feet, apparently, as he just stood there dumbly. When the first shot sounded, the senator squealed like a pig at the noise and flash of it all. Weapon fire boomed, enormously loud in this tomb of a monument.

Don't hit the senator, I prayed, not wanting Jordan to have his father's death on his conscience.

A flash on my left told me Carson had fired. Fuck. I curled onto my side, protecting the baby, and swung my legs out hitting Carson behind the knees and taking him down. He hit the marble floor with a grunt.

I shifted my attention back to the battle, working at the restraints on my wrists.

The major had on state of the art body armor. Finger already on the trigger, he was hit multiple times in the chest, and the force knocked him back.

Jordan launched himself in front of me, continuing to shoot as he dove.

What the fuck was he doing? This was not part of our plan.

Jordan's last bullet was a kill shot to the Major's head. With a neat little hole in his forehead and a look of surprise on his face, he disappeared, tumbling backward down the stairs, his weapon still firing, mostly spent bullets raining down on us.

I heard the thud of impact as one of the major's bullets hit.

Behind me, Carson swore.

Shit, shit, shit.

Finally I got the damn cuffs off. Frantically, I ripped open Jordan's shirt, looking for a wound. "Shoulder," he gasped. "I'll be okay. Check Carson."

I crawled over to Carson, who had blood pouring out of a crease wound in his head. "Wasn't me."

"Later," I said.

"No. It wasn't me. I didn't authorize the press conference." He gripped my hand with more force than I would have thought possible with the amount of blood pouring down his face and obscuring his eyes. "There's a traitor somewhere."

Quickly I tore off one of my sleeves and wrapped it around his head as tightly as possible.

Switch our weapons, Carson pantomimed.

"What?"

"I got the kill shot," Carson said hoarsely.

He was trying to protect Jordan.

I ripped out the other sleeve and crawled back to Jordan to tie the material around the wound in his shoulder. Keeping my back to the cameras, I quickly switched the weapons.

A moan from near the steps brought my attention to the senator as he tried to slink away.

"Oh, no, you don't, pal." I ran over to where he was still semi-huddled on the ground trying to crawl away, and planted a boot in his back, right between his shoulder blades.

If everything had gone as Carson agreed, the CIA had representatives in the security booth were watching the entire exchange. They should be here any minute.

"Smile for the security camera."

The senator's voice shook. "It's my word against yours, who do you think they'll believe?"

"Mine." I ripped open my shirt. I had been wearing body armor. I'd also been wearing a wire.

I HATED HOSPITALS.

Everything about them. Antiseptic and Betadyne, the smell of medicine and sickness. All the odors reminded me of the day life as I knew it ended.

And I hated the waiting.

Carson came up behind me, rubbed my shoulders. "You

can go in soon." A large bandage covered the top of his skull. He'd been lucky.

Jordan was still in recovery to repair the damage to his shoulder.

"Can I see him before they take me away?" I thought about going back to prison, even for a short time, and my stomach turned. But until we could get my name cleared, it was the safest place for me...and the baby. I placed a hand over the little bump.

"You're all cleared," Carson replied calmly.

"Really?"

"Well, you've got about five more minutes." He gestured to the television. Senator Jordan was giving a press conference on the steps of the Lincoln Memorial. He had a bandage on his head.

"He was injured?"

"I don't believe so."

The bandage played better. I guess.

"This country owes a large debt to the efforts of civilian Staci Grant who helped us uncover a large heroin smuggling ring. Through her assistance, and agreeing to make herself a target, we were able to capture the people responsible."

No mention of Major Vandenburg. Somehow I didn't think his involvement would be making the morning news.

Carson said, "I spoke with your boss. He said to apologize."

"About what?"

"They had suspicions about Vandenburg but hadn't been able to prove anything. Every time they went to a suspect village the poppy fields had been destroyed. They had been hoping that by leaving you in the prison that they'd finally be able to get the evidence to nail him. The recording from the wire you wore should help tie up the loose ends."

"What about the traitor?"

"Believe me, I'm still looking for him."

Had to be someone fairly high up, I thought. "After all that it had nothing to do with--"

Carson's hand on my wrist stopped me.

CHAPTER 46

He inclined his head.

Then the nurse interrupted, "He's in his room if you want to go in."

I walked into the hospital room hesitantly.

Jordan lay on the blinding white sheets. "Hey," he said, smiling fuzzily.

"Hey." I went closer to the bed, looking him over carefully. "How're you feeling?"

"Pretty good right now." He grinned wryly. "Give it an hour and we'll see."

I didn't know what to say. Since we'd been back together we'd been on the run. Now...now reality was here.

"That dive wasn't part of the plan," I said lamely.

He tugged me down against the uninjured side of his body. "Neither was that surrender."

"Yeah." I was afraid I'd hurt him, but his grip was firm. "I was protecting you."

"I don't need protection."

"Neither do I."

"I know. It's one of the very best things I love about

you." Jordan squeezed me tighter. "You can take care of yourself."

Love?

"But the little guy in there needs both of us."

I felt compelled to contradict. "Or girl."

Maybe he was right.

Love. A pretty scary word.

Except, if this were anyone else, anyone, I would have been long gone.

My mouth suddenly dry, my heart just edging on frantic, it occurred to me that epic didn't have to mean sacrifice on a grand scale. It just needed to be epic for us.

I'd been protecting him, loving him as much as he'd been protecting me. "How about we...protect each other?"

Then I realized it wasn't just us anymore.

Jordan and I had made a baby.

The idea of the baby, the true miracle of the life I couldn't feel inside me swelled over me in a tidal wave. A real, living entity of both of us, a mixture, a perfect physical expression of our love for each other.

I rested my hand on my belly, and Jordan's hand slid over mine, curling underneath the tiny bulge that seemed to get a little bigger every day.

"And Junior."

I snorted. "I got checked out while we were waiting. I...we seem to be fine." I thought about all my body had been through in the last two months, torture, abuse, drugs, starvation, and still this baby had held on. "This baby is a fighter."

"Like her mother."

"Like her father." I contradicted, then took a deep breath. "Forgive me?"

"Of course."

The tension eased from my body. "No more secrets."

"Agreed."

We had lots of details to work out, but I had confidence in us. I lay my head down next to Jordan's on the scratchy linen pillow.

Maybe I didn't hate hospitals so much anymore. After all, life as I knew it was over...but a new life was beginning. Again.

***

Thanks so much for reading Betrayals!

Want to know what's going on with Zeke? Click here for Burned

And Barb finally gets her Happily Ever After in Dangerous Game in a story with an homage to the classic Christmas movie, Die Hard.

P.S. Would you like to know when my next book is available? You can sign up for my new release email list/newsletter at Lisa's Confidants

October 20, 1995
Rural Kansas

He was yelling. Again.

I stared out the window from the attic of our old farmhouse and tried to block out the shouting. A full, bright orange moon hung low in the dark blue night, lighting up the sky like it was daytime. Rain, rain, and more rain, that's all we had lately. 'Cept tonight was clear.

Squeezing my eyes shut, I squished up my face and wished on the moon.

Tomorrow was my birthday. I was going to be seven whole years old and I wanted a pair of roller blades so bad. With Grammy and Grampy coming, I might just get them. They were coming 'specially to celebrate my birthday. And he was angry.

I hid in the curtain of my long hair, the color of midnight Grampy always said, as if I could disappear behind the strands and *he* couldn't see me. I clutched my Lunette doll from the Big Comfy Couch to my chest, snuffling the soft strands of her hair along my cheek, comforted by the familiar smells from before, when daddy was alive. Before he moved in.

Boom-boom, boom-boom.

My heart thumped, ringing in my ears, drowning out the sound of Mama pleading, sobbing.

"Claire is too old for dolls," he shouted. "We need to get rid of her." But he wasn't looking at Lunette when he said that, he was glaring at me with his angry face.

But Mama defended me, letting me hold on to the only toy left from Daddy.

She was paying for it now.

The screen door slapped shut and he pounded down the wooden stairs and stomped toward the barn. His hands were clenched tight and his shoulders shook. The leaves rattled in the trees and swirled in a mini-whirlwind through the yard.

The rumble of Grammy and Grampy's shiny new car, a Caddie-lack, struck my ears at the same time the moonlight glinted off the silver bumper as they ambled up the drive and alongside the raging creek.

Relief swept through me. I loved my Grammy and Grampy. When they visited, everything was okay.

I felt loved and protected and safe.

A crack of thunder shook the house, except...the sky was clear. A movement from the door of the barn drew my gaze. The long barrel of my stepfather's rifle, the one he used for shooing foxes when they came 'round the chicken coop, disappeared into the open doorway.

I saw the tire pop. Heard a loud screech. The car rolled like a somersault over and over until it disappeared over the edge of the road and into the creek.

Boom. Upside down, the car bounced and bobbed. The

water in the creek roared. Their car rushed away from me, away from us. He stepped into the shadow of the doorway. I watched him turn, and I could feel him staring at the attic window. Right where I was sitting. He lifted the rifle barrel toward the window and pointed it straight at me. Then he shook his head sharply, and pivoted toward the creek.

I could hear myself screaming, throat raw, hurting as I ran down the stairs. Wanting only the comfort of Grammy's arms.

I ran into the kitchen, and saw the stark terror on Mama's face, the horror. Suddenly another boom sounded.

"He did it. He did it," I screamed, unable to say anything else, as I threw myself at Mama.

"Hush." Mama clamped a hand over my mouth so tight. It hurt.

Mama never hurt me. Not like him.

With her other hand, she grabbed our coats off the hook in the mud room. "You've got to hush."

The car had gotten trapped on a tree root, bright yellow flames licked at the sky. Fire. How could the car be on fire in the water?

We watched from the window. Tears ran silently down Mama's face, her eyes puffy, her nose running. He went over to the burning wreckage and looked down, still holding the rifle. Then, Mama tugged me toward the back door, toward the garage and our only car.

Mama pushed the car out of the garage, and said a quick prayer of thanks for being on top of the hill. She hopped in the driver's seat, and let the car coast down the hill.

His shout echoed furiously when he discovered we were leaving. Mama twisted the key and the car started with a cough.

"He's coming," I whispered, clutching Lunette tightly.

He sprinted toward the car. "I won't let you go," he screamed. "You can't escape. I will never let you go."

Mama jammed her foot down and the car leapt forward. "Buckle up, baby."

And we ran.

ACKNOWLEDGMENTS

Thanks so much to Alicia Rasley for always imparting wisdom and for giving Jordan his scarab.

Thanks to Ross for giving me info on WWII guns.

Thanks to my whole family for giving me room to work. Thanks for all the emptied dishwashers, sorted laundry and folding clothes. And putting up with cereal for dinner.

Thanks to Lynn, Adrienne, and Sophie for reading at a moment's notice and generally keeping me sane. And to all of the Pens Fatales for their encouragement and support.

Thanks to Martha for her daily check-ins and silent but deadly expectations. You spur me to be more creative, more productive, more everything and I cannot express how much I appreciate it.

Finally, thanks to Jim for everything. Love you!

<u>Family Stone Box Set (Stone Cold Heart, Carved in Stone, Heart of Stone, Still the One, & Jar of Hearts)</u>

<u>The Nostradamus Prophecies</u>

<u>View To A Kill #1</u>

Never Say Never #2

<u>ALIAS</u>

Stalked (ALIAS #1)

Hunted (ALIAS #2)

Vanished (ALIAS #3)

<u>Billionaire Breakfast Club</u>

His Semi-Charmed Life (Camp Firefly Falls #11 and Billionaire Breakfast Club #0)

Everything He Wants (Billionaire Breakfast Club #1 The Jock)

Queen of His Daydreams (Camp Firefly Falls #23 and Billionaire Breakfast Club #1.5)

ABOUT LISA

USA Today Bestselling Author Lisa Hughey started writing romance in the fourth grade. That particular story involved a prince and an engagement. Now, she writes about strong heroines who are perfectly capable of rescuing themselves and the heroes who love both their strength and their vulnerability. She pens romances of all types—suspense, paranormal, and contemporary—but at their heart, all her books celebrate the power of love.

She lives in Cape Ann Massachusetts with her fabulously supportive husband, two out of three awesome mostly-grown kids, and one somewhat grumpy cat.

Yoga, hiking, and traveling are her favorite ways to pass the time when she isn't plotting new ways to get her characters to fall in love.

Lisa loves to hear from readers and has tons of places you can connect with her. It's a wonder she gets any writing done at all….

Be Lisa's Friend on Facebook
Follow Lisa on Twitter

Sign Up for Lisa's Confidants
Visit Lisa on the Web
Follow Lisa on Pinterest
Follow Lisa on Instagram
Email Lisa
Be Lisa's Friend on Goodreads
Like Lisa on Facebook at Lisa Hughey Author

www.ingramcontent.com/pod-product-compliance
Lightning Source LLC
Chambersburg PA
CBHW032158180726
48284CB00001B/90